Wycaan Master: Book Four

SACRIFICIAL FLAME

A Novel

ALON SHALEV

Tourmaline Books
Berkeley, California

SACRIFICIAL FLAME

Sacrificial Flame
Wycaan Master, Book 4

Copyright © 2014 Alon Shalev

Tourmaline Books, Berkeley, California
http://www.tourmalinebooks.com

ISBN: 978-0-9884428-1-8
LCCN: 2013944793

First Edition: June, 2014

Published in the United States of America

Dedication

The storyteller's path can be lonely for those who become consumed, who stand with one foot in another world, who hold responsibility for characters and their destiny. But the path is just as demanding for those who support the storyteller's journey, those who walk side-by-side with the writer even when he is called to another world, those who are left behind in this world, those who ensure that reality continues.

They make the excuses for the writer when he is late, bridge the gap when he is distant, bring balance when another world consumes.

To Ariela, my life partner and soul mate, who gives me the freedom to soar above the land of Odessiya and who acts as my lodestar, my compass that always leads me home.

The Wycaan Master Series:

ACKNOWLEDGEMENTS

—To Monica Buntin, my editor, for once again making sense of an awful lot of words.

—To William Kenney, my book cover artist, for your amazing ability to continually transform my jumbled ideas into such beautiful pieces of art.

—To Jeny Lyn Ruelo and her team at The Fast Fingers, for the interior design and formatting, and always being willing to deal with my tech-challenged questions.

—To my good friend, Janet Frankel, who gave the manuscript one final polish and saved me a few blushes.

Prologue

Ancient stories possess great knowledge for those who study them. They cement the past and offer lessons for the future. These legends become beacons of values, create culture, and, ultimately, define truth.

But what happens when these ancient stories are imbued with lies? Surely, history sits in judgment, weeding out such falsities, exposing them as the work of charlatanism.

And what about the half-truths? Sometimes such omissions are genuine mistakes, the paucity of a forgetful memory. History does not tolerate complacency, and it condemns forgotten facts to obscurity and extinction.

Occasionally, the truth is purposely omitted: to protect an ego, to hide a hideous event, to deny a truth or existence. And that, my friends, is the most dangerous fallacy, for when part of a story is neglected, the potential lessons and warnings are swiftly forgotten.

I remember these stories, and I recall them all in their completeness. I have seen where great powers have risen and fallen. I bore witness to the sentences of the vanquished. In my youth, I was arrogant, but I never neglected my studies. I never really believed that my power in Odessiya could be taken from me. But, I was smart enough to make plans.

Often during my reign, I left on trips of invigoration and exploration – to discover the strengths and potential of those who strayed from the path, who fell by the wayside, who were forgotten by the stories.

The Wycaans were painstakingly assiduous in their efforts to cleanse history of those who stood against them. I am not referring to the wild men of the North, or creatures from lands afar. I refer to the very ones of their kind who turned away from the path of the Alliance. These maverick Wycaans were disgraced, they were incarcerated, and they were forgotten.

But not by me.

I nurtured their hope, restored their dignity, and promised that I would one day return to lead them against those who destroyed them.

The time is now, and I have come. Revenge for the vanquished. Revenge for me.

Emperor Shindell
Personal Diaries

Chapter One

Sellia crouched, shifting her bow and the loaded quiver on her back. Her leg muscles protested, and she grimaced. It had been too long since last she had gone hunting. She fingered the prints of the deer she was tracking. The damp, mossy earth left clear signs that her prey was getting away.

The dark elfe sighed, and, as she rose, one of her knees clicked. "Ouch!" She took a deep breath, filled her lungs, and jogged along the trail, pushing her long, black hair from her face. She did not get out much from Wycaan Island. She had so many responsibilities now.

Seanchai's Healer Academy had sprung up with great speed on the small piece of land jutting out on what Prince Shayth had generously renamed Lake Mhari, after Seanchai's first Wycaan teacher. Indeed, the speed with which the academy had been built was also due to the generosity of the prince, who had sent legions of builders and materials to ensure Seanchai fulfilled his dream.

Ducking under a low branch, Sellia stopped again to inspect the tracks. It was not her role at the academy that ate away at her time. Seanchai traveled incessantly to all parts of Odessiya, and she had accompanied him until the first pregnancy. Now it was her time as a mother that kept her busy, and Sellia still was conflicted with her new role.

She was mate to a Wycaan Master and, as such, held important responsibilities, not the least of which was to bear him *calhei*, offspring. The blood of the Wycaans did not necessarily flow from parent to child, but appeared nonetheless in considerably higher proportions than randomly outside the bloodlines.

Sellia had given birth to a daughter, a beautiful dark elfe named Mharina, who was followed two years later by twins: an elf and an elfe, Ilan and Senzia. She had no plans for more. Those first few years had been a blur of sleepless nights, sore breasts, and endless soothing. Seanchai proved the more natural parent, almost effortlessly negotiating the trials and tribulations of newborns. The problem was that Seanchai was not often around. This time, he had been gone for two months.

The huntress stopped again and crouched. She was nearer the deer now. Why had it ceased fleeing if it knew she was in pursuit? Her blood quickened as she set off again. She would catch up. If she could glimpse it, she would bring it down. Though her days were full, Sellia never stopped practicing her archery, refining her art on a beautiful elven bow – a final gift from another love in an earlier lifetime. Sellia belonged in the woods with a bow in her hand. Her Wycaan mate could parent for both of them.

The plump doe stood motionless, looking up at something in the sky. It turned its head and stared straight at her. Sellia froze. The deer saw her and wasn't running. Why? It looked up again, and Sellia could see its ears pricking, its muscles tensed. It was not too tired to run…it was too scared.

The deer seemed more fearful of whatever it could see than of the elfe huntress tracking it. Sellia felt a chill of apprehension. A shadow crossed over her, then over the small clearing. The deer let out a whimper and lowered its head. *Run!* Sellia almost screamed.

A roar shook the ground, and a winged creature, three times the size of the doe, swept down and grabbed the animal with huge, curved talons. In one swift movement, it swung the heavy deer effortlessly against a tree. There was a snap, and the doe lay lifeless on the ground.

Sellia expected the creature to feed on its kill, but instead, it slowly turned its horned, scaly head — thick smoke escaping from its wide nostrils — in Sellia's direction. She hugged closer to the tree that was concealing her, daring not to breathe. She kneeled and cautiously peeked around the mossy trunk.

From the movement of its frosty blue eyes, the creature couldn't see her, but knew she was there. Its flared nostrils and narrow, pointed ears twitched, and a long, scaly, spiked tail swayed from side to side. It was a deep red, its scales glinting in the sun.

Sellia had never seen such a creature, but Seanchai had told her how the Emperor, a Wycaan Master himself, had transformed into a red firebreather when Seanchai had confronted him. The beast had almost killed her mate.

It couldn't be! If this was the deposed Emperor or one of his minions, she was in terrible danger. And then the realization flowed through her, numbingly cold. It wasn't just her. Mharina, Senzia and Ilan's faces filled her mind. Her children!

She reached to her side, but she had not thought to bring her sword. There was peace in the land, and this was known Wycaan country, so marauders kept a wide berth.

The firebreather craned its neck, peering in her direction. Rays of sunlight flashed off sharp scales. She doubted, had she brought her sword, that she could have even penetrated such armor.

It turned away and pounded over to the fallen deer. Sellia heard the ripping of meat and the crunching of bones. Blood spurted up onto the peeled bark of a pine tree. She silently slid back and began to retrace her steps to Wycaan Island.

How many times had she faced danger in the old days before the Emperor had been vanquished? She had always been more surprised at surviving afterward than fearful of death in the heat of the moment. But this was the first time she faced danger as a mother, and it terrified her.

What would they do without her? The twins were so young, and Mharina was so close to her. They would not lack for food or attention, but Sellia knew only too well what it was like to grow up without a mother. And Seanchai? He had never fully recovered from Ilana's death as it was. She shivered as she recalled how he had almost lost his mind then.

A sudden realization dawned and she felt a cold shiver. What if there were firebreathers attacking Wycaan Island? Could they know that Seanchai was away? There were only a few soldiers garrisoned to protect the acolytes, and the academy. But why bother to attack her? Why attack the island if Seanchai was away?

For the first time in her life, Sellia understood sheer panic. A paralyzing wave constricted her breathing and filled her eyes with tears. Her stealthy escape collapsed as she scrambled frantically. Her children were almost undefended, and the school was not built to withstand attack. She ran through the forest, branches and twigs snapping in her wake.

If the Emperor knew Seanchai was away, then he was coming for the Wycaan's children, and she could not protect them.

Their names erupted from deep inside her body: MHARINA! SENZIA! ILAN! She screamed in an alien high-pitch she did not recognize.

She reached the clearing beyond the forest and stopped instinctively. The firebreather landed with a thud in front of her, grunting from the impact. It raised its head and roared. Then, staring at her, it actually seemed to smile, revealing long, bloodstained teeth.

It licked its nose several times, then took a deep breath and loosened a volley of fire, igniting a line in the dry brush in front of Sellia to block her way home. She rolled backwards, the pungent smoke assaulting her nostrils.

She sprinted back into the forest, slipping and sliding. More volleys of fire followed, and the creature let out another roar, one that eerily resembled a maniacal laugh. It was driving her back into the forest, away from the island, away from Mharina, away from her twins.

She gripped her bow tightly as she ran, her knuckles white, passing the bleeding corpse of the doe with barely a second glance. The huntress had become the hunted.

Chapter Two

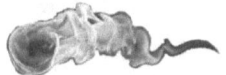

The punch to her stomach had Riona gasping for air. When two muscular hands threw her effortlessly across the room, it was her reflexes alone that guided her into a roll. She rose, feeling a wave of nausea, and looked around for a weapon. But she was in the eating room, and it would take more than a meat knife to pierce the scales covering the huge, looming lizard.

Not that Riona was a warrior. She had come to Wycaan Island to study as a healer. She swooned as the reptilian creature – seven, maybe eight feet tall – dashed forward on two legs and grabbed her long black hair. It picked her up like a toy doll, its antennae brushing her head.

"Ssshow me where they are," it hissed.

Riona, still dizzy and lightheaded, almost fainted again from the creature's foul breath, and she felt her teeth rattle as it shook her.

"What are you?" she wheezed.

"Taragusssii. Where are the younglingsss? Where?"

Riona tried to shake her head, but it was painful with her hair held so tightly. The taragus turned and walked out of the hall, dragging Riona by her hair behind it.

She heard screams and short clashes of steel on steel as the taragus pulled her into the square. She gasped in pain as her shiny, dark hair was almost wrenched from her scalp and her body scraped against the uneven, stone ground.

The creature stopped, but Riona's momentum sent her head plowing into its thick leg. The creature absentmindedly dropped her to the ground, and she crumpled, gasping in pain.

Realizing she was forgotten, the healer crawled under an overturned cart. A screaming elderly elfe was brought out, struggling in the grasp of a second taragus, who, though smaller than the first, and more brown than black, was still considerably bigger than the largest soldier stationed here, and far broader.

It croaked something to the larger taragus, who grabbed the old elfe and raised her to eye level, her spindly legs swinging off the ground.

"Where are younglingsss of the Wycaan?"

"I'll never tell you. I'd rath–"

Riona heard a sickening crunch of bone and the elfe gasped. Two tentacles from behind the creature's head swung over and inserted into the old elfe's forehead and she let out a shrill scream. Then the huge taragus tossed her body toward the cart. There was a loud snap as her body smashed against a thick wheel and went still. A wooden spike protruded from the elfe's chest, and Riona watched blood seep into a puddle on the ground.

The reptile went onto all four limbs and scampered into a tower. Two other taragusii dropped to four legs and scampered after their leader. Riona groaned. The children studied in that building. She heard flapping wings and saw two hawks fly from the top of the tower. Two taragusii archers shot both down instantly. Moments later, the three creatures exited the tower, each holding a *calhei*.

The twins were both whimpering, and one of Ilan's cheeks was red and swollen. Mharina, the oldest, seemed the most in control of herself. Her skin was dark, and her hair curly. She closely resembled her mother, as her dark brown eyes darted around for help or escape, but the black taragus had her in a firm grasp.

The leader let out a high screech, and four more creatures appeared. "Massster calls usss. We ride for Golgoth Passs. It will be two weeksss until we feassst in our hallsss. We move."

One taragus brought something to its lips and emitted a shrill note. Soon Riona heard hooves galloping from the mainland and watched as black, scaled, horse-like creatures entered the courtyard. They were thin and their bones protruded, but they moved with power and grace. The taragusii mounted, and the children were thrown over the saddles. Ilan and Mharina cried out, but in moments, the group had galloped down the narrow path that connected the island to the mainland.

Riona waited until she could no longer hear the gait of the taragusii. Then she crawled out from under the cart and rose, using the cart to steady herself. She was dizzy and bruised, but otherwise unhurt.

Strong hands grabbed her from behind, and she screamed.

"It's okay," Denalion said. The red-haired elf slowly turned her toward him and pulled her close. "They've gone. Come sit over here, and I'll bring you water."

After she had sipped some cool liquid, she looked up into Denalion's lined face. His dark skin always had a red hue because of his hair, but she was sure it was more flushed than usual.

"The children," she rasped.

"I know. I saw."

"How did you escape them?"

"I can be most elusive. Sadly, I am too old and weak to fight."

"They would have killed you. We must give chase. How will we track them? I heard something like Golgoth Pass, but that is surely only an initial meeting point."

"We will find them," the dreamwalker said. "I can follow the children when they sleep. I have prepared Mharina for just such an event. She knows to take in the route and try to dream about it.

"Can a person do that?"

"Yes," Denalion replied, and shrugged. "It has worked before."

She thought he was stroking her to be comforting, but realized that Denalion was feeling for broken bones and wounds. After a moment, he stood up.

"I am going to search for survivors, Riona. Stay here and wait. I need you to be ready to tend to survivors, if I can find any."

He returned a little while later, staggering under the weight of an elfe in his arms. Riona recognized Pyre, the young elfe warrior. She had joined Seanchai soon after the academy had opened. They had been close when Seanchai had first traveled to the Forest of Markwin, and remained very close now. The young warrior was slight of build, and her white hair was not the snow-white of one like Seanchai who had gone through his Wycaan transformation. Riona, as a human, did not understand fully, but thought that Pyre was still not a full Wycaan, perhaps because of her age.

Riona shook herself when she realized the elfe was wounded, and her healer training kicked in. Riona felt a steadying sense of purpose. "Take her into the hall," she directed Denalion.

"There's a pack of herbs and bandages in the guard room by the gate. Bring it to me and then continue to search for survivors."

Denalion smiled despondently. "You are strong of heart, Riona – stronger than you know."

There were no more survivors. Denalion counted twenty-three dead elves, dwarves, and humans. Most were young students who had come to learn with the only known Wycaan Master in Odessiya. They had wanted one day to serve the people, as healers, potential Wycaans, and leaders. This had been an abrupt and violent end to such aspirations.

Seanchai had taken a large delegation to the capital. He had not left more than a few soldiers, provided by Prince Shayth, and taken his senior students. After thirteen years of peace, they had become lax in their security.

As Denalion piled the bodies onto a fire bed, he wept for them. He knew each and every one. They would serve no one – their dreams, like their bodies, were dead. He lit the fire and watched the wood catch. He took some oil and poured it on, desperate to accelerate the task.

An arm gripped his shoulders, and he gasped.

"Are my children in there?" Sellia demanded, her voice ice cold.

"No," Denalion said, keeping his eyes on the fire. "They live, but the taragusii have taken them."

"The who? Never mind. Send word to the capital, old one. Let Seanchai know."

"I tried. They shot down the hawks," Denalion replied. "Tonight I'll try and enter someone's dreams: Seanchai, Shayth, Maugwen, whoever."

"Is anyone else alive?"

"Pyre and Riona are in the main hall." Sellia turned away, and Denalion had to jog to catch up. "Don't do anything reckless, Sellia—"

"Reckless?" she wheeled and stared down at him. "Those beasts have my children."

"And you will not serve your children by getting yourself killed. Listen to me. This was well-planned, and they were kept alive for a reason."

"He wants Seanchai," Sellia replied, continuing to walk to the hall.

"Who?"

"I was kept away from here by a firebreather, a red one. He's back, Denalion, and he wants revenge."

CHAPTER THREE

"My dear prince," the advisor pleaded, scurrying to keep up with his lord's fast gait while precariously balancing several scrolls.

Prince Shayth Shindell was still not used to either the title or the responsibilities. It had been over thirteen years since he had sat on his uncle's throne and created a political framework that was supposed to alleviate the need for him to preside over day-to-day issues.

Over time, Shayth had discovered he possessed a sound strategic mind, which he applied to help each region develop its own natural resources, and consequently fewer people lived in poverty. The wealthy also prospered as a result of Shayth's innovative projects, and Odessiya enjoyed a period of growth and trust.

Still, he always needed to sit with his governors and oversee diplomatic meetings. Today, a delegation from the fishing region of Brillmore had arrived and already presented a nauseatingly detailed account of changing ocean climate. This presentation had only just concluded, and he needed to dress for what was sure to be an excruciatingly formal state banquet. He tried to suppress a yawn at the prospect. At least he had not lost his temper at the delegation or his staff. In the old days, it had been anger alone that had fueled his very existence.

"Sire, you will need to show considerably more enthusiasm for your guests than you did in the meeting earlier. I am sure you will present your most charismatic nature," First Advisor Gilead remarked as they entered the prince's chambers.

The advisor received a glare for his troubles, while an attendant was brushed aside for trying to straighten Shayth's bowknot for the umpteenth time. They had stopped trying to suppress his spiky, unruly black hair. Shayth flexed his broad chest and shoulders, which strained against the tight coat they had squeezed him into.

There was a brisk knock on the door, and it immediately opened. Shayth turned, surprised that whoever was outside had not waited to be summoned.

"Forgive the interruption, but I must speak with you," Maugwen said. She was still dressed in her brown work clothes from the hospital, a short shirt and baggy trousers.

"Oh, no. That would not be possible, my dear," Advisor Gilead even dropped a scroll, he was so flustered at the idea. "The prince is due in the banquet hall very soon."

"Can it wait?" Shayth asked her, failing to suppress a hopeful smile.

Maugwen rarely came to court, though she had an open invitation. She preferred to spend her time at the hospital, channeling her healing energy that had proved the difference between life and death time and again. She had grown up these past years, and filled out since they had first met in the dungeons at Galbrieth. She was a woman now, not a scared little girl, and there was a quiet, assured confidence solidifying her considerable talent and sense of purpose. Only her defiant spiky hair – like Shayth's – was a reminder of a past they had shared on the run in the old days.

"Rhoddan arrived," she persisted. "He rode through the night and is meeting Seanchai here. He received instruction to prepare horses and supplies for a long and arduous journey."

"Seanchai is coming here?" Shayth was surprised. "He isn't expected for at least two weeks. I sent–"

"There's more," Maugwen said, but didn't continue.

"One should never interrupt a prince mid-sentence," Advisor Gilead said, raising an eyebrow in admonishment.

But Shayth was frowning. He had picked up on the healer's tone.

"Leave us, everyone," he commanded, and a bustle of people immediately exited. "That includes you, Advisor. Be ready to step into my place if I am detained."

"Sire. These diplomatic initiatives are extremely important. They take months of preparation, and you will be expected–"

"My friends, Advisor, are my family. Leave us."

When the door was closed, Shayth looked at Maugwen, who was smiling wryly. "You sound like an old friend of ours. I'll be brief, and you can go about your duties."

"Take as long as you need." Shayth poured them both some wine and slumped in a big chair. His room was full of comfort. "I'm happy for the distraction."

"Denalion walked in my dreams," Maugwen said.

"The dreamwalker? I haven't heard anything of him in years. Is he still in the Forest of Markwin with the Elves of the West?"

"No. He's a tutor to Sellia and Seanchai's children. He resides on Wycaan Island. I couldn't understand him. I saw his lips moving, but heard no words. It felt like someone had stolen my ability to hear. But his body language was clear. Something bad has happened."

Shayth furrowed his brow and raked his hand through his hair, which immediately released it from the gel that had been optimistically applied. Neither of them spoke for a while and then, finally, Maugwen looked at her prince.

"For now, I think you should join your guests. I'll stay close and bring Rhoddan and Seanchai to talk with you as soon as Seanchai arrives."

"So you'll join me for dinner, then?"

"No way. You're the prince. You have to suffer these stuffy ceremonies. I most certainly don't."

She exited, adeptly avoiding the royally thrown cushion.

A low rumble reached Shayth's ears sometime between the duck soup, the roast boar, and the countless speeches. He turned from the banquet table and glanced down a long corridor. There was a standoff, and angry voices echoed into the hall. Shayth bristled at the rudeness of the interruption and the potential insult to the Brillmorians.

He turned to the visiting delegation leader as he wiped his mouth with a napkin. "Excuse me, Ambassador."

A deft hand signal brought Gilead gliding over, holding a skin of wine.

"Ambassador, you simply must try this sweet red. It is a rare…"

Shayth walked down the corridor, his heels clicking on the smooth stone floor. His royal guard slipped seamlessly from behind pillars and settled in formation around him, and he realized that he was no longer annoyed at their constant presence. It had only taken more than a decade for this to happen.

One of Advisor Gilead's assistants was barring entrance to two tall figures, both hooded. Shayth recognized Seanchai and Rhoddan from their stances and smiled as he thought that either could easily toss the fragile diplomat aside.

"...without an official invitation. The prince simply doesn't—"

"The prince simply does," Shayth interrupted, "when his friends are concerned."

"Of course he does," the young advisor bowed, his cheeks glowing. "I have evidently misinterpreted the instruction I received. My apologies."

He shuffled backward awkwardly, then hovered, not sure what to do next.

"It might be better if we talk somewhere a little quieter," Seanchai said.

Shayth turned to the assistant. "Please bring some food for my friends. One eats meat, but bring the other some fish."

"I believe fish was not on the menu," the attendant began, but then his eyes met his prince's, and he started stammering. "I-I will surely find something..."

"A plate of hot vegetables, bread, and cheese will be fine," Seanchai said. "Thank you."

The young man stared as Seanchai removed his hood, revealing long, vibrant, white hair and deep blue eyes. The Wycaan Master was imposing – tall and muscular, even next to Rhoddan, who was just as well-built.

Shayth ushered them into a small room. As the elves removed their cloaks, Maugwen appeared with a plate. "I asked the chef to prepare you some snapper," she said to Seanchai, offering him the food.

"Thank you," he replied, taking the plate in one hand and hugging Maugwen with the other. Her feet left the ground, and she laughed.

"Sit down," Shayth said. "While I would rather spend the entire evening with you, I need to...well, you know."

The others smiled and nodded, enjoying how much Shayth, the wild rebel they all remembered, hated his civic responsibility.

"There are worrying tidings from the north," Rhoddan began while Seanchai ate. "The wild men are gathering, and Umnesilk believes an invasion is imminent. The pictorians request that you send troops north to honor the accords with them. If they do invade, it may well be before the spring."

"It's already spring," Shayth said, pointing to pink blossoms on a tree just outside a window.

"Not in the north. The snows have ceased to fall, but the passes are still blocked. Nonetheless, you have few fortifications in place, and your cavalry cannot be utilized while the snow lies thick on the ground. I believe an attack will come earlier than the melting season."

"Then I'll take my army north," Shayth said, seemingly happy with the prospect. "But surely the wild men know we are stronger than them. Why would they attack now?"

Seanchai put his fork back on the plate. "There's more. Umnesilk has heard boars from different villages report a fire in the sky at night, and a rumbling. I fear the Emperor is behind this."

"You fear he's behind everything," Shayth said, sipping his wine. "It's most likely a meteorite shower. The northern skies are so clear in the winter when there are no clouds. Come on, Seanchai. We haven't heard from him since—"

A sharp knock on the door stopped him, and the assistant appeared again. He bowed to Shayth.

"My lord. Please excuse me. A hawk just arrived. The message is urgent."

Shayth snatched the small scroll and scanned it. When he looked up at Seanchai, his face was pale. "Seems like I'm wrong. I need you to ride north with me. If my dear uncle is behind this, you will need to face him."

Seanchai grimaced. "That's the opposite direction to my family. I was hoping…"

"I know," Shayth interrupted. "But I need you with me."

"It's a Wycaan's destiny," Seanchai sighed, "never to be around his family for long."

"I thought there weren't Wycaan families for that very reason," Rhoddan said, and received a glare for his trouble.

"I'm sure they're doing just fine, my friend," the prince replied, frowning. "They are safer away from all this in the quiet south. We leave in the morning with a preliminary force. The army will need to organize supplies and can catch up as soon as they have."

Chapter Four

When Sellia quietly turned her door handle just before dawn, she already wore her heavy riding cloak and thick breeches. Across her shoulders were two bags, her weapons, and a sleeping roll. She had only planned to nap, but slept this long, she suspected, because Riona had slipped some herbs into her drink the night before as they had pored over maps and gathered supplies.

She was going to leave without them. She could travel quicker alone, and no one would restrain her when she found those who had dared to kidnap her children. They would pay – no mercy. The old elf would have been useful to take, and she considered waking him. But the two youngsters were…well, just too young.

Her door creaked, and she silently cursed it. She took one step out, stumbled over something soft beneath her foot, and crashed to the floor, the sound of her sword's steel clattering down the corridor. Whatever she landed on let out a cry of pain, and Sellia knew that she was not leaving alone.

She lit a torch on the wall and looked down on Pyre, who was now sitting up and rubbing her stomach. Sellia glared at her.

"What are you doing sleeping in the corridor?" she demanded, knowing perfectly well the answer.

"I thought you would put your boots on outside, not in your room. Is it dawn already?" Pyre asked innocently before calling out: "Riona! Denalion! She's up. Let's go. You were right, old one."

"Oh, by the Goddess's bow, what are you doing? Trying to stop me sneaking off? Who asked you to..."

She trailed off. Pyre was already heading toward the kitchens.

"She was wearing her boots," she heard Pyre complain.

They ate a final hot breakfast in silence, oat porridge with nuts and fresh fruit, and then all stared at the dishes. For some reason, Sellia thought, they couldn't decide whether or not to wash them.

"Riona, Pyre," Denalion said at last, "please feed and saddle the horses."

Both rose, and Riona took her herbal bags, while Pyre swung her Win Dao swords onto her back. Both females balanced saddlebags of supplies on their shoulders and exited. When it was just himself and Sellia, Denalion began to gather the plates.

"I know this is hard for you, Sellia, but we need to move with caution. And we need to work together."

"What are you talking about?" Sellia snapped.

He stacked the bowls, ignoring the edge she heard in her own voice.

"One person chasing a band of taragusii doesn't seem too rational," Denalion said at last.

"I was considering waking you, old one."

"I'm flattered. But as you point out, I am old. I can help track the children and hopefully contact Seanchai, but I am limited." He leaned over the table and collected the spoons.

"Pyre knows how to track and fight. Riona is a very good healer and will undoubtedly prove extremely useful."

Sellia sighed and nodded. "Denalion, I agree to take you, but on one condition."

"What?"

"Leave the damn dishes!"

They rode out with eight horses laden with supplies and weapons. Sellia led, following the obvious tracks, while Pyre rode in the rear. Sellia knew Seanchai was very fond of the young elfe. She had been the first to befriend him when he had gone to the Elves of the West and, even as a *calhei* of only six cycles, had stood up to the Elvin Council on his behalf.

Pyre was nineteen now and had wasted no time coming to Wycaan Island to join Seanchai. She trained as a warrior and tracker, and had asked Sellia to teach her the bow. Sellia would not be surprised if Pyre soon surpassed her in archery. She was impressed with the elfe's strong-headedness and self-discipline, but knew there was something holding her back from becoming a Wycaan like Seanchai.

Sellia hardly knew Riona, though they were probably the same age. The human was quiet and kept to herself. Her hair was a beautiful lush black, but her skin was pale. She had frightened the children at first. Mharina, the oldest, had claimed the healer was a ghost come to haunt them, but the woman soon won them over after treating a few cuts and bruises. Riona was a tenacious student in the healing arts, and Seanchai had confided in Sellia that he hoped she would graduate to become a teacher. It was not her pale skin that disturbed Sellia. It was more the woman's total lack of desire to make friends with anyone except Denalion. While always respectful, Riona kept her own company.

Right now, though, this was fine by Sellia. She wasn't looking for conversation or anyone expressing concern about how she was feeling. All she could think about was her children in the clutches of ruthless taragusii. She didn't even know exactly what these creatures were, but had seen the carnage they had inflicted on Wycaan Island. She planned to ask Denalion about them when they stopped.

She pushed them to ride through the day, fueled by a fear that the tracks would disappear or that the taragusii would pull ahead. All too soon, it began to darken, and Denalion called out to stop.

"Tired, old one?" Sellia asked, frustrated.

"Yes," he replied evenly, "as are we all, horses included. This is a defensible area to sleep in, and we must rest. Also, we are going to have difficulty seeing their tracks in the dark."

"How do you know they won't ride though the night?" Sellia knew she must rein in her tone, but couldn't stop herself.

"A taragus has no night vision. They will stop. Also, I need to dreamwalk, and this must be done while it is night in Shindellia City."

"To dreamwalk?" Pyre asked.

"I thought you did that last night!" Sellia exclaimed. "I told you—"

"And so I did, while you all slept," Denalion interrupted. "For hours, I tried to find Seanchai and Rhoddan, and then I sought out Prince Shindell himself. But I could not connect to any of them. I fear the Emperor might have cast some kind of shield to prevent me. This has never happened before.

"I was able to somehow connect to the healer who lives with the prince, but I am not sure she heard me. She is a complex one. Her defenses are reminiscent of Seanchai's, and I do not know how to pass through them, as I have only met her on a couple of occasions. Sellia," his tone became more insistent. "We must stop, and this is a good place."

Sellia sighed. "Very well. Let me try and hunt. We should preserve our supplies in case we don't have the ability to hunt later."

Pyre had dismounted and already taken saddles and bags from her two horses. She adjusted her bow. "I'll come with you."

"I don't need a wet nurse!"

Pyre's eyes widened, and then glanced at Denalion. When Sellia glared at him, the old elf held eye contact. Sellia was the first to relent and turned to Pyre.

"Fine. But I wasn't planning on running off and, to be clear, I do the killing. Come."

"First, please unsaddle your horses," Denalion said.

Sellia let off an impressive huff, but went to her own horse. Denalion came up next to her, and, when he spoke, his tone was low and only for her ears.

"I can't imagine how hard this is for you, but I must insist that you find the warrior you used to be, the powerful dark elfe who accompanied Seanchai to the Elves of the West and, from there, into battle. It could prove costly for you, your children, and the rest of us if you forget yourself. Reach into your past."

Sellia nodded but didn't say anything. She felt the tears welling up, and maybe Denalion did, too, for he went to tend his own horses.

"You have great patience, Dreamwalker," Riona said when they were alone.

They had collected wood and were preparing a fire. Riona was crouched down, holding her long hair back as she blew on dry moss. The fire caught, and twigs crackled as they gave in to the flame. Denalion sat on a log, sipping water.

"No, young one. I have great loyalty – to the Wycaan and all he has achieved. I love his children and know what will happen if they are harmed, for I dread to imagine this Wycaan blind in the pain of mourning his children, and its consequences on all of us."

The pale woman looked up. "What would happen?"

Denalion hooked his red hair behind pointed ears as he crouched next to her. When their eyes met, she saw the reflection of the flames mingling with fear.

"The destruction of everything we hold dear, Riona. The end of Odessiya."

CHAPTER FIVE

*M*harina, eldest daughter of Seanchai and Sellia, stood on a rock that was impressively dense for a dream, staring out over the valley she had passed earlier that day. Behind her loomed ancient, gnarled oaks with thick, dark brown trunks and rich green leaves. The valley was maybe three hundred feet below, and, in the failing light, she could no longer see the great river she knew meandered there.

She didn't understand why she was standing in this place or what she was waiting for, but she felt certain she was meant to be here. She realized she felt no pain in her dream, even though the day had been tough. She and the twins had been roughly held on the saddles of whatever these lizard creatures rode. When her younger brother Ilan had cried or complained, she had stood up to the lizard captain and twice been struck for defending him.

"Hoo. Hoo."

The owl made her jump, which was dangerous, considering she was standing on a protruding rock. She was analyzing everything rather than feeling it emotionally, she realized. But she couldn't fall, could she? This was a dream, after all.

"No, I'm pretty sure you cannot fall, little one, but let's not test the theory."

She turned and saw no one.

"Hoo? Hoo?"

She looked up and saw a red-winged owl staring down at her. It cocked its head to one side.

"Ouch! How do owls do this?"

"Denalion? Denalion! Is that you?" Her wonder turned to amusement. "Are you always red when you take animal form?"

"It seems so, little one. How are you? And the twins? Are you being treated well?"

"Those reptile things don't seem to have any love for calhei," she replied. "What are they? Where did they come from?"

"They are taragusii, my sweet. Try not to antagonize them. They have probably been ordered not to harm you, but I doubt they excel much with manners. Are you standing by your camp?"

"No. We passed here about an hour before we stopped."

"Very well. I'll need to see these kinds of physical landmarks when we meet at night. I need you to remember anything that is clearly identifiable. Do you understand?"

She nodded. "Are you coming to rescue us? Is my ahdahr with you?"

"Your father? Best I tell you nothing. Do not look for us, but know that your mother and father will never suffer you to be taken like this. Don't tell the twins anything, either. They're too young to keep it a secret. So are you, my dear."

"I'm not! I'm in my twelfth year."

"You have just celebrated your eleventh birthday."

"That means it's my twelfth year."

The owl hooted. "So be it. Stay strong, Mharina, for yourself and your siblings."

"Wait! Why did they take us?"

"I think whoever is commanding the taragusii wants your father to come. I'm afraid you're the bait, but that is also why I believe you are in no immediate danger. Try and reason with the leader for small things:

your own horse, rests when the twins need to relieve themselves. But do it softly and not in front of his troops. Do you understand?"

"Denalion, I'm afraid."

"Of course you are, little one. That is only natural, even for a brave calhei *in her twelfth year. Go to sleep now. I will visit tomorrow and ask you some questions about how many* taragusii *there are and what weapons they have. But you must stay patient and brave. Okay?"*

"You're quite cute as an owl, Denalion. It suits you."

"Hoo, Hoo, Hoo. Good night then, my brave little elfe.*"*

Mharina was woken by a sharp kick in her backside. She rolled over and took a moment to orient.

"If you and your kin want to eat before we ride, better hurry. And empty your bladdersss now. I don't want to have to ssstop for you."

The voice was a deep rasp, and the silver, scaled head and black eyes scared her. She stared into its face, rubbing her eyes, and it cocked its head. "Underssstand?"

"Y-yes, yes. I'll get the twins up. T-thank you."

She jumped to her feet; woke the twins; and rolled up the thick, woolen cloak the creatures had covered her with.

"Get up, both of you. Fold your cloaks as I'm doing. Come, we must eat while there's still food."

Ilan rose and stared around before trying to copy his big sister. "I'd hoped this had all been a dream," he muttered.

Senzia rose, but didn't collect her makeshift bed.

"Senzia!" Mharina snapped, but her little sister just stared at her.

Senzia was clutching a doll, and Mharina could see her knuckles were white. Mharina glanced at the taragusii, who were all eating around a fire. Then she took her sister's hand and led her into the wood.

"Come, do pee-pee. We must stay calm, and not show we're afraid."

"But I *am* afraid. Why isn't our *ahdahr* coming to save us?"

"He will, I'm sure. But it might take some time. You have to do as they tell you."

"Don't want to," Senzia muttered as she crouched behind a bush.

"Do you remember when the leader hit me yesterday? That was because you were not doing what he told you to do. I can't keep getting hit for you. Do you understand?"

Senzia looked up at her sister. She was named after Sellia's mother, but her eyes were blue like her father's and her hair was fair, though not yet Wycaan white. She and Senzia had often debated in their bedroom whether the latter was a natural Wycaan. Now it occurred to Mharina that this might put Senzia in greater danger. She would ask Denalion tonight in her dream.

They walked back to the camp and she saw a taragus holding some bread in the air, baiting Ilan to jump for it. The others were laughing in a throaty, rasping way. Mharina approached the leader, who was sitting to the side.

"I'm sure your master won't want us starved," she whispered. "Please order him to stop."

The taragus stared at her and licked his nose with a thin forked tongue. Then he hissed something to the one who was taunting Ilan, and the creature lowered his hand and offered the bread. Then, with the same hand, he ruffled Ilan's head in what looked like an affectionate gesture. Mharina was puzzled, but when she turned back to the leader she simply said, " "Thank you," she said, keeping her voice steady. She walked over and took two bowls, filled them with the warm gruel, and gave them to the twins. She returned, took a bowl for herself, and tore off some bread.

No one bothered her, but as she sat, she saw the leader staring at her. She couldn't tell, but she hoped there was a modicum of respect in its expression.

Chapter Six

Sellia woke and took a moment to stare at the foliage above her, trying to face the reality that this had not all been a dream. She rose with considerable effort, one of her knees clicking in protest. In the old days, she had always slept outside on the ground, with a bed and a solid roof a rare treat. But now she felt every muscle in her body complaining. She supposed she would soon get used to it again.

She stumbled to the small fire that Riona had rekindled. The healer passed her a cup of steaming nettle tea. Sellia thanked her and then stared at Riona's puffy face.

"You didn't sleep well, Riona?"

"I'm fine, thank you."

"Did you sleep at all?" Denalion asked, approaching from behind Sellia. "Someone put in a double shift guarding, for I was not woken."

"You were busy. Don't worry about it." Riona stirred some gruel in a pot, her eyes focused on her cooking.

"What are you talking about?" Sellia asked.

"He was dreamwalking," Pyre said as she joined them, rubbing her hands near the flames for warmth. "He started while I was guarding and continued after my shift."

Sellia looked again to Riona. "You mustn't deplete yourself. We can't have you slowing us down or getting sick."

"I said I'm fine."

"Take that as an order!" Sellia snapped, and the others stared at her. She sighed and winced. "I have no right to…Denalion rightly chastised me last night. But we need to be disciplined and pace ourselves."

"How do you know I was dreamwalking?" Denalion asked.

"You were making strange hooting noises," Riona replied, and Sellia was relieved to see the girl trying to suppress a grin.

"Maybe I was just snoring," Denalion protested.

"No," Pyre added. "We certainly know how you snore."

"Oh, my," Denalion chuckled, and all but Sellia laughed.

"Did you find my children?" she asked the old elf.

"I did. At least, I walked with Mharina for a few moments. I only stayed long enough to establish where they were."

"How is she?" Sellia's voice was soft now.

"She is tough," Denalion replied with a smile. "Like her mother."

They packed up camp and were soon on their way. The horses were switched so those that had carried the supplies the previous day now carried a rider. Sellia led them up through a rocky terrain following a well-worn path. As they passed through a forest, the air became increasingly humid.

Sellia sensed a presence and glimpsed brief movement on either side of them. Two quiet clicks from behind Sellia told her that Pyre had released the safety clips on the scabbards of her Win Dao swords. Sellia adjusted her bow and took an arrow from her quiver.

They rode on. Each time she thought they were safe, she heard another sound or spied a glint of steel. They were being herded along by faceless shadows, and she didn't like it.

"Any ideas?" she whispered.

Denalion was riding behind her. "Wait for an open space or a rock enclave, and then we'll stop."

"Is it them? Taragusii?"

"No."

"How do you know?"

"I just do. And, they would probably attack instead of just shadowing us. "

"You saw them in your dreams further along." She didn't frame this as a question, and he didn't answer.

They continued to ride, undisturbed, and this frayed everyone's nerves. The forest was dense now and darkening due to the thick foliage overhead. At a small stream they stopped and dismounted one at a time to refill their water skins and give their horses a chance to drink.

"Maybe we are simply being escorted through someone's territory," Denalion said. "As long as we don't linger or try and attack anyone, we might be left alone."

No one answered. It was conjecture, but a comforting thought nonetheless. Pyre had been the last to drink, and, as she mounted, a gruff voice spoke from in front of them.

"Or maybe you should consider turning back."

They all stared at a huge man with a large black beard indistinguishable from the hair flowing down from his head. Big, beefy hands grasped a large staff made of thick wood that had been charred to a dark black on the outside. He stood directly in their path.

"Who are you?" Sellia demanded.

"Me? Why, I live here, beautiful elfe. It is for me to ask who you are."

"I am Sellia, and I lead this party. We track a pack of taragusii who passed through here probably a day or so ago."

"And what would three females and an old elf expect to do when they catch up with taragusii? They're fierce creatures. We let them pass unhindered for our own good."

"They have my children," Sellia said. "I doubt their prowess in battle matches the wrath of a mother."

"How many children?"

"Three."

The man glanced into the trees, apparently for confirmation. "You cannot pass. Go home and forget your children. The taragusii don't take prisoners for long. I'm sorry, but your children are as good as dead."

"I will pass," Sellia said. "My children are alive. They are bait for—"

"For us," Denalion interrupted. "Good sir. I appreciate your intentions, but as my lady said, we must pass."

"We won't incur the wrath of the taragusii, old one. You'll have to give me a very good reason for letting you pass."

Sellia noched her bow, but Denalion moved his horse in front of her, gently staying her arm with his hand. He smiled at her pleasantly, and then turned to face the man.

From where she sat, she could only see Denalion's back and the man's face. But it was the latter she gaped at. As he and Denalion stared as each other, the man slowly began to go red. His face bulged, and his eyes looked as if they might pop out of his head.

His staff began to shake, and then it fell to the ground. His hands clasped his head, and his whole body shuddered, wave after wave. Then Denalion looked to one side, and the man dropped to his knees, gasping for breath.

Denalion clicked his horse to a trot and, as he slowly passed the man, he leaned down.

"I'm sorry, my friend. I mean you no harm. Drink plenty of water now and something much stronger when you go to sleep. Do not follow us – not you or any of your people – for I can revisit you in the night, and I *will* find you. I live on both sides of the veil, so killing me will condemn you to a lifetime of nightmares."

He clicked again, sharper this time, and his stallion moved to a brisk trot. The others followed. As the path took them around a corner, Sellia glanced back. Two men were helping their leader to his feet.

She looked ahead and saw Denalion raise his water skin to his lips. She couldn't see his face, but the water skin was visibly shaking.

You'll sleep all night tonight, old one, she said to herself. *You've earned it.*

Chapter Seven

Sellia kept glancing over her shoulder throughout the next day. Denalion rode behind her in silence as she led them easily through the thick forest. He had gone to sleep as soon as they had stopped to camp the night before, and had not woken until morning. None of them thought he had dreamwalked, though they could not be sure.

When they finally left the forest, the sun on their faces was refreshing, and they halted to remove cloaks and drink water. The trees gave way near a high precipice, and Denalion walked over to a rock protruding out over a river below. He turned and stared up at the trees, squinting in the sunlight.

"What are you looking for?" Pyre asked.

"A red-winged owl," he smiled.

"In daylight?" she laughed. "Is he there?"

"Of course not, but he was," Denalion said and walked back toward them.

Sellia had taken out a map and was frowning.

"What are you thinking?" Denalion asked.

"This path we are following circles the sea town of Braithwaite, which is over there." She pointed in the direction of a group of rocks. "After the path leaves the town, it is a day away from the entrance of a long, narrow gorge. The taragusii probably went around, as they would be unwelcome in the town and would not go looking for a fight while they have the children. But we could cut through and pick up supplies."

"What do we know of Braithwaite?" Denalion asked.

"I've been there," Riona said. "It's a rough, outlying settlement. Many of the inhabitants live off the miners and prospectors who work the mountains ahead. It's a fishing port, too, or used to be. I'm not sure how elves will be received there, though draktans will likely speak louder than racial preferences."

Glances were exchanged between Pyre, Denalion, and Sellia. It occurred to Sellia that she knew nothing about Riona before she joined them at Wycaan Island. Seanchai had said that she had already come with considerable healing knowledge and experience, but he would not share whatever Riona had confided in him.

"We'll go through the town," Sellia said at last. "We'll have a hot meal and then head out. If it brings us closer to my children, I'll take the risk."

They climbed back onto their horses and began to ride. A short while later, they reached a junction. Tracks led in two different directions from the way they had come, but they could make out the outskirts of the town and the deep blue of the ocean beyond down the path to the right.

"Are you sure about this?" Denalion asked.

Sellia shrugged. "I don't feel inclined to cower in the shadows just because my ears are pointed. Odessiya has moved on."

"This isn't Odessiya," Denalion replied. "I doubt they have even heard of Seanchai and what he has done."

"Then maybe it's about time they did."

Sellia wore a grim expression as she nudged her horse forward. Denalion glanced at the others. Pyre's green eyes offered no outward expression, but there was a scowl on Riona's face.

The town was more disheveled than the last time Riona had passed through. The outlying neighborhoods were really just shacks that might have once served as homes. They passed through a gate that stood in a wooden wall made of logs bound together. The logs looked flimsy, but were probably designed only to keep wild animals out.

The buildings got bigger and better maintained as they rode further toward the quay. Shops, a small market, and eateries intertwined with houses and hotels. There could hear seagulls and smell a fresh, salty breeze. Sellia stopped by a building with several tables outside.

"Let's eat here. We can sit outside and keep an eye on the horses. We'll leave them saddled in case we need to move out fast."

They dismounted, tied their horses, and moved to an empty table. They sat for a short while and, though the chairs were rough, they were still more comfortable than the ground the company had become used to. The warm sunshine on their faces helped them all relax, and they sat for a while, each in their own thoughts.

Finally, Riona rose. "I think we need to go inside for service. I'll order."

Inside, the saloon was dark and smoky. Undistinguishable eyes followed her as she walked to the counter. A big man with a dirty apron watched her approach.

"What kin I getcha?" he asked, his eyes roving down her body.

Riona regretted packing her cloak. "There are four of us outside. We are hungry, but have little time. What do you have that is hot and ready to eat?"

The man glanced back into the kitchen and yelled. "'erb. Get me four plates o' stew an' some bread." He turned back to Riona. "A draktan from each o'ya and I'll bring ya some ale on the house."

"What's in the stew?"

"Fish. What else d'ya expect? We don't 'unt much in the woods, but the sea's safe enouf an' plent'ful."

"Why don't you hunt much?"

"Too often the 'unter becomes the 'unted. Know what I mean? 'eard a pack o' taragusii just passed by." The man took her money and counted it slowly.

A voice spoke from behind her. "A pretty fing like you shouldn't worry 'bout them when you 'ave strong men like us to protect ya."

Riona turned around, her body tensing. The voice came from one of three stout, rough-shaven men who were unabashedly admiring her backside. He stood up rather unsteadily.

"Come over 'ere 'n join us? We'll give ya more 'an fish stew." His friends laughed.

"No, thank you. My friends are outside."

"Two fine looking she-elves, I see. Ditch the old elf, and we'll 'ave a party. There's three o'ya 'n three o' us."

"They prefer to be called elfes, not she-elves," Riona answered, keeping her voice calm, "and those two elfes are hunting taragusii, not cowering from them. They might be a bit out of your league."

The other two men laughed with a little less enthusiasm. The one standing looked at them. He had to grip the side of the table to maintain his balance, and his cheeks were flushed.

"Ah, I like me women feisty, and I'm very accepting of *elfes*, if they're pretty 'nough."

Riona turned to the proprietor. "I'd best wait outside."

But as she turned to leave, the man blocked her path.

"Let me through, sir. Our mission is urgent, and my friends impatient."

"I want ya to join us 'ere at our table," the man insisted. "I fink you'll find us manly enough for ya and ya elfe friends."

The tip of a blue sword blade nudged into the man's cheek. A quiet, well-accented voice pierced the hushed room. "The lady wants to wait outside. She's a healer, and one day you might have need of her services. Now sit, or that day will come sooner than you expect."

The blade grazed down the man's cheek and pressed on his shoulder. The man carefully sat, and Riona walked past. She glanced up at her hooded rescuer, but could not distinguish anything. Then she stopped and turned to him.

"Would you eat with my party, sir?"

"I have eaten. Thank you."

"Then at least allow me to buy you a drink in gratitude. I insist." She nodded to the proprietor for another tankard.

The man smiled and followed her outside.

At the doorway, she whirled around. "How do you know I'm a healer?"

The voice came from deep inside his cowl. "I know who you are, Riona Sh—"

She gasped, and her hand grabbed his chin. "No one knows," she hissed. "Not even my friends who sit at that table. No one."

"Understood. Am I still invited for that ale? And please, remove your other hand from the hilt of your knife."

Riona had not realized she was holding her knife. She slid it out just a bit. "Promise you won't reveal me."

"For now. We can talk later. But your friends are watching. Compose yourself."

He signaled with his hand toward the table, leaving Riona no choice. She turned to face her friends and put on her best smile.

Chapter Eight

Sellia realized she was more irked by Riona's smile as she made her way to the table than she was by the presence of the hooded stranger following her. Riona rarely smiled, and Sellia's hand went slowly to loosen her short knife. The stranger pulled a chair from another table and sat between Riona and Denalion.

"I ran into some trouble in there," Riona said. "This gentleman stepped in, and I invited him to join us for a drink."

"I thought it was elves they hated," Sellia said.

"They didn't hate her," the man said, his voice soft. "Quite the opposite. Sending a pretty young wench in tight breeches into a tavern like this is hardly the most strategic move."

Riona blushed at the compliment and glanced down at her trousers. Sellia smiled, enjoying the young woman's discomfort.

"Thank you for aiding my friend," the elfe said to the man. She was about to ask his name, but stopped as a young boy appeared, precariously balancing an array of bowls, steam wafting up in promise. Her stomach rumbled.

The proprietor followed with a jug of ale and tankards. Sellia glared at him.

"Do you usually allow your customers to behave so badly to other customers?"

"Where d' ya fink this is?" he snapped back. "Ya're far from ya home, dark elfe. Keep that bow close. Enjoy ya food, and then move on. Ya trouble 'ere."

Sellia watched him walk back inside. "He didn't mind taking our money," she muttered.

"Don't be hard on him," the man replied. "It's tough to grind out a living in these parts, and those scum inside probably spend most of their wages in there."

Sellia bristled, but kept silent. They began to eat, and Denalion poured the ale. He offered the first tankard to the man.

"Excuse us. We have been traveling hard and are probably not the greatest company, but we appreciate you coming to Riona's defense."

The man nodded. "Why are you tracking taragusii?"

"They have my children," Sellia said.

"I'm sorry. Are you sure they're still—"

"Yes." Her dark eyes blazed at him.

"Again, I'm sorry. But that doesn't sound like taragusii behavior."

"They're following orders from one scarier than them."

Denalion leaned forward. "Excuse me for asking, sir, but could you lower your hood? It's hard to talk to a stranger you cannot look in the eye."

The man hesitated a moment, and then pulled his cowl back. His straw-colored hair was long, crinkled, and parted in the middle. He had a yellowish beard, and his eyes were green. Sellia judged him to be around thirty or thirty-five years old, but his sun-beaten face made it hard to estimate.

"What do you know of the taragusii?" Sellia asked.

"Been paid to clear them out from the forest around here. They usually hunt in twos and threes. There are a few fortune-swords in these parts, and we team up and hunt them. Most of my friends have moved on, as our prey became sparse. Rumor has it that the taragusii were summoned somewhere."

"You choose rather fierce opponents," Denalion said.

"The fiercer they are, the greater the payment."

"Why haven't you moved on?" Denalion sipped his ale.

The man shrugged. "I like the fishing town. There is action here, especially nearer the docks. Gambling, women, you know."

"Not really," Denalion replied with a smile, "but I can imagine."

They went silent again.

"Where did you learn to fight?" Sellia asked after a while.

"Held a sword as soon as I could walk. I was trained in the Emperor's army back in the old days. But I don't take orders very well, and, while I have no problem killing a man who stands before me wielding a sword, I took no satisfaction in some of the tasks assigned."

"Maybe you could join us," Sellia said. "We have need of more swords, and you know the taragusii."

"Can you pay? You don't seem to have assembled much of an army."

Sellia saw Pyre tense, as did the man, who held up his hands in apology. "I was referring to quantity, not quality, milady."

Denalion and Sellia both laughed, while Pyre pouted and Riona scowled.

"The money I have with me might be needed for food and supplies. But I have means. If we return alive, I will see you handsomely rewarded."

"I notice a distinct lack of numbers involved. I will require a contract and some kind of proof."

"You can trust her," Pyre snapped. "She is…"

Sellia's hand stopped her.

"It is not a question of trust, young warrior," the man replied. "What if your lady doesn't survive this expedition?"

Sellia removed a ring from her finger. "Show this to Prince Shindell. He gave it to me when my eldest was born. He will reward you."

The man picked up the ring and examined it closely. It was gold with tiny red stones all the way around. He shook his head and set it down.

"I assure you it is quite valuable," Sellia said, leaving it on the table.

"I don't doubt that. But I would have great difficulty getting its true value from anyone in these parts."

"I said to take it to Prince Shindell," Sellia arched an eyebrow. "He rules in–"

The man laughed. "I won't go anywhere near the one we both knew as Shayth. I value my life highly and have survived by staying away from people like him."

"He's changed," Sellia snapped, surprised at the intensity of her own reaction.

"Not inside. Not deep down. Men like that don't change. His rage is like a dormant volcano, sealed away, but still boiling. He has learned to master it, not destroy it."

"You know him?" Riona asked.

"Knew him. Look, I'll think about it. If I decide to join you, I'll have the quill-master draft a contract. He'll leave space on the parchment for numbers and seal. Agreed?"

"We're not hanging around," Sellia said.

"You'll head through the pass," the man predicted, nodding to the imposing mountain range that shadowed the edge of town. "I'll catch you up, but I have some business to tie up first. Thank you for the ale."

He stood to go.

"If I die," Sellia said with a sly smile, "how will you receive your money if you don't take the ring?"

The answer came without the man turning round. "I hear the Wycaan is an honorable elf."

They all watched him walk off. Sellia looked over at Riona. Could the girl get any paler?

Chapter Nine

Riona glanced over her shoulder…again.

"He'll come, don't worry," Sellia said.

Riona was certain that Sellia, who was riding in front of her and had not looked round, was smirking. Her horse snorted conspiratorially, and the healer slapped it playfully.

"How do you know?" Pyre piped up from the back.

Sellia was shaking her head. She was, she assumed, the most experienced with males among the three of them.

"How do you know?" Pyre repeated.

"We made him an interesting business proposal, and he can make a lot of money from serving Seanchai." Riona answered rather too quickly. She winced.

There was an uncomfortable silence, and then Pyre replied: "*Oh*, I see."

That made Sellia laugh out loud. It was the first time the elfe had laughed since her children had been kidnapped, and it sounded alien.

"Riona?" Denalion asked over his shoulder.

"Yes?"

"What do you know about that man?"

"Nothing you don't," she replied, deciding that wasn't a lie. "I don't even know his name."

But the man knew her, and he wasn't much older. She searched back into a past she had long locked away. It wasn't comforting, and she withdrew.

Sellia had stopped and dismounted. Riona looked around warily, and then dismounted, too. Only Pyre remained on her horse, and, while one hand held the reins, the other was on the hilt of one of her swords.

"It's okay," Sellia called out. "I just saw something in the tracks."

Riona bent down. Some of the taragusii had been walking on foot, and the prints were a mixture of those four-toed prints and the sharp horse hooves of the creatures that bore them. But what Sellia had seen were three pairs of smaller elf footprints. The sight made her weep.

Sellia took a deep breath and drank some water. She poured a little onto her hand and washed her face. She stared again at her children's footprints and sighed. It had been a shock.

She had not stopped worrying about them, but had internalized the situation and allowed herself to relax as they had bantered over the man and his attraction to Riona. Her body was reacclimatizing to living outside and, though she worried constantly for Mharina and the twins, a part of her felt an adrenaline rush that had been absent since the days she had aided Seanchai in overthrowing the Emperor.

But now she was a mother, and a mother in pain. She climbed back on her horse and nudged it on. She didn't wait to see if the others were following.

The path began to ascend into the mountains. This worried Sellia, as the narrow gorge would be a perfect place for an ambush. If the taragusii surprised them, they would not stand much of a chance.

She reined in and waited for the others.

"I think we should ride through here at night. Denalion: you said the taragusii have no night vision, right?"

The redheaded elf nodded.

"Then we rest. I'll take first shift if anyone wants to sleep."

She stared at Denalion. He dismounted stiffly, and Pyre offered to groom his horses. He just nodded in appreciation and settled down against a tree, his cloak wrapped around him.

"He gets very tired," Pyre said to Sellia as they watched him while grooming the horses.

"I think when he dreamwalks he is asleep, but not resting," Sellia replied.

"Do you need him to walk tonight?"

"No. I just *want* him to. I want to know my children are okay, and if Seanchai is coming."

"Denalion has not managed to connect with him yet," Riona said as she unsaddled her horses. "Why is that?"

"I don't know. I have asked him too many times. While on Wycaan Island, he suspected the Emperor had cast some kind of psychic shield. But, well, I don't know why he isn't succeeding."

"How old is he?" Riona asked, her voice almost a whisper.

Pyre glared at her. "Denalion is a living legend among our people. He has served the Elves of the West for centuries."

"Centuries?"

"Yes. I think he has been our dreamwalker for three hundred years, and it takes decades of training and dedication to walk such a path."

"I mean no offense," Riona answered. "He's been my only friend since I came to the academy, and I have great respect for him. But all I have seen until now is a wise old elf tutoring the *calhei* and advising Seanchai. This is far more...physically demanding."

"I'll be fine, Riona," Denalion said from where he lay. "There is still life in these old bones – plenty of it. And I am honored to be counted as your friend."

Pyre groomed her and Denalion's horses, while Riona lit a fire.

Sellia crouched by Denalion, who was watching Riona work. "She cares about you, I'm sure. Why do you not sleep?"

"I will sleep, but I cannot dreamwalk. The children will not sleep for a few hours."

"What about Seanchai? Have you not been able to contact him?"

"No. I am focusing on Rhoddan, Maugwen, and Shayth. If Seanchai has sensed the Emperor's presence, he will have shielded himself. I don't understand why I can't reach the others, however. It worries me."

"Perhaps you are too tired," Sellia said. "We'll wait here tonight and tomorrow. You use that time to recover."

Denalion looked at her. "At some point, you might want to consider going on without me. I am of little use in a battle, and when the Emperor gets wind of me, my dreamwalking will be very limited. Once I become a burden, promise you will press on. The children must come first."

Sellia nodded and patted his arm. "Get some sleep, dreamwalker."

CHAPTER TEN

“I'm tired. I want to ride their horse-thingies. Ask him, Mharina.”

Mharina sighed. Ilan was a pain in the butt at the best of times, always following her around and never able to sit quietly. The twins were both softer and more sensitive than she was. Both had fair hair and blue eyes.

Mharina was dark-skinned like their mother, and loved physical exercise. For three years now, her mother had personally taught her how to shoot the bow. She had treasured those moments. When her mother had gone out hunting, Mharina had begged to join her. If her mother had let her come the last time, Mharina wouldn't be stuck with the twins right now.

Senzia tugged her arm. “I need to pee, Mharina. We haven't stopped for ages.”

This was true. Two of the creatures they rode had gone lame on the stony path, and now the leader had everyone walking. And he was very clear that meant *everyone*.

To make matters worse, they had entered a narrow gorge, which seemed to make the taragusii uneasy. Mharina had gone to ask the leader for a break earlier, but he had brushed her off. He wanted to get through the gorge as quickly as possible. Something was spooking them and, given how strong and powerful the taragusii were, she was worried what it might be.

"We're going to stop soon," she told her sister. "Wait a while."

"But Mharina!" She hated it when her little sister whined.

"You're welcome to run ahead and tell him yourself," she snapped.

The conversation was over.

"Come here, girl," the leader hissed.

They were sitting around the fire, having just finished eating. Mharina was planning on getting the twins ready for bed. Her leg muscles ached from the day's walk, and the soles of her feet were sore. She would do some of her mother's stretching exercises when Ilan and Senzia were settled, or else she was going to be very stiff in the morning. She was looking forward to sleeping, in the hopes that Denalion would visit in her dreams. He had not come in two days, and she worried something might be wrong.

But now, she stared at the huge taragus. He was holding the same big metal cup that he produced every night. The other taragusii were scared of him and would bring him food and drink, but otherwise left him alone.

"I sssaid to come here." His tone was insistent, but not cross. He spoke slowly, weighing every word, or perhaps just uncomfortable with the language.

Mharina knew his angry voice and certainly wanted to avoid that. She took a deep breath, glanced over at the twins, who were still eating, and walked slowly over to him. He patted a rock next to the log he sat on, and she scrambled up onto it. She was nearly his height now.

"You do well, little elfe," he said. "You do not ssshow fear. Are you afraid?"

Mharina considered what was the best answer. She was scared, and finally admitted to it.

"Undersssstandable," he said. "You would be foolisssh not to be. Asss long as you do not try to essscape, you will not be harmed. Undersssstand?"

She nodded. "Where would we run to?" she said. "You're faster than us and used to this kind of land."

"Ssso true. Yet I sssee hope in your eyes. You are not defeated asss others would be. Why isss that?"

Mharina stared into the fire. She had nothing to lose by telling the truth. "I believe that our parents will come and rescue us. I don't think whoever sent you to kidnap us actually wants me or my sister and brother. We're *calhei*, elf children. We don't count for much."

"Excccept to your parentsss," he replied. "My massster wantsss your father. Ever sssince I came to ssserve him, he hasss talked of nothing elssse. I wonder if your father isss really that powerful?"

"I guess so. To me he is the most powerful elf in Odessiya. But what would you expect a daughter to say?"

The taragus laughed. It was a rasping hiss, but she preferred it to his fury. "But you are not in Odesssiya anymore. Ssstill, I think he mussst be formidable, judging by hisss daughter."

They sat together in silence for a while, and then the lizard-like creature turned to her. His scales were shiny and metallic in the firelight.

"It will take sssome time for your father to come after usss?"

"Yes," she nodded, "assuming he knows you have us. He's a long way away."

"That wasss the idea. We need the time to get you to the Massster."

"Who is this master?"

"*The* Massster. He once ruled all of Odessssiya."

"The Emperor?" Mharina frowned. "He's alive?"

"The Massster. And yesss, he isss very much alive."

Mharina was shocked by the revelation and decided to change track. "How many more days will it take?"

"Sssome days, maybe a week. Your sssiblings ssslow usss down, but that wasss expected."

"They're young, only ten," she replied. "It's hard on them."

"Yesss, they are young, asss are you. You impresss me, Mharina. You are ssstrong, ssstronger than you think."

"Thank you." She wanted to think she was strong, but right now, she was confused.

"Go ssssleep now. Tomorrow isss another long day, and it will get colder before we reach the desssert."

Mharina jumped off the rock and began to move around the fire. Then a thought occurred to her. She turned back to the taragus.

"Do you have children?"

"Yesss, I have a mate and many children. We call our children *bata*. They all ssserve the massster."

"They are captives? Is that how he commands you?" She was surprised that she actually felt concern for him.

The taragus didn't respond. He stared into the fire and quietly hissed to himself. Occasionally, his thin, forked tongue darted out and licked his nose. Then, as if remembering where he was, he started and looked at her.

"Go to sssleep, little elfe. Go tend to your sssiblings."

Mharina looked at him and then nodded. "Do you have a name?"

"I am Third Sssscale."

"Good night then, Third Scale," she said. "If you dream of your *bata*, say hi from me."

As she took the twins into the trees to relieve themselves, she reflected on the conversation. It seemed absurd for her to feel anything for those who had captured her and killed many people at Wycaan Island. But she *did* feel empathy for Third Scale.

She would ask Denalion if he visited her in her dreams. She hoped he would, and it was this that kept her calm. Surely Denalion would bring her father and save them. He would fight this master and beat him.

Then it occurred to her that maybe this master was more powerful than her father. He commanded the taragusii, after all. Her father had once fought in battles, but what if he was less powerful than this master? Suddenly, she was not so sure she wanted him to come and rescue them. It was a heavy realization. As she lay in her blanket, Mharina closed her eyes, and, for the first time, allowed herself to silently sob.

CHAPTER ELEVEN

Seanchai's leg muscles were stiff, and he took a moment to stretch them. His exercises should not be this hard, but they were. He had intensified his training ever since rumors that the Emperor might be behind the Wild Men of the North's uprising had surfaced. It was not as if he had stopped training completely these past years, but his personal daily practice was not the priority it had been in the past.

There was always so much to do. The establishment of the school on Wycaan Island was of paramount importance, and his training with the acolytes had, he thought, maintained his personal level of fitness or fighting. When they were together, he also had Rhoddan to keep him on his toes. But Prince Shindell – Seanchai would never get used to the title – was increasingly calling upon Rhoddan to lead all kinds of missions throughout the kingdom.

And then there were the many missions when a Wycaan was requested. Seanchai had ridden through most of Odessiya, helping to build and solidify the alliance with the land-bound aqua'lanis – though he had not fulfilled his promise to help them go home – the tutan, the dwarves, and many other races. He had spent considerable time working with elves in the first few years after the Emperor had been defeated. For an oppressed people to suddenly be emancipated, freedom was a drastic and oft-misunderstood concept. In these situations, Seanchai was better placed than Shayth to intervene and lead.

Finally, Seanchai was a father, which sadly had to be his last priority. He was surprised how easily he had embraced the role, and he could think of nothing he preferred than to walk, talk, and play with Mharina, Ilan, and Senzia.

His closeness to and natural ability with their children had created tension between him and Sellia. She was not naturally cut out to be a mother, though the children loved her deeply, and she them. He knew she resented him leaving her to parent alone and run the school in his place. As soon as he returned each time, she would grab her bow and head out to hunt. They rarely argued, but he could feel the rift growing, and it saddened him.

He had planned to take the family to the Shanrea – the Elves of the West – and to see Sellia's recently discovered family. He had planned it several times, in fact, and now knew better than to suggest it beforehand. Sellia had gone once without him, taking Mharina when the *calhei* was just a year old.

He would need to put all this behind him if he was indeed to face the Emperor again. The thought sent ice through his veins. He had only beaten the Emperor before because of his alliance with the bears. Since then, he had rarely tried to change back or find them in the dream world. Now he realized this might have been a huge mistake. He had grown stronger and delved deeper into the Wycaan Mysteries, but still he feared confronting the Emperor.

"If you've finished exercising, we should return to camp," Rhoddan said, perched on a rock nearby. "It's time for breakfast."

"It's always time for a meal with you," Seanchai laughed.

"I'm a growing *calhei*," Rhoddan protested.

"Not so young anymore, my friend, but certainly growing."

Seanchai had not said this in jest. Rhoddan was considerably bigger these days. He could probably look Uncle in the eye, and could certainly wrestle the huge leader to the ground.

As they returned to camp, Seanchai reflected on how long they had been together. Rhoddan had been sent, at the very beginning, to escort Seanchai as far as Uncle's camp, but ended up taking him all the way to Mhari, Seanchai's first teacher. When Rhoddan was captured, Seanchai had gone to Galbrieth to rescue him. They had stayed together ever since.

"You're like a brother to me," Seanchai reflected, and blushed when he realized he had shared his thoughts out loud.

Rhoddan laughed. "Where did that come from?"

"I don't know," Seanchai said. "The prospect of facing the Emperor has me feeling vulnerable. I need to train harder."

"Can't argue with that," Rhoddan said. "We knew one day it would happen. Why didn't you go after him when he was wounded and alone?"

"I meant to, but there was always so much happening with Shayth and the new kingdom. Then, when Mharina was born, and the twins after her, I didn't want to leave them." He stopped and considered the surfacing emotions. "I don't want to die. I never did, but now, the thought of never seeing my children again – the thought of them being denied even the childhood that I had…"

His voice trailed off.

"Well," Rhoddan said, "better that you face him in the north than anywhere near Wycaan Island. No? At least you know your children are safe." He slapped Seanchai on the shoulder. "Come. I'm hungry."

The Wycaan lay on his bearskin. He was tired, and his eyes soon closed.

He stood on a sharp ridge and felt the wind ruffle his fur. Standing on his hind legs, he looked out over the land of Odessiya stretching out in all directions. He was alone, and this time, unlike in the past, he wasn't sure if they would come.

His elf eyesight was sharp, and he scrutinized every movement. He sniffed, hoping to catch a scent. Would they understand that he had new responsibilities, duties, and…no! He knew he was wrong not to come back and spend time with them. They were his family, too, and, when he had most needed them, they had risked everything to protect him.

But they were not coming. He grunted and lowered himself awkwardly to walk on all four paws. He descended from the ridge and saw a river glistening in the sunlight. He began to gallop, stiffly at first, feeling the pain in muscles seldom used. Gradually, his body adapted to the motion, and, by the time he reached the water, his gait was comfortable.

At the edge of the river, he stopped and sniffed the air. There were some elk or deer upwind, but no bears. He tentatively dipped a paw into the water and snorted. As an elf, he would have balked at the coldness of the icy water, but as a bear, he felt nothing and sauntered in.

The river was shallow, and, even as it flowed, he could see clearly into the water. The glint of fish evading his paws excited him. He looked around again, self-conscious that he could never master fishing as other bears had. He thought of the brown bear cubs that had playfully mocked him, and he guffawed to himself.

But the merriment soon faded. How could he, the Wycaan, have been so stupid to neglect them? He slashed at a fish in front of him. It was a clumsy swipe, borne of personal frustration. He focused now and eventually caught two fish.

Then he saw something in his peripheral vision. He jerked his head round at a tall rock. Something had been there. Again, he saw it. Something red and shimmering. He screwed up his eyes and then blinked. It was there and not there. An animal, he was sure — a red animal, maybe a bear — and it was pawing, almost frantically, signaling something.

Denalion had once transformed into a red panda, but they had agreed not to connect if the Emperor ever resurfaced. The dreamwalker had been adamant. It could endanger both of them. If Denalion needed him, he would be able to connect with Rhoddan, Shayth, Maugwen, or another from his entourage.

It was wishful thinking. The bears hadn't come. Denalion wouldn't come. Seanchai felt suddenly very alone. He missed his cubs, his mate, and his home.

Up in the sky above the snow-covered peaks, he saw a faint stream of fire. He stared, jaws open, and then quickly transitioned out of the dream.

Chapter Twelve

"T hey didn't come?"

"No," came Seanchai's curt reply.

Rhoddan glanced over at his friend, but Seanchai had pulled his hood over his head, and all Rhoddan could see was the swirl of the Wycaan's breath in the cold dawn air.

"They'll come," he said, at a loss how to respond.

"What makes you such an expert?"

"Hey! The bears know you screwed up, but you'll call them every night now. They will hear and come. Few of us can resist you."

Rhoddan's jest did little to comfort Seanchai, and they rode on in silence. The party climbed into a steep mountain pass, and the horses found the thin air hard going. Shayth called numerous breaks, and Seanchai became increasingly agitated. At one such break, the prince signaled for Rhoddan to ride with him a hundred paces ahead of the soldiers.

"What's his problem?"

Rhoddan relayed what had not happened with the bears, and Shayth nodded.

"I understand, but he can't defy me in public. If he has a problem, he'll always have my ear, but my subjects are watching. I would choose Seanchai over this crown any time, but if I have to play the part ... well, so does he."

"I'll talk to him," Rhoddan answered.

They sat on their horses, side by side, staring at the mountains in front of them.

"Do you ever tire of following him? How much longer until the great hero Rhoddan finds a beautiful elfe to settle down with? They probably line up for your attention."

"If they do, I've not noticed," Rhoddan answered. "I swore loyalty to Seanchai – committed myself a long time ago. It's never a question."

He felt Shayth staring at him, and shifted uncomfortably in his saddle.

"You've been with me for a long time, too, Rhoddan. I owe you my life a dozen times over."

"As I owe you mine."

"Then what is it?"

"Nothing."

"So answer me truly: is there an elfe in your dreams?"

Rhoddan was silent for a long time. He frowned, struggling with the truth he had never shared.

Shayth pressed, intrigued. "I've never seen you pursue an elfe in all the years we've been together."

"It's complicated and best left alone," Rhoddan finally snapped. "Ilana made sure of that."

"You were in love with Ilana?" Shayth raised his eyebrows, thinking of Seanchai's first mate.

"No. I loved her as you all did, but … ." Rhoddan looked down at the ground. "I will never forgive her for forcing Sellia to take her place."

"Sellia? You can't be serious, Rhoddan. You would blush if she even looked your way."

Rhoddan looked up at Shayth. "And now you know why," he said. "None of you ever questioned why Sellia was the only elfe to have this effect on me. I thought it was so obvious, but I was ever the loyal, stoic warrior."

"Does she know?"

"No. At least, I hope not." His voice became sharp. "And if you ever tell her or Seanchai, well, that crown won't save you."

"You shouldn't talk to royalty like that!" Shayth frowned, and then burst out laughing. "Of course I won't."

"How about you, Shayth? Surely the Prince of Odessiya, scruffy though he may be, must make for a good catch."

"Not only that, but I am expected to find a suitable bride and produce an heir. It regularly appears as an item of business when I meet with my council."

Rhoddan laughed. "You're kidding! Is there no one? Are you looking?"

"Haven't found anyone yet, but yes, I'm looking, and having fun along the way."

The noise of soldiers mounting and preparing to move brought them back to reality. They turned and watched as Seanchai caught up with them.

"Who gave the order to continue?" Shayth asked, his tone sharp.

"I did. We need to quicken our pace."

"We're bringing a lot of supplies and food for an army, and the carts move slowly," Shayth said. "We have to feed the horses and keep them fresh and warm. These are cavalry horses, and they're not used to this cold. The pictorians cannot provide us with provisions, and we don't know how long this campaign might continue."

Seanchai didn't answer, and Rhoddan and Shayth exchanged glances.

"Maybe Seanchai and I should go ahead?" Rhoddan suggested.

"What's that look you gave each other?" Seanchai snapped suspiciously.

"Listen, Seanchai," Rhoddan said, "you're not much fun right now, and Shayth needs to be seen by his subjects as the prince."

Seanchai straightened up and stared at the looming mountains. Then he turned to Shayth. "Have I been out of line?"

Shayth smiled. "Yes. It's good for me, a reminder that I'm only a pretender. But it's confusing for those who must follow their prince into battle."

"I'm sorry. I need to watch myself."

"You're worried about facing him again. It's alright."

"I'm worried about facing him alone," Seanchai sighed. "The tales the bards sing are kind to me, but not accurate. I only won last time because the bears intervened and that way is shut to me, at least for now."

Without the constraints of a military column, Seanchai and Rhoddan rode faster. Shayth insisted they take another two horses, and, when they camped that night, the snow was thick on the ground and the trees long behind and below them.

Rhoddan got a fire going with a small amount of wood they had brought. There were fourteen wagons behind them full of wood, but still, he rationed it. They unsaddled the horses and tied them nearby with bags of grain to eat, as there was nothing on the barren ground to graze. They bound furs around each hoof and Rhoddan suggested they bring the horses closer to the fire when they went to sleep, which meant sacrificing their own warmth through the night.

When they had eaten and taken care of the horses, they wrapped themselves up in furs and lay down staring at the small fire.

"What were you and Shayth talking about earlier, apart from my misbehavior?"

"Nothing," Rhoddan lied.

Seanchai looked up, perhaps alerted to the curtness of his friend's response.

"Really? Was my behavior that bad to be the only topic of conversation?"

Rhoddan was quiet for a while, then said: "Actually, we were talking about elfes and women."

Seanchai yawned. "Aw. I'd have liked to be part of that."

Rhoddan glanced at his friend who was already falling asleep. Then he looked back into the dying embers and sighed … deeply.

Chapter Thirteen

It was a tense ride through the gorge. Every movement had Sellia and Pyre, who rode at the front and rear with bows ready, reaching for their quivers. Riona rode behind Denalion, who was visibly weak. Her periodic check-ins concerning his welfare, elicited short, curt responses, and this was the only conversation.

Sellia had vented her frustration on the dreamwalker for not contacting Mharina the previous night. She knew he had expended considerable energy trying to reach Seanchai, and when he had not succeeded, he tried with Rhoddan, Shayth, and Maugwen. It had not helped when Denalion confirmed that Seanchai was in the north, above the snowline, and heading further north.

Riona was no help, either. She was sullen, and Sellia could not decide whether to attribute this to her fortune-sword not catching up, or the way Sellia was treating the old elf, who the healer was very fond of.

"Dreamwalker, do you need a break?" Riona asked once more, braving Sellia's stiffening body language.

"It's too dangerous," Denalion said, breaking his silence. "Move faster. We must get through this gorge soon."

Sellia swung around in her saddle. "We go too fast, and we tire the horses or run the risk of one becoming lame. Neither do

I want the noise of a galloping party to give away our position. We maintain this pace."

"Then move to the rear and prepare to help Pyre," Denalion replied. "We are being chased."

Sellia heard the hooves immediately and spurred her horse forward. She had been prepared for an attack from above the steep rock walls or from the taragusii in front of them. How had the creatures gotten behind them? Was there a second group following? Had they doubled-back?

She had to get her party through the gorge and off the road. The end was near, and she hoped there would be shelter to conceal them. The galloping horses behind them would catch them easily. At least the curvy gorge kept them out of sight.

When they broke through the other side, Sellia gasped. It was all flat, empty desert. She cursed, and then swung to her left. They would make a stand with the rock face behind them. She maneuvered her horse around and noched an arrow. Pyre immediately followed suit. Denalion's gelding had followed Sellia's, but Riona's was spooked and bolted forward into the open desert. Pyre prepared to spur her horse forward to help, but Sellia barked at her to stop.

Eight riders galloped through the pass in pursuit of Riona. Sellia and Pyre quickly brought four down with two arrows each, but the rest sped out of range.

"Go," Sellia yelled. "Leave the spare horses with Denalion."

She kicked her heels into her steed and rode hard into the thick, blinding dust cloud. Sellia pulled her shirt up over her mouth and nose, but the sand flew into her eyes. She was vaguely aware that her horse was struggling to find traction on a sand dune. When they reached the top, she found herself in the end of a fight.

The fortune-sword was pulling his blade from one of three prone bodies. Riona stood with her long, dark hair splayed in all directions and her cheeks flushed. She was holding a dirk in one hand and what looked like a sling in the other.

Sellia shivered at the rage in Riona's dark eyes. Such hatred; such fury. It reminded her...

The fortune-sword rose, his back to Sellia, and turned on Riona. "You almost hit me with that...that thing."

"There's *almost* and *actually* hitting you. Believe me, you would know the difference." Riona deftly twirled, and then folded, the sling up, and it disappeared inside her cloak.

The man harrumphed.

Riona turned back and sneered. "Maybe you're upset at being outscored by a woman in combat?"

"I'm upset about a pr—"

"JUST SHUT UP!" Riona screamed, and the man, to his credit, went silent.

Sellia thought the healer was about to attack him. "Are you okay, Riona?"

Riona nodded and turned away to compose herself. Pyre had dismounted and checked the bodies. Now she stood next to the man. "Who are they? Are there more coming?"

"Just them," he replied. "One of them owed me money from a game the night before I met you. I went to collect, and he refused to pay. So I followed him to his room and took what he owed me."

Pyre glared at him. "Seems like a lot of trouble to chase you for money already lost."

The fortune-sword pushed his long, straw-colored hair out of his face and smiled, pretending to be sheepish. "Obviously, there's a fine for not paying your debts, plus interest and expenses incurred."

"You stole from them," Pyre snapped. "And then you endangered our lives bringing them here."

"The way I see it—"

"I don't care how you see it." She turned to Sellia. "Are you going to let him ride with us?"

Sellia glanced at the man's sword. It had a blue hue to it, and the handle was wrapped in silver twine. She had no doubt he knew how to use it. A man doesn't keep a sword like that for long if he didn't.

"Did you draw up that contract?" she asked.

He grinned, walked to his horse, and dug into a saddlebag. He returned with a small scroll.

"You can't be serious," Pyre spat.

Sellia looked at her. "They are my children, Pyre. I must do what is best to rescue them. Please return and help Denalion with the horses."

Pyre produced an impressive snort and jumped on her horse. Riona had returned and was looking at the contract. There was still a scowl on her face, but she was in control. Then she began searching the ground around one of the prone bodies, eventually retrieving what looked like a sharp stone. She then went to a second corpse and, with her boot pushing on the man's face, yanked something out from the man's forehead.

Then she returned to the fortune-sword and Sellia. "I think you should add a condition," she said to Sellia. "No gambling."

The man laughed out loud, and the young healer blushed.

"What is your name?" Sellia asked the man.

"Montclair," he replied.

Riona's blush disappeared, replaced by a white, shocked expression.

Chapter Fourteen

"How far does this desert stretch?" Sellia asked, gazing at endless sand and a few isolated, spindly trees.

"Very far," Montclair replied. "I have never needed to reach the other side, but I have always found a small oasis when needed. We will not lack for water if we ration it."

"Do the taragusii drink water?"

"They will care for your children if they are being used as bait. The taragusii are intelligent creatures," he added, adjusting his shoulder-length, straw-colored hair. "But I have a question: for whom are they bait?"

"My husband," Sellia replied.

"It is said that the Emperor always plans several steps ahead."

"I have heard others use that phrase," she frowned.

"Shayth?" His tone was bitter, and Sellia didn't bother to respond. When he spoke again, his voice had returned to its normal deep tone. "Excuse me. The Emperor will have anticipated that you would give chase, no?"

"If he understands about mothers and love." Sellia felt Montclair's gaze upon her. "What is it?" she asked.

"I have heard that the Wycaan is a dedicated father."

"When he's around, he's the best," she replied, and then it gushed out. "But he wasn't around when the taragusii took my children and slaughtered everyone else on the island."

Montclair spat on the ground. "And how did you survive the attack?"

"I was out hunting. A red firebreather kept me away. What does that tell you?"

Montclair grimaced and wiped the sweat from his brow. "That you are expected. That you are walking into a trap."

"Still want to join us?"

"I want your gold," Montclair said. "I might be ready to settle down. I'm a fortune-sword – a very good one, or I wouldn't still be alive. But those of my profession rarely retire."

"Why not?"

"There's always a better fortune-sword or warrior out there, so it's just a matter of time. A smart gambler knows when to leave the table and cut his losses."

"*You* didn't," Sellia smirked and tapped one of the dead bodies with her boot.

"I'm a gambler, milady, but I never said I was smart."

"*That's* clear," Riona said as she walked past them toward the approaching horses led by Denalion and Pyre.

"How do you know her?" Sellia asked as they both watched Riona's retreating form.

"I don't."

"You do, and you work for me. Don't lie."

Montclair grinned. "I don't recall honesty being stipulated in the contract. I'll see if I can round up the horses that bolted."

Sellia watched him mount his horse with ease. There was something she was missing – something in front of her eyes – and she couldn't figure it out.

The campfire crackled behind her, warming her back. Riona stared out into the desert, but she couldn't see nor hear anything. Her hand gripped her unsheathed short sword and her sling sat ready in her belt as she studied the night.

She could hear Denalion's rumbling snores, occasionally punctuated by a few muttered words. She clung to those words, wondering if they might give away with whom he walked in the dream world, but she couldn't distinguish anyone.

She moved deeper into the stillness and the darkness folded around her. She had excellent night vision for a human and walked with natural stealth. The darkness offered her protection, and she embraced it.

The short sword felt familiar in her hand. She had used it before and never hesitated taking a life in self-defense. Men who thought to force their affections upon her soon learned that she would protect herself. But this was not the life she had chosen, and she hated the macho drive to fight. It had cost her family and friends. She had been alone and running until she joined Seanchai's school.

She had considerable knowledge of herbs and healing – too much for a mere student – but she had not revealed the extent for fear that Seanchai might send her out into the world. But the Wycaan had noticed, anyway, and often gave her advanced lessons, taking her with him on trips to difficult or plague-ridden areas, and had left her to attend patients without offering explanations. She had been caught knowing too much several times before she realized what he was doing.

Still, he never called her out, and she felt utterly devoted to him and his vision. Seanchai was the first powerful male she had ever met who also abhorred fighting. He did not seek accolades, and often traveled to Shindellia with a hood concealing his face. She knew he maintained a close relationship with the prince, and had therefore found excuses not to join Seanchai when he was summoned to the capital.

Two footsteps brought her from her reverie. Riona crouched and held up her blade. It shimmered in the firelight, a deadly beauty. She glanced behind to see if the other four were sleeping and lost her night vision to the fire.

She cursed under her breath and moved further away from the group. When she made out the figure, it wasn't trying to conceal itself, and, as it drew nearer, she recognized Montclair fastening his trousers.

"Fool," she hissed. "I could have taken you for the enemy and attacked."

His initial expression was one of apology, but it quickly disappeared. "Maintain your night vision, milady, and don't be too eager with that sword. It might hurt someone."

"You arrogant—"

"Shush. You'll wake the others. The old one is having enough trouble trying to sleep. He must have done some bad things in his life to have dreams haunt him like that."

"How dare you! He's a great and respected elf, and you're an idiot." Riona stopped, realizing her hands were clenched, one around the pommel of her sword.

"Come," Montclair said, nodding away from the fire. "We can talk over here."

"I don't want to talk to you."

"Then come away from the others and continue calling me names. You apparently need to vent your anger."

"I'm not angry," she hissed. "It's you …. It's hard, all this: the children, poor Sellia, the chase."

"Come," he said, and held his hand in front of him, inviting her. "Please."

They moved a dozen paces away and stood, staring in silence at the stars.

"You should return to sleep," Riona said. "You'll be tired tomorrow."

"I have the next shift," he replied. "I think we're pretty close to switching."

"I don't want to talk to you," she repeated half-heartedly.

"Then you can either go to bed or stand here with me in silent companionship."

"You're not going to try and force a conversation if I stay with you?"

"No." His voice was gentler now. "I promise."

"Why not?"

"I'm a nice person," he said. "Not a gentleman, mind, but buried deep inside somewhere, there is a modicum of chivalry."

Riona laughed and looked at him. He was handsome with his long crinkled hair, goatee, and well-proportioned face. But what caught her was his smile. It was … it was … genuine. She didn't see that on men's faces very often.

"Maybe," she said.

"Maybe what?"

"Maybe you are a nice guy...deep inside somewhere."

They stood together, side by side, staring silently out into the night.

Chapter Fifteen

"But I'm thirsty," Ilan whined. "I need some water."

"Ssshut him up," a taragus hissed from around the campfire. "He hasss more than usss."

Mharina tried to quiet her brother, but Third Scale had forbade her giving him any of her own water supply. He had caught her once and warned that her brother's selfishness would endanger her own life. She put an arm around Ilan and drew him to her.

"Elvesss are ssso weak," the same taragus said loudly. "If he wasss our *bata*, he would be ssstew." There was a round of laughter, and this, no doubt, only encouraged him. "We eat our offsssspring if they are weak. Not much meat for ssstew on this one."

"I wonder how they tassste?" a guard called back from beyond the firelight. "They are ssso ssskinny."

"Ssso weak," another echoed, flicking its tongue to wet its nose.

There was another round of laughter, which stopped abruptly when Senzia spoke.

"We're not," She was standing with a rock in her hand above her head, ready to throw.

Mharina could see that her sister's hand shook, but her eyes flashed defiance. Senzia rarely spoke and was often moody, but she was strong and fast for her age. If she threw the rock, it would hit its target.

The air was tense, and only the crackle of wood made any sound. One taragus stood slowly, his armor creaking. He stepped forward, but Senzia held her ground. The light of the fire ignited the whiteness of her long, splayed hair.

"You think you're so brave, kidnapping *calhei*? Such great deeds for mighty taragusii warriors to boast of 'round the fire? If you're so brave, tell me why you're fleeing from those who pursue you? I've seen you looking over your shoulders. My father comes, and you fear him. Why do such brave lizards run?"

A hand from behind Senzia grabbed the rock, and a slap sent her reeling. Third Scale stood over her, glaring. To her credit, Senzia did not cry, or even touch her swelling face. She stood up slowly, shaking a bit, but she held herself erect and met his gaze.

"Your bravery isss commendable. A ssshame to taint it by calling us namesss. We are not lizardsss. Elvesss were ssslaves, no? Humiliated and insssulted. You ssshould not look down on usss. You ssshould be better than that."

His tone was admonishing rather than angry. Mharina thought he might actually be disappointed in Senzia, like a father in his child. She rose, slowly walked over to her sister, and took her arm.

"Come on," she said, tugging gently.

But Senzia would not move. She was still staring at Third Scale. "I'm sorry," she said at last.

"For the name calling, or that you didn't get to throw the rock?" Third Scale asked.

"Both," she replied, failing to suppress a smile.

There was a round of laughter behind the leader, and Mharina saw him relax. He moved closer to her and knelt down so he could look her in the eye. When he spoke, his tone was softer, meant only for the three of them.

"We ssserve a mighty massster. If he wantsss you to ssstay alive, then I will keep you alive. If you had thrown that rock and one of my taragusssii had attacked you, I would have had to ssslay him and been very sssad, because they are my resssponsibility. Many have matesss, and *bata* like you.

"It isss not your father who followsss. He isss a long way away, going further north with each passsing day. My massster wantsss him to come to Grogin, but not until you are sssafely delivered there. Pleassse do not rile my sssoldiers, brave ssshe-elf."

"I'm an elfe," Senzia said stubbornly, her hands now tightly folded across her chest.

"Yesss, you are," said Third Scale, and he mussed her hair.

"He really did, Denalion. He rubbed her hair. I feel as though Third Scale cares about us, and we are more than just his prisoners."

"Interesting," the red owl replied from his perch on a branch above her. "We should not assume they are all bad, I suppose. Rarely is a person all good or all bad."

"What about my ahdahr? *Does he have any bad in him?"*

Denalion hooted, the closest thing to a laugh that he could manage in owl form. "Your father included, though I am at a loss as to what his badness might be."

"Third Scale said that my ahdahr *was far away in the north. Is that true? Why won't he come?"*

'I don't know. I can only guess that the Emperor has created some unrest, and Prince Shindell has sent your father north to deal with it. I believe the prince rides with him, so it must be important."

"Can't you dreamwalk with him like you do with me?"

"No. Your father has many protective wards to shield him from the Emperor. He won't think to lower them without good cause. What puzzles me is that I cannot connect with his companions. Perhaps I am getting too old for this."

"Of course you're not, Denalion. Don't say that. The Emperor probably has found a way to prevent you. Otherwise, my ahdahr would be on his way here to rescue us before we reach Grogin."

"Grogin?"

"Third Scale said that's where we're going. Do you know of it?"

"It sounds familiar. Listen, little Mharina, I know you have a lot to deal with while taking care of your brother and sister, but I want you to find an opportunity to ask the leader about this Grogin. Remember every detail about the place and your journey there. Do you have enough water?"

"We always feel thirsty, and the taragusii ration it. We were almost out before we found a spring yesterday, and even then they wouldn't let us drink much once we left, even when our skins were full."

"Very well. It might be some time before you reach another. Try and find out how many more days of marching are before you. You are very brave, Mharina — you know that, right? Your mother is proud of you and will be even more so when I tell her of this…Mharina? What is happening?" He was losing her as she came awake. "Mharina?"

"Fighting. I must— aagh!"

Chapter Sixteen

Mharina grabbed her brother as he screamed – a horse had almost trampled him. She reached for Senzia and pulled them both tight against a tree trunk. There were flashes of silver and sparks as blades clashed in the firelight opposite where they stood.

Taragusii screeched and hissed as they melted into a defensive circle with remarkable discipline. Third Scale's eyes met Mharina's for a moment. His face was impassive as he barked orders, his serrated broadsword raining blows on all who approached him.

Their attackers were clothed in ragged raiment and didn't seem well armed or organized. Mharina thought they were human, but with their long, straggly hair and beards, it was hard to distinguish. Their weapons – swords, halberds, staffs, and crossbows – seemed old and battered.

One man, his sword rusty and nicked, planted himself in front of the children. Ilan cried out, and Mharina felt a whimper escape her. The man stared at them but, even though his sword was raised, he did not attack. Instead, he shook his head and let out a series of clicks from his mouth.

Whatever he said were his last words. Third Scale leapt on him, clawing his face with two front feet while his rear claws tore into the man's waist. Pools of blood began to spread on each spot as the taragus yanked the man's head left, then right. There was a sharp snap, and the man went limp. Third Scale stood, panting, the man's head in his hand as the body crumpled.

Both Mharina and Ilan screamed as blood spurted onto them. Mharina realized she had not heard her sister react and glanced at her. Some of the man's blood dripped down her face, but Senzia's gaze was hard. Her blue eyes were glowing in the firelight, and her features seemed frozen.

Mharina squeezed her hand. "You okay?"

Senzia nodded slightly, but kept her eyes on the fight. She could be going into shock, Mharina thought, feeling a wave of panic rise. She was not sure what that was exactly, but Riona had once used that term to describe an elf who had broken his leg in an accident and was just sitting, staring into space, instead of crying from pain.

The fighting intensified. Third Scale had melted back into his soldier's formation. They were stronger than the humans, but not impervious to the men's weapons. Two lay lifeless to Mharina's left.

Suddenly, it occurred to Mharina that these assailants might be just as bad as the taragusii. She had heard stories of slave traders, and that children were profitable because they lived longer.

She bent nearer to her sister's ear. "We need to get away."

Senzia nodded, hardened her grip, and began to lead Mharina and Ilan away from the battle and into the desert. Mharina was taken aback at how her sister had assumed command and realized that Senzia was not in shock. Far from it — she was the calmest among them. For some reason, this scared Mharina even more.

As they moved through the darkness away from the fighting, Ilan being half-dragged, Mharina began to wonder about her sister. She had often seemed removed, and their mother had said she was introverted. Mharina remembered asking if that was contagious.

There was a series of clicks from behind them, and Mharina saw that two men were pursuing them. "We've got to hurry. Ilan, you must go faster."

"Can't," he cried, his voice a whimper. "Trying."

He was, she knew, but his smaller legs were having a hard time in the sand. So was she, but fear pushed her faster. Still, he dragged.

The two men soon caught up, and one stood in front of them. He held a staff with blades on either end. While he pointed it at them, he did not seem to threaten. He kept making clicking sounds and seemed to expect them to understand.

"What are you saying?" Ilan suddenly demanded. "Why can't you speak Odessiyan?"

"That is their way of speaking," Senzia said, her voice quiet and calm. "They are tutan." She looked up at the man. "Seanchai," she said and repeated it. "Seanchai. Galbrieth. Seanchai."

The tutan stared at her, and then clicked to the second, who shrugged. He then began clicking to Senzia, who shook her head.

"I can't understand you, but your people fought with my *ahd–*, my father, Seanchai the Wycaan, at the battle of Galbrieth. Seanchai fought General Tarlach. General Tarlach."

There was a flicker of recognition, and, again, the two men exchanged clicks. Then the other swung round as a taragus jumped at him. There was a brief clash of blades and the man fell, blood pouring from his chest. The other tutan charged forward, pushing the children to the ground. Spitting sand from her mouth, Mharina saw the staff spin as the man assailed the taragus.

They battled, trading ascendancy. More tutan were coming out of the dark, and the taragus was soon surrounded. Suddenly, a flash of rich purple light sent two men flying. Another burst, and more men fell. There were shrieks, and the tutting became rapid and high-pitched.

Mharina had lost any night vision from the light bursts, but someone swept past, and more bursts of purple light shot in all directions. Despite her inability to see well, Mharina knew the tutan were retreating now, the battle lost.

The taragus who had come to attack the two men stood by them. "We ssstay put," it said, staring toward what was left of the battle. "Ssshe will finish thisss."

"She?" Mharina said. "Who is 'she'?"

The taragus was breathing heavily, his scaly chest heaving. His tongue kept darting out and wetting his flaring nostrils. He was bleeding from a wound on his arm.

"You're hurt." Mharina reached out, but the creature barely glanced down, as though he hadn't noticed.

"It can wait."

"You don't feel pain?"

"Sssssssh."

There were a few more bursts of light, and then everything went quiet. The taragus pushed them forward, not ungently, toward the fire that was now sputtering. Those taragusii who were alive had fallen upon the bodies of the tutan and were ripping out organs and flesh, the battle rage fueling their intensity.

"Ughh!" Ilan retched.

Mharina felt her own body heave and turned her brother's and sister's faces from the frenzied feast. Senzia looked back, however, and continued watching.

"Don't make us go there right now," Mharina said to their guard.

"They are dead. We feassst on the defeated. It isss an honor for them that we do not leave them for the wolvesss."

"It's disgusting," Ilan shouted, his body heaving.

A figure approached, and a female voice spoke. "I will take the children. You have fought well, now go eat."

The woman who approached was not much taller than Mharina, but her presence was palpable, and the guard bowed before scampering off. She wore a purple cloak over darker garments. Her arms embraced the children and guided them away.

"Sit here," she said.

The woman, who Mharina was sure was human and not elf, extended a hand with long, purple fingernails and a thick band that covered most of her wrist. A thin, purple light left her hand, and a small fire erupted. The flames gave off a purplish glow, its warmth embracing them.

"Warm yourselves, little ones. You are safe with me. This must have been very hard for you. You were very brave, all of you."

Mharina and Ilan moved closer and extended their hands to warm themselves, but Senzia just stared at the woman.

"Who are you?" she asked, her tone tight.

The woman stared at her. The firelight revealed that she had black hair with purple streaks running through. Mharina thought the woman had purple rings around her eyes and purple lips, but that might have been the light of the fire.

"I am your savior right now, little one, but I am not a friend. You show no fear, do you? Is that a wise thing for one in your position?"

Senzia stared back. "I will not give them or you the satisfaction of seeing my fear. My *ahdahr* says all beings fear. There is no shame in that."

"No shame indeed. I look forward to meeting your father. It is why I agreed to help bring you to Grogin."

"Who are you?" Senzia asked again, moving her white hair behind her pointed ears.

"I am Sa'gola, also known as the Purple Lady."

"*Are* you a lady?" Senzia asked.

The woman arched a thin eyebrow, and then laughed throatily. "I am anything but, child."

Chapter Seventeen

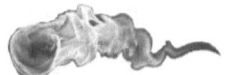

The snow lay so thick on the ground that Seanchai and Rhoddan were forced to dismount and lead their horses. It was hard walking for both elves and horses. Seanchai recalled the last time he had come this far north. The pictorians had given Sellia and him wide-bottomed snowshoes with spikes that gripped the smooth terrain.

They had climbed to a high elevation now, and breathing was difficult. It occurred to Seanchai that if the Wild Men of the North knew they were coming and attacked the army before they became acclimatized to the thin air, the Wild Men would have a considerable advantage.

As if on cue, Rhoddan pulled up. "There's movement up there to our right. I've seen the glint of metal twice. There it is again."

Seanchai screwed up his eyes, but could see nothing besides white snow and blue sky. He took a deep, cleansing breath and tried to reach out with his mind.

"They're not pictorians," he said. "I can't distinguish if they are humans, but there seems to be about twenty of them."

Rhoddan surveyed the expanse. "There is nowhere to take cover," he said. "I regret leaving our main strength. We should have listened to Gilead."

It had been a strange incident. The old, usually mild-mannered, advisor had protested strongly against them going ahead. He cited safety, but was also concerned that it be deemed a slight that the prince was not in the welcoming party. Seanchai had been taken aback by the old man and, at one point, felt suspicious. But now, Gilead's words seemed unfortunately prophetic.

"Let's stop here or make an arc and head back," Rhoddan said. "If we keep the arc wide, it could look as if we're just lost."

"We are still a day from Umnesilk's village," Seanchai said. "I don't believe these horses can gallop, but then, the attackers will be just as slow."

"Don't count on that," Rhoddan said as several figures glided down the mountain in elegant curves.

Seanchai noched his green elf bow and let fly two black-feathered arrows. They arched and landed, one next to the other, their black feathers distinct in the white snow. When the party reached them, they stopped, recognizing the line that Seanchai had drawn.

One removed the long, thin planks of wood attached to his feet and left them standing upright. Then he began to walk forward by himself.

"Name yourselves, Southerners," he called out from a dozen paces. "Why are you here?"

"Our names and business are our own," Seanchai replied.

The man was wrapped in furs, but his beady eyes stared at Seanchai.

"This isn't even half the force I have with me," the man said. "There are plenty more on the ridge, and you saw how quickly we ride the new snow."

"That really was very impressive," Rhoddan enthused, and both the man and Seanchai stared at him. The big elf shrugged. "What's the matter? It looks cool."

The man laughed, and his padded body shook. "If you tell us who you are and what you are doing here, and if I decide you are no threat, then perhaps we can teach you."

"We have business with the pictorians," Seanchai said.

"What kind of business? Are they friends?"

"That will depend upon whether they conduct business with us."

The man thought for a moment. "Do you know who you're dealing with?"

"Our liege lord has had dealings with them in the past."

"If they don't like you or your terms, they're likely to rip your heads off."

"We know how to negotiate," Seanchai said, showing the hilt of one of his swords.

The man laughed. "Their First Boar would destroy the two of you without breaking a sweat. I will do you a favor because I like you. Turn around, and go back to your lord."

"He wouldn't appreciate that," Seanchai said. "What would we tell him?"

"That all you found were burned villages and decaying bodies," the man replied.

"Is it true?"

"Not right now," the man sniffed and stood up straighter. "But by the time you reach your home and someone is sent to check, it will be. The days of the pictorians are numbered."

"What makes you think that?" Seanchai asked. "They sound pretty fierce, by your own admission."

The man spat on the ground. What left his mouth was frozen by the time it settled on the snow. "I said we were two dozen, but we are part of an army a hundred thousand strong. An entire nation of fighters head south, and the pictorians are just the first in their path."

The man looked south. "And the army following you isn't going to help much. Now, turn around and go back."

"I can't," Seanchai said, kicking some snow with his boot. "I must reach the pictorians. I thank you for warning us, and, out of respect, will let you rejoin your troops. But I must continue. I hope we can soon meet as friends."

"And if I refuse to let you continue?"

"That would be regrettable ... for you."

Something in Seanchai's voice made the man hesitate.

"I told you, we are more than twenty and used to fighting out here on this land. You are a couple of swordsmen way out of your depth."

"I do not wish to hurt you or your people," Seanchai said, his tone quiet but powerful.

The man stared at his hooded form. "I will return over there to my men," he said. "If you turn back, you will have safe passage. If not ...."

He turned and walked back to the men he had arrived with, and they retreated. Seanchai watched them go, and then pointed to a small hill they had passed a few hundred paces back.

"Let's go up there. We will be safer."

"What are you planning?" Rhoddan asked as they reached the top of the knoll.

"I'm going to encourage them to leave," Seanchai replied.

"You are? How do you plan to do that? Bring down the mountain?"

Seanchai did not respond to his joke, and when Rhoddan glanced over, all he could see beneath the cowl was the Wycaan's lips moving silently.

CHAPTER EIGHTEEN

"*a'afula. Ma'afula.*" Seanchai's whisper became gradually louder.

Rhoddan stared at his friend. The Wycaan's hood was still covering his head, but words were pouring out in thick, white puffs of air. A few more of the north men had slid down the mountain to join their friends. For now, they were just watching, but as the group was growing in size, Rhoddan sensed it would not be long until they attacked. No one would stand still for long in this cold.

"*Ma'afula. Ma'afula.*"

It began with what looked like wisps of white top snow being lifted by a light breeze, but Rhoddan realized what he was seeing was quite a distance away. Small, black human dots were sliding down the mountain, more quickly and less gracefully than their companions had.

Those who had gathered with their leader down the slope were no longer looking toward Seanchai and Rhoddan, but back up at the mountain. Their body language suggested they were clearly agitated.

"*Ma'afula. Ma'afula. Ma'afula.*" Seanchai was calling out loudly enough now that his voice echoed back.

The peak of the mountain was lost in a white sheet that was growing fast as it moved down toward them. It reached the slowest of the fleeing men and engulfed them.

Rhoddan's eyes went to the group, where he saw that, while most of the group was staring up the mountain, their leader was watching the elves. Rhoddan glanced again at Seanchai. He was not sure if his friend could move the elements and fight at the same time. The man had claimed they were twenty in his band, but Rhoddan was quite sure there was considerably more now fleeing the mountain.

"Hurry it up," he murmured. "They're gonna charge."

Seanchai's voice became louder, and the words flew from his mouth up the mountainside. "*Ma'afula. Ma'afula. Ma'afula.*" His arms rose in front of him.

Rhoddan stared up and gaped. The white sheet had become a dense, tumbling mass, hurtling downward with ferocious speed and swallowing all the black dots in its path. The men at the bottom roared with rage and began to jog forward toward Seanchai and Rhoddan.

Their position on the knoll not only buffered them from the waves of descending snow, but also aided them as the men struggled to advance and their jog slowed to a determined walk.

Rhoddan drew his big broadsword, the rasp as it left its sheath barely audible as the huge wave of snow engulfed most of the steep slopes.

"Seanchai, that bow of yours would come in handy right now." When there was no response, Rhoddan raised his voice. "Seanchai! Your bow! Now! Let fly."

The Wyccan's long, green bow was in front of him in a flash. Arrow after arrow was noched and unleashed. The men were not far away now, and slow targets. Every one of a dozen arrows found their mark.

Those in the rear faltered, seeing their comrades fall, and then the arrows vanish. Seanchai's bow had been a gift from the Forest of Markwin, and his quiver emptied and filled in a smooth, magical fluency.

But there was no way back for the attackers. The wave of snow had continued on its own momentum and was bearing down on them. One called to head north, in the direction the elves were taking to the pictorian villages.

"They cannot escape," Seanchai said. "The Emperor will know of our armies and my presence."

"Aim for those escaping," Rhoddan called, struggling to pass Seanchai. "I will hold this group off."

Seanchai turned and raised his bow. Though they were already a hundred paces away, two men fell quickly. A third was wounded and limping. Two others passed him and kept moving.

Six men were upon Rhoddan with an assortment of swords and halberds. He held up his broadsword, feeling restricted by the thick fur layers he was wearing. He should have discarded them to fight, and he cursed himself.

Seanchai almost flew past him, his two Win Dao swords ignited by the sun. Four men quickly fell to his sword, and he continued to the last group. Rhoddan parried a man's clumsy attack and swung his sword to cut through his neck. He continued to roll down the shaft of an extended halberd and stabbed the man holding it. Man? He was merely a boy, and Rhoddan winced as he saw the boy's eyes open wide and then roll from their sockets.

He pulled his sword out and looked up. Seanchai was standing in the middle of several prone bodies, most still, a few spasming in the last throes of life. Seanchai's hair was splayed, but blended with the snow. Droplets of blood fell from his blades onto the white snow.

Rhoddan walked over to him. They were both panting, the exertion and the thin air proving a tough combination.

"The two who escaped are heading toward the pictorian villages. Let's give chase."

Seanchai nodded and set off briskly.

"The horses," Rhoddan called after him.

"Leave them. It'll take too long to retrieve them."

The horses had bolted when the fighting began, and, though they were probably near, Seanchai was right – especially since the avalanche spooked them. But without food and riders to direct them, the cold and hunger would claim them.

"Maybe Shayth will collect them on his way," Seanchai called without conviction.

They had been jogging for only a short while when the sound of battle floated back to them. It was short, and two human screams signaled its end.

Around a long bend, they found a group of pictorians. The biggest was leaning over a human corpse. He rose, turned around to face them, and smiled.

"Well met, Wycaan," said Umnesilk, First Boar of the Pictorians. He raised the head he was holding, rich, red blood dripping onto the snow. "Thank you for fine gift."

Chapter Nineteen

Sellia crouched, fingering a torn piece of cloth. It had surely belonged to one of her children, and she felt tears welling in her eyes. Pyre and Montclair, to give Sellia some space, were trying to unravel what had transpired here the day before. There had clearly been an ambush, with two-legged creatures attacking from the west.

"The taragusii made a stand here by the fire, but I can't make out if the children were here. We should look a bit further away for their tracks." Montclair had his sword out as he scanned around. "There was a heck of a lot of attackers. Where were the *calhei* when this all happened?"

"They were asleep when the tutan attacked," Denalion said.

"Tutan?"

"Yes. Look at these bodies," the old elf said.

That was a considerable task. The desert's scavengers had savaged the bodies once the taragusii had their fill. Swarms of flies covered every body, and the stench was foul.

"Tutan are desert people," Denalion explained. "They live in the deep south and occasionally come north to hunt. Seanchai's teacher, the venerable Mhari, had a rich history with them. But I wonder why they would attack like this. Perhaps they have a history of their own with the taragusii."

"Don't stare at me like that! Get away!" Sellia screamed at Pyre, who stood over her.

"I'm not looking at you," Pyre answered, her voice calm. "Denalion, please come here."

They all walked over, quite happy to distance themselves from the mound of bodies. Sellia breathed deeply, trying to keep control. She watched Pyre examine a tree covered in purple-tinged burn lines.

Denalion approached the tree and rubbed a charred part. He brought his hand to his nose and inhaled. When he spoke, there was a frown on his face.

"This is not common fire," he said and turned back to the bodies. "We need to work out if they all died from the taragusii weapons."

Pyre moved away, half crouching as she began to follow tracks.

"What is it?" Montclair called.

"There are tracks of someone small, maybe one of the children. No. They meet up with…Sellia, the children were moved over here. Look: there are three distinct sets of footprints. One of the lizards was with them. They left the tree…and walked in a wide arc…over here. And then, this fourth set of footprints."

Pyre looked up. "Gambler. Retrace those small tracks and see where she came from."

"She?" Sellia asked.

"Gambler?" Montclair added.

"Shut up," Riona said. "Do as she asks."

"Oh, I didn't realize it was a request." Facing four pairs of glaring eyes, he raised his hands, one with his sword, and bid a hasty retreat. "Retracing," he said.

Denalion turned to Sellia. "The taragusii were attacked and fought off the tutan band. They moved the children away to protect them. They are safe, I am sure. There is no sign around their prints that anyone was wounded. Each set of footprints is even and consistent with walking. Pyre, do you agree?"

Pyre, her green eyes wide with anticipation, nodded.

"The question," Denalion mused, "is who intervened to ensure the taragusii won. What is this fire we can see? I fear…"

His voice trailed off. They all waited, but he did not continue.

"What is it, old one?" Sellia asked, her voice strained but composed.

"I fear that one with a greater power now rides with the children, perhaps the Emperor himself. We are not far behind them, but I do not know how we can fight a force that fifty or sixty tutans could not defeat."

"What would you suggest?"

"That we track them. Seanchai will, at some point, discover something is wrong and follow you. You have the dwarf stone, right?"

Sellia nodded, fingering what hung from a chain under her shirt. She and Seanchai each possessed half of a green stone, part of a collection that the Priestess of Clan Den Zu'Reising had given to Seanchai before she had died. Ilana had given her stone to Sellia before she died in Hothengold. The two stones would help the owners find each other, even over long distances.

"Perhaps, when they reach this Grogin, we can sneak in and out." Even Sellia heard the doubt in her own voice. "I think we have learned all we can here. Let's move on."

They moved to their horses, but Sellia put her hand on Pyre's shoulder. The young elfe turned her head, apprehensive.

"I'm sorry I screamed," Sellia said, her voice wavering. "It's not you."

Pyre turned to face Sellia, and her expression melted. Riona put a hand on Sellia's shoulder and gently turned her around. Sellia found herself engulfed in the young woman's arms, and gave in to the strong embrace.

"I have no idea what you're going through," Riona whispered, her mouth close to Sellia's ear. "I have not borne children. But, if it is within my power, we will find and rescue them. I swear."

And the emotional dam broke. Sellia's whole body was racked with anguish. Wave after wave of sobs filled the desert air. All stood silent, powerless to respond. Riona held her close, her arms tight around the elfe, riding every tumultuous wave of Sellia's despair.

Sellia felt Pyre behind her, also hugging her. Through tear-filled eyes, she saw Denalion's red hair and felt his hand squeezing her arm. And beyond, holding the reins of her horse and his own, stood Montclair. Was he wiping away a tear from glistening eyes?

Sellia took a deep breath and pulled herself away. "Montclair, my water skin, please," she said.

It allowed him to turn away, and when he retrieved her skin, pulling the cork as he passed it, she smiled, acknowledging wordlessly what she had seen. After she took several long gulps, she inhaled deeply and turned to face them all.

"Take a good look here," she said, her voice steady. "See the carnage, for this might be our destiny very soon. I will not hesitate to risk your lives or mine to rescue my children. If you want to turn around and return to Odessiya, I would understand."

No one moved or so much as flinched as they each held her gaze. Sellia saw the determination on their faces, and she felt truly blessed by their company.

"This is the power Seanchai draws from," she said. "True friendship is stronger than sword or arrow, or any kind of magic."

But I doubt it is enough, she thought as she led her mare away. *And I am not a Wycaan Master. I am not Seanchai.*

ChApter Twenty

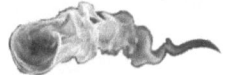

The sun moved relentlessly through the empty, blue sky, and the company rode in silence through the thick wall of heat. Sellia was becoming resigned to the idea that they would not catch the taragusii, and it made the ride considerably more laborious. All she could see around her was sand and sky. Her lips cracked, and her skin felt like leather. Any exposed parts burned.

The others fared no better. Montclair had encouraged them to tie white cloth around their heads, a flimsy and ineffective turban against the sun, in her opinion. She tried to turn her mind to what lay ahead in Grogin. She wondered if it was a small outpost or a mighty fortress.

Either way, the five of them alone could not hope to assault whatever lay ahead. Perhaps a big castle was preferable – easier to slip through unnoticed – but Sellia found it hard to imagine that a big population lived out here. This was a land good for those who wanted to hide and not be found.

She yawned and felt her head drop a few times. *Damn! It was so hot.* She reached for her water skin and drank sparingly. Behind her, the others were talking, so she stopped her horse and turned around in her saddle.

"Over there," Pyre was pointing.

"I see nothing," Montclair said. "The heat can play tricks –"

"She's an elfe," Riona snapped. "Her eyesight is far better than ours."

"I see it, too," Denalion confirmed. "Sellia, it might be an oasis. We should head there for water and to wait out the heat of the day."

Sellia looked at the old elf. Denalion's face was almost as red as his flaming hair, and his skin was also cracked and burned. He had traveled far and often in his life, but had grown up in a moist forest. She brought a hand to shield her eyes and followed Pyre's outstretched hand.

"It is far, whatever it is. The taragusii did not detour there."

"They have less need for water than we do," Montclair said. "If speed is no longer important, we should refill our skins."

But my children need water, Sellia thought. *Mharina is dark-skinned like me, but the twins…Senzia is so pale, she must be burning up.* Involuntarily, she glanced at Riona, also pale of skin. Riona's whole face was a near-beetroot color, yet she did not complain. Senzia would probably bear it quietly, as well.

They steered their horses in that direction, and, while the detour seemed frustratingly long to Sellia, they found a tall rock face and trees surrounding a small lake. Even in her troubled state, she appreciated its natural beauty. As they rode in the shade under the trees, she felt the temperature drop and sighed.

Montclair dismounted and swiftly removed the saddles and supplies from two of the horses before taking them to drink. Sellia did the same, deep in thought.

"Montclair!" Riona cried.

Sellia looked up. The man was totally naked and about to enter the small lake with his water skin. He turned and stared at Riona, whose sunburnt cheeks were turning an even deeper red.

Pyre and Denalion were both laughing at the innocent look on the fortune-sword's face. Despite her woes, Sellia could not help but laugh, too.

"Get in the water already, human," she called. "Your snow-white backside is exposed to the sun, so it won't only be Riona's cheeks that are red in a few minutes."

This brought more laughter from the elves, while Riona huffed and busied herself tending the horses.

"What?" Montclair called as he waded in. "Am I going to be the only clean member of this party?" He dove underwater.

"He has a point," Denalion said. "Perhaps I should join him while the three of you avert your eyes. I can assure you, I do not cut such a figure as that strapping young man."

Riona immediately claimed guard duty, filled her water skin, and moved into the shade of the rock. The two elfes laid down under the trees and soon fell asleep.

Denalion and Montclair washed themselves and their clothes. Reluctantly, they relinquished the water and, clad only in underclothes, woke the elfes.

"Your turn," Denalion said to them, picking up his long knife.

Montclair had sat down, but the elves stared at him.

"What now?" he said.

"Why don't you join me on guard," Denalion suggested. "We can give the females some privacy."

Montclair looked up at Pyre and Sellia. Both had started to undress and now stood, glaring at him. He lifted his hands in submission and rose.

"I'll take sentry from Riona. Let the old one lay here and sleep. I'm sure he won't peep; he's more honorable than me."

"Yes. You stay and rest, Denalion," Pyre said. "We trust *you*."

"No. No," Denalion protested, standing up. "Just because I am old, doesn't mean I would not be sorely tempted."

They all laughed, and Montclair patted the old elf's spindly shoulder as they walked up to the ridge where Riona was standing.

"You can go join the elfes," Montclair declared. "Or, if you prefer to wait for me, I can scrub your back."

Riona's eyes narrowed, and her cheeks reddened. This elicited a snicker from Denalion, which earned him a glare as well. She pointed at the fortune-sword with her sling.

"If I catch you sneaking a peek, I'll have your eyes."

"What makes you think I would be looking at you?" he teased, raising an eyebrow. "There are two beautiful elfes down there bathing."

Riona pouted all the more. "They are way too good for you," was all she could manage.

"As are you, milady," replied Montclair with an exaggerated bow.

"And don't you forget it," she snapped and walked away.

Denalion watched Montclair's eyes followed the healer. He cleared his throat. "I think we would serve best as guards if we looked in the other direction."

Montclair turned and laughed. "They should be glad you are here to guard the sentry."

"I don't think you are quite the scoundrel you make yourself out to be," Denalion said, smiling.

"You offend me, sir," Montclair protested, crossing his hands over his heart.

Denalion laughed. "I think you hide behind it to prevent us from discovering the real man. I would like to meet him sometime, though."

"You would be disappointed," the fortune-sword replied, his expression now serious. "Everyone invariably is."

Denalion just looked at him and waited for him to speak.

"Anyway, can't you peek into my dreams?"

"Not without your consent, and even then, I would only see what you want me to."

"You can really enter into people's dreams?"

"No. I walk together with them in the dream world. I help people by understanding them better. Don't look so worried. I would not enter your world without permission. It is a sacred responsibility."

Montclair nodded. "I'm a private man. I appreciate your... your nobleness. We're very different from each other."

Denalion smiled at him. "We have some things in common. There is a noble streak in you, too, I suspect. You are not here only for the money. And there is something else we share."

"What's that, Dreamwalker?"

"We both love Riona very much. If I was only a couple hundred years younger..."

They both laughed.

"Well, at least she loves you back," Montclair replied. "Not that I'm saying I'm interested, but she can't seem to stand me."

"I think not," Denalion mused. "That dark past you share might yet forge a brighter future together."

Montclair sighed deeply, but said nothing.

"When you are ready, my friend. I have found that listening can often be more effective than dreamwalking."

Chapter Twenty One

With so many taragusii dead, there were now enough mounts for everyone to ride. Ilan sat behind Mharina, holding her waist, but Senzia had insisted on her own mount. Mharina could not help stealing glances at the mysterious woman as they rode.

Sa'gola was barely taller than Mharina and as thin as a reed. Though the taragusii towered over her, they were clearly intimidated and scampered to oblige her every command. It was clear from the way she addressed them that she expected nothing less.

"Why do you stare at me, *calhei*?" Sa'gola asked, her tone not unkind.

Mharina was surprised the Purple Lady knew the correct term for elf children. She swallowed hard, unaware Sa'gola had noticed her looking. "How do you paint your hair like that, with those purple strands?"

Sa'gola fixed Mharina with a hard glare to show that she knew that wasn't the reason for the young elfe's interest, but let it pass. "Back in my rooms at Grogin, I have paints for hair and face. I will show you, if we have time."

"Won't we be prisoners there, stuck in the dungeons to die?" Ilan asked.

"Only if you misbehave or try to escape," Sa'gola replied, arching a thin eyebrow. "But I doubt you will."

"Why?" Mharina asked.

"Because you are all intelligent enough to understand that it would be a terribly foolish thing to do. You are not enemies; you are bait. As long as you fulfill your role of staying put, then the Master will not mind, I think. If we get on, and I request your company, then I believe he will allow you to stay in rooms near my quarters."

"Thank you," Mharina said, recalling Denalion's advice to show courtesy even to an enemy.

"I will try and escape," Ilan announced, clutching his sister's waist.

"Fair enough," Sa'gola replied. "But you have seen only a glimpse of what I'm capable of. And if I tire of your attempts, I can always have you thrown into the dungeons. It is dark and lonely down there. All kinds of sharp-toothed rodents and magical creatures scurry around."

Ilan went quiet, and Sa'gola smiled. Then she looked over at Senzia, who returned her look without flinching.

"You puzzle me the most, little one. Senzia, right? Your hair is beautiful, as white as snow."

When Senzia didn't reply, Mharina interjected, using her big sister voice. "Senzia. She paid you a compliment."

Senzia turned her head slowly, glared at her older sister, and then turned back to Sa'gola.

"Thank you, milady," she said, her tone flat.

"You don't speak much, child. Why is that?"

Senzia did not answer immediately. When she did, it was a dull reprimand, and ignored the question. "You have already referred to us as *calhei*. Surely you must know that we prefer that to the human word."

Mharina sighed and looked apprehensively at the woman. If Sa'gola was annoyed, she did not show it.

"My apologies if I offended you. It was unintentional and I hold nothing against your race." She waited a moment and, when the elfe did not respond, asked: "Does my apology suffice?"

"It does," Senzia replied. "Thank you." She then nudged her creature forward.

"Is she always so closed?" Sa'gola asked Mharina.

"More than Ilan and myself," Mharina replied. "Plus, we aren't exactly in happy circumstances."

The diminutive woman nodded. "I understand, but I think there is more. Do you know when a natural-born Wycaan enters into his or her powers?"

"No," Mharina said, but she thought of the stories that Pyre had told her. Pyre was Mharina's age when Seanchai had met her in the Forest of Markwin, and she was already in training with the Wycaans.

Mharina looked ahead at her little sister. Her family had often discussed whether Senzia might be a natural-born Wycaan. Her white hair and blue eyes seemed so similar to her father's and the other Wycaans that she had met. But if she were a Wycaan, could Senzia become a more attractive prize than her father? The Emperor might try to kill her father, but he could bend and train Senzia.

Mharina wondered if Ilan was also a natural-born Wycaan. She had already dismissed herself a long time ago, because she was dark-skinned and shared her mother's temperament. But

Ilan? He was immature, and that would make him even easier to bend than his twin sister.

Mharina realized that Sa'gola was watching her. "I do not possess the ability to read thoughts," the woman said. "From your expression, I wish I could."

Mharina tried to smile at her. "Who are you, Sa'gola? Tell us about yourself."

Sa'gola flashed a beautiful smile and, as the sun caught her black and purple hair, she appeared almost royal. "What would you like to know?"

"What was that purple light you used against those who attacked the taragusii?"

"Magic. I possess talents not unlike your father's. The purple, however, is my own artistic touch."

Despite herself, Mharina laughed, and the woman smiled.

"Are you a witch?" Ilan asked.

"A witch? Hmmm, is a witch good or bad?"

"Bad," Ilan replied, and then, remembering who he was talking to, added: "–eh, usually. At least, in the stories we grew up with. You can be a good witch, too, I guess."

"And a witch is someone who has powers, who can wield energy?"

"Sure." Ilan was trying to be confident, and Mharina was glad he was behind her and couldn't see her smile.

"What makes a witch good or bad?" Sa'gola asked innocently.

Ilan hesitated. "Perhaps I shouldn't answer," he said in a quiet voice.

"Please do. I asked for an honest reply. I promise not to get angry."

"Well. It seems to me that if you are on my *ahdahr's* side, then you are good. If you are against him, then…"

"I understand your dilemma," Sa'gola said. "But I don't think it is ever that simple. Someone – or something – is rarely all good or all bad. Sometimes what we do is for the greater good, and, at other times, not so much. We can only try."

Mharina glanced at the woman. She wore a painful, faraway expression. She seemed so powerful and so vulnerable at the same time. "I think you're right," the elfe said, "and I think my *ahdahr* would agree with you."

It seemed to relieve Sa'gola, and Mharina was surprised at how important it felt right now to please the mysterious woman.

Chapter Twenty Two

When the party stopped for the night, Senzia watched the taragusii, Mharina, and her brother eat silently and quickly. It had been a long day, and they soon bedded down to sleep. There was little joviality around the fire, perhaps due to the earlier attack or the presence of Sa'gola and, thankfully, no one thought to taunt Ilan.

Her little brother (for that was how she saw him, even if they were twins) was whimpering as he tried to fall asleep. That was typical. Apparently, at birth, she had shoved him out of the way to come out first. Mharina hugged and soothed him; she had so much patience, especially considering she was just a couple of years their elder.

Senzia admired her sister as she admired her mother. Both were tough and strong. Mharina didn't flaunt her power or leadership ability, but it was there. The head taragus, Third Scale, had sensed it and given ground to her when his soldiers were making fun of Ilan.

She glanced to her other side and saw the small woman and taragusii leader talking. Third Scale was huge and towered over Sa'gola, even though he was sitting on a rock. But he did not seem to intimidate her. If anything, he appeared deferential, constantly nodding and laughing gruffly at her jokes.

When they finished, Third Scale rose and spoke with two guards before lying down to sleep. Sa'gola sat on the rock and stared into the fire. Her dark eyes surveyed the group, and Senzia closed her eyes almost entirely, feigning sleep.

A short time passed, and Sa'gola rose gracefully and walked away from the fire. Before she realized what she was doing, Senzia was on her feet, pursuing the woman through the sparse trees of this small oasis.

She allowed Sa'gola to move ahead, as Senzia could easily and quietly follow the small footprints in the sand. A full moon provided more than enough light, and back on Wycaan Island, she had snuck off many times to train with Pyre in secret. Pyre had taught her stealth; tracking; and, recently, how to use the bow.

Pyre was a natural-born Wycaan and a fine soldier. She was proficient with the Win Dao swords and the flying discs, and her body was flexible and strong. Pyre practiced and taught a meditative discipline that built this flexibility and strength, as well as to fight without weapons. Senzia had tried to practice her own skills on Ilan. But he was too gentle and often cried as soon as she tossed him. She didn't dare try on Mharina, because her sister would discover her secret skills.

The purple woman ascended a dune, and Senzia had to be careful not to pant with the exertion. It was tiring walking through the thick sand. She heard voices and stopped as she approached the ridge.

Senzia dropped quietly to the ground and crept forward so that she could peer around a small rock. Sa'gola was crouched with her back to Senzia, so the young elfe could not see what she was doing, but she was clearly engaged in conversation.

"The Wild Men of the North have grown strong," a steely, male voice said. "I am glad I never crushed them. Their thirst for battle and vengeance is gratifying. They might even inflict significant losses on my nephew's army. He is a fool to travel north and think he can fight them in the mountains and snow."

"Why did he not send troops in his stead?" Sa'gola asked.

"It takes more than a crown to make a king. I am sure he was happy to escape the dull routine of the palace."

"Is the Wycaan with him, Master?" Sa'gola asked. "Why wouldn't he have advised Shayth otherwise?"

"He is young, too. And, the idea of a few weeks traveling with his companions was probably a relief from his bawling brats."

Senzia bristled, but kept herself still. This was the Emperor talking, which confused and terrified her.

"He is also captive to his foolish sense of loyalty and code of honor. Once the pictorians called for help, he was honor-bound to answer and support his precious alliance. Did you know he was the one who turned the pictorians against me at the Battle of Hothengold?

"My plan remains to bring him to Grogin, and for him to see his children incarcerated. He was able to walk away when his first mate was murdered, but I doubt he could walk away from his own blood. Knowing they are Wycaan and what kind of power that could give me makes him more expendable. He will become reckless. How far are you from Grogin?"

"We will arrive tomorrow. There was an attack. Tutans, if you can believe that, and it slowed us down. I had to show myself to ensure we were victorious."

"Tutans? Another ally of the Wycaan. It is troubling that they are so close to Grogin."

"I think this was a breakaway band or a hunting group. But there were enough of them that I could not stand by. There was a risk to the children."

"How are the spawn of the Wycaan?"

"Fascinating. The oldest is a dark-skinned she-elf – like her mother, I hear. She is strong and smart, and worries for her brother and sister. I do not think the blood of the Wycaan flows in her, but she could one day be formidable with the right training.

"The boy feigns himself to be weak, but there is fire behind his eyes. I have seen it a couple of times. He may just be very afraid, but I think it suits him to hide behind his sister's skirts for now.

"And then there is the twin girl. Her hair is snow-white, and she has the temperament."

"Delicious. Has she shown her power yet? In the fight, perhaps?"

"No," Sa'gola replied. "But all the time, she watches and learns. There is no fear in her eyes."

"If she is a natural-born Wycaan, then the twin should be as well. Get to know her, Sa'gola. She will keep to herself, remain in her sister's shadow, and you will need to bring her out."

"It won't be easy. She is so closed."

"I do not think it will be as hard as you think. As a Wycaan, she will be drawn to your power as I and others are. Her body will crave the feel of the energy, and her mind will desire the knowledge.

"But she is also young, and the young are careless and impulsive. Talk to her, Sa'gola. You can begin right now, if you wish. She is lying behind a rock twenty paces from you. Goodbye."

Sa'gola jerk her head around, and Senzia felt a paralyzing fear. Still, there was no point in trying to run, so she stood up slowly and brushed the sand off her body.

"You were eavesdropping?"

"Your master commands you to befriend me," Senzia replied, trying desperately to keep her voice louder than her beating heart.

Sa'gola tucked something inside her black and purple cloak and walked over to the *calhei*. By the time she had traversed the short distance, she was smiling. "Well, what do you think?"

"I like the idea, He's correct. Your power intrigues me," Senzia said, staring into Sa'gola's dark eyes.

Chapter Twenty Three

"Well met, my friend," Seanchai said, reaching out to hug the First Boar.

He immediately regretted it as the eight-foot, horned pictorian crushed the air out of Seanchai with his embrace. Pictorians, a bipedal bear-human hybrid, were fierce in fighting and friendship. Umnesilk was the biggest of his kind and, therefore, First Boar. He was also still holding the dripping head, which he tossed to one of his boars before turning to Rhoddan.

"Well met, warrior. Last see in battle at Cliftean Pass. You grow. Maybe pictorian blood flow inside you?" His booming laughter had everyone smiling.

"Well met, Umnesilk, First Boar of the Pictorians," Rhoddan bowed his head. "It was an honor to fight with you then."

"Honor mine. We fight again. Alliance."

"Yes," Seanchai replied, projecting his voice so that others could hear. "We have come to honor the Alliance and are proud to stand once again by the pictorian nation."

Umnesilk translated, and a cheer erupted from the assembled boars. They all turned to head north to their villages. More pictorian patrols joined up with them, and then gradually filtered off toward different villages.

Umnesilk and three young boars led the elves up between two mountains and onto a wide plateau. At the end of the flatland was the narrow gorge leading to Umnesilk's village. The First Boar stopped and turned to Rhoddan.

"We near my village. Last time Wycaan come, he and mate swear never tell where village is. You swear now in elf tongue."

Rhoddan stepped forward and looked up at the pictorian. "I do not know if the times that have fallen upon us will allow your people to maintain the secrecy of your hearths, First Boar. Prince Shindell rides with an army from Shindellia, and a massive army assembles further north. But you have my word as an elven warrior that this secret will not be revealed from my mouth. *Ashbar.*"

Umnesilk nodded, a frown etched across his face. "I think you right, but still I thank you."

With that, he turned and led them through the narrow, winding gorge. Seanchai was glad they didn't have to coax any horses through like last time. As they exited onto the inverted plateau surrounded by an ice wall rising over forty feet above them, Seanchai was struck by how different it looked. Previously, there had been ice and stone houses and caves around the perimeter, used for animals and storage, and the area between dwellings had been spaced out. Now there were large tents of sown animal hides, all clustered together, and most of the caves had furs concealing the entrances.

When he and Sellia had first entered, the place had been empty, as the apprehensive pictorians, unused to strangers, had stayed inside their homes. Now it was packed, and pictorians of all ages milled around slowly.

Seanchai just gaped and slowly turned to face Umnesilk.

The First Boar grimaced. "Now you understand why I call for help?"

"These pictorians are refugees?"

"Refu–?"

"Where are they from?" Seanchai asked.

"Flee from further north. We are most south of pictorian land. Every day, more come. All villages like this. You see at council tomorrow. Many faces, many dead. All who come, very frightened."

Scared Pictorians? Seanchai gaped at his huge allies. *What is out there?*

Seanchai and Rhoddan slept on the floor in the meeting room. There was no hut or tent vacant, but they were happy with the fire and knowledge that posted guards protected them.

In the morning, Onywei, Umnesilk's mate, brought them a thick, hot gruel. She spoke through a young boar she had brought to translate, as she did not know the common Odessiyan tongue.

"Onywei asks, how is dark-skinned one?"

"Sellia is well. Thank you," Seanchai replied.

"She have elf pictorye? Not know right word. Sorry."

"That's fine," Seanchai smiled and held out his hands to the approximate heights of his children. "Yes, we have two daughters and a son. They grow fast – too fast."

No one smiled. In fact, Onywei grimaced.

"What is it?" Seanchai asked.

There was a long back-and-forth between Onywei and the young boar. When the boar turned to Seanchai, he was collecting his words.

"Sad when leave young to fight. Not know if come back. Many pictorye and females lost boars. Easier when no young left behind. Understand? Onywei happy for you with elf pictorye, sad you come here, not be with them."

Scanchai nodded. "I miss my children every day and wonder what will happen if I do not return. It is scarier than death."

"At least them far from here. Best them safe, no?"

They ate in silence together, and, even when others joined them, the atmosphere remained subdued. With the meal finished, Umnesilk told them that they must leave for the City of the Elders, where the council sat in government.

It took most of the day to ascend into the mountains. The snow along the way was slippery but compacted enough to bear their weight. Umnesilk provided them with the snowshoes, which made it easier. When he saw the large, white tunnel, Seanchai felt a wave of excitement. He was pleased at the look of awe on Rhoddan's face.

They walked through the tunnel, its thick walls of ice smooth, the steady sound of dripping water echoing around them like a living pulse. The tunnel had a character of its own.

"I forgot how amazing this is," Seanchai said.

"Wow! I'm glad you didn't tell me," Rhoddan replied, his voice hushed in awe.

They exited into a huge bowl with ice sheets rising around the perimeter. This town had been moderately populated the last time Seanchai had come, but now it was teeming with pictorians.

Umnesilk led them briskly through the path that opened up before him and past the huge meeting tent. Seanchai glimpsed inside and saw the spacious, decorated room packed with sleeping furs and unruly piles of possessions.

They instead entered a smaller tent, also covered with hides. Food and drink sat on a table to one side, and thick logs had been positioned so a group could sit in a square.

"We not meet all council. When Prince come, he meet them. You hear from scouts. Then maybe go see with own eyes."

Seanchai filled a cup with a steaming brown beverage. It tasted bitter, but warmed him inside. Two older pictorians crouched where they peered at a map. They stood when they saw the elves, and Umnesilk entered behind them and touched foreheads with them – a sign of respect – and then introduced everyone. The oldest signaled for the elves to sit and picked up a long stick.

"These pictorian villages," he said, pointing with the stick, as Umnesilk translated. "You first not-pictorian to see where villages are."

"We understand," Seanchai responded to the ensuing expectant silence. "We have sworn oaths to Umnesilk to protect the location of his village. We extend that oath to all your villages."

Umnesilk translated, and both elders nodded. Then one pointed to a mountain range and moved his stick further north. More than a dozen villages were drawn, and all had red crosses scrawled through them.

"All villages not there now," Umnesilk said. "Gone. Maybe some of pictorians them, you say, survivors. Them here."

"Has this army crossed the mountains?" Rhoddan asked.

"Only small numbers, come to look."

"Scouting groups," Seanchai said. "Are they all humans?"

Umnesilk shrugged. "No one go close to see."

"Why not?"

Umnesilk translated to his fellow pictorians, and all three looked up at Seanchai. Umnesilk swallowed hard. "This why proud pictorian warriors need ask for help. This why call you, Wycaan. They have Firebreather."

Chapter Twenty Four

Umnesilk woke them while it was still dark. There was hot food and drink waiting, and, while they ate, an elderly, female pictorian bustled around, packing the elves' bags. Seanchai had offered to help, but she had shooed him away. He saw in her face that she was too sad to talk. Words were unnecessary.

Three pictorians entered each with a pack twice as big as what the elves would carry. Two sat and began to heap food onto their plates while the third called over something as he left the tent.

"He wish safe journey for you," one said, nodding to the tent flap.

"Thank you," Seanchai answered. "Did you fight in Hothengold? Is that how you know Odessiyan?"

"Yes," he replied, and then filled his mouth with food.

"If you and Umnesilk are coming with us, are there pictorians here who can also speak our tongue? Will there be someone to interpret for Prince Shayth?"

The pictorian nodded. Seanchai took another cup of steaming beverage and walked outside. The dawn light was gray and foreboding. Only a few pictorians were up, and they walked quickly and hunched. He looked up to the top of the ice walls as Umnesilk walked up to him.

"We go, Wycaan. Ready?"

"Umnesilk. That map we saw yesterday – do you have more copies?"

"Yes. We have mapmaker. Why?"

"Is it possible there were copies in the villages beyond the mountain?"

Umnesilk did not answer. He looked at Seanchai, and then followed the elf's gaze to the walls. Seanchai waited for the pictorian leader to acknowledge what Seanchai was implying. When he didn't, the Wycaan leaned in and kept his voice low so as not to be overheard.

"Umnesilk. You are First Boar. You must give the order to begin evacuating."

The tall pictorian frowned, hung his head, and remained silent. Seanchai continued.

"This design was used to hide the presence of the villages. You explained this to me yourself. But if your location is already known, this is not defensible. They don't even need to enter. They can shoot fire arrows and then just pick those down here off without even stepping foot into the village. Give the order. Your people must leave."

He looked up at his huge friend, who stood with his head still bent. The sunlight lit up the tips of his horns. Pictorians were tough, and there were none tougher than First Boar Umnesilk. But Seanchai saw his friend purse his lips several times and thought the pictorian even wiped a traitorous tear away.

Then Umnesilk raised his mighty horned head and took a deep breath. A determined expression etched across his face, he turned and strode off.

They left without Umnesilk and headed north. One of the pictorians was a scout and the other spoke Odessiyan. Umnesilk caught up with them before the sun had reached its zenith. Seanchai took one look at his face and knew this was not the time to talk. He exchanged a glance with Rhoddan whose face was also grim.

Each pictorian carried a long, thin skin-wrapped parcel along with their pack. Seanchai wondered what they were. They climbed a steep slope and the wind picked up, sending icy air into every crevice of their bodies not covered with furs and skins. Seanchai adjusted his scarf so that only his eyes were exposed, and they watered incessantly.

They were not far from the top of a ridge when the pictorians stopped and looked around. Grunts were exchanged, and they moved further east searching for something. Finally, they found what they were looking for: two small pieces of wood protruding out from the snow. The pictorians each removed their packs and dug with gloved hands until more wood was exposed. Metal rods reinforced the planks.

"Wycaan, you be guard," Umnesilk said pointing all around. "Rhoddan Warrior, help me."

Rhoddan and the First Board began pushing and pulling one plank, while the other two pictorians did the same with the other in a steady rhythm. Slowly, amidst grunts of exertion, as more snow began to loosen, Seanchai saw a wooden door was revealed and pulled loose.

One of the pictorians made a signal with his hand. "I tracks go."

"No need," Seanchai said. He extended his arm and gathered the energy to him with deep breaths. "*Moriarhtur*," he murmured, "*Moriarhtur, Moriarhtur.*"

A deliberate breeze rose and followed the movement of his hand. Slowly, a thin film of snow began to move until the path behind them was smooth. Then Seanchai followed the pictorians inside what seemed to be a small cave.

They had stacked their packs near the door, but the long packages were leaned against the other side of the room. One of the pictorians began to unpack them, and he pointed to two more that had been waiting for them in the cave.

"What's he saying?" Seanchai asked.

"Two scout come here. Leave planks for escape like us. Not come back to find." Umnesilk said.

"You can ride on these?" Rhoddan asked, thinking of the Men of the North, who had attacked him and Seanchai.

"Yes. Here to take us back fast if need."

"How far away do you think we are?" Seanchai asked.

Umnesilk looked inquisitively at the boar Seanchai had spoken to at breakfast.

"When I come last," the boar said, his voice deep and hesitant, "they about three days north. Took Ryhajask's village. Very big column, so move slow. I think no move much from there."

"What is your name?" Seanchai asked.

"Narasilk," he replied.

Seanchai looked at the young boar, and then at Umnesilk. "Are you related?"

"First son of first brother," Narasilk answered, clear pride in his voice.

"Maybe one day First Boar," Umnesilk said.

"How is that decided?" Rhoddan asked.

"Usual way. All who want, fight. Last one to stand is First Boar."

"How can you be sure the First Boar is also wise if the honor is only decided by physical combat?" Seanchai asked.

"If not wise, soon dead." Umnesilk shrugged.

Narasilk had been translating for the third pictorian, and they all laughed. It was a good sound to hear.

When they had rested, Umnesilk rose and picked up his pack. The others did the same.

"Remember this place. Maybe come back without pictorians. Take planks, and ride down mountain. Now, we go over mountain and find place for night on other side. Shelter there from wind."

They exited, and put the door back how they had found it. As they moved off, Narasilk pointed out landmarks to help them remember. In such a bland landscape, Seanchai was impressed that Narasilk found anything to distinguish where they were. Then the young boar stopped.

"You do magic on boot steps, yes?"

Seanchai nodded, and when they left, the snow was once more flat and smooth. By the time they reached the ridge, dusk was already gathering. Umnesilk strode several paces in front of the others. As he crested the top, he dropped to his belly. Seanchai gasped, fearing he had been shot, but the First Boar signaled for them all to lie flat.

They crawled up onto the ridge and gaped. The sun was blocked by the mountain range, and the valley before them was a mass of campfires that stretched as far as they could see.

"There are so many," Rhoddan whispered. "When that man boasted a hundred thousand, I assumed he was exaggerating. He might not have been."

No one spoke for a long time.

"We need to know if they're all soldiers," Rhoddan finally said, his warrior training kicking in.

"What you mean?" Narasilk asked. "Some cook and fix, but most fight, no?"

"I'm not so sure," Rhoddan said. "This might be an entire nation on the move. The Men of the North could be migrating."

"We need to find out," Seanchai said. "If they are migrating, it begs the question of what a hundred thousand people are fleeing from." He paused a moment. "I'll go down after dark."

Narasilk stared at him. "What? You just walk in and say hi?"

"I don't plan to stay for dinner, but yes, I will walk in."

Chapter Twenty Five

"Tell me about this woman, Mharina. Is she a human?"

"Yes," Mharina sat on a rock, looking up at the red-feathered owl. "She is powerful and confident. I'm not sure which scares me more. I told you about the purple fire and the respect the taragusii have for her, but there is something even more disturbing."

"What's that?"

"She's so nice to us. Ilan is totally in love with her and will sit next to her at every meal. He would ride next to her if I weren't the one holding the reins. But it is Senzia who worries me the most.

"You know how she is so...quiet. She has kept to herself even more since we were captured. But she and the purple woman, why, they ride together most of the day, and when we break for the evening, they go off together while the taragusii set up camp and prepare food."

"What do they discuss? Have you asked Senzia?"

"She won't tell me, or she just feeds me little things about the castle we are going to. We will be there tomorrow, Denalion. Will you be able to rescue us once we are behind their walls?"

"I don't know, little one. It might need for Prince Shindell to send an army, but he is in the north."

"I know."

"How?"

"I told Sa'gola I hoped my ahdahr *will come to rescue us. I thought she would be angry, but instead she just told me that it was perfectly natural to hope for that, but my* ahdahr *had gone on a quest beyond even where the pictorians live."*

"If she knows Seanchai is in the north, then this is a very coordinated abduction. I wonder how the Emperor is giving his orders."

"Senzia found out she talks with the Emperor. She has a small black stone, an Anw... something,"

"An Anwar? That is a very rare stone. There is only a handful left from ancient times. Listen, Mharina. Ask Senzia to try and find out about the stone and how it works. If she could get..."

"What, Denalion?"

"If she could use the stone...I don't know. I must talk to your mother first."

"If she uses the stone, she would talk with the Emperor, no? Does my ahdahr *or Prince Shindell also possess such a stone? Maybe—"*

"No! It's too dangerous." Denalion heard his own intrigue at the idea, which lessened the effect of his warning. *"At least wait until I discuss this with your mother."*

"My ahdahr *has a set of dwarf stones, doesn't he? Is one of them an Anw-"*

"Do not try anything, Mharina. Wait for my instruction. What is that?"

"I must go."

"What is...aaaagh!"

Denalion woke, gasping. A bright light momentarily blinded him, and he squeezed his eyes in pain. Riona sprung to his side, offering him water as she maneuvered him to a sitting position. Montclair called over from the perimeter where he was on guard, waking Sellia and Pyre in the process. The dreamwalker groaned and rubbed his forehead.

"What happened?" Riona asked. She made him hold the water skin and began to massage his forehead.

"Did you talk with Mharina?" Sellia asked. "Is she alright? Did something happen?"

Denalion wiped his mouth on his sleeve. "Mharina sensed something and fled. I felt a light, a burst of energy. That's what hurt me. It was the sorceress."

"How do you know?" Sellia asked.

"The light was purple."

An ominous silence descended, broken only by the crackle of burning wood and the old elf gulping water.

"Is she okay? Did they hurt her?" Seeing him shrug, Sellia wrung her hands. "Did you reach Seanchai or Rhoddan?"

"No. Seanchai has his wards up, and Rhoddan is not…well, I have only once succeeded in entering his dreams, when I called him to take the dwarves and pictorians back into the Cliftean Pass. He sleeps deeply and without dreams. I sense there are secrets he hides in his subconscious, even from himself.

"I have tried to reach Shayth and Maugwen. She does not ward herself and knows me. I really should be able to reach her."

He stopped and took another deep swig of water, which dribbled down his chin. "Sellia, I have another idea, but it would put Senzia in danger." He told her about the Anwar.

"That's ridiculous," Sellia snarled when he was finished. "Are you crazy? You would send Senzia, my daughter, an eleven-year-old *calhei*, to spy on a sorceress and the Emperor, who is also a Wycaan Master?"

"She is not any *calhei*, Sellia. She is a natural-born Wycaan. She has grown up fast and is far more mature than we give her credit. You and I discussed this when planning her education. Pyre?" He turned to the elfe. "When did you begin training?"

"When I was four years old," Pyre snapped. "But you're not offering to train her. You're sending her out on a mission – a very dangerous one, at that."

He looked at her. Pyre was usually very reverent toward the dreamwalker, but her tone now was terse.

"You are both right," Denalion relented. "I am also unsure how the Anwar works. Seanchai held it in his hand when he used it. Perhaps it is activated through touch."

"I'm not sure how it works," Riona said. "But I agree the idea is too dangerous. However, maybe it gives us a plan."

They all looked at the healer, and she seemed abashed at the attention. "It's not for me to suggest combat strategy."

"Suggest," Sellia said. "We have no luxury for ego."

Riona swallowed hard. "The children will be heavily guarded, so I think we need to accept that we aren't going to rescue them without a huge amount of luck." She saw Sellia stiffen, but braved on. "Before we even try, let's find the sorceress' chambers and her dwarf stones. We need to find a way to contact Seanchai and alert him, and her stones might give that to us. That way, Sellia, if we fail – if we die or are taken captive – we at least know he is on his way."

They went silent for a while, each desperately seeking another option. Finally, Denalion spoke.

"If we fail to even reach her Anwar, the children need to understand the alternative. I will–"

"No, you won't." Sellia had sprung to her feet, hands on hips, eyes blazing in the false dawn. "Mharina is very independent, and Senzia is…" her voice quivered, "… too brave. Do not mention it to them. You haven't, have you?"

Denalion looked even older than usual. His eyes betrayed his thoughts as he recounted his conversation with Mharina. Wrinkles creased his face.

"You've already talked to Mharina about it," Sellia hissed.

Denalion didn't answer. Sellia let out a guttural groan, and then leapt at the old elf. She instead found herself lying on her back, her arms pinned above her head. Riona straddled her, a curved knife with an ivory hilt at Sellia's throat.

"Steady," Montclair said, his voice quiet and calm.

Sellia stared into Riona's eyes. They were as black as a tourmaline stone, and the woman's nostrils flared as she struggled to control her rage. But, Sellia noted, the blade at her throat did not waver.

Chapter Twenty Six

"Please get off me," Sellia said, trying to project a calm voice. "I am in control of myself."

Riona did not move, the glinting blade still pressing against Sellia's throat.

"Let her up, child," Denalion said, his voice firm. "Her response was of a mother desperate in grief."

"Whatever it was, she could have—"

"But she didn't, thanks to you," Denalion interrupted, his tone steady. "We both are in your debt."

"We are," Sellia said. "I'm very sorry, Denalion. I really am."

Riona slowly withdrew her knife and returned it to her boot. When she stood, she spied a grinning Montclair.

"Fool," she hissed and pushed past him to her pack.

"Glad I never pressed my favors," he replied.

"Lucky for you," Riona snapped, her back to everyone as she fumbled with her bag.

Sellia stood up and offered a hand to the dreamwalker to help him up. He was so light. When he was standing, he put a bony hand on her shoulder and squeezed gently. He shuffled past her, but Sellia was not finished.

"I want you to reach Mharina again tonight. Tell her I absolutely forbid it."

Denalion winced. "I might not have that opportunity. I think the sorceress discovered us."

"You can't be certain."

"There was the flash of purple," he replied.

Sellia rubbed red friction burns and the clear indents of fingernails at her wrists. The dark elfe stared across at Riona. "She is very strong for such a frail-looking woman, and fast."

"She is," Denalion replied. "There is much to Riona that I suspect we do not know, and it would be our folly to consider her frail." Seeing Sellia still staring, he asked, "What is it, my dear? You are not going to hold this against her, right?"

"No," Sellia said. "But there was something in her eyes that...such rage...I've seen that look before, Denalion, but I don't know where." She looked from him to Montclair, who was listening intently. "You know something, don't you?"

The fortune-sword shrugged and turned away, which saved him from Sellia's glare.

They rode all day, wrapped in tense silence. Any breaks were short and purely functional. When the sun was just past its zenith, they saw the flat, sandy terrain begin to rise. Sellia stopped her horse and turned to Montclair.

"What is that?"

"Looks like a mountain range, judging by that vertical rise I see ahead," he replied.

"Show respect," Riona hissed at him from behind.

"I'm no ranger," he said, drily. "At the end of the desert is a mountain range – not a big one, but one that can hold a fortress and town."

"A town?" Sellia asked.

"A lone fortress is found only in children's stories," Montclair said. "The inhabitants would require servants and craftsman. Those servants and craftsman would, in turn, have families. This far away from any large town, there is probably also agriculture and animals. Just a guess, of course."

"Of course," Sellia replied. "Do you think there are lookouts in those peaks?"

"Probably," he shrugged. "But it matters little. They are expecting us and will allow us to get near."

"So much for the element of surprise," Pyre mumbled from the rear.

The mountains were further away and higher than they had looked. The group entered in the shadow of a setting sun and looked for a safe spot to camp. The atmosphere still tense, they ate, divided guard duty, and went to sleep.

Pyre woke early and decided to hunt. She almost woke Sellia to join her but stopped. Sellia was not much fun right now and, though Pyre would give her life to defend the Wycaan's mate, she didn't have to sacrifice her precious hunting time.

Montclair had the last watch. To his credit, he volunteered for what was generally the most dangerous shift, when guards were often tired and careless. She held up her bow to him, and he smiled, rubbing his stomach in an exaggerated display of hunger. Pyre could not resist smiling back. She really wanted to dislike this vagabond, but was having an increasingly difficult time doing so.

She walked along a steep path and over a ridge. The gray morning air was crisp, and she enjoyed the smell of the dewy earth. She stopped by a boulder ten times her height and saw clear marks of a herd – mountain goats, she was sure. She followed them around the ridge, noting that their droppings were soft as she poked around with a stick.

It was only a few minutes before she caught up with about thirty of them intently grazing. She moved close to the rock face and slowly drew an arrow. As she drew it back, she heard a human whimper from above. Abruptly she turned and aimed her bow at a boy, who curled up in fear and let out a wail.

"Are you alone?" Pyre demanded, adrenaline deepening her voice.

The boy cried something unintelligible and nodded.

"Come down here. Move slowly. I will not hurt you unless I feel threatened."

He was wearing a long, dirty dress and a turban. She could see the whites of his eyes, wide open in fear, as they darted from her to his footholds. He wore no shoes and white-knuckle gripped a twisted staff that looked freshly whittled.

Pyre kept her bowstring taut and watched his face to see if he was looking for someone else. He wasn't. His big, scared eyes remained fixed on her, and he was shaking.

"Are you here alone?" She kept her tone stern.

He shook his head, and she swung around in a wide arc, ready to let fly an arrow. But when she had completed a circle, she saw the boy trying to conceal a big grin behind a dirty hand.

"What is it?"

He turned and pointed to the goats. "I'm with them," he guffawed, then went serious. "I'm sorry, but you did ask, and I'm not allowed to lie."

Pyre lowered her bow. "Okay," she said. "Listen: I won't hurt you."

"Please don't kill a goat, either. My master will think I lost it and beat me." He lifted his shirt to show her several white scars on his dark-skinned hip and back.

"Your master did this to you?" Pyre felt her anger rising. "Maybe I *should* take a goat and then skin your master's hide as well."

The boy thought that was hilarious and laughed through a toothy grin.

"You hungry?" Pyre asked, and he nodded. "Come. My friends are making breakfast. Can you leave the goats for a while?"

The boy considered the idea before shaking his head no.

"Okay," Pyre said, "how about I go back and bring us both some breakfast?" He nodded with considerable enthusiasm. "What's your name?"

"Ricard," he replied, his eyes bulging. "Will you really bring me breakfast?"

She nodded.

"And you will eat with me? Share your food?"

When she nodded again, he puffed his chest out with pride. Pyre mussed his hair, and he gasped at her touch. She frowned as she turned to leave.

Chapter Twenty Seven

When Pyre returned to Ricard, she brought Sellia with her, as well as some hot oats with apples and honey. The boy's eyes lit up when he saw Pyre but grew apprehensive at Sellia.

"This is my friend, Sellia," Pyre said. "No need to worry."

"She's beautiful," Ricard replied, and then blushed. "There are not many dark-skinned rich people."

"Rich?" Sellia raised an eyebrow. She had been traveling for weeks now. Her clothes were soiled, her hair oily, and her face dry.

But Ricard looked down at his ragged dress and bare feet, then nodded at her boots. Compared to him, she was wealthy. His eyes wandered to the food, and they all sat on the ground by the rocks. The goats bleated contentedly nearby.

"Did you really bring me food?" he asked.

"No," Sellia joked. "We're going to eat while you watch."

Ricard went silent and bowed his head. "Of course," he mumbled.

"She's joking," Pyre said. "Of course we're going to eat with you. Why would we not share our food with you? I offered, didn't I?"

The boy looked up and frowned. "You aren't from these parts. I've never seen pointed ears, but I've heard of them in stories. Here, the poor mustn't even look at the rich. You could have beaten me for even talking to you. Your kind never eats with F'lusha –,the olive-skinned ones. We mustn't drink from your wells or walk into your buildings, unless it's to serve."

"You're right," Sellia said. "We aren't from these parts. My people were also treated badly, but now all people are equal with laws that protect everyone."

"Wow," Ricard's eyes widened. "Your home must be very, very far from here. Why have you come?"

"We are on our way to Grogin. Do you know it?"

Ricard, who had been shoveling the gruel into his mouth, froze mid-bite.

"You might want to eat that before it falls off your spoon," Pyre suggested.

He did, but his enthusiasm for his breakfast had vanished. After he swallowed, Ricard frowned, trying to decide what to say.

"I showed you the scar that my master gave me," he said to Pyre. "There are more. My master is very powerful. He is the lord of our village, and we all serve him and are frightened by him. He himself is very, very frightened of those beyond the black walls. Those who go to serve there often do not return.

"There are strong lizards in their army that walk on two legs. Over them are five old warriors, all with white hair, and above them is the Master, who rules over all. I have not seen him, but they say he can turn into different animals. They say he can become a firebreather and light up the night sky when he is angry. I have seen fire in the sky.

"Whenever a white-haired one comes into our village, someone dies. Our master offers them money, women, and animals. Once, they took my friend Potal, and we never saw him again."

"Ricard," Sellia leaned forward. "Is your village near here?"

The boy had resumed eating, so he just nodded.

"Is there anyone in your village who has ever entered Grogin and come out? Maybe through a secret passage of some sort?"

The boy didn't answer. Sellia leaned forward and took the spoon from his hand. In its place, she put a gold draktan.

"Hide the coin, or someone will take it from you. I want you to go to whoever this person is and tell him that he will receive five gold coins if he comes and talks with us. There could be more, depending on the information he gives us. You will also receive more once you bring him here. Do you understand?"

Ricard nodded, but as he withdrew his hand, Sellia grabbed his wrist. She moved her face closer to his and spoke in a harsh whisper.

"Do you see that Pyre and I both have bows? If you tell anyone apart from this person, and they come looking for us, we will find you. We are armed and very, very dangerous. Again, do you understand?"

The boy nodded slowly, fear in his eyes. "W–what if she won't come to you? Will you kill me then?" His voice was trembling.

"No. As long as you try, we will not blame you for someone else's decision."

"Or take away my coin?"

"You have my word."

Ricard stood. "One day, I want to visit the land you come from, where all people are free and with honor."

He bowed and ran off, gathering his goats as he went.

They took turns lying in wait for Ricard's return in a concealed crevice higher up the small mountain. Pyre and Sellia were coming to switch with Montclair and Riona when they saw a party approach. They hid behind a large rock and watched as five heavily armed, bearded men walked past. They had wide, curved swords, but no shields or bows. A man in a white turban and flowing, cream-colored cloak rode a horse alongside them. He brandished a coiled whip in a way that suggested he could use it at a moment's notice. On another horse lay Ricard, bloody and bound.

They stopped, and the man pulled Ricard's head up by his hair. He said something, and then spat on the boy's face. The man in white gave orders, and four of his men spread out to scout. A fifth cut the ropes that held Ricard. The boy slipped down the side of the horse and moaned as he landed in a crumpled heap. The men had turned at his cry and all thought this was very funny, and the one who had cut his ropes gave Ricard a kick in the ribs. The boy gasped.

Sellia's arrow went straight through the man's throat, and he crumpled where he stood. The leader called his men back – the two nearest responded, but only to provide more open targets. The other two had not returned, and the man in white looked around frantically for his soldiers.

"Stay hidden," Sellia whispered to Pyre, and strode out into the open, bow raised. The man turned his horse to her and unleashed his whip. "You won't get within twenty paces of me," she warned. "The whip is of no use. Drop it."

The man began ease his horse toward her. "You are too beautiful to be so violent. Come, we shall talk. This is a very hospitable land, and we respect the honor of the guest rites."

Sellia pulled her bowstring taut. "The whip. Now."

The man dropped the whip and raised his hands, the rein looped through his fingers.

The whip cracked behind him, and he jerked around. Montclair stood there, whip in one hand and bloody sword in his other. "This is cool," he said, giving it another crack.

The man looked from Montclair to Sellia. "The boy said there were bandits out here. Is that what you are?"

"Why did you beat him if you were heeding his words?" Sellia retorted.

"He's a F'lusha boy. He's nothing. I can give you ten if you want. They breed so fast that I cannot feed and employ them all. They cheat and lie. I thought he was lying, and when I found the coin on him, I assumed he stole it.

"I came to find the one he stole it from. You perhaps? There is no need to fight. I have money, if that's what you want. Tell me, how can I help you on your way?"

Riona had run out from behind Montclair and was tending the boy.

"Have you ever entered Grogin?" Sellia asked.

"Of course, milady. I am a respected civic leader."

Sellia glared at him, and glanced at where the boy lay. "Is there any way in, other than the main gate? How would someone enter who preferred to stay anonymous?"

The man laughed. "How would I know that, milady?"

"Know it and tell it, or I have no reason to let you live."

"I will not tell you," he snarled. "He who lives there is far more worthy of fear than you. Let the arrow pierce my breast while I stand before you, defenseless. Murder me, and let my body rot in the dust with the F'lusha boy."

"No," Sellia said, her voice suddenly calm. "If the boy dies, we will bury him. He does not deserve for the crows and vultures to pluck out his eyes and tear his skin from his bones. But you do."

She turned away and then swept round, the arrow at her bow again taut. This time she loosened and her arrow pierced his heart. He fell from his horse slowly. The thud of his body hitting the ground echoed in the silence.

Sellia joined Riona and Pyre where they were leaning over Ricard. Blood dripped from his mouth, and one side of his rib cage was unnaturally inverted.

"I'm sorry, mistress," he whispered. "And you ate with me… gave me food and touched my he…aaah,"

Sellia touched his arm. "You did all you could, little one. Now, close your eyes and fly to Odessiya, where your spirit will live free with my ancestors. There will be food there and noble elves and humans to sup with you."

Ricard smiled. "And boots … like yours?"

"And boots," she whispered back, her voice breaking.

Ricard closed his eyes, but the smile remained until he drew his final breath.

Chapter Twenty Eight

Mharina stole glances at the sorceress whenever they rode near to each other. If Sa'gola had entered her dreams and seen her talking with Denalion, then she had not said anything so far. But the young elfe was afraid.

The taragusii now avoided interacting with the prisoners, allowing Sa'gola to tell them when to sleep, eat, or relieve themselves. They also seemed increasingly restless once they left the desert. Mharina wondered whether they were pleased or apprehensive at the prospect of reaching their master's castle.

Ilan was becoming increasingly petulant. Either he was exhausted from the journey or fear was driving him to behavior that, even by his standards, was pretty extreme.

They had entered into a foreboding mountain range. The rocks were dark and uniform, gray and black. An argument broke out among the taragusii not long after they had crested a steep hill and reached a three-way junction.

When Sa'gola clucked at her horse to trot up, Mharina decided to follow. She twisted in her saddle and whispered to Ilan to stay quiet.

"What is the problem?" Sa'gola asked.

"It'sss been a long time sssince we have eaten fresssh meat, missstresss. There isss a village nearby," Third Scale said, nodding in one direction.

"It's the opposite direction from Grogin," Sa'gola said.

"Sssso right, missstresss," one of the other taragusii replied, bowing his head. "But with permisssion, a few can go and hunt for all. The little onesss are ssslow. We will catch you up."

Sa'gola turned to Third Scale. "They are under your command. Do you think we are in danger of being attacked?"

"The scoutsss in the rear will sssignal if the elvesss catch up, but they will not at the pace we have ssset. The villagersss here are weak and easssily intimidated. Mossst are F'lusssha, and thosssse who aren't pay homage and taxesss to the massster."

"Very well," Sa'gola relented. "Bring only enough for one meal, understood? Use no unnecessary force, and" – she lowered her voice – "bring a goat or lamb for the children. Cut everything up before you rejoin us. I don't want them to see …."

The taragusii stared behind Sa'gola, and she turned to see that the young elves were within earshot.

She turned back, and her voice was hard. "Nonetheless, my request still stands."

"Asss you command, missstresss," one replied, and they all bowed their heads.

Third Scale called for his soldiers to form ranks and continue riding. Mharina brought her horse alongside Sa'gola.

"They're going to eat human flesh?"

"Yes, my dear. You saw it, unfortunately with the tutans. That was not just battle rage. They also eat dwarf and elf, though I hear dwarves are somewhat tough to chew."

"That's disgusting," Ilan said from the rear of the saddle he shared with Mharina.

Mharina rested a hand on his knee to calm him when two taragusii hissed at the response. Sa'gola looked at him sternly, but her tone remained friendly.

"All creatures are different. It is not for us to judge one another. Who decides that what they eat is crueler than what you do? Who is to say that the prince and your father, who have killed thousands, are any purer? Perhaps they might have honored their victims by eating them rather than leaving their corpses for the scavengers."

"My *ahdahr* –" Ilan started.

"… is not as perfect as you want to think, little elf. He may be a fine father, but that does not excuse him from his actions."

"My *ahdahr* … " Ilan began again, but his voice puttered out.

"Tell us about the people who live here," Mharina asked, wanting to change the subject. "Who are the F'lusha?"

"There is a strict class system that you are born into here, no exceptions. The poorest are the F'lusha. They are slaves or servants who belong to their lords. They have no rights and must not eat or drink in the presence of the other classes. There is little more to be said about them."

"Excccept they don't tassste good, being ssso thin," a taragus answered from behind. The others laughed. "Ssshame really. They are ssso abundant."

"The richer, the tassstier," another said, and another round of laughter followed.

Mharina glanced at the sorceress. She could have silenced them – had done so in the past – but this time, she let it ride. She had a point to prove, Mharina decided. Ilan's fingers grasped her waist even tighter. Point made, apparently.

That night, the taragusii prepared as if for a feast. A cooking fire was lit, and the goat was turned on a spit for the young elves and Sa'gola. Eating in a different area than the taragusii didn't stop Ilan from glancing over his shoulder at them, but at least he had an appetite.

"How can they eat people?" he asked Sa'gola.

The sorceress took a long drink of water before answering. "To understand why they eat what they do, you need to understand their origins. The taragusii live in the hot, arid wastelands of Harridiya. And they were not always reptilian."

"Where?" Mharina thought she knew her geography.

Sa'gola smiled at her. "In the ancient times, there was a very different landscape than what we understand exists today. Once, a bitter power struggle broke out between two brothers, both Master Mages, and their armies fought throughout the great desert. What we have passed through is only a small part of what was once a great expanse of sand dunes and oases.

"One of the brothers was an elf called—"

"An elf?" Ilan interrupted.

"My story will take all night if you three keep interrupting," Sa'gola laughed. "Yes, an elf. Most of the ancient lore concerns elves. The dwarves and pictorians came later, and the humans even later still.

"Taragus was a huge elf with long, shining, blond hair. He was as fine a warrior as he was a wielder of magic. But his army fell to the swords and bows of his brother, Wyccin, who—"

"… had white hair?" Senzia bobbed up and down.

"Indeed he did, little one. Very clever. Very perceptive. Wyccin used magic — dark magic — to defeat his brother. He spread an infection that boiled the skin, which, I understand, is quite sensitive for elves.

"With too few soldiers left, Taragus led his people into Harridiya, and there, he used his magic to transform their skin into a hard, scale-like material that was impervious to the disease.

"Wyccin did not know this and scryed the wastelands for elves. Finding none, he took his armies and returned to Odessiya to rule unopposed.

"But he left his dead and dying, caring little for his people. The taragusii were hungry and desperate. They did not yet know how to use their new bodies to hunt and, most likely, there was little to hunt in Harridiya. They were starving and ate what they could find, and what they found were corpses and dying elves.

"Later, when they had eaten the elves, tribes of humans migrated from the far south toward Odessiya. The taragusii preyed on them, as your people hunt the buffalo and other herd creatures."

Ilan looked over to the taragusii eating round the campfire.

"It must have been very hard for them to transform into what they are," he said.

Sa'gola smiled at him. "I'm glad you understand," she said and gave him a hug, which he seemed to gladly reciprocate. "Always remember, little *calhei*, that everyone – elf, human, dwarf, pictorian – start out equal. If some rise higher, it is not because of the shape of the ears, but the quality of their heart."

Mharina found herself nodding in agreement with the diminutive woman.

Chapter Twenty Nine

The sun had not yet reached its zenith when the taragusii crested the peak of a mountain and stopped. They parted into two lines and allowed Sa'gola and the *calhei* to ride between them.

A valley lay below, crisscrossed with fields and orchards. Mharina counted six hamlets – a few no more than a dozen huts. But her eyes did not stay there for long.

On the other side of the valley was a looming fortress that hugged the side of the mountain almost to the top. In fact, as she looked closer, Mharina saw that the peak of the mountain was incorporated into a tower that spiraled around it, with only the actual summit protruding.

"Welcome, little elvesss, to Grogin," Third Scale said with a flourish of his powerful, scaled arm. "The Cccity in the Mountain."

"They built it against the rock face?" Ilan asked.

"No," Sa'gola answered, the purple streaks in her shiny black hair shimmering in the breeze. "They built it out of the rock. Much of the interior is carved directly into the mountains. It rivals the finest dwarf craftship."

"How was it built?" Ilan asked her without taking his eyes away from the architecture.

"Best we save that for another time," she answered. "The story is long, and we are all tired and hungry. Lead us on, Third Scale," she commanded. "Tonight we sleep in beds with walls and a roof, after soothing, hot baths."

"Asss you command, milady," Third Scale said.

As one, the taragusii troops followed a path down into the valley that headed straight to the fortress. They crossed over a strong river on a bridge with guard towers at each end. Mharina saw no life in the village and no one working the fields. She almost asked where everyone was until she noticed a taragus near her gnawing the meat off a bone. She swallowed hard and forced her eyes forward.

The mountain and fortress of Grogin rose quickly before them, and all three *calhei* stared up in awe, as the road went alongside the outer walls.

"What stones are those?" Senzia wondered. "I see no bricks."

The walls indeed looked to be constructed of one piece. They were not smooth but if there were joints, Mharina could not see them.

"The mountain is the fortress, and the fortress the mountain," Sa'gola replied. "The Master wields powerful magic and controls the elements."

Mharina looked at the small woman wrapped in her purple cloak. There was clearly immense awe in her tone, but Mharina wondered if Sa'gola also feared her master as the taragusii did.

They reached huge iron gates with intertwining wooden beams reinforced with rods of metal. A conversation between Third Scale and a guard inside a watchtower ended with a vibration underfoot and the whoosh of moving water.

The water came up from the river below them and filled something behind the walls. Gradually, the metal bars released themselves, one by one. Water dripped from their tips, but a steady flow filled a tank on the opposite side. This tank emptied once the doors were open, and Mharina assumed the water was flowing back underground to the river.

She looked to her brother and sister. Ilan was very impressed and clearly wanted to ask more questions. But Senzia was frowning and agitated. Finally, she turned to Sa'gola, who wore an excited smile.

"It doesn't make sense," Senzia said. "The water from the river is being used to open the gates."

"That's right," Sa'gola answered.

Senzia looked behind them several times. "But the water is flowing *uphill* from the river to the gate. That's impossible."

"Clearly not impossible." The sorceress arched a purple-shaded eyebrow. "However, I concede that it's not natural, either. It's a message to those who enter: The Master is stronger than the elements and their laws."

Senzia nodded, accepting the explanation. "Impressive," she said. "Let's go in."

Sa'gola laughed. "You are very clever. Ride with me inside."

They entered through a long tunnel, the rock as smooth inside as on the wall outside. When they exited, it was so bright that they needed a moment for their vision to adjust. Mharina realized how this put an enemy – or any visitor, really – at a clear disadvantage.

"Has Grogin ever needed to be defended in a war?" Senzia asked, her voice strong in the crisp air.

"Never," the nearest taragus answered.

"Very perceptive," Sa'gola said.

As her vision returned, Mharina observed the heavily fortified wall, full of arrow slits and chutes used to pour burning oil from the inside onto the exterior. But there was no sign that there had ever been a battle: no chipped stone, no stains, no burn marks.

She glanced at her sister. Senzia had ignored Sa'gola's compliment as her eyes darted around. Tonight, when they were alone, Mharina would discuss the Anwar with Senzia. For now, she followed the procession through a large, empty courtyard to a second wall and gate. This one was not as large or dominating as the first, but still had hooded guards at every arrow slit.

Through this wall was a small courtyard with trees and flowers fed by channels of running water. Under the trees were benches, and, over to one side sat archery targets and figures stuffed with hay for sword training. The fortress followed around the base of the mountain.

Ahead of her loomed the keep. It was also built of smooth stone, but vines hugged the stone itself, dotting it with an assortment of purple and orange flowers.

They stopped in front of an elderly taragus, dressed in a white toga with a diagonal purple sash over his right shoulder. There was a brooch on the sash above his breast, and its orange stone sparkled when the sun kissed it.

"Greetingsss, dear Sssa'gola," he said in a surprisingly high-pitched voice, and bowed.

"Greetings to you, First Scale," she replied. "I have the *calhei*."

First Scale peered around her and nodded solemnly at the three. His scaly claws intertwined, and he turned to the taragusii leader.

"You've done well, Third Ssscale. The massster gave you a difficult task."

"The sssorcccceresss was very helpful," Third Scale replied. "And they're good little elvesssessss."

"Are you being followed?"

"Yesss."

"How many?"

"Jussst four or five. Their mother isss among them."

"Excccellent," First Scale's tongue darted out and licked his nose.

"Missstresss Sssa'gola, will you sssettle them into their quartersss?"

Sa'gola nodded, and two taragusii stepped forward to take their reins.

"Are we not going to see him?" Senzia asked as they walked together.

"The Master is in the north," Sa'gola answered. "With your father."

"Will they fight?" Senzia asked, her tone steady.

"Maybe."

"I don't think so," the white-haired *calhei* answered.

"Really? Why? I doubt your father has an advantage there or here," Sa'gola snapped back. "Excuse me, I'm tired."

"I disagree," Senzia replied, ignoring the woman's sharp tone. "The Emperor will probably return here, because he'll prefer to make his stand on his own ground," Senzia said. "But he makes a bad mistake."

Sa'gola frowned. "How?"

"My *ahdahr* will also be better suited to fight here."

"And why, little one, is that?"

"Because *we* are here. He will tear this place apart to rescue us. Then Grogin will face its first battle... and quite possibly its last."

It was Senzia who took Sa'gola's hand to lead her into the keep.

Chapter Thirty

"Chasichot, Chasichot, Chasichot." Seanchai whispered the words over and over again.

The energy came to him slowly, sluggish in the frigid cold. He fretted. Was his power weakened in these conditions, or could his powers be waning?

He stared across the white landscape. It was winter here, and he realized that the living energy of the land was buried deep underground, stored for long-term conservation. It was so different from the vibrancy of the Markwin forest or the ley lakes.

The realization suddenly gave him confidence. He simply needed to embrace the energy there, even if it was different. He almost smiled to himself. If it was not him but the frozen environment, then the Emperor would have the same disadvantage when they fought.

"*Chasichot, Chasichot, Chasichot,*" he repeated with more conviction.

He could hear the pictorians and Rhoddan nearby, but as he spun his web of darkness, they became distant, their voices taking on a muffled quality. Narasilk was plying Rhoddan with questions about Seanchai, his power, the world of the Wycaans, and the world of Odessiya, until Umnesilk finally silenced him.

They would stay and wait for Seanchai until dawn. Then they would retreat to the concealed cave and wait another day. After that, they would return to the elder's settlement.

"I am going," Seanchai said. "How do I look?"

"Not see you," Umnesilk replied.

"Amazing," Narasilk exclaimed. "How you–"

Umnesilk growled at him, and he fell silent. Seanchai smiled at Narasilk, understanding the youngster's enthusiasm – but his compassion went unnoticed, as Narasilk could not see him.

"May the spirits guide you," Rhoddan said. "We'll wait as long as we can."

Seanchai turned and began to descend the mountain, the sea of campfires rushing up to greet him. He gulped as he neared the first line of sentries. These men were big and broad-shouldered. Their dark hair hung in long, greasy strands, and most had bushy, unkempt beards.

He passed near the first group and realized that he was leaving a trail in the snow. He turned and focused on covering his footprints while staying hidden. He had never juggled two spells before, and it tired him.

He needed to get close to the throng of people so his footprints wouldn't betray him. There was a second perimeter of guards patrolling a sandy path being smoothed by two oxen dragging a log. Seanchai stopped as he watched the oxen pass.

When they reached a dark area away from the tents, Seanchai crossed the path and turned to quickly cover his tracks. Inside the camp, he had a new problem to worry about. His tracks would blend in with those of the hordes of soldiers milling around, but he had to avoid bumping into anyone.

Heavily armed men fortified the area he entered and he made his way between groups who laughed raucously as they drank ale and quaffed pipes. When two engaged in a mock fight, one nearly collided with the Wycaan.

Seanchai saw a gap between these tents and the next group. He gasped as the huge black mass that he had thought to be a rock moved when he brushed past it. He looked up at the first giant he had ever seen. It must have been ten feet tall and twice his width. Slowly, it turned toward Seanchai, lifted its fur pelt, and relieved itself.

What streamed out hissed as it hit the frozen ground only a hand's length in front of Seanchai. The smell almost made the elf choke. Hearing grunts behind the giant, Seanchai looked to see that there were at least a dozen of these creatures. Two held huge clubs as if they weighed nothing.

Seanchai moved away quickly and into the middle of the camp. There were more groups of men distinguished by the furs they wore, clearly of different races, though most seemed human. There were women – many bearing weapons – but no children.

Seanchai decided to follow the outer circle of the camp instead of going through its middle. If the Emperor was here, then he wanted to avoid him until he at least knew how many men were gathered. He headed toward some tents that were separate from those he had just passed.

This group had their own guards, a detail that did not escape Seanchai's attention. The sentries wore helmets with two horns and were bigger and broader than Seanchai. They each rested double-headed axes on their massive shoulders.

Only when he was closer did he realize that they were not wearing helmets. Seanchai felt a chill course through him. *Pictorians!*

Umnesilk had spoken about the clans that had ventured further north and then disappeared. They were apparently now part of an army formed by geographical alliance or bonded under the Emperor's power as were the men and giants.

Seanchai peeked into one of their tents and counted twenty-four boars. Moving carefully through their camp, he counted thirty such tents: assuming the same number in each tent, there were over seven hundred pictorian warriors.

He continued past more camps of men; some with bright red faces, clear even in the darkness, though he wasn't sure if this was paint, or burns from the sun and snow glare. Then he approached a huge area of corralled horses, cows, and goats; large, fur-covered mastiffs; and then a large, empty pen for exercising the animals.

A dozen men led their horses out of the pen to make way for large, gray-scaled creatures with huge hooves and protruding horns on their noses. These creatures galloped around the training area, each carrying a pictorian in a huge, heavy-set saddle.

Seanchai watched them exercising. The pictorians held long poles with iron tips. They were almost twice the length of the pictorians and they smashed into dummies as they thundered by.

After a quick count, the Wycaan turned away from the animal enclosures and back toward the center of the camp. He wanted to see if he could identify a chain of command. Was it only the Emperor giving directions, or did he have competent officers leading the soldiers? Seanchai needed to discover whether they were facing a volatile horde or a well-disciplined army.

A wooden palisade of sharpened logs fenced off the camp's center. Whoever was inside evidently feared those outside.

Seanchai could not see how to enter and quickly scryed the area, trying to determine if the Emperor was there. Even though he could not identify the Emperor, he was far from sure whether his adversary's wards would not simply elude him.

Then he heard a high-pitched, animal scream. There was a fight in the training enclosure or maybe beyond it. It was not his fight, and he turned back to focus on the command post. But a second scream stopped him in his tracks, and then his hair stood up on his neck. A desperate whisper carried clear inside his head.

"Help us! Wycaan!"

Chapter Thirty One

Seanchai wheeled around. That scream had not cut through the night – he had heard the plea inside his head. *Inside.* It felt similar to walking in the dream world with Denalion, but who could be reaching out to him here? Denalion was safe at the other end of Odessiya with Sellia and the children, protected on Wycaan Island.

He began to walk back toward the training pen, slowing his pace, being careful not to accidentally brush up against someone or trip on an object strewn on the ground.

There were still pictorians riding drills on their one-horned creatures. These beasts, huge and heavy, were as fast as they were bad tempered. Seanchai noted that while they could accelerate quickly, they were slow to change direction.

The Wycaan cautiously cast his mind out, scrying among the pictorians, but sensed nothing. High above, in the sky, a creature screeched and blew a pillar of fire. Seanchai quickly withdrew his thoughts and watched as the firebreather descended and landed on the other side of the camp.

Wait, the same voice said inside his head. *When he transforms from the firebreather, he will be exhausted. Let him retire.*

Again, Seanchai looked around. He saw only pictorians and their beasts here. But then a buzz rippled through the pictorians, and they looked over to the other side of the training pen.

Others were filing in, a long column of mounted…what were they?

The riders were too tall and thin to be human, but otherwise still human-like. Their hair was a strange yellow color, and they were almost entirely covered in blue paint, intricately woven patterns, and animal pelts. All wore long swords, and when two drew them from their scabbards, the blades were blue and thin.

Moving closer, Seanchai noticed they were mounted on ice bears. The bears seemed agitated, and many of them were marked with bloodied cuts. Their riders held whips and did not hesitate to mete out punishment.

The column entered the ring on the far side and began their own exercises. Unlike the pictorians, their animals were unruly but the riders elegant and skillful. All wore long swords and when two drew them from their scabbards, the blades were blue and thin.

Gradually, they began to spread out, encroaching on more than half of the ring. One pictorian trotted over to speak to three of the blue-painted humanoids. Seanchai could not hear what was being said, but the humanoids seemed to taunt the pictorian, who became increasingly agitated. Exasperated, he dragged his one-horn around, but he pulled too hard and the creature shook its massive neck, almost unseating the pictorian. The humanoids laughed, and, as the pictorian steadied himself, another pictorian approached and called for his return.

A few moments later, both sides were back on their respective sides and focusing on their exercises. Suddenly, an unmounted one-horn roared and broke from the troop, galloping toward the bears. Seanchai could feel the ground shake under his pounding hooves. He snorted large clouds of gray breath and, as he approached, he lowered his head to offer the tip of his horn.

Cries of alarm had the men wheeling their bears to meet the challenge. A volley of arrows bounced off the one-horn's scales. Two landed and pierced its natural armor, and it bellowed in anger.

A huge spear landed between its eyes, and, the creature faltered for a moment before regaining a steady gallop. The men and bears scattered, but the one-horn seemed to have singled out one specific bear and rider.

At first, rider and bear dodged comfortably, but as they sidestepped the beast, the tip of its horn grazed the ice bear's thigh, and a line of bright red began to trickle. The bear bellowed and turned on the one-horn, its great teeth snapping for revenge. Its rider tried to move it away, but the bear refused, ignoring the whip lashing its body.

They dodged the next attack, and this time the ice bear leapt onto the one-horned creature's back. There was a screech of claws on scales, and Seanchai couldn't help but gasp in pain. The one-horn threw him off, but the bear fell with what looked like an iron plate in its claws. A great swell of scarlet red spurted from the one-horned creature's back, and it wheeled around.

Roaring its pain, the bear rose onto its back paws, sending its helpless rider sprawling. It sidestepped the one-horn again and cuffed it with a paw that wrenched the beast's head. It staggered a couple of paces from the blow, but the one-horned still stood. As it turned back to confront the bear, the heavy beast crushed the blue rider. The crunch was sickening, its finality clear.

The one-horned hesitated a moment, and that was enough for the bear to leap onto its back again. Shorn of its armor plating, it bucked, trying to shake off the bear, but the bear's claws had sunk deep into its back.

Suddenly, the one-horned swerved and rolled onto its back, crushing the bear under tons of body mass. This crunch was more drawn out than the first, as several ribs caved, one after the other.

Noooo, a voice screamed in Seanchai's mind. *Noooo.*

Seanchai stared at the other ice bears. He was certain now that it was one of them, but his attention was soon drawn back to the one-horned creature. With blood still spurting rhythmically from the wound on its neck, it raised its mighty head and bellowed in rage and pain. One-horn never saw the huge axe descend. Its head rolled onto the ground, and the body, blood now gushing onto the churned snow, bucked once and lay still.

Come to us in an hour, the voice in Seanchai's head panted. *Finish seeing what you need to see and, if you will help us, be prepared to leave.*

Seanchai looked over to the bears and their blue-painted riders. The bears were furious, roaring into the air and stamping their feet. Their riders frantically tried to calm them, whips snapping through the air.

One bear was less agitated and moved to the side of the column, closer to where Seanchai stood. Then it stopped, and its rider patted its haunches. The bear was panting hard, and large clouds of white breath filled the air. But Seanchai caught a glimpse of its face, and its blue eyes were looking in his direction.

Will you come? It asked. *Will you help us?*

I will, Seanchai replied wordlessly.

Chapter Thirty Two

Pyre sobbed as she dug Ricard's grave. She did not care who saw or heard, and she channeled all her grief into the effort. Ricard lay motionless, wrapped in the fine cream cloak of his tormenter. Sellia had taken the man's boots and put them on the boy, as well. These were undoubtedly the finest garments he had ever worn.

"Let me dig some," Riona said softly from her side.

"No," Pyre snapped and wiped her eyes. "He was such a beautiful boy. He expected nothing, never received kindness from anyone."

"He received it from you," Riona answered.

Pyre stopped and sniffled. "What are you talking about?"

"You and Sellia respected him. You ate with him and gave him hope that there exists a better world."

"It didn't help him. He's dead."

"There are people in the east who believe that when you die, you are reborn as another creature. If you lived a good life, you would be born to a higher station than the one you just left."

Pyre sniffed. "What animal will he be? He was too pure to return as a human or elf."

"How about an eagle? He can soar above the clouds and be free."

"An eagle, yes."

Pyre put down the spade and picked up the small body. She hugged him and turned to the grave. A voice stopped her.

"May I hold him one last time, milady?"

They both turned to see a slight woman wrapped in brown, stained cloth.

"Can I hug my little boy before you give him back to the earth?"

The woman's eyes were red and swollen, but she did not cry. She reached out, and Pyre reverently passed him along. Ricard's mother pulled him tight to her body and turned away. Pyre could see her shoulders shaking, but the woman made no sound.

Sellia, Denalion, and Montclair joined them, having brought their horses and bedding from the camp. Sellia gave her reins to the fortune-sword and went to the woman, hugging her from behind.

"I am a mother, too," she whispered. "I'm so sorry."

A shrill wail erupted from the woman, echoing off the nearby rocks. Sellia signaled to Riona, who came and took the body. Then Sellia turned the woman around and hugged her as Pyre and Riona lay Ricard carefully in the grave and covered him up.

When the sobbing subsided, they moved into the shade and broke bread. The woman held a chunk, but did not eat. At Sellia's insistence, she drank from their water skins.

"Thank you," the woman said. "You showed him respect by burying him. He was so...so..."

She began to cry again silently, her body jerking and her breath coming in gasps. No one spoke, their only movements to wipe their own tears away. Finally, the woman let out a deep sigh. She looked into her hand, where Sellia had placed five gold coins.

"Ricard was running an errand for me," Sellia explained. "I promised him the coin. It is only right that you have it." She put a small pouch on the ground by the woman's foot. "And this is from his murderer. It is scarcely compensation, but should help to ease your burden. Be careful how you show it."

"What was Ricard doing for you?"

"We need to enter Grogin. He knew someone who can slip us in or at least tell us the way. I asked him to bring them."

The woman closed her hand around the coins. "I will take you in," she whispered. "Ricard's last act will not be in vain. He would want to earn his coin. I have a daughter who works in the kitchens, and I visit her in the night when I can, though it is not allowed."

They packed up their possessions and followed Ricard's mother through the valley.

"I'm taking you around our village. It wouldn't be good for you to be seen there —for you or us."

"What is your name?" Sellia asked.

"Better I not tell you. If they torture you, I don't want my name screamed out. The fortress is very big. The Master lives within a castle inside it. The taragusii live in and guard the outside fortress."

"Who guards the inside one?"

"Men, elves, dwarves, and others."

"That doesn't sound so bad," Montclair offered from behind them.

The woman turned to him. "They are all white-haired and have powers I cannot explain. They are members of noble peoples, but have lost their nobility. They are the cruelest and most vicious of the guards. My daughter…"

She stopped talking abruptly.

"My mate is white-haired," Sellia said.

"I am sorry for you."

"No, he is a good Wycaan. He led those who freed our people in Odessiya."

"Is he coming here?" The woman seemed more interested.

Sellia glanced at Denalion, who lowered his eyes. "We are trying to reach him. When he hears, he will summon a great army and lead them here."

"But he isn't coming now," Ricard's mother lowered her gaze. "This is not a land for heroes, milady. They do not come here."

"He will come," Pyre snapped.

The woman turned to look at her. "You showed kindness to my son, so I will not cross you, but hope left this land many years ago. The Master rules, and he commands the white-haired ones, who are scared of him. Perhaps it is better for you that the good Wycaan stays away."

Sellia laughed. "You don't know my mate. He drops everything to come to the aid of his friends, and has done so too many times. But there is more at stake now than his mate and friends."

The woman studied her expression. "You are a mother, too," she whispered.

Sellia nodded and pursed her lips.

"I will take you in," the woman said. "You see that cave? We will sleep there tonight, and you will leave your horses. I will bring them feed and water for a while."

"How will you bring food and water here?" Montclair asked.

"I will pay a boy to do it. I am a woman of coin." She jangled the pouch in her cloak. "Let us settle in there and then climb up to see the fortress before dark. We will sleep half a night and then go."

Chapter Thirty Three

Montclair smeared a black paste over each of his weapons, as well as Denalion's belt buckle and cloak broach. Then he colored the old elf's face and palms, wherever his dark skin was blotched. Pyre did the same with her own equipment and Sellia's.

"Handsome fella," Montclair said to Denalion, admiring his work. "You should get some sleep. It's going to be a long day tomorrow."

Then he reached for Riona, his cream in hand.

"Don't touch me!" she snapped, and they all looked round. Riona blushed and then glared at the fortune-sword. "Here, you can darken my blades."

"I am honored, though greatly unworthy of such a task," Montclair flourished.

Ricard's mother looked at Sellia and whispered too loudly, "Are they …?"

Sellia shrugged, keenly aware that everyone was watching her.

"This is not the place to fall in love," the woman said, her tone sad.

"We're not in—" Riona responded, too harshly, and ended it with a huff.

"Evidently. But think on this." The woman interrupted, her own voice despondent. "You'll probably both be dead tomorrow. Do you want to die having never heard the words from his lips?"

They all stared at her, and the silence was uncomfortable. Montclair rose rather sharply. "We should post guards. I'll take the first shift."

When he was outside, the women all looked at Riona, who shuffled where she sat.

"She's right," Riona mumbled. "This is not the place or the time…"

Sellia put a hand on the healer's arm. "Before Seanchai, there was another. I was betrothed to an elf called Dyrovas. There were things I would have told him if I'd known he was to die so soon. I have grown to accept his death, but all the same, I would have liked to share some things that were never said. We were both fiery young elves. We argued, fought, made up, and made love, channeling the adrenaline of life as rebels into our relationship. But we thought we would live forever.

"There are things I have never told my children, either." She shook her head and retreated into her own thoughts.

Riona took her in her arms and drew her close. "We will help you find the opportunity to tell them," she whispered.

"And what about you?" Sellia's voice was muffled in Riona's chest.

"It's more complicated than that," the healer replied. "Now isn't the time."

Denalion's body tossed and turned. His snores echoed off the cave walls, but he was not aware of them. He soared into the sky, an eagle beating his powerful wings. He flew north, high above the clouds, where mountain peaks peeped through intermittently. The sun beat down on him, but he would not rest.

This might be my last chance, he thought. *I must get through.*

He glided down through the gray clouds, surveying the land that spread out under him. He was hungry, and his sharp eyes identified mice, voles, and young rabbits. His stomach growled, but he pushed on – he was seeking a bigger animal.

The mountain peaks became snow-capped, and, as he pushed on, the mountains grew larger until all beneath him was a great, white world.

He spied large cavalcades of men traveling north, an army with the accompanying long lines of wagons and livestock trailing behind. The eagle tried to descend and see who was leading this great force, but an invisible force stopped him.

He circled up, realizing that he was expending huge amounts of energy. Was this how his way to Seanchai, Shayth, and the others was blocked? He had thought it to be his own weakening powers and blamed himself for failing to serve as dreamwalker. This had never happened before, and the taste of failure had been so bitter.

As he rose in the sky, he let out a screech of joy and continued north. He saw ice bears lumbering across the ice flats and reached out with his mind. But they would not respond, could not hear the voice of an eagle.

No bear could, except one.

The eagle turned for the great mountain range in the west. The great grizzly was old and had withdrawn. As Seanchai had taken on a grizzly form, this one had stepped aside. His wound, dealt by the firebreather at the Battle of the Cliftean Pass, had never healed, and never would.

The old grizzly had returned to the mountains and his role as a solitary king, to see out his days with nobility in self-imposed exile. But perhaps he had the ability to talk with dreamwalkers in all forms. Denalion hoped so.

The great grizzly lay by a pool, huge mountains towering over him and a waterfall spraying him softly. He had eaten and now lay in the sun, allowing his food to digest and the pain from his wound to subside.

These days, he did little aside from sleeping and fishing, but he dared not dream by day or night. His days were numbered, his reign over. He had passed on his responsibilities to the young, impetuous grizzly – the one that could bind a nation of bears to him, but not catch a fish if it jumped into his claws.

The bear laughed but stopped quickly, as his wound hurt from such movement. He yawned and closed his eyes. The smooth rock was warm and helped the pain subside. He would not allow himself to dream. He must not.

"*You must.*" A voice said in his head. "*He needs you. We all do.*"

"*He must find his own way now. He is a master.*"

"*His way is blocked, and he has no idea. You had a family once, did you not?*"

"*I had a mate and cubs, but it is not our way to stay together. I had a job to do. I had responsibilities, as does he.*"

"Yes, but it is different for him. He cannot fulfill his destiny without the support of his family. If they die, he will lose his mind, and we will lose everything that you and I have dedicated our lives to."

The bear opened its eyes. The eagle that perched on a rock nearby was rusty brown with a yellow beak. It opened its scruffy feathers to reveal bright red plumage.

"You know me," the eagle said.

"We have walked together many times, Denalion, Dreamwalker of the West, but we are both very old now."

"Yet I have come, and in this form, a dangerous drain on my energy. I have flown from beyond the southern borders of Odessiya. The Wycaan's children are prisoners of the firebreather. He will use them to destroy the Wycaan."

"What will you have of me?"

"Go to him. His dreams are blocked by our old enemy, and I cannot reach him."

"You ask much of an old bear. If I go, I will not return. He has been absent from our world, turned his back on the bears of the world."

"He has never stopped working for the peoples of Odessiya, but yes, he neglected his duty to the bears. And you are right that I ask you to risk your life for this. My heart is heavy, old friend, but I ask it nonetheless. Go to him one more time. Alert the Wycaan to his family's danger and council him as you once did. He will need to hear a calm voice. If you cannot reach him, reach the ice bears. You must find a way.

"One last time, my friend. Please. One last time, for Odessiya."

The bear rose steadily and sat on its back haunches. It sniffed the air and slowly gazed around. *"This is a beautiful place, is it not?"*

"It is," the eagle replied.

"It is a place worthy to die in, to offer the final sight before the eyes close forever." The great grizzly sighed. *"Have I ever refused you, my friend? Have I ever refused Odessiya?"*

"*No, old one, you have not. Nor will you now.*"

"*No, nor will I now. Farewell then, Denalion Dreamwalker. When next we meet, it shall be in the dream world — the one from which one never wakes.*"

Chapter Thirty Four

Mharina woke slowly, aware that she was ensconced in a warm bed, her head resting on soft pillows. She was hesitant to open her eyes, afraid that last night had been a dream. Upon arrival, they had been escorted through stone corridors, all the time walking downwards, until they reached a large cavern lit with burning torches. Mharina could not see a ceiling. In front of her were small pools with a beautiful waterfall providing a rhythmic and comfortable sound that echoed off the cavern walls.

"Our guards have remained outside, *calhei*," Sa'gola had said. "They will not disturb us. Come, discard your dirty garb and enter the bath. We will wash the journey's grime from our bodies."

Ilan and Senzia were delighted at the prospect and dropped their clothes where they were. Mharina watched Sa'gola gracefully unpin her robe, fold it, and lay it in a basket. Her body was small and beautiful – her pale, smooth skin glowing in the light of the torches. Her curves were not as pronounced as Mharina's mother's, but her small breasts stood up, and her hips were curved and narrow.

The woman's body was also taut and her muscles clearly defined. When she bent to toss the twins' clothes into the basket, Mharina saw her calf muscles bulge. She had no doubt that

Sa'gola could move quickly, but when the woman straightened, she saw a crisscross of scars on her back – long-healed dark brown stripes clear on the woman's pale-white skin.

Sa'gola turned, and their eyes met.

"Are you embarrassed to undress in front of me, little one? That's okay. I will go in the pool and not look, I promise."

"No," Mharina blurted out. "It's your scars. Someone hurt you, and you are so beautiful."

Sa'gola's smile turned to a grimace and back again. "Yes," she said. "I have learned hard lessons during my life, little elfe, but I learned to become strong so that I can protect myself. That is why I let them fear me, so what you see on my back will never happen again.

"But please – no more of this. It will sadden me. Come into the pools and help me bathe the little ones. I don't really know how to do it."

Mharina watched Sa'gola stride elegantly to the pool, her eyes going involuntarily to the scars. She quickly undressed, threw her clothes in the basket, and followed.

There were several pools, all filled with warm water. They moved to the furthest, where they found brushes and soaps. Here they soaped the twins, ignoring Ilan's objections when they washed his hair. All three *calhei* needed to wash their hair several times and comb out knots.

Mharina put considerable effort into her sister's beautiful white hair and didn't stop until she could comb through without obstacle. As she did, she watched how Sa'gola encouraged and played with Ilan, tricking him into following her wishes and letting her clean him.

She hoped Sa'gola would ask for help to wash her own black and purple hair. The young elfe felt a strong desire to be asked, that it would be an honor. *Honor?* It was a strange thought, but even stranger was the pang of jealousy she felt when Sa'gola asked her sister for help instead.

Sa'gola appeared not to notice, because she invited Mharina to stand in front of her, and she gently went about cleaning the elfe's hair. Mharina closed her eyes and enjoyed the sorceress's skillful fingers. She would have been happy to stay like that, but was jarred out of her reverie by Sa'gola's compliments to Senzia.

After they had cleansed themselves, they moved to another pool and played under the waterfall. Soft furs waited for them when they exited, and this was the only thing that enticed Ilan to leave the pools that he so enjoyed.

"Can we come back tomorrow?" he asked.

"Of course," Sa'gola said as she rubbed him dry. "But there is much to discover and explore in this castle. We will have fun."

They had been left long, white garments to slip into and were escorted to a spacious room with a huge circular bed, easily big enough for half a dozen *calhei*. Sa'gola had made sure that each was comfortable before leaving, and Mharina drifted quickly into a dreamless sleep.

Now, Mharina slowly opened her eyes. The room was tall with a creviced stone ceiling, and the sun sent beams through a large doorway. Mharina rose and shivered when her feet touched the cold, stone floor, made up of smooth dark stones. She walked across to a table where there was fruit and water.

She drank water and peeled a banana, one of the few fruits she recognized. It tasted slightly bitter, she thought as she walked to the doorway. It was cold, and she retreated back into the room. There were three piles of clothes there, neatly folded. She chose the one that looked biggest and found undergarments; thick, coarse pants with a rope belt; and a loose-sleeved shirt of material similar to the pants. Her clothes were all a light brown, and she noted the other two were aqua-green and brown, respectively.

Feeling warmer, she again approached the doorway and stepped outside. She was standing on a small balcony that overlooked the fruit trees they had seen when they entered.

"We must find a way to escape," Senzia said from behind her.

Mharina jumped. "You scared me. I didn't hear you."

"Good." Senzia was chewing on a pear, and juice trickled down the side of her mouth.

"Anyway," Mharina snapped, strangely distracted, "where would we run to? They would catch us."

"We don't need to run," Senzia pushed past her and stared out. "When the fighting begins, we just need to be out of the way. Once we see who wins, we will decide what to do."

Mharina stared at her. Her little sister seemed so detached from their situation, yet so practical.

"We must find a way to contact *ahdahr*. Maybe through Denalion?"

"I know a way," Mharina said, "but I'm frightened to try."

Senzia turned and studied her sister. "You don't have to be scared. I will be the one to do it. Tell me what it is."

Mharina's mouth was wide open. "But you are younger than me and–"

"What does age have to do with it? I know you've been hiding something from us. But I never found the chance to ask. What is it?"

Mharina felt her sister's eyes boring into her.

"You have met him in your dreams. You walked with *ahdahr*?"

"No," Mharina glanced around. Only Ilan's gentle snores could be heard. "Denalion."

"Why you?" Senzia asked without judgment in her tone. She smiled and answered her own question before Mharina could. "He knew you would obey whatever instruction he gave you. Fair enough. Come inside. We should not talk when we cannot see who might be above and below us."

Mharina followed her white-haired sister, who she had known all her life, but whom she hardly recognized right now.

Chapter Thirty Five

Mharina went to sit on the bed, but Senzia called her over to the table where the water and fruit lay. She had pulled two chairs over to the far side.

"We must speak quietly," Senzia said in a soft tone. "I don't want to speak of this once Ilan wakes."

"I agree," Mharina said glancing toward the bed. "He seems much younger than we are."

"He's male. Yet he may well be the one to follow in *ahdahr* 's footsteps."

"You think so? Why not you?"

"If one of us is a Wycaan then the other will be too. But only Ilan has *ahdahr's* temperament."

"What do you mean?" Mharina was intrigued. They had never had a conversation like this.

"We came into life together, shared the first … the first … everything. We are bonded in a way that can only be experienced by twins. What awakens in me awakens in him, too. He just doesn't want it to break through."

"Why not? What is *it*?"

Senzia shrugged. "I cannot define it, but do you remember how Pyre has told us of her own childhood? She was a Wycaan-in-training for a few years by the time she had reached our age. But they weren't just teaching her skills; they were honing and explaining what was waking inside of her.

"I felt it even before we were kidnapped, but since we began to face real danger, I feel a ...." she stared into space, searching for the right word. "I feel an acceleration, and I'm sure Ilan does, too. Why does he fight it? He knows he'll lose his childhood once he allows it to take root."

"Is that what has happened to you?"

Again Senzia shrugged. "I have been aware of it now for some time. That is why I craved *ahdahr's* attention and trailed after Pyre so much."

They both laughed. It had been a source of contention, and Pyre had been angry at first by the attention she had drawn. But in the past year, she had taken to sitting with all three of them, and Senzia in particular. With Sellia's permission, she had begun to train them with bow and gentle wrestling.

"You are more like *ahdahr* and Pyre," Mharina said.

"And you are mother's special one," Senzia replied rather too quickly.

"Only because I'm the oldest," Mharina protested, and they both laughed, for this had been argued many times.

"I miss them both," Senzia said, her voice suddenly resembling a lost *calhei*.

"As do I."

Ilan tossed in the bed and muttered something that might have been their mother's name, and they stared at each other.

"Was that a response to your feelings?" Mharina asked.

"I don't know," Senzia replied. "I don't fully understand it. Tell me what Denalion has told you."

Mharina leaned forward, and her voice went low. "There are these stones of all different sizes called Anwars. They connect to each other, and you can talk to someone on the other end if they have one, too."

"Really?" Senzia leaned in, as well.

"The Emperor has one, and we think that Sa'gola does, too."

"And?"

"And so does *ahdahr*."

Senzia leaned back. "The Emperor has one and so does Sa'gola. I saw her talking to him."

The two elfes stared at each other, both playing out different scenarios. Then Senzia walked over to the bed, picked up a pillow, and threw it on Ilan's head.

He sat up immediately and cried out.

"Get up, sleepy head," she said. "We want to take a walk."

Ilan dressed in the brown garments since Senzia claimed the green. The color picked out her white hair and blue eyes.

He grabbed a banana and ripped off the skin. "I'm starving," he said.

As if on cue, Sa'gola entered the room. "Did you sleep well, little ones?"

Sa'gola was dressed in black pants and a faded purple shirt with dark purple lines running across it. Her hair was shiny and vibrant, her facial paints fresh. She looked both beautiful and intimidating.

"Can we go somewhere to eat?" Ilan asked devouring a banana.

"Finish what's in your mouth before you speak," Mharina hissed, not sure why she was feeling angry.

Sa'gola pretended not to notice and mussed his hair. She bent and smelled Senzia's and sighed.

"Much better. It has been a rough trip for you, I know. Come, we shall eat."

She led them out of their room and into a stony corridor. They turned left and then right, passing plenty of rooms as they went.

"Are we near your room?" Senzia asked, her hand clasped in Sa'gola's.

"No, little one. These are guest's quarters. Mine are in another part of the castle. But you will have an attendant assigned to you, and if you have need of me, you will just have to ask her. Ah, here we are."

They entered a huge hall with long tables, half-filled with noisy taragusii. The young elves followed Sa'gola past them to a smaller hall with tables for about fifty. Around one sat an assortment of humans, elves, and dwarves. They all had white hair. Senzia gasped.

"You will meet a number of Wycaans here, Senzia. You need not fear them. Some will be your teachers."

"Teachers, for me?"

"Not only you. The Master wants you all to have the opportunity to explore who you are."

"You mean to discover whether or not we are Wycaans?" Ilan said and there was a defiant ring to his words.

Sa'gola stopped and turned to him. Mharina was relieved that she was smiling.

"Maybe you are Wycaans, and maybe you aren't. Maybe only one or two of you are. But if you are not, there is still much you can learn. I am not a Wycaan, but do not doubt my power." She looked at Mharina. "I could teach you a lot," she repeated.

"I might be Wycaan, too," Mharina insisted, and then blushed at her own vehemence.

"Could you defeat our *ahdahr*?" Ilan asked, unabashed.

Sa'gola blinked, and her tone was sad when she responded. "I do not know, and I hope we never have to find out. I would not like to fight the father – you call him *ahdahr*? – the *ahdahr* of those I have grown to care about. Come, now. I thought you were hungry. Take a plate each. Do not overfill it, Ilan – you can come back for more."

Chapter Thirty Six

Seanchai found a dark corner of a store tent and grounded his energy. Through a tear in the canvas, he watched as the camp began to settle down for the night. There were plenty of guards, both on the perimeter and around individual camps. Clearly, no one group trusted the others. This could be exploited, he thought.

After it had been quiet for a while, he drew up the energy again and concealed himself in darkness. Then he walked toward the animal enclosure, where he saw two blue-painted guards at one end, and two pictorians at the other. Their animals were corralled separately, but it was clear that the guards were hostile to each other.

Seanchai walked past the guards and approached the ice bears, which had all moved to the end of the cage, as far from the guards as possible. They all turned in his direction, sniffing the air, but only one followed his progress.

Thank you for coming, it said inside his head.

"*How many of you are there?*" Seanchai asked.

Forty-eight. No — forty-seven now.

"*I saw. I'm sorry.*"

The one-horned were trained from a young age to be subservient, but we were all captured within the past year, as part of some big plan that you see unfolding. We will not be slaves.

"*Do you have a plan?*"

Yes. We need you to take care of the guards – all four of them. Then release the one-horned. They will panic near fire, which should be most entertaining. Then come for us.

"*In return for my help, can your bears destroy as much of their supplies as possible before escaping? Are they kept in a central place?*"

The bear turned and conferred through a series of grunts. *Yes. It can be done.*

"*I must also return to my friends over the mountain and warn them. Can you take me there?*"

Yes. Go now and stampede the one-horned beasts.

Seanchai watched the guards for a moment, thinking. He could not kill one pair without the others seeing. Then he had a better idea. He moved across to the entrance to the bear enclosures and wrapped steaming dung in a snowball. He edged closer to the pictorians and threw it. The packed snowball hit one in the face. The boar stood stunned, and then, sniffing the contents of the splattered snowball, roared, and both charged the tall humanoids.

The soldiers clashed, but the fight lasted only seconds before all four lay sprawled on the ground, dead from either their enemies or a pair of Win Dao swords. A deep mix of red humanoid and purple pictorian blood combined on the snow. Seanchai quickly wiped his swords on one of the bodies and ran to the one-horns' enclosure, grabbed three burning torches as he passed, and threw two into separate piles of hay.

Then he leapt into the enclosure and flashed the third torch at the beasts. The one-horned animals bellowed with fear and charged hysterically in the other direction, crushing the wooden fence enclosing them underfoot and stampeding into tents of sleeping men.

Amid the cries of trampled soldiers, Seanchai ran to the ice bears' enclosure and hacked through the cords that bound the gates with one of his swords.

"Over there!" a voice cried, and Seanchai realized with horror that he had stopped repeating the word that had kept the darkness bound around him.

Already, though, the organized formation of ice bears was heading into the heart of the camp.

Jump on, the ice bear said as it lumbered past. Seanchai sheathed his swords and grabbed the bear behind the neck, swinging himself up with help from the bear's momentum.

The bear did not follow his pack, but veered off and out to the perimeter.

"What about them?" Seanchai called.

They'll do their job. You have fulfilled your promise, so now I must fulfill mine. Hold on. We need to circle around the camp quickly.

The bear lumbered steadily into the darkness. Seanchai squeezed his legs against the animal's body and held on to its furry neck scruff, matching its momentum with his own change in body weight as it rocked forwards and backwards.

He was not sure how long they had gone, but when the bear stopped to rest, Seanchai looked back and saw only a faint glow of fire in the dark.

We will walk for a while, but we cannot linger. He will search for you.

"What is your name?" Seanchai asked.

The bear growled something incomprehensible at Seanchai. It had barely finished when a loud roar came from behind them, and a billow of fire lit up the sky.

Something comes.

"Yeah, I can hear."

No. Something else approaches from the north.

Seanchai turned to find the dark shape of a huge grizzly lumbering toward them, panting billows of hot breath in the frigid night air.

Do not linger, a deep voice boomed inside Seanchai's head. *He comes. We must reach the tunnel before he does, or stand and fight.*

The grizzly continued its gallop, and the ice bear matched its pace. But Seanchai did not have to look back to know the firebreather was gaining on them. He could hear the ominous flapping of its great wings, and the sky around them lightened brighter as it approached.

Before them, a dark wall loomed up. The ice bear accelerated and passed the grizzly.

Go on, the elder urged. *I will catch you.*

As the firebreather screamed another billow of fire, the ice bear dug deeply into its reserves as its mighty paws pounded on the ice.

They reached a tunnel into the mountain and looked back. The grizzly was still a considerable distance away, and the aerial shadow closed in on it.

"We must go back," Seanchai cried, and kicked the ice bear with his heels.

No, the grizzly, panting from exertion, commanded them in their heads. *Go warn the pictorians. Odessiya must prepare for what is coming.*

"But what about you?" Seanchai yelled, already knowing.

Wycaan, my time passes. Be the bear you are inside. But watch to your back. There is treachery close by and afar. Danger creeps up upon you not only in the north. You must-

A bright pillar of flame blinded them and, even despite their distance, it made the ice bear retreat.

Go through the tunnel. He cannot follow. Go now.

A roar, giant and majestic, shook the mountains. A second wave of flames was extinguished momentarily, and the firebreather screamed as they clashed.

Gooooo. The Great Grizzly cried.

The ice bear turned and cantered into the mountain, its head lowered. Seanchai struggled, pulling its furry neck, kicking with his heels. They could both feel the struggle as firebreather and grizzly clashed. They felt the heat on their skins, the claws raking. They screamed as claws raked, both received and meted out. They roared in rage. They roared in pain. And then, finally, they roared in sorrow. Though they roared together, there were but two voices and it felt so terribly lonely.

CHAPTER THIRTY SEVEN

The ice bear slowed to an even pace, and they continued for an indeterminate amount of time. Yet another great teacher had given his life to save Seanchai. As the ice bear continued into the dark, the Wycaan reflected on Mhari, Master Onyxei, the Weapons Master of the Elves of the West, and her lead student, Cheriuk.

And then there were the many who had fallen in sacrifice, a deadly consequence of befriending a young Wycaan who had failed to vanquish the enemy when he had the chance. There were too many to name, but Ilana stayed forever first in his memory, forever in his heart. He had failed even in his oath to his dying soul mate.

Deep in sorrow, Seanchai barely registered that the ice bear had stopped.

Get down, it said in his head. *I must rest for a few minutes.*

Seanchai slid from its muscled, furry back and stood for a moment on wobbly legs. He walked away and stared. They were in a huge cavern with mighty ice stalactites descending out of darkness to kiss the tips of the ice forest growing up from the floor. The whole area seemed lit from a source in the ground, and, as he stumbled further in, he saw a small lake with a bright green light emanating from it. Was this a ley lake like the one he had used for his transformation?

He glanced back. The ice bear lay with its huge head across its front paws, eyes closed. Seanchai hesitated wondering if this break was wise, but the grizzly had said that the Emperor could not follow.

Instinct told him that the great grizzly had struck a blow – that one of those slashing, scraping claws had wounded the firebreather. The elf walked on into the ice forest, marveling at the bark-like drip rivulets on the sides of ice pillars. Pinging drops of water dripped steadily as he neared the pool.

It sounded and felt like tears falling from a mourning mountain. All nature was connected, and the elements that served the Wycaan magic mourned one of its greatest passing away.

Seanchai thought of the grizzly's last words. He, too, was a grizzly in his animal form, but he was so much less proficient as he struggled to transform. He had barely practiced, uneasy with his constant and frustrating failure. Now, as he gazed at this magical forest, feeling the natural world weeping, he reached his decision. He would honor the great grizzly by learning to change form and leading those who followed him as a Wycaan *and* those who followed him as a bear.

His transformations would be made with love and reverence, in tribute to the great grizzly who had preceded him and sacrificed its life for him, and no longer with struggle or trepidation.

With this vow filling his mind, Seanchai dropped slowly on four big paws and stared into the water at a young grizzly with bright blue eyes and an expression of grim determination.

A white muzzle appeared besides his, looking down at the grizzly's reflection. Seanchai turned to the ice bear.

I ride you no more. Now we run side by side. I am ready.

The ice bear nodded its approval, then raised its head and howled his pain and defiance. The young grizzly followed suit, and their roars echoed up into the darkness of the mountain. Seanchai focused, desperate to send a defiant message into the void: *No longer the last of a majestic line, Great One.*

They continued through the ice forest, and the roof closed above them until they were again walking through a tunnel. The path was smooth and surprisingly cylindrical.

Seanchai did not feel the cold, though he saw the thick condensation of his breath. His front paws, unaccustomed to walking, became sore, and he felt the protestations of many muscles that had not been used in this way.

When they next rested, it was again near a small pool, and Seanchai dangled his sore front paws in the freezing water. The numbing effect dulled the pain, and he groaned in relief.

The ice bear smiled. *You will get used to it,* he said in Seanchai's head.

"Tell me of the great grizzly?"

He was the first bear. He ran with the eagle, the firebreather, and the wolf. He spoke with the gods and saw the world fracture between the two-legged and the animal kingdom. He witnessed the two-legged multiply and split among themselves. He saw the animals retreat and go their separate ways.

His was a lonely life, high in the mountains, where he watched and intervened as leader when needed. But he judged with wisdom and love. For that, he was held in the highest regard. All animals knew of him: the wolf, firebreather, and eagle.

I know the dreamwalkers reached out to him, and some he called friends, for they, too, were honored and revered outcasts of their tribes.

Seanchai nodded as he thought of Denalion. The redheaded dreamwalker had left the Forest of Markwin and stayed with him after they defeated the Emperor and established Wycaan Island. He was a constant source of guidance for Seanchai, an adopted grandparent for Seanchai's children, and an integral part of the Wycaan Island community. Yet, always, he had walked alone.

He would like to talk with Denalion now, share his sorrow at the passing of the great grizzly. Denalion would understand and appreciate the life and death of the leader of bears. Perhaps he had known him.

Denalion could also tell him how his children were, and Sellia, too. Seanchai pondered the grizzly's warning of treachery, of danger near and far. It would not hurt to warn those on Wycaan Island and ask Denalion to keep an extra eye on his family.

He missed them. But at least they were a long way from the reach of the Emperor. At least they were safe.

Chapter Thirty Eight

"It's a beautiful night," Riona said as she approached the fortune-sword.

Montclair gazed up at the almost-full moon. He had been standing here for quite a while, judging by its ascent into the sky, but he had not noticed.

He had been instead staring into the valley, which had been swallowed up by darkness, and now only a few scattered fires offered any evidence that there was life down there.

"I said, it's a beautiful night," Riona repeated.

He turned his head toward her. "Yes it is," he said. "Too beautiful."

"What do you mean?" Her voice was softer than he had ever heard.

Montclair turned and sighed. "This is suicide," he said. "I might not be much of a man, but I don't feel ready to die."

"You've faced death many times – every battle you fought in the army, every time you faced a taragus or a dishonest gambler."

"Yes, but I liked those odds. If my swordplay couldn't get me through, then my wits would save me. But this…"

He moved to the side of the cave and leaned back against the warm rock. There was a chilly breeze, and the sun-kissed mountain was comforting. He could feel the healer's eyes on him.

"Did she upset you in there?"

"She upset *you*," Montclair retorted and snorted at his own impulsiveness. "I wish you weren't here. It would make the inevitable more...palatable."

Riona moved in front of him and leaned back slowly against him. She took his hand and guided it around her waist. She rested her head against his chest, and he could smell the musty scent of her hair. He closed his eyes and took it in, feeling this might be his only chance.

"You never gave me away," Riona said. "Thank you again. But how do you know who I am?"

"I served under your father. I was one of his personal bodyguards for two year."

"You failed him."

"I was not there," he hissed, and then sighed. "Even if I had been, you cannot guard against a random arrow from the mountainside."

"Random?" she snapped and pulled away.

"Sorry. When you were sent away, I was part of your security detail."

"I don't remember you."

"There were twelve soldiers, and I was the youngest, furthest on your perimeter, so I was never close to you."

"He shouldn't have sent me away. Neither of them should."

"But it saved your life. Both your parents are dead, and your brother should have died countless times."

"When did you leave the army?"

"Can you guess?"

"Shortly after the assassination?"

Montclair nodded.

"You said you know the prince. How?"

"The *prince*, you call him?" He felt her body stiffen, and did not want to lose the intimate moment. "I tracked him for years, watching him destroy everyone and everything around him. While he won many fights on his own, there was often a mysterious arrow shot from the darkness that felled the man creeping up behind him, that kind of thing."

"Then what happened?"

"He discovered me and consented to me riding with him for a while, as long as I never got in his way. Finally, I couldn't stand it. He was confronting three kids – simple peasants, they were. I don't remember what the fight was about, and I don't even think he was in the wrong, but he was clearly going to win. He goaded them, waiting for one to make the first move.

"I intervened, and he took his sword to me. The peasants ran as we fought. There aren't many who can match his swordsmanship in Odessiya, but I am one who can. We fought for what seemed an age, both of us venting our frustrations about the Emperor, his father and each other."

Montclair went silent as Denalion shuffled outside. "I'm sorry," the old elf muttered and disappeared into the nearby brush. "Carry on," he said as he returned inside. "Sorry. You won't be disturbed."

Riona had moved away from Montclair and was facing him now.

"Please continue," she said, tucking some hair behind her round ear.

"Finally, when he saw we were evenly matched, he stopped. We faced each other, sweat dripping from our faces, panting. Then he broke into a maniacal laugh. I asked if he would now send me away because I had broken our agreement. He told me that I could stay with him, but that he was going to seek out those boys if I did and kill them in front of their parents and me.

"I just stood, staring into his dark, evil eyes, and knew I possessed nothing that could help him. All I could feel was that this was my greatest failure to his father; the man I had seen as a living hero. Here was his son – a crazy, bloodthirsty animal.

"It was only my love for Prince Shindell that stopped me from killing Shayth then. I turned and walked away, and, for months, lost myself in liquor. It was a blur of drunken brawls, until one day after I cut a man down, his two sons jumped me. They were the same age as the peasants that I had prevented Shayth from killing. The battle rage took me, and, when I woke up, they were dead, as well.

"I got on my horse and rode until one or both of us collapsed with exhaustion."

He went quiet and reached for his water skin. Then he handed it to Riona, who took a gulp and choked.

"This is not water," she rasped and glared at him before taking another, more cautious, swig.

"How did you recognize me? I was just a girl when you took me to the monastery. How did you know I was a healer?"

Montclair took another swig, smiling when Riona held out her hand for the skin again.

"I thought I could make amends to your father by looking out for you, if not Shayth. So I traveled back to the monastery and took a job there for a while as a guard."

"I don't remember you."

"Once they saw how good I was, they sent me to guard the monks who went to buy supplies and ensure that the wagons got back to the monastery. They knew I drank and tried to stop me."

"Smart with a weapon, dumb with a bottle," Riona said.

"Thank you. That's the nicest thing you've said about me." Riona laughed a deep, throaty laugh and Montclair felt a thrill course through him.

"So they sent me to the cave where their most devout went to meditate. I went three months without the fire wine, and if there was a hell, I found it. But I got my life back, and I guess I am thankful for that.

"When I returned to the monastery, I discovered that you had gone. I tracked you, and, when I found you, well, I figured it was not good for you to meet me."

"Why not?"

"What would I tell you? That I should have saved your father? That I walked away from Shayth? So I watched you at Castlestone, in Galbrieth, at the Rockwall villages. Do you remember when you were captured by bandits in the swamps after Rockwall?"

Riona shivered. She had been badly beaten and lost consciousness. When she had woken, all nine men were dead. She had thought they had killed each other.

"You? You killed them?"

Montclair nodded and handed her the skin. She drank deeply this time.

"Thank you," she said. "Was it you who took me back to Rockwall? It was all a blur."

"It was," he said. "After you recovered, I followed you until you reached Wycaan Island. I met your master when he was returning and requested employment. He refused me, and I finally told him that I wanted to be near you. I never told him who you were or why I wanted to join you.

"He sent me away, but promised to take care of you. There was something about him that made me realize you were better off under his protection, and I decided I had paid my dues to your father and could leave the Shindell family forever.

"Guess I was wrong about that, too, huh?"

Chapter Thirty Nine

When Denalion woke, Pyre and Sellia were huddled in a corner of the cave, whispering. It was clear they were talking about him from the furtive glances he received and their clumsy attempts to speak even quieter than they had been. The cave was cold and damp, but it boasted excellent acoustics, and Denalion heard a cacophony of hisses and whispers.

He rose unsteadily and shuffled out of the cave to relieve himself. He was shocked to see Riona leaning against Montclair, her back to the fortune-sword. Their pose was striking in the moonlight and clearly intimate.

They, too, went abruptly silent, and Denalion almost laughed to himself. *I hope they have better things to talk about than an old elf,* he thought, and muttered an apology for disturbing them. Then he coughed to warn of his return after finishing his business.

The looks on their faces told him everything. "Sorry," he said again. "You won't be disturbed."

It was ironic that here, on the cusp of death, Riona had found love. He saw it as soon as they encountered Montclair. The spark had been clear, and he wished she had spent her time enjoying rather than fighting it.

The old dreamwalker moved back into the cave and was received with a stony silence. "You should not gossip about me," he chided. "It has been more than a century since I have given anyone cause." He sat himself down and folded his legs with considerable effort. "But I don't think my past loves are the subject you are dwelling on."

They did not answer. "Now, what is on your minds?"

Pyre and Sellia exchanged glances, and Pyre cleared her throat.

"Dreamwalker, we are concerned about you entering Grogin. You have served our people for centuries, and it would be unimaginable if you were lost to the elf nation."

She looked at Sellia for support.

"We mean you no offense, Denalion," Sellia said. "But the time might come when we need speed and stamina."

"You think I might endanger your venture?" Denalion could not help but frown.

Sellia winced, displaying fine dimples, and nodded. "But also, you need to keep reaching out to Seanchai," she added quickly.

"I spoke with one who has gone to him – a powerful grizzly. He will not fail us."

"But what if he does?" Sellia persisted. "How would we find out, if we are incarcerated? The Emperor will have built wards to protect the castle, and you believe the sorceress knows of your connection to Mharina."

Denalion sighed deeply. "Pass me my water skin, Pyre."

She brought it over to him and, crouching, put an arm around his bony shoulders. Her voice was soft and reverent. "I have known you all my life, Dreamwalker, and I grew up thirsting for the legends they told of you before I was born. If you come, I will be looking out for you, and it will limit my ability to protect Sellia and the children. Do you understand?"

After he finished drinking, he firmly took Pyre's arm from around him. He could see it was the worst blow this young warrior had ever received. He took a deep breath, and, when he spoke, his voice was hard and strong.

"I am Denalion, Dreamwalker of the Elves of the West. For more than three hundred years have I served my people. But never have I felt so alive, so filled with purpose, than when I met the Wycaan. And I will die serving him and his children, who are a living part of him. You know this to be true.

"Neither am I harmless. You saw what I did to that man in the forest before we reached Braithwaite. There is more in this ancient arsenal."

"But it will not be enough against the Emperor," Sellia implored, "and maybe not even against the sorceress. If we fail, you must reach Seanchai somehow. If we fail, you must succeed for the Wycaan you serve, and his children."

Denalion stared into her beautiful hazel eyes. They were brimming with tears.

"And for me, Denalion," Sellia whispered. "If that means anything after all these years."

He knew something was wrong as soon as he stepped into the spirit world. The colors were bright, the smells rich, but the trails of energy were … sad. The dreamwalker took his eagle form and soared, beating his wings as hard as he could. His chest burned with pain.

He was unsure how long he flew, but just as he began to fear for his strength, he saw them by a small lake with a waterfall. It was close to the mountain range where the great grizzly had once lived. He knew this place also from Seanchai's dreams. Here had been his first encounter with the bears.

He landed on a tree branch almost overhanging the water. Below, four brown bears and two cubs lumbered into the clearing. They sat still, their mighty heads bowed, and then, as one, they turned to the snow-capped peaks, raised their heads, and howled. Shivers coursed through the eagle, for he had never heard such wretched sounds from the mouths of noble bears.

And then, echoing off the mountain came answering howls. Denalion closed his eyes and traveled: a dream within a dream. Dozens of ice bears had gathered on huge ice flows and faced the same mountain, crying out their loss.

He returned to his eagle body, only to hear a fainter cry from the forests, He did not travel this time, knowing that the black bears were sharing in mourning the great loss. Denalion turned his beaked head to the mountain and tried to join the chorus, but his hoots were insignificant compared to the cries of the bear sleuths.

'I'm sorry,' he whispered to the wind. 'Did we not both know this would be the price? Yet, I am so sorry for the great loss I have inflicted on the world. None will ever walk in your path.'

Denalion woke to the touch of many hands. He found his head cradled in Riona's chest, his cheeks wet, and momentarily remembered a mother centuries dead. He moved himself from her grasp and sat up, his breathing unrestrained.

He took the water skin somebody offered and drank. When his breathing and emotions were under control he looked into Sellia's concerned face.

"I have failed again. A great spirit fell this night. The one I sent to Seanchai is dead."

"Did he pass on his message?" Sellia asked.

Denalion thought for a moment and shrugged. "I do not know. We must assume that he did not."

And Denalion, Dreamwalker of the Elves of the West, turned his back in shame, covered his head with his hood, and wept. He was the last of his age, the last of a generation. The world was changing, and even an old elven dreamwalker had his limits.

CHAPTER FORTY

I lan was being pushed back. The blows from the swordsman were not fast, but they were strong. Each blow reverberated through the young elf's arm, but he kept his guard up and parried as best he could. When he felt the cool stone of the wall on his back, he attempted a double roll to avoid being trapped.

His roll was clumsy, and he lost his sword and his bearings. When he came to his feet, he was giddy and wobbled. Several taragusii across the courtyard laughed.

"Silence!" bellowed Ilan's opponent, and there was instant quiet. "The idea was sound, young elf. You will just have to practice more."

He offered a hand to steady Ilan who was still dizzy, but when he heard a snigger, he whirled on the onlookers. "Perhaps one of you would like to take his place. Don't expect me to go slow on you, though. Who will it be? Who finds this so amusing that they are willing to show the boy how easy it is to spar with a Wycaan warrior?"

There were no volunteers, and this only served to anger the man. He sheathed his sword and walked slowly over to the three taragusii watching. "What, no takers? Are the mighty taragusii so scared that they would not trade places with a *calhei*?

The man drank deeply from a jeweled jug, stones sparkling as he raised it. Water dripped down the man's white beard, and he wiped it away with a sleeve. Then he turned to face the taragusii. "All right. If there are no volunteers, then I will fight all three of you. Tie up your breeches and draw your swords. Put your training sheathes on, or you might find yourselves facing the Master, who is not as patient as me."

The man tucked his long, white hair behind an ornate red band and then knelt to retie a strap around one of his boots. Ilan moved closer.

"Are you sure about this, Master Sythen?" Ilan asked quietly. He liked the portly man because he was a Wycaan and happy to train with and teach an eager *calhei*.

"Yes. It is important that they remember their place. You may be young, but you are a Wycaan. I am sure of it. They must show you respect and never forget it. And it will give me a chance to show you what I can do."

Ilan backed away and sat on the table. The three taragusii had large, curved swords, thick in the middle and tapered to the end. They fanned out, and the young elf could see that they were apprehensive by the way their tongues constantly flicked out to wet their noses.

Master Sythen drew his sword and staff. Ilan now suspected that the latter served purposes other than supporting the man when he walked.

Sythen walked into the middle of the taragusii triangle and whirled his staff, which whooshed as it moved from side to side. The man made to leap at one taragus, but feinted and attacked a second. His sword met blade, but his staff struck and they parried, which sent the taragus furiously backpedaling.

The third taragus lunged at the man's back and was met with the base of Sythen's staff in his stomach, one of the few unscaled areas. Ilan gasped as he realized the Wycaan had not turned to face the attacking taragus. It collapsed, but his advance encouraged another to lunge, only to receive a foot in his throat, exactly between his scaled chest and helmet.

Only one taragus was left. He was good, Ilan saw, and maintained his form, matching the Wycaan's moves. But the Wycaan sped up. The taragus was panting and dancing backwards, blocking and deflecting blows, and turning in time to not have the wall to its back, as Ilan had.

As they moved around the training yard, kicking up dust, another taragus jumped into the fray, and the Wycaan fought both of them with incredible speed. He contained them both in front of him, not allowing them to spread out. His footwork was stunning.

Suddenly, his staff blocked the newcomer while his sword whirled and sent the other's sword flying. It was back to one warrior against another, and Ilan leaned forward, realizing that the newcomer was Third Scale, the taragus who had led the mission to kidnap them.

Master Sythen let out a whoop as he fought faster and faster. "That's more like it!"

Third Scale's face remained impassive as his eyes darted after the Wycaan's sword. Faster and faster they moved around the training yard, and the dusk became thicker. More taragusii and an assortment of fortune-swords came to watch.

Beads of sweat flowed down Master Sythen's face, and his cheeks blazed red against his white beard. Third Scale's forked tongue darted out with increasing agitation, but his expression remained stoic.

Finally, Sythen tripped, and Third Scale saw his chance. He lunged in, but the Wycaan was faking and rolled around the taragus' blade. In one smooth movement, he twisted around Third Scale's body and had his blade at the lizard's throat.

Slowly, Third Scale let go of his sword and raised his front claws in front of him. But he held his head erect. Sythen slowly let go of him and turned him around.

"You are a fine opponent, Third Scale," he said loudly and bowed theatrically. "I thank you for the serious practice."

With that, he turned and walked off.

Ilan hadn't noticed that Sa'gola was now standing next to him.

"Do you understand what just happened, Ilan?" she asked, her voice quiet enough for only his ears.

"I saw what I saw," he replied, still exhilarated by the fight.

"Really? Who won?"

"Master Sythen. Third Scale yielded when he held a blade to his throat."

"Use more than just your eyes, and let us consider together who won. Why did Third Scale enter the fight?"

Ilan thought about this. "To protect his soldiers?"

"Why?"

"Because…because he knew that Master Sythen would not kill him."

"Good," Sa'gola purred. "Now, why was Sythen pleased that Third Scale entered the fray?"

Again, Ilan considered this. "So that he would have a good fight?"

"Yes, and so that he could show you the esteemed level you should reach for. But remember, Ilan, that over-confidence is also one's downfall."

"But he won."

"Did he? It would seem like that to all around, but the taragusii have two tentacles that they can unfurl from behind their heads. They can use these to kill or stun, and some, like Third Scale, can use them to read your mind.

"Even as Master Sythen held a blade to his throat, both the Wycaan and the taragus knew what could play out in a real fight. So again I ask you: who won?"

Ilan furrowed his brow in concentration. "They both did," he said finally. "And they both lost."

Sa'gola put her arm around the *calhei* and hugged him. "Well done, Ilan. Victory rarely comes without loss, and I think you have won as well."

Chapter Forty One

Marina had been watching the fight from a window in a corridor above the training yard. She had seen how Ilan sparred and how the Wycaan had fought against Third Scale, but, most of all, she had watched Sa'gola whispering into Ilan's ear and the ensuing conversation.
What was she talking to him about?

Ilan had received considerable attention since they arrived. He had trained with Master Sythen with not only swords, but also staff and bow. It annoyed Mharina that no one had offered to train her, particularly with the bow, because she already had some proficiency.

Both Senzia and Ilan met with Master Willowood, an elderly Wycaan elfe, who taught them the stories and tested them on the language used. A bald Wycaan dwarf gave both the twins a set of small stones and was teaching them how to use them for very rudimentary magic.

At best, she was allowed to attend their sessions, but she was ignored during the lessons. Often, though, the twins were taken to study away from her presence. She went for long walks in the gardens and did the exercises that Denalion and Pyre had taught them. She would remain strong and ready to run.

First Scale gave her books to read, but when she asked to see maps, he had politely refused.

It seemed she could walk around the fortress wherever she wanted. Often, she met with locked doors, but there was no one following her or supervising her.

She wondered, several times, whether to try and escape without the twins. It would certainly offer more chance of success, and she would be glad to be rid of her brother's constant whining and neediness.

But she loved her little brother and sister. They were family, and she could not turn her back on them. She walked down to the gardens, to a small pond where two large, purple fish swum around. She sat on a bench with a wonderful aromatic vine twisting around a trellis behind her.

And there, she began to weep. No one would see her cry here. She was strong, the elder sibling. She would not give the taragusii or these Wycaans the pleasure. Her body shook as her tears fell quietly, only the occasional gasp of air escaping.

Deep in her misery, Mharina never heard the footsteps and barely noticed the swish of a dress. The bench sagged ever so slightly as Sa'gola sat down and put her arm around the young elfe.

"I'm sure your mother felt alone, as well. She was the only dark-skinned elfe, I imagine, and you are, too."

"I'm not alone," Mharina sniffled, trying to suppress the tears. "I have the twins."

"In a way, you do," Sa'gola said, stroking Mharina's hair. "But in a way, you don't. They are walking a separate path now, the same one your father walked. Tell me: when he trained with the Wycaans in the west, was your mother allowed to reside with him?"

Mharina remembered her mother telling them how bored she had been, waiting – how she had spent hours practicing her archery and wandering around the Markwin Forest city. She shook her head.

Sa'gola sighed. "I thought not, and, as their training intensifies, you will see your brother and sister even less. They cannot share with you what they learn. It is a cruel time, but they at least have each other."

This made Mharina feel even worse and, despite her best efforts, her sobbing started again. Sa'gola put her arms around Mharina and drew her close. The elfe's cheek rested on the woman's chest, and she found her arms had circled Sa'gola's tiny waist.

They sat like this for some time, then Sa'gola gently pushed her away and raised the elfe's chin with one delicate finger. Mharina looked into the woman's deep green eyes and noticed that when she smiled, Sa'gola had beautiful dimples.

"What is it?" Mharina asked.

"Well, it was the Master who planned for the twins to begin immediate training, even before he returned to test them, but I've just had an idea that he hasn't mentioned. Why don't I train you in the ways I follow? It's natural that one such as I would take an apprentice, though I always imagined it would happen when I am older, and" – she giggled – "I always thought it would be a young man."

"Why a –?" Mharina blushed.

"An apprentice looks after his teacher until the teacher dies," Sa'gola told her. "The apprentice inherits the teacher's tools and books, and even their experiences. It is a very deep commitment, and I guess I fantasized that it might be a romantic thing, as well. I am, as you can see, very busy, and have not found a mate. In this place, only old and undesirable men and elves surround us. But the Master needs me here for now, so what can I do?"

"Are you lonely?" Mharina asked, somewhat intrigued.

Sa'gola took a moment to consider this. "Yes, I would say I am, though I do not dwell on it much. I have great power, and with power comes responsibility. Your father, I'm sure, understands this. But I am also not as young as I look."

"How old are you?"

"That is not a question to ask a lady," Sa'gola frowned in a mock scold.

"When we first met you, you said you were anything but."

Sa'gola threw back her long, dark hair and laughed. The sunlight caught on her purple streaks, and Mharina felt a resounding desire to hear her laugh more.

"You got me there," Sa'gola said. "Still, let's just say that the magic keeps me young – on the outside, at least. So, what do you say? Shall I teach you?"

Mharina went silent for a while.

"What is it, little one? I see you chewing your lip."

Mharina looked at her. "I would need to be honest with you to be your apprentice, and to protect you?"

"Do you plan to lie to me?" Sa'gola raised a purple tinted eyebrow.

"I really like you," Mharina said. "But you are aiding the enemy of my *ahdahr*. When the two sides clash, you will take one side, and I, another, or so I am being led to believe."

"That is a fair point, my *calhei*, and I appreciate your truthfulness." Sa'gola considered. After what seemed to Mharina like ages, the sorceress turned to her. "My offer still stands. You will not lie to me in anything save that which conflicts with your father's interests, and I will take that into account as I teach you."

"What will the Emperor say when he finds out?" Mharina asked. "Perhaps you should ask him first."

"Then we must wait for his return. Is that what you want?"

"Can't you contact him while he is away with a hawk or something?"

Sa'gola looked at her carefully. When she spoke, her voice was harsher. "No."

"Then I accept your offer," Mharina said with a smile. "Thank you."

Mharina rose and walked into the garden. She felt okay training with Sa'gola and lying to her at the same time. This had been Sa'gola's first lesson, she decided.

Sa'gola watched the dark elfe recede into the garden and allowed herself a very smug smile.

Chapter Forty Two

Seanchai slept deeply and dreamlessly near the mouth of the tunnel as the ice bear stood guard. When he woke, he was alone. He followed the ice bear's tracks, desiring to thank him, but when he reached the end of the tunnel, the bear's tracks went back up the mountain, in the opposite direction that Seanchai needed to take. The ice bear had his brothers to round up. They would all head further north, away from the crazed whips of men.

Seanchai remained in his bear form so he could descend more quickly and easily. Only when he saw that he was near the hideout that the pictorians had built did he change back into an elf, gasping at the biting cold. He had left his clothes behind when he had changed forms, and now he ran naked on freezing snow.

He pulled the door open and jumped inside. A roar met him, and he was pinned down, a steel blade against his throat. The knife was steady, but his body was shivering.

"Name of man who helped you reach first teacher?" a voice growled.

"What? It's me, Seanchai. Umnesilk? Narasilk?"

The grip on his body tightened. "Name of man? Narasilk roared.

"Mainsch. It was Mainsch."

The grip loosened. "When first time you scry? When?"

"When Rhoddan and I had to decide whether to cross a valley at night before we met Uncle."

Narasilk loosened his grip and sheathed his knife. "Next time, give warning. Not jump in."

"I'm sorry," Seanchai said, catching his breath. "I'm so cold."

Narasilk stared at him. "Where clothes?" Then, without waiting for an answer, he turned and rummaged through a box.

The clothes he found were ludicrously large even for the big elf, but they were better than nothing. As Seanchai dressed, he asked who else had waited.

"All go," Narasilk replied. "Elf want to stay, but Umnesilk say only one because of food and wood and water. Pictorian know to survive in mountains. Better I stay. But elf argue a lot."

Seanchai laughed. "How did you persuade him?"

"Umnesilk say he not ride on snow planks and must walk if argue more. Also, Umnesilk First Boar, bigger than elf."

Narasilk laughed a deep throaty rumble, and Seanchai, despite himself, smiled. "What's with the questions?"

"Big elf worry you prisoner. Emperor could come as you. Give me questions to ask."

"A good idea," Seanchai conceded. "Good questions too."

"Yes, but what is scry?"

Seanchai explained as he drank some water and massaged his stiff limbs. When he was ready, Narasilk turned and pulled out two sets of snow planks.

"I've never done that before," Seanchai said, fidgeting.

"Not hard. Stand on and go whoosh down mountain. All you need think is how stay on planks. Also, try to stop at bottom of mountain."

Seanchai stared at his new friend, but couldn't decide if the pictorian was joking. They packed their bags and weapons and stepped outside. Narasilk tied a piece of rope around himself and then around Seanchai.

"Put one foot on each wood, yes? I lead and go right way. You think to stay on."

Narasilk stood on his snow planks and faced the tips to each other, preventing himself from sliding away. He signaled for Seanchai to do the same. Tentatively, the elf stood on the boards, but instinctively lifted a foot to walk forward and one plank shot down the mountain.

"Ooops," he grimaced.

Narasilk stared after the plank, then grunted something Seanchai decided was best left untranslated. The pictorian tied the elf's left foot onto the board. "Maybe easier now," he said.

"Why?"

"Need think only of one board." The pictorian laughed again. "Come, we go very fast."

"Very fast?"

"Yes. Look."

Seanchai turned his head, and his whole body wobbled. At the peak of the mountain, several dark dots were approaching.

"Can you outrun them?"

"Me, yes. Us, not sure, but try." Narasilk suddenly pulled them both down.

It took Seanchai a while to feel like he had any kind of control over his weight or his ability to steer himself, even within the boundaries of Narasilk's ropes, and to understand that, no matter what, his face was going to be numb.

At that point, something else took over – a wave of exhilaration – and he whooped as he felt the edged snow plank cut crisply through the snow.

"Yeeeeeah," he yelled, and whooped again.

When the arrow landed to his right, narrowly missing him, his enthusiasm vanished. He began to turn his head, but wobbled precariously. Then an arrow bounced off the furs he was wearing.

Narasilk was swerving to put the archers off, and Seanchai allowed himself a quick glance back. Three of the pursuers were shooting from their planks. Inexplicably, this infuriated him, and he slowly took his bow from his back and an arrow from his quiver.

He noched and then turned slowly, letting off a ridiculously wide shot. It did not help that the pictorian had swerved left just as Seanchai let loose his arrow.

As they passed through a path between the rocks, Narasilk swerved sharply and grabbed a long stick. As he did, something thin rose in the air, but Seanchai lost sight of it as they slid to a halt among a few trees to the side.

"Get bow ready, but wait," Narasilk called.

Seanchai complied, but almost lowered his bow as three of the men pursuing him ripped into the cord that Narasilk had raised and lay still. The others were quick enough to stop, but Seanchai made short work of them firing arrow after arrow. This time, standing still, his aim was deadly.

Narasilk stared at him, his huge mouth hanging open.

"How?"

"A lot of practice, my friend. A lot of practice."

"Shoot well, yes. But how bag of arrows not empty?" Narasilk asked, wonder evident in his deep voice.

"That's a whole other story, but for now, we must keep on. I have a report to give and we don't have much time."

CHAPTER FORTY THREE

Seanchai was so exhausted that he failed to recognize the ice tunnel with his usual level of awe. Once through to the City of the Elders, it was still bustling, but very different. There were no more pictorye or signs of everyday life. Instead, it resembled a military camp. There were pictorians and humans training in clearing. Next to the training field were rows and rows of tents.

Seanchai glanced at Narasilk, who looked similarly shocked. They had only been gone a few days, but those left in charge had followed Umnesilk's orders to begin the evacuation, and at a surprisingly efficient pace.

"Where have they all gone?" he asked Narasilk.

The young pictorian shuffled his feet.

"It's okay," Seanchai said. "It's better I don't know."

"I trust you, Wycaan, but still you may—"

"Get caught, be tortured, and give your people away," Seanchai grimaced. "Now *there's* a comforting thought."

"Wycaan," Narasilk grabbed his arm and squeezed to the point of pain. "I trust, but must follow orders. I trust you much."

When he loosened his grip, Seanchai could not help but rub his arm. "I appreciate that, Narasilk, and I know your First Boar means no offense. He is wise and makes difficult decisions."

Seanchai walked toward a large tent where Shayth's banner hung limp on a pole. A flutter of wind stirred some life into it momentarily. The tower with a red sun behind it looked wrong now that the Emperor's regime had been overthrown, but Shayth would do nothing to suggest that he was a permanent king.

"Narasilk. Please go to the First Boar and request a joint council. I must report to Prince Shindell."

Seanchai stood outside the big tent. There were many voices inside, and, after so long away, it sounded cacophonous.

"If you prefer, I can bring you food and drink to my tent, and then call Shayth?"

He turned and smiled at Maugwen. "Have you become a mind reader as well as a healer?"

"I knew you were going to ask that," she replied rubbed her fingers around her temples.

Seanchai laughed. "I'm so glad you were thrown in jail at Galbrieth," he said, "despite it…um… not being good for you, I mean."

"I'll take that as a compliment," Maugwen replied, shaking her head and smiling. "Come, something troubles me."

As they walked, she stopped a young man in uniform. "How is your shoulder?"

"Better than before," he replied with a warm smile as his hand moved to check. "Yeh magic touch worked wonders, milady. May I help yeh or the Wycaan?"

"Please. Could you ask at the kitchen for a plate of food – not meat – for the Wycaan, and some wine?"

"T'is a mark of mah debt to yeh that I will face the cook with this dangerous quest." The man bowed. "Where shall I bring the food?"

"To my tent." Maugwen pointed as she laughed. "Thank you."

"Mah pleasure, milady. If I don't survive, don't roast the cook. We ain't got another."

Maugwen's tent was quite big, but only one of the five cots showed any evidence of someone having slept there. Seanchai also noted a rack of herbs, a water barrel, and a pile of cloths.

"This isn't your tent. This is for wounded."

"When the battle begins, those most seriously wounded sleep here. Otherwise, I will not go to bed. I will call Shayth."

Seanchai sat on the edge of one of the cots, not realizing he was dozing until his food arrived. He sat for a moment, disoriented, and then sipped a glass of dark red wine. There were definite advantages to traveling with royalty.

Shayth, First Advisor Gilead, Rhoddan, and Maugwen entered the tent. Seanchai began to rise, but Shayth stopped him.

"This will be a short meeting. We are due before the Pictorian Council of Elders in two hours, and you need to eat and nap."

"It is most improper to call such a meeting so soon," Gilead complained, "and at such a late hour."

Shayth ignored him and sat next to Seanchai. "Is there anything I should know before we meet with Umnesilk and his council?"

Seanchai thought about this and shook his head.

"Then eat and sleep, my friend." Shayth stopped and looked up as a pictorian entered the tent with two objecting guards.

Gilead leapt to his feet. "This is unseemly. One should–"

"Gilead!" Shayth snapped and turned to the pictorian. "What can I do for you?"

"First Boar ask you come now. Think not good to meet late."

"Seanchai will finish eating and wash. Then we will join you. Please thank Umnesilk for the consideration."

The pictorian furrowed his brow as he bowed and exited.

"My prince," Gilead said. "You are the sovereign here, and yet they treat you as a...as a mere guest."

"He allowed Shayth into his village and the City of the Elders," Seanchai said. "You are probably the first humans to receive such an honor. It is a huge sign of trust."

"But he had the insolence to demand that the prince swear himself and us to secrecy."

"Do you plan to tell anyone?" Seanchai growled.

Gilead had the sense not to respond, but Shayth put a hand on the old man's shoulder. "I need sound advice from my advisor. Protocol is very low down on the list of priorities right now."

Gilead stood up straight, "Then, my prince, I suggest you arrive with your generals. Not for the sake of protocol, but to create a war council at once. You might want to let the First Boar decide who sits from their clans. Nonetheless, their council is there only to give you advice, not make decisions. They need to know that from the start."

Shayth looked at Seanchai. "You know the pictorians better than anyone else. What do you think?"

"They know the land best and are defending their homeland. But this is going to be even more difficult for them."

"Why?"

"They have already evacuated their pictorye and pregnant females. They fear losing their land and their boars. They fear their race is facing extinction." Seanchai looked up at Shayth.

"This is no ordinary invading army we are facing. Even without factoring the Emperor, this is a nation on the move, bent on conquest. I saw males and females of many different races. I suspect there are children with them, as well as their herds and all their belongings.

"What frightens me most is not who we are facing, but who they are fleeing from. If we are to win this, we have a lot of killing to do, and we will not like it."

"It doesn't seem as if the pictorians will have that problem," Gilead replied.

Seanchai turned to face the old man. "But they do not know yet who they face. There are pictorians in that army. The Ice Clans that disappeared in pictorian legend have returned. And they are armed, mounted, and as bloodthirsty as Umnesilk's boars. When they clash, it will be horrific.

"Victory, if at all possible, will come at a very high price. There may be no winners, and the biggest losers will be the pictorian nation…whatever remains of it."

CHAPTER FORTY FOUR

Denalion stared into the darkness, his legs rolled up and his chin resting on his knees. The woman put a steaming cup into his hands and sat down next to him. They both remained almost motionless, save for the slurping of tea.

"It must be hard to let them go," the woman said, her voice soft.

"It is harder knowing they want to go on without me," Denalion replied. "Have I really aged so?"

"Aw, don't be hard on yourself. Truth is, they probably saved your life. They have no chance once they're inside. Anyways, you can't be much older than my mum, bless 'er."

Denalion's smile was tight. "I am almost four hundred years old," he said.

The woman gasped, and then glanced at his ears. "I've never met an elf before. There were three of you, right? The dark one and the young female with the two swords."

"Yes."

"And do you all live forever?"

"Not forever. Elves live longer than humans, but still, I am old in the eyes of my people."

"They hold you in high regard."

When Denalion did not acknowledge this statement, she asked. "Are you a priest or something?"

"Something," he replied. "An old something."

The woman laughed. After all she had been through, Denalion thought, she could still find the capacity to laugh. He felt ashamed at feeling sorry for himself.

"I should sleep," he said, putting the cup down.

"Why is it so important that you sleep? I saw how everyone wanted you to, and how they waited with anticipation for you to wake."

"I travel in the dream world and council others."

"And you can bring help for those imprisoned?"

Denalion nodded.

"The one you try to bring: is he strong enough to defeat those in the castle?"

"He is, and if his children or mate are harmed, he will not only defeat everyone inside, but destroy the castle."

"But it is part of the mountain," she said, fear permeating her tone.

"Then he will bring down the mountain. The wrath of a wounded Wycaan is beyond comprehension."

The woman stared at him. Denalion was rather ashamed to speak like this. It was reckless, and he desperately hoped he was right.

The castle walls were smooth and warm from the iron torches. The mouse scampered along, afraid of cats, boots, and a thousand other dangers. Mice don't belong upstairs. There is plenty of food in the

kitchens and storerooms, and holes in the walls to escape through when needed. Life was not hard for a mouse down there.

But here he darted, not exactly sure where he was going. He would have to trust the dream. He saw the door he had been looking for, slid underneath, and looked around the room. There was a huge, round bed, and, judging by the movements, at least one child tossing in his or her sleep. In the corner sat a wooden table with several chairs. One was occupied by a dark-skinned elfe, who looked at him as she nibbled on an apple.

He scurried over, and, with considerable effort, climbed the chair legs. He was still too far from the table, and he took a deep breath as the elfe picked him up and placed him on the table.

"You are very cute. I shall call you Red Whiskers," she said, and giggled. "Here, would you like some cheese?" She laughed again.

"You will call me Denalion," the little mouse said, mustering up as much dignity as a mouse could. "Oh, my. That cheese does smell good."

He nibbled a small crumb that Mharina had cut from the block. This made Mharina laugh even more, but he couldn't help himself. There was something very instinctual in his appetite, and it tasted as good as it smelled.

"Be quiet. You will wake your brother and sister, or her."

"Sa'gola sleeps in another tower."

"Listen, Mharina. If we do sense her, I don't want you to wake up. Instead, ask me about your ahdahr. Do you understand?"

"You plan to trick her?"

"Feed her false information. Even a mouse can play a cat."

Mharina frowned. "I'm not sure I follow."

"It's a mouse joke. You…never mind. What can you tell me?"

"The twins are training intensively. There are five Wycaans here. One is very good with the Win Dao swords; another teaches them elements. Ilan is enjoying feeling important, having secrets, and Senzia has become remote.

"He's just a little idiot, but I don't understand her. I thought we were planning…"

"Planning what?" Denalion asked. "I told you not to use the Anwar stone."

Mharina pouted. "You never returned to me. How was I to know if any of you were still alive? Maybe our ahdahr has fallen in the north. If we are alone, we are…" She stopped for a moment and then asked tersely, "What word do you bring from my ahdahr? How goes it in the north?"

"He must stay there for now, but he will send forces here as soon as he can. There will be a great battle in the north, but he will be able to come faster than we thought. Do not speak of this to anyone, not even the twins."

"When will he come?" Mharina pressed.

"I couldn't tell you even if I knew. But it will take some time. You must be ready to stay here for quite a while."

"I have a request," Mharina said, her voice timid.

"What is it?"

"The sorceress. Please don't harm her. We're all very fond of her."

Denalion's whiskers twitched. "I cannot promise, Mharina, since she is loyal to the Emperor. You must not allow yourself to get too close to her emotionally. Now, I must go."

"Why?"

A black cat leapt onto the table, but Denalion was already gone. He sat by a hole in the wall. The cat remained on the table licking its front paws and cleaning its ears. It sat in front of Mharina seemingly quite proud of the purple bow around its neck.

Mharina stroked the cat. "Very funny," she said and giggled again.

Chapter Forty Five

"I don't know whether to be hurt or impressed."

They were in Sa'gola's quarters, and the diminutive woman was pacing as she thought. Mharina sat in a chair at the worktable, watching and wondering whether she should be feeling more afraid.

Sa'gola stopped pacing and stared at her. "What are you thinking?"

Mharina shrugged. "I really appreciate you teaching me, and I'm very fond of you. But you don't expect me to suddenly give up my family and enjoy being captive, do you?"

"No," Sa'gola replied, almost reluctantly. Mharina thought she had a beautiful pout. "The question is, however, whether I continue to teach you. Why share my secrets, my weapons, my knowledge with you if you are going to betray me?"

Mharina rose and walked to the window. Sa'gola had a beautiful view of the valley.

"I would be very sad if you stopped. I have learned so much, and I feel the magic growing inside of me every day." Mharina turned around to face the woman. "But I might try and deceive you one day in order to escape. I belong with my people on Wycaan Island." She sighed deeply. "I'd understand if you stopped my apprenticeship, but I don't want to lose your friendship. I hope you can believe that, at least."

Sa'gola stepped forward and took the young elfe's hands in her own. Mharina thought she saw a tear in the sorceress' eye, and it made her think of the scars on the woman's body.

The sorceress pursed her lips. "I appreciate your honesty, child. I'm also touched that you tried to bargain for my life. But I do not look for mercy in this world."

"Others who served the Emperor turned to my *ahdahr*, and he forgave them. I will plead for you, and he will not deny me."

Sa'gola smiled. "Thank you, but I doubt it will be necessary."

"Why?"

"You don't know the Master's power. My life is not in danger, and your escape is not possible.

Mharina couldn't sleep, and Ilan's snoring was driving her crazy. She sipped some water, put on her leggings and shirt, and crept out of the room, her sandals in hand.

She planned to walk around the gardens, but lost her way in the maze of corridors and found herself on an unfamiliar, downward path. Perhaps she would reach the underground lakes where Sa'gola took them to bathe. Floating in the water seemed a fine idea and might help her fall asleep.

But after a while the path became steeper and the wall torches less frequent. Suddenly, she stopped, hearing voices ahead of her. She put a hand out to steady herself against the wall, but it was no longer there. She was in a cavern of sorts.

The voices ahead of her were growing fainter, she thought, and she decided to turn around. As she did, a sharp clack of footsteps on the stone path alerted her that someone was approaching from where she had come. From the distant torch, she saw a silhouette of a very tall person.

She made a practiced hand signal that Sa'gola had taught her and faded into the darkness. The figure had almost walked past, but stopped only a few hands from her. His head was devoid of hair and shaped like an egg. His face seemed emaciated – skin tight around his facial bones – and his eyes…were they red? She could not be sure in the dark.

The man was very tall and exuded power and fear. He turned his head slowly in her direction, and Mharina did not dare to breathe. She could see mist coming from his mouth as he exhaled in the chilly air.

"Sa'gola? Are you here?"

When he received no reply, he mumbled something and slowly continued on his path. Mharina watched him walk, slowly and deliberately, the clicks of his shoes sparking in the darkness.

She was sure she had not seen him before. She could see the bones on his face just beneath the pale skin. Her instinct was to run back the way she had come to get away from this man. But he was expecting Sa'gola, and it occurred to the elfe that her teacher might be in danger. The scars. She remembered the scars, and, suddenly, she felt compelled to follow him.

They walked at an eerily measured pace for what felt to Mharina to be eternity. Then, around a corner, there were several lit torches. The man stopped, and so did Mharina.

"I do not think it a mistake to train her," Sa'gola was saying. "You promised me an apprentice of my choice, and I have chosen. She is an excellent student."

"And the dreamwalker?" The deep, male voice that responded to her was harsh.

"She has been in touch with him since she was kidnapped, Master. I suspect this is how the old elf and his party were able to track the taragusii." Sa'gola replied. "I also don't understand why he hasn't reported where the Wycaan's children are to their father. And then, there is the mother. She—"

"The mother knows," the Emperor said. "She and her party will try and penetrate the castle. You will deal with them as planned. And the dreamwalker cannot reach the Wycaan as long as my spy weaves his own web of magic."

"You have a magician in the Wycaan's camp, Master?" Sa'gola's tone revealed her surprise and admiration. "How has he not been detected?"

"I have used magic to surround them when I can," the Emperor replied. "But my man has a potion that he puts in their water, wine, and beer. It is more like he has dulled their senses."

"Their?"

"The Wycaan, my nephew, and their friends. He has a good supply."

"Could he fall in the battle?"

"No. He is close to my nephew, Shayth."

"You don't like your nephew much?"

"I don't like him living in my palace or sitting on my throne. Now I must kill him. Someone approaches. Ithea?"

"I am here, my lord and master." The big man bent low, but Mharina could still not make out a third person.

"I am not," the Emperor replied, and Sa'gola returned something to the pocket of her cloak. The conversation was over.

Sa'gola turned to the big man and her tone was cold. "Why have you come uninvited?"

"I do not need your permission."

Sa'gola reddened, and, though she calmed herself, her voice remained strained. "What can I do for you, Ithea?"

"Why does he not want to talk with me? He speaks regularly with you through that pebble, but me, he ignores. What have I done to deserve this? I have served him constantly for many years, yet you come and go as you will, and still, he favors you."

"Face it: I'm way cuter."

The man harrumphed. "Do not try me, witch."

"Or what? If the Master is fond of me, you will not touch me."

"The Master is far away. He will not hear you scream."

"Maybe not, but he has a very long memory."

"He uses you as I have used you – as others have, and always will. You whore your magic, Sa'gola. You sell it to the highest bidder."

"The Master does not pay me."

"But he will give you something, I'm sure. At least, he hopes you will want something of him."

"That is not your concern. You have not come here in the middle of the night to expound upon your jealousy, or your lack of self-worth."

"Shut up," the man hissed, "or I will teach you a lesson."

"Don't threaten me, Ithea. It does not become you or scare me."

The man drew a crackling whip, exuding an energy, or magic, perhaps. "Do you not fear me now?"

Sa'gola hissed and crouched, ready to spring. "No. I see a coward who feeds on fear. I will not cower to you."

"You will." He lashed out, and the whip flowed backwards, not far from where Mharina crouched.

As it snapped forward, a purple light met it with a loud sizzle and burning smell. Again and again he struck, moving forward. Sa'gola retreated, blocking him and gasping with each blow. Then she tripped, and, though she rolled, the whip caught her across the back, and she screamed.

She shot two volleys of purple light, but they missed, and, suddenly, the whip rained down on her. Sa'gola did not scream any more, but grunted and curled up to shield herself from the blows.

Mharina could stand it no more. She stepped forward and raised her hands above her head. She had never before succeeded in summoning the sorceress' fire, but a powerful rage gave her absolute certainty that this time, she could. Pointing toward the man, she whispered the words, and two bright orange flames left her fingers and smashed into the man. He fell and lay still on the ground.

Sa'gola stared up at her, breathing hard. "Thank you," she panted.

CHAPTER FORTY SIX

They allowed Denalion to try one more time to reach Seanchai and when he did not succeed, they left. Pyre felt haunted by the dreamwalker's pained expression as they left him behind. He had always been so powerful and confident. She, like all the *calhei*, had enjoyed the mystery and power that surrounded this living legend back in the Markwin Forest. But here, they were a long way away from the protection of the great trees.

The party walked in silence, each deep in their own thoughts. Pyre contemplated her companions. Ricard's mother would guide them through the hidden gate, but not beyond. She had a daughter who worked in the castle and two more children in the village. Retribution would surely include either losing more of her children or her children being deprived their mother.

Montclair followed her. His beautiful sword was sheathed and blackened, but he clutched his short sword, eyes darting around in search of treachery. Twice, when they stopped, Pyre noticed Riona brush up against the fortune-sword. Though it was subtle each time – the back of her hand or her forearm – Pyre knew something had happened between them. It was a shame they may not live to explore it further. She thought Riona would not easily give herself to a man.

And then, Sellia. Though she looked relaxed, Pyre recognized the elfe would have an arrow taut and aimed in a flash. What could possibly be passing through her mind? Her children were so close, and yet so far from her.

Pyre had no children and no lover, but had dedicated herself to experience the transformation from a Wycaan warrior to master. It happened to apprentice elves in different ways. Pyre's hair was white, but not the snow white of a master. She had tried not to let it bother her. She trained hard with weapons and energy, but she had never taken on an animal form or felt the physical changes others had. Dying would mean never experiencing this ultimate step and, if her life was forfeit, here lay her only personal regret.

She was still thinking about this as they followed a narrow track down from the mountain with paths that forked off into the night. The hour was so late that they neither expected nor met anyone on the road, but still she maintained her vigilance.

The darkness in front of them became increasingly dense, and Pyre finally realized they were coming upon either the fortress's walls or the side of the mountain. As they got closer, she realized they were one and the same.

They rested at the wall, and Pyre ran her hand along it. The stone was still warm from the sun's rays the day before, and so smooth. Sellia leaned back and closed her eyes, exhaling as the heat relaxed her body.

Hissing voices faded off the side of the road, and Pyre, copying Sellia, silently noched an arrow. Montclair caught both their eyes and shook his head. If possible, it was better to let the taragusii pass unimpeded.

Pyre shuddered. She had fought two of the creatures on Wyccan Island and killed one. But the other had locked swords, pushed her against a wall, and pierced her skull with two antennae from the back of its head. It had felt as though the creature was inside her, wading through her memories. It did not hurt, but felt so violating. Not finding what it wanted, the taragus had tossed her across the room, where she fell unconscious.

Now she watched as they passed, tall and muscular, scaled and dark. She heard their hisses and saw thin tongues dart out to lick their noses. A third came from the opposite direction and hissed at them. All three sunk onto all fours and ran quickly into the darkness.

Ahead, Montclair squeezed Ricard's mother's shoulders. She shook her head as they whispered. Montclair turned to the others.

"She has never encountered taragusii patrols here. She fears the entrance might be compromised. She won't go on, even though I offered more money."

Sellia moved to speak to the woman. At first, the woman shook her head repeatedly, but then began pointing, directing Sellia. When she had finished, Sellia hugged the woman, who quickly faded back into the darkness.

"Why?" Montclair asked, clearly agitated.

"She's no fortune-sword," Riona answered, her tone harsh. "She has other children who need her."

"But we paid–"

"Enough," Sellia said. The conversation was over.

They stalked along the path, listening for more taragusii. They found none until they discovered three guards posted at the gate. Montclair swore under his breath and Pyre almost laughed when she saw Riona glare at him. For her suppressed effort, Pyre also received a glare, but she consoled herself that it was less severe than Montclair's.

Pyre felt a tap on her arm. Riona pointed at Pyre's bow and then at the furthest taragus. Then she touched Sellia and signaled the one next to it. She drew out her sling and a pebble, but Montclair shook his head. When she pointed a warning finger at him, he stopped and she slowly touched his lips. She looked again to the two elfes and touched her ear. *Wait for my signal*, Pyre understood.

Riona disappeared silently into the brush. A few moments later, they heard a click far to their right. The taragusii all turned. and then each silently fell, almost in one movement.

Riona flew to the one she had shot, and Pyre saw the glint of a blade. Sellia and Montclair checked the other two and they dragged the bodies off the path. As they approached the small entrance, Pyre smiled at how well they had worked together to dispatch the three guards. But she froze when she saw what awaited them.

Before them stood a small, dark-haired woman dressed in black and purple. She shimmered at the edges, and Pyre realized that the woman was not physically there.

"Welcome to Grogin," she said to the group, her voice sweet and clear. Then she turned to Sellia. "Welcome, Sellia. I've been waiting to meet you."

Chapter Forty Seven

"How do you know who I am?" Sellia snapped.

"Because, my dear, you have a daughter who is as beautiful as you. She loves and admires her mother and has told me many wonderful things about you."

"You have my children. I've come to take them back." Sellia growled, bow ready.

"Really? Perhaps you might consider that being here is not such a bad option for them. The twins train with Wycaan teachers and are claiming their noble heritage. You would be proud of them if you saw, and I can show you."

"Who gave you the right to decide on their education?"

"Actually, it is not my decision. It is the Master's."

"Who?"

"I believe the Emperor has a new title," Riona said. "Given that he's in exile, it probably makes sense."

Sellia wheeled around and glared at the healer, but Riona just shrugged. Sellia turned back to the sorceress.

"What about Mharina?"

"She is well. We have become quite close, and I am teaching her things."

"What things?"

'It's a complicated, but fitting education. Give yourselves up, and I can answer all your questions."

"And if we refuse?"

Sa'gola shrugged. "You are all most capable fighters." She turned to Riona. "A sling – nice touch. You are still only five against a well-trained army of taragusii and fortune-swords, all led by Wycaans."

She paused and frowned. "Where is the spirit man?"

"Who?"

"The red one who walks in people's dreams."

"He's not with us," Sellia replied.

"I can see that," Sa'gola arched a thin eyebrow. "Where is he?"

"Gone back to Wycaan Island," the elfe said.

The sorceress stared at her for a while. "You lie."

Sellia shrugged. "If he's not there, then he hasn't gone far. He's an old elf."

"He's the best weapon you have, elfe. If you sent him away, you've made a big mistake. Now, will you give yourselves up and come without any drama?"

"Why would we do that?" Sellia replied.

"I have already told you. The Master has left a number of scenarios available. It is up to you. Death is not the worst option. He is very creative, actually."

"If I give myself up, will I see my children?"

"See them, yes, but they will not see you. It will disrupt their training, I fear."

"You have no right to keep me from them."

Sa'gola turned to Pyre. "You are a young Wycaan, are you not? Were your parents allowed to visit you in your Wycaan trees whenever they wanted?"

"That is different," Pyre said. "No one there was forced to become a Wycaan. No one was separated from their parents so violently. We could request to see our parents, or them us, and time was always found."

"Oh, you have it quite wrong," Sa'gola replied. "They are most willing students and doing so well. Ilan is like his father, I believe, from what I've heard. He is highly skilled and yet, very sensitive. Mharina is so like you, and Senzia seems to be a powerful hybrid. She has the skill of her father and the strength of her mother. She will be a great Wycaan, and she and Ilan will be the first to be personally trained by the Master. You should be gratified."

"Gratified," Sellia snorted. "Enough talk. If we enter that door, what happens?"

Sa'gola smirked. "Why don't you find out?"

Montclair took a step forward, and then turned to face his friends, his back to Sa'gola. "I don't like this. There is no surprise here. We cannot win."

"What do you suggest?" Sellia snapped, clearly out of ideas, herself.

"Either we disappear for a while and try again later, or we go inside and surrender. If the children are not being harmed – and it doesn't sound like they are – then we wait for your dashing husband to charge in and rescue everyone."

"And if he doesn't come? If Denalion cannot make contact or he falls in battle?"

It was Pyre who spoke, her green eyes hard. "He will come, of that I have no doubt. But it might be a very long time to sit in a dungeon. If we go in, we should try and fight our way through. If it looks useless, we flee or surrender."

"And has it occurred to you that some or all of us might die if we do that?" Montclair hissed.

"You don't have to join us," Riona goaded him. "We would understand if you turned around now."

Sellia looked at them as they glared at one another. *This is not the time,* Riona had said when Sellia had earlier suggested she allow Montclair into her heart. She had helped bring them together and now her next step might separate them forever. She thought of her first love, Dyrovas, and her loss at his death.

Sellia turned to Sa'gola. "We will return," she said, and led them back into the darkness.

"They will follow us, surely," Montclair said, jogging to catch up.

"Then shut up and think of something," Riona answered.

Sellia led them blindly, listening for the inevitable sounds of pursuit. Soon, they heard a rustling to their right.

"They track us," Pyre said, drawing her Win Dao swords.

"That is not taragusii," Montclair declared.

"How do you know?" Riona asked.

"If it was, you wouldn't hear, and they wouldn't wait to attack."

Sellia glanced at the fortune-sword, whose face was grim. "What do you suggest?"

"Stop and let them approach."

"And if it's a trap?"

He shrugged. "Then we fight."

They did as he said and stood in an outward facing square, each with weapons drawn.

"We're waiting," Sellia called.

"What for?" asked a child's voice, and four young, dark-skinned boys tentatively walked into the open. They wore stained white robes.

"You were Ricard's friends, weren't you?" one boy asked. "If you still have coin, we will help you."

"Ricard paid a high price for helping us," Sellia said. "I don't want to be responsible for any other children dying."

"F'lusha boys always become soldiers or slaves. Sooner or later, we all die for the Master."

"They know we're here," Sellia said. "Can you hide us somewhere that is nowhere near your village?"

The boy smiled in much the same way Ricard had.

"First, coin," he said.

"Half now, half later in the day after we wake."

There were already signs of dawn approaching. The boy nodded and took the coins. He counted them and distributed shares to his companions.

"Come," he said.

Sellia felt a moment of unease and, as she glanced at Montclair, she knew he was worried, too. The boys took them to a small shack, half-submerged underground.

"You sleep in here. We will close the door and guard. But if we get in danger, we'll shout and run. Understood?"

Sellia nodded, and they went inside. The graying dawn showed nothing but a windowless room. They each curled up, ready to go to sleep.

"Sellia?" Riona called, yawning. "Why did we not go in?"

"Montclair was right, and I didn't want the two of you to be separated so soon."

There was quiet. She glanced up and saw that Montclair was lying next to Riona, an arm around her, spooning her.

"Thank you," Riona said, and they all fell into a deep sleep.

When she woke much later in the day, Sellia pushed the door open. The sun poured in, but the boys were gone and everything had changed.

Everything.

Chapter Forty Eight

Seanchai sat on a rock, looking down at the Emperor's forces as they filled the northern half of the valley. They moved with precision and purpose. He could hear faint orders being cried.

The sun was behind him, making its way up into the sky and sharpening his vision in the crisp early morning light. He noticed that the pictorians, on their horned and scaled beasts, held the most forward position.

Seanchai was not sure whether this was because they were the fiercest, or to provoke Umnesilk's boars into breaking formation. They stood in disciplined rows, but had been kept far from the blue-painted humanoids, who stood in four rows in the flank, now devoid of their ice bears. Seanchai smiled to himself at this and wondered how the pictorians had reacted.

The other group on the front line was a dozen giants. Though the legends told of the giants being slow like the trolls, they were considered more intelligent. Seanchai would have liked the opportunity to meet them.

Rhoddan, Umnesilk, and two boars trotted out on horses. Rhoddan carried the Prince's banner, while one of the boars held a large white one, signaling parlay.

There was a murmur from the ranks of the Emperor's army, and a giant picked up a boulder and threw it. The rock landed short, but one of the horses spooked, and its pictorian fell.

The blue-painted men shrieked with laughter and catcalls, and this prompted one of the Emperor's pictorians to stride forward. He shook his huge axe at the blue soldiers and marched out to meet Umnesilk.

Rhoddan calmed his horse and winced as he saw the pictorian next to him fall. The pictorians were not natural horse-riders, and the horses suffered for their weight. Rhoddan had insisted they ride in order to retreat quickly if the parley did not go well and they were attacked. He tried to ignore the glare from the boar that had fallen, but knew none of them could ignore the taunts from those tall, blue-painted soldiers.

He watched the opposing side's pictorian leader step forward and shake his axe at the blue contingent. The pictorian's blade shone in the bright morning sun and fresh snow. He stopped before Umnesilk. Narasilk moved clumsily next to Rhoddan and leaned over, ready to translate.

"I am Umnesilk, First Boar of Pictorian Nation."

"Of what pictorian nation you speak, brother? I am Arad'gug of Ice Clans, called upon by old ones to serve and lead."

"There only one pictorian nation," Umnesilk growled, "and you not raise axe against us, unless challenge my leadership."

"When our people trapped in Great Freeze and could not join you, where was nation?" Arad'gug boomed back. "When pictorye and old ones starved because we no food, no hunt beasts, as all fled Great Freeze, where, then, were brothers of south? You safely in huts, food stored and dried, or hunt herds that fled from north. Why not come find us?"

Umnesilk paused a while. "All happened long ago. Now, face each other. You run from something at backs, but we can give home and family."

"Perhaps we not run from what is behind, but serve its strength and its promise."

Umnesilk leaned in. Arad'gug was almost his height. "I know who you serve. I once officer in his army. I followed until met Wycaan."

"The Master told. You turned and knifed his soldiers in back. Coward."

Umnesilk let out a roar that Narasilk did not bother to translate. Then he took a deep breath. "We left battlefield. We refused to join Wycaan in fight even though he right. We kept honor."

Arad'gug spit on the ground. "Honor? Maybe we do honor and fight first – you and me."

"No!" Rhoddan cried out as the translation reached his ears.

The pictorians – both sides – all looked at him.

"You are better than that, both of you." The elf turned to Arad'gug. "Anyway, would your master even let your boars change sides? He isn't too happy with Umnesilk right now for standing up to him."

As if on cue, a huge roar made them all cringe, and a fire seared across the northern sky.

"Pointed ears right," Arad'gug answered and turned to leave.

"Wait," said Rhoddan and stepped his horse forward. "Make a pact. If the Emperor falls to the Wycaan, or if he flees, agree to bring your boars over to join Umnesilk."

"You be welcome," Umnesilk added, "as long-lost brothers you are."

The boar looked from Rhoddan to Umnesilk. "You must prove. As atonement for abandoning people to Great Freeze, your council choose First Boar from my people."

Both Narasilk and the third pictorian began to protest, but Umnesilk nodded. "When you hear great horn blow, it mean Emperor fallen or fled, as happened once before. Then your boars join us and your females and pictorye as one nation. And I stand down as First Boar. My word."

"My word." Arad'gug replied and returned to his boars.

"Are you alright?" Rhoddan asked quietly as they trotted back.

"It done," Umnesilk replied without looking at him. "One pictorian not important. Nation more." He awkwardly spurred his horse on.

Chapter Forty Nine

Seanchai saw the confrontation between the two pictorian chiefs, as well as Rhoddan's intervention. The Ice Clan chief looked far happier than Umnesilk.

The firebreather's roar and burst of fire had been timely. Seanchai wished he had something to match the bravado, if only to give his own troops courage. As the Emperor's army began to advance, Seanchai began muttering the phrase to bring down an avalanche. *Ma'afula, Ma'afula, Ma'afula.*

He saw the top snow begin to cascade down, fine powdery top snow, but it was the beginning. *Ma'afula, Ma'afula, Ma'afula.* He heard anxious voices below and saw men pointing in his direction.

As he repeated the words, he felt a strange breeze pass by and through him. The wind carried a human whisper, both insistent and confident, and the snow stopped in place. Seanchai stared down at a small piece unnaturally balanced, paused mid-roll.

He focused his energy on it and felt the small snowball wobble, but as it tried to roll, it encountered more resistance. After a few minutes, he felt tired and was sweating, despite the cold. He stopped trying.

And then he saw him. The Emperor was dressed in a white cloak edged in gold. His hood was drawn over his head, where a thick golden band sparkled in the sunlight. His face was flushed with exertion, and he looked older.

"Where are your friends, little cub? No more Great Grizzly this time, but will the others come?"

Seanchai did not reply.

"He was most brave at the end – ferocious, in fact. Where does one find the strength to fight a battle one cannot win?"

"From their morals, their convictions." Seanchai couldn't resist answering as he stared across the valley, many faces entering his memory, most vivid of whom was Ilana. "From love," he added.

"Yes, of course. I was thinking of your teachers, as well: the woman, the dwarf, and the Weapons Master."

"They have names," Seanchai snapped.

"Of course they do. So does everybody. Then there is the one you loved the most. I never met her. She wasn't a Wycaan was she?"

"No."

"And then you bonded with another who is not a Wycaan. Why?"

"Is it relevant to what is happening now?"

The Emperor shrugged. "Not really. Only that she gave you two Wycaan children – twins, I understand. And there is an older one who has yet to be tested, as well."

"How do you know about my *calhei*?"

The Emperor just laughed. "Is it relevant to what is happening now?" he mimicked.

Seanchai turned away. He remembered the priestess of Ballendir's clan warning him of the vulnerability that a mate brings. His children, even more so. He shivered but not from the cold.

"How did you persuade so many to come south?" he asked. "What did you promise?"

"Nothing, at first. They did not seem to want for riches or land. I made sure something else threatened them in the north and offered to protect them as they fled south. Once I was seen as their savior, it was easy to motivate them to follow me.

"I staged a few rescues and told them of the wonderful land they would inherit. Impressed?"

Seanchai didn't answer, because, truthfully, he was.

"What did you unleash to frighten them so?" he asked instead.

"Oh, you'll find out in good time. Or maybe not, if you are dead."

Seanchai looked down on the armies waiting in the valley. "I guess they are waiting for us to fight," he said.

"They can wait if you want to negotiate. Serve me, and I will train you to a higher level than you can imagine. I will offer security to your dear family and peace to the land of Odessiya. Quite generous, in my opinion."

Seanchai laughed. "You haven't changed, have you? Age hasn't softened you or made you wiser."

The Emperor scowled. "Then, little cub, yes – we should fight."

Seanchai drew his swords, and the Emperor unsheathed a great, double-headed axe. Seanchai had never seen such a magnificent weapon.

"This is my favorite toy. I will show you how effective it is," the Emperor said, swirling it in a series of intricate movements.

Then he leapt at Seanchai, but the elf did not wait to make contact. He rolled and slashed at the Emperor's legs, cutting into one of his calves. The older Wycaan gasped in pain and leapt again. This time, Seanchai feigned a retreat, but then stepped closer, and twisted into a jump, slamming both his legs into the Emperor's sides, sending him flying back.

The huge axe clattered to the ground. The Emperor swirled.

"Very impressive," he hissed. "Perhaps we should fight as Wycaan Masters."

Seanchai sheathed his swords and swung round his lime-green elf bow in one fluid movement as the Emperor began to transform. He had planned for this and, before the Emperor finished his transition, sent two arrows into the firebreather's wings and a third into his throat.

Blood dripped, bright pink on the snow, and the creature roared.

Wycaans fight with honor in their animal form, the voice in Seanchai's head snarled. *Next time, you will come to me, and you will beg for mercy."*

Why? Seanchai asked, puzzled at the retort.

A hysterical laugh jarred through the elf. The firebreather was shaking with mirth, despite the pain. *You pathetic elf. I almost feel sorry for you. Come to Grogin."*

The firebreather shot upwards, its wounded wings tight to its side. Seanchai lost it in the sun's glare, but saw the trickles of blood on white snow.

He had no time to consider the Emperor's words. A huge cry from below made him turn. *Ungallah! Ungallah! Ungallah!* The pictorian battle cry rose up from both sides. He watched as Umnesilk slowly led his army forward, and the Emperor's forces had little choice but to charge, too. This was not an army that could scatter and retreat; they had to protect their rear, their mates and children. The Emperor had surely known this, planned this. *He is always several moves ahead,* he had often heard Shayth say.

Not this time, Seanchai thought, as he swung his bow over his shoulders and allowed himself a wry smile.

Chapter Fifty

The pictorian Ice Clans took the lead with their armored, one-horned beasts. Their heavy hooves pummeled the snow with an eerie, pounding beat that shook the valley.

From within Prince Shindell's own ranks, the deep pictorian horn blew. In response, the Ice Clans swung round as one coordinated, graceful unit and charged into the blue-painted humanoids. Umnesilk roared, and a second horn blow sent his boars cutting into the rest of the army.

An alliance!

The Emperor's army was holding its own, with its large numbers and the giants. Seanchai, from above, realized he had waited too long to finish the avalanche. It would now kill soldiers from both sides. He needed to enter the fray and dispose of the giants.

He grabbed the snow plank that Narasilk had given him. Just as he was about to step on, he saw the huge double-headed axe. He picked it up, shocked at how heavy it was, and slung it over his back under the bow.

Following Narasilk's instruction, he slid down the mountain in wide arcs, holding himself steady with his Wycaan stance exercises. As he made his way down, he realized he could still not shoot and stay balanced. He almost regretted using the board, but smiled to himself when he caught Shayth and Rhoddan staring at him in wonder.

In moments, he was near the fight and jumped off the board, allowing it to shoot into a group of longhaired blond men in furs. He took his bow and fired off dozens of arrows as quickly as his quiver could refill itself.

He vaguely heard Shayth call for men to form up with Seanchai, and, soon, he was advancing with Shayth one side of him and Rhoddan on the other. As much as he despised war, he always felt an odd sense of completeness fighting alongside his friends. His thoughts went to Sellia. Ironic that he missed her now.

It did not take long to reach the giants. There were about twenty of them, and they formed a large circle. The Wycaan reached out to stop Shayth from charging them. His friend's eyes blazed. He was as lost in the battle rage as Seanchai, but he paused, and allowed Seanchai to push forward.

The biggest giant swatted two arrows aside, and then a huge arm sent the bow flying from Seanchai's hands. Infuriated, the elf pulled the battle-axe around, and, pressing his feet into the ground, the word escaped his lips: *Karfix*.

The ground beneath him rose into the air, and Seanchai, the Emperor's axe now light in his hands, swung into the giant's throat. Dark purple blood sprayed out at him, and the giant collapsed. The others hesitated, and Seanchai's axe fell upon them, too. The giants were slow and no match for the Wycaan. There was, however, something almost tragic as Seanchai moved from one to the next, leaving a sad wake of carnage.

The fighting continued as the sun began to sink and the battlefield became a mixture of churned snow and an assortment of hues from the mixing of different species' blood. Corpses fell one upon another. Seanchai and Shayth, Rhoddan and the pictorians, gradually began to take over the battlefield. But there were so many of the wild men and their allies, that the progress of the Odessiyan army was slow and costly.

Seanchai turned and grabbed a pictorian with his horn and a piper from Shayth's guard. Together they blasted out a long note and then another, and a third. Other horns responded from around the great battlefield. The sides slowly separated, with the Ice Clans standing with Umnesilk's boars. Seanchai stood in the center, panting. He grabbed Shayth.

"We must offer them terms. Now. They will listen. Tell them you know their families are behind them." As Shayth began to walk forward, his guard fell in around him. Seanchai turned to Rhoddan. "I must go with him. Please, find my bow."

Umnesilk, Narasilk, and another giant boar from the Ice Clans jogged toward Shayth. Seanchai stopped Narasilk and held out the axe. "Please guard this for now."

Narasilk gazed at the weapon, taking in every part, and then swung it onto his back.

Three men, yellow-haired and bloody, walked forward to meet them.

"I am Shayth Shindell, Prince of Odessiya," Shayth greeted them. "This is Umnesilk, First Boar of the Pictorians, and Seanchai, Wycaan Master."

"Yeh killed the Master?" one man asked Seanchai.

"He escaped, wounded," Seanchai replied. "But I will hunt him down."

"Surrender to me," Shayth said, "and swear allegiance. If you do, I will spare you and your families who follow."

The three men looked at each other. "Why'da think we'd bring them?"

"You bring your young, your herds, and your wealth. The Emperor cannot hide them from the Wycaan Master," Shayth replied.

Seanchai glanced at his friend, impressed by Shayth's bluff. The Prince of Odessiya continued. "I will allow you to keep it all and give you land to live on – land that is fertile and more hospitable than in the north. You will send me one son of each of the tribe chiefs, and they will study with our young, train with our army, or apprentice to a profession. If you keep the peace for five season cycles, they will be allowed to return to you. If you keep the peace for another five, all your people are welcome to enter our cities as citizens and live whenever you desire."

Again, the men looked at each other. One said: "We are still greater than yeh in numbers."

"You have not seen the full forces I possess, I also have the entire pictorian nation united on my side. And you can see the Wycaan is pretty useful."

The men followed where Shayth was pointing to the fallen giants.

"May we have a little time to talk amongst ourselves? Men are not the only ones here; you confer your terms on all species?"

Shayth nodded. The men returned to speak with a mixed group that had gathered nearby. But they were not long in returning.

"Our women will be safe?" one asked.

"My army is disciplined," Shayth promised. "And I am not taking your weapons."

The tallest stood in front of Shayth. "We flee a threat that will come. Whether in one season cycle, ten, or a hundred, it will come. Will you swear to stand by us then?"

"When this enemy comes, it will come for all of us, no?" Shayth asked, and the man nodded. Shayth drew his huge broadsword. It still shone, despite the multicolored blood smeared all over it. Now when he spoke, his strong voice traveled into the assembled ranks.

"To all who join the people of Odessiya, I swear that, upon your alliance, we will face all enemies – north, south, east or west – together as one people. I offer you my life and those of my armies to protect you and all peoples of Odessiya. In exchange, I demand your fealty. No more shall you call yourselves Men of the North, but rather proud men of Odessiya."

All three men went down on one knee, and their people followed. Shayth raised his mighty sword to the sky.

"*Ashbar!*" cried the Prince of Odessiya, and it seemed to Seanchai that the blade blazed with the rays of the sun.

There was a moment of silence; then the younger man said, "What does *Ashbar* mean?"

Shayth sheathed his sword and stepped forward. He pulled the young man to his feet and put one hand on the lad's shoulder and his other on the leader's.

In a voice hoarse with emotion he replied, "Everything."

Chapter Fifty One

It was a long, slow walk back to the camp at the entrance to the valley. The soldiers led their horses, the wounded and dead strapped across their saddles. Though the day had been full of physical and emotional stress, all were fueled by the adrenaline of battle. When he reached the tents, Shayth ordered guards to be set and made a short, stirring speech, praising the bravery of all.

The Ice Clans, escorted by many of Umnesilk's boars, had gone to bring their mates and pictorye. Seanchai went to the tent that Maugwen had set up to help those who had been wounded. He poured healing energy into some, and eased the passage to the other side for those he could not help. Shayth and Rhoddan came, and soon Maugwen had them bringing water and dressing wounds.

When word spread that even the prince was in the wounded tents, men stopped their celebrations and came to help. It was an amazing sight as the tents filled, and each patient had his own personal attendant.

Maugwen focused on the worst wounds, and Seanchai gravitated over to help her. Each time he saw her sag in exhaustion, he laid his hands on her shoulders and sent waves of energy into her. He returned time after time to buoy her and her helpers.

They worked deep into the night, until a soldier entered the tent and saluted Shayth.

"The pictorians have returned, sire. Umnesilk has called a council and requests your and the Wycaan's presence."

Seanchai looked around the tent and sighed. Then he followed Shayth out.

Shayth led his entourage to the pictorian tents. The celebrations had given way to exhaustion, and the camp was quiet. Suddenly, the silence broke as a man began screaming hysterically. They stopped, and Shayth frowned.

"It's Gilead," he said and turned.

The old man came running to them, still shrieking, and waving his hands in the air. He wore long nightclothes, and his eyes bulged, white in the darkness around them.

"Stop them!" he screamed. "Stop them!"

He launched himself at Seanchai as if he was going to strangle him. One of Shayth's bodyguards leapt forward and effortlessly turned the old man, pinning his arms and chest to his own armored body.

"Stop them!" Gilead screamed. "Red-haired demons. Call them off!"

"What are–" Seanchai began.

"H-he ordered me. He is the Emperor, the Master. Call them off. They'll kill me. Aaaagh! They feast on me from inside."

Shayth stepped forward and firmly grasped his advisor's face with both hands. When he spoke, his voice was ice.

"What were you doing for my uncle? What was his command?"

Gilead was shaking, and Seanchai moved to stop Shayth, but froze at what Gilead screamed next.

"The *calhei*! I stopped…you knowing. The elf cannot find out until…aaaagh!"

Shayth's fingers whitened as he tightened his grip on the old man. "Until what?"

Gilead was panting. "At Grogin…he has them…his taragusii took Wycaan Island."

Now Seanchai shoved Shayth out of the way and lifted the old man out of the guard's grasp and into the air, leaving his legs dangling. "What about Sellia? Is she alive?"

"Don't know. Stop them, please. I see them, feel them gnawing ...."

"What do you see? What attacks you?"

"Red beasts. All red – hair, faces, beards, aaaagh! Make them stop. Red devils inside of me. Pointed ears, aaaagh!"

Red? Seanchai tightened his grip. "Denalion! You prevented him from reaching me, from warning me?"

The man was choking. "And the elf warrior, the prince, the healer – all of you." He sputtered, and Seanchai loosened his grip slightly, but he shook the man violently.

"How?"

"The Emperor sent me a liquid. I have been putting it in the water. Told my aides to help. Protect you, I said. Please. Stop them."

"Oh, I'll stop them," Seanchai hissed and, in one swift movement, threw the old man to the ground.

The snap of bones and spine was clear and final. Gilead, First Advisor to the Prince of Odessiya, lay still.

Seanchai turned to Shayth, his face flushed and teeth bared. "The Emperor mocked me. He said I would...my *calhei*. My wife. MY FAMILY!"

Battle-hardened soldiers took a step back before the seething Wycaan. Only Shayth stood his ground. Rhoddan burst up to them, panting from the run, and stood next to Shayth.

"He told me," Seanchai rasped. "Before he fled, your uncle said I would come begging, and he laughed at me. Even though I'd just defeated him again, he taunted me."

"Seanchai," Shayth raised a hand to his friend's shoulder. "We will go to Grogin and crush him. We will destroy his fortress, his taragusii, everything. I swear. But first, please, I need you to serve one more time. Come to the Pictorian Council with me. Then we leave, first thing in the morning."

Seanchai stood there, his chest heaving, his eyes watering from grief and rage. "I left almost no guard. How many died because of me? How many students, how many servers and teachers? THEY DIED BY MY NEGLIGENCE!"

"No," Shayth shook his head. "This is the Emperor's doing, not yours."

"I should have gone after him when you asked me to. I should have finished it then." He looked at Rhoddan's stony face, his voice hoarse, his breathing labored. "You know that to be true. You urged me to go and find him. You always counseled to be vigilant."

Rhoddan met his gaze. His mouth opened and closed without sound. Then he nodded slowly. "But now is not the time for regret. You must compose yourself and go with Prince Shindell to the pictorians. Solidify the alliance."

Seanchai stood there, bringing his emotions and breathing under control. He closed his eyes and drew energy from the ground deep beneath the snow. He woke those asleep deep underground and took what he needed.

Then he opened his eyes and nodded to Shayth. "I am ready, my prince."

They turned and walked together in silence. When they reached the pictorian camp, Shayth turned to Seanchai, his voice low.

"I need you to stay focused here. This is sensitive. I need the Ice Clans to accept me as ruler to be able to help them."

Seanchai nodded. They stepped inside a crowded tent. The pictorians were mingling, and there seemed to be no hostility. Quiet conversations ensued as they made their way forward. Narasilk came into step with Seanchai, the Emperor's axe swung across his back.

"Everyone seems to be getting on," Seanchai said.

Narasilk leaned over. "All look for lost family. Chance to bind together and grow clans. Is very strange. Not sure is good. But even worse yet. You see."

They reached the middle, where Umnesilk and a couple of his council members stood with Arad'gug and two of his boars. Here was the tension and it was palpable. Umnesilk raised his hand, and the tent went quiet. Narasilk moved close to translate for Seanchai and Shayth.

"Today," Umnesilk boomed, "great battle fought. Emperor sent away, enemies of Ice Clans destroyed, and pictorians fought together as great warriors. Even more important, Ice Clans and us now one. Pictorian nation, all of us."

He clenched his fists together above his head, and cheers erupted around the room. When it subsided Umnesilk continued.

"Many years ago, pictorian clans separate in Big Freeze. Many trapped in far north, and we here not help. Not right. Now I, First Boar, in front of Prince of Odessiya and Wycaan Master, say sorry for what happened."

Again, there were cheers, and some pictorians actually hugged. Seanchai was amazed. But Umnesilk had not finished. He turned to Arad'gug, who stood even straighter, his expression grim.

"Many of Ice Clans die. Very bad. Sorry cannot give back life. Now clans come together. We make amends, even if only symbolic." He paused and took a deep breath. "I, Umnesilk, First Boar of the Pictorians, offer you Arad'gug of the Ice Clans, to take my place as First Boar, to serve all pictorians, Ice and South, as one people."

There was a murmur of bewilderment, but Arad'gug stood tall and glared around the room.

In his deep, rasping voice, he called out. "I accept, and will meet any challengers at dawn." Then he turned to Umnesilk. "Tradition demands I have your head. You know this and why it must be so."

Umnesilk nodded, his head held high, but Seanchai stepped forward, shaking off Narasilk's grip. Arad'gug glared at him, but the elf met the contempt in the big boar's eyes.

"Not pictorian," was all Arad'gug said and slightly turned away.

"No" Seanchai said, moving with him, so they still faced each other, eyes locked. "Not pictorian, Wycaan Master." His voice carried across the tent "And the one who vanquished the Master who enslaved you."

There was a murmur around the tent, but Seanchai kept his eyes firmly on the new leader. "Arad'gug, First Boar. I have proved myself a friend in battle to the pictorians many times. It is I who, together with the prince, came north to fight alongside Umnesilk and the pictorians. It is I who set your people free at the dwarf capitol of Hothengold."

"Show me, now, your gratitude. Show me that you are a friend of the prince and the Wycaan. Show your people that you have the wisdom to rule. Give me Umnesilk, that he may serve me with honor and show the rest of Odessiya the ferocity of a pictorian warrior. Bind him to me, and I will be your ally, as I am his. Bind him to me and I have a great gift, worthy of the First Boar of all pictorians. What say you?"

Arad'gug thought for a moment. "So be it. You take Umnesilk, his mate, and pictorye as sign we allies. They not dead, but exile. Do not bring them back even if you mighty Wycaan."

Seanchai turned to Narasilk and took the double-headed axe. "What better way for the First Boar of the Pictorians to enter a battle wielding the mighty weapon of his oppressor? Behold, the axe of the vanquished Emperor." He raised it above his head and cried out. "Arad'gug, First Boar of the Pictorians, show wisdom to your people and vengeance to your enemies."

Arad'gug took the great axe and examined the beautiful silver shaft and gleaming blades at either end. He raised it in the air and cried: *Ungallah! Ungallah! Ungallah!* The entire tent cried out with him.

Seanchai turned to Umnesilk, his face again tight.

"Be prepared. We leave at dawn."

Chapter Fifty Two

Mharina's mind was in turmoil as she struggled to drag the heavy body. Sa'gola led them deeper into the mountain, and the young elfe felt both terror and exhilaration at the same moment. She had killed a man. That was surely bad, even though he had been attacking Sa'gola. But she had done it with her own fire. She had *ignited her own flame* as her teacher had urged her to do so many times.

They were each dragging a leg and Ithea's head was bouncing unceremoniously off stones protruding from the otherwise smooth path. It was getting very hot, and sweat streamed down Mharina's face. Her soaked shirt stuck to her body. Sa'gola, eyes hard and grimly focused, walked next to her, but in another place, and, judging by her expression, it was a very dark memory.

"I need to rest a moment," Mharina said at last, dropping the leg she dragged. "Is there any water down here?"

"No, child – only fire."

"Where are we taking his body?"

Sa'gola started to stretch, but gasped when the welts on her back pulled and fresh blood appeared on her torn dress. "We will give him to the mountain's fire. It is the only way to ensure that he…"

Mharina stared at her and then at Ithea's body. Abruptly, she knelt and checked for a pulse. There was none.

"He's dead," she said, hearing the fear in her own voice.

"And the mountain fire is so hot at its heart that it will ensure he stays that way."

Mharina suppressed the urge to ask more questions. Now she wanted to get rid of the body as soon as she could. She picked up a leg, and Sa'gola followed suit.

It was impossible to judge how long they dragged the body down this endless path, but finally Sa'gola stopped and pointed through a thin corridor. Mharina was not sure the body would fit.

Sa'gola went first and began pulling. Mharina tried to push, but did not have much leverage. She switched to squishing Ithea's body parts to get them through. She twisted his head, and it passed. Then, with considerable effort, she turned his shoulders. Gradually, they squeezed Ithea's long body through the crevice, and Mharina followed him through.

They stood on a precipice, staring down at a bright orange glow that shimmered off the walls. Tentatively, Mharina leaned over and saw below a lake of melted rock. Her elf vision enabled her to distinguish different shades of red, orange, and black. Occasionally, the lake bubbled like a lazy burp.

"This is how the mountain was built?" she asked in a respectful whisper.

"Yes, and the entire mountain range. The rage of mountain fire is indestructible and unstoppable, and you are learning to harness its power. Come, help me."

They rolled Ithea's body over the side and watched it fall slowly toward the fire. But it stopped, suspended on a protruding ledge. Sa'gola cursed and extended her hands downwards.

The body began to rock, slowly at first, then with increasing momentum. Finally, it rolled off and disappeared, swallowed up by the darkness.

Mharina sighed with relief, but Sa'gola stared down, holding her breath.

"What is it?" Mharina whispered.

"I just wish I could hear his body splash."

Mharina leaned over, but even squinting her eyes, and with her superior elf vision, she could not see anything. She looked up at Sa'gola. The woman had a wet, red glow to her skin from the fire, and she was even more beautiful than ever. Mharina wondered if the rivulets running down her face were tears or sweat. Her eyes were still hard, but the elfe thought she discerned fear there, too, or doubt.

"Even if he didn't land in the fire lake, he is close to it. His body will decompose quickly," Mharina said.

Sa'gola did not reply, her silence deafening.

"And he is dead. I checked his pulse. There was no beat."

Still nothing.

"Sa'gola. He's dead, right?" Mharina heard the fear in her own voice. "Who was he, Sa'gola?"

The woman turned and picked up the hem of her dress to wipe her face, revealing bloody knees and scrapes all down her legs. Mharina reached out.

"Let's return to your quarters. I'll tend your wounds." She put her arms around the woman, who suddenly seemed very petite. A wave of emotion crested as she pulled the woman to her, and her own voice shook as she whispered in the sorceress' ear. "I will take care of you. This won't happen again. I'll protect you."

It sounded absurd and childish, even to Mharina's young ears, but she meant every word.

It was still nighttime, Mharina surmised. The corridors were empty, the castle and its inhabitants still asleep. They reached Sa'gola's rooms without encountering anyone. Mharina gently guided the woman to sit on the edge of the bed. Then she pumped water into Sa'gola's stone tub.

Sa'gola loved her bath. The mountain heated the water, and the woman had told Mharina that she spent time every day in the water. She had shown Mharina an array of ground minerals that she used to relax and keep her skin smooth.

Mharina picked one up, but Sa'gola tutted, the first sound she had uttered in a long while. The elfe put it down, moved her hand to another, and received the same tut. Finally, she poured a small sack of purple minerals into the tub. They soon evaporated, and a warm, inviting aroma filled the room.

When the tub was full enough, she moved to her teacher, gently pulling her to her feet, and began to undress her. The material of Sa'gola's dress was thin and stuck to congealing blood. Sa'gola did not make a sound, but her body tensed as Mharina slowly peeled the material from her body.

The new wounds crisscrossed with the faded scars, and Mharina felt a wave of sadness for her powerful teacher. She helped her into the tub, and Sa'gola sunk under the water. Finally, her face resurfaced.

"If you are tired, you may go sleep," she said quietly when Mharina yawned involuntarily.

"No. I want to salve your wounds. Besides, I'm not sure I can sleep right now."

"It was quite a night, my child."

"Sa'gola. What just happened? Who was Ithea?"

Even as she said it, she wondered if *was* had been the correct tense to use.

CHAPTER FIFTY THREE

Marina woke, stiff and cold. She had lain down to sleep wrapped in a blanket on the cold floor in Sa'gola's chambers. The fire had gone out, and the blanket had rolled around her, exposing her bare legs to the rock ground.

Sa'gola was asleep, her black hair splayed on a white pillow. With her eyes closed, she looked so innocent and young. Mharina stared at her. She had an overwhelming desire to take care of this small woman, but she needed to remember who Sa'gola was. The image of the woman walking through the tutan ambush, spreading her fire and killing many men, filled her head. The fear and respect that the tough taragusii had for her were clear.

Mharina wrote a short note – *taking twins to breakfast; will return immediately* – and closed the door quietly behind her. As her bare feet skipped along the cool stone floor, memories of the previous night flooded. She had killed someone, a powerful, evil man, a cruel beast who had beaten Sa'gola.

She wondered why Sa'gola had not fought back, and her thoughts focused, almost unwillingly, on who Ithea had been. As she neared her own rooms, she forced the thoughts from her mind.

"Where have you been?" Ilan demanded, sitting up in bed. "We were worried about you."

Senzia, sitting at the table with a half-eaten purple fruit in her hand, laughed. "That is not quite how I remember it."

Mharina felt a wave of comfort engulf her, and she grabbed her sister, hugging her fiercely.

Senzia pulled away and stared at her. "What happened?"

Mharina tried to smile, but faltered. "The training is long and intense. I guess I fell asleep in Sa'gola's rooms."

Ilan had joined them at the table, unaware anything was wrong. "We train hard, as well," he said. "Look at this."

He proudly flourished a multicolored bruise.

"You weren't so proud when Master Sythen gave it to you," Senzia said, and rolled her eyes.

"Let's go eat," Mharina laughed. "I need to return to Sa'gola."

"Ilan," Senzia said. "Go brush your teeth."

The boy pouted at being commanded by his twin sister. Still, he went. Senzia leaned forward.

"Mharina. Are you getting too close to her?"

"What do you mean?"

"I mean, she is not only dangerous, but deceptive. I sense great power, but also great hurt. I think—"

"What do you mean, you *sense*?" It was the way that her sister said this that had startled her.

Senzia glanced over to make sure Ilan was occupied. "It doesn't matter. I am enjoying my studies here, believe me, but we need to reach out to Denalion."

"Sa'gola won't harm us," Mharina protested. "She cares about—"

Senzia covered Mharina's hand with hers and suddenly looked so much older. "She serves this master and will do his bidding. She will kill our parents and whoever else is coming to rescue us. There seem to be plenty of other powerful people and creatures here, as well. I hear the Wycaans at the meal tables." Again, she glanced to the side room, where Ilan was about to exit. She leaned further forward. "Can you find the Anwar and use it?"

"I...I'm..."

"I thought so. It's okay. I will take care of it. I think you're having the tougher training, even if we have the bruises."

As Ilan walked out, Mharina's eyes filled with tears, and the words tumbled out.

"Bruises? I just killed a man."

When Mharina returned to Sa'gola's quarters, she found her teacher in the bathtub. The steaming water was green, and Mharina laughed.

"What's so funny, child?" Sa'gola sounded tired, but was making an effort to be upbeat.

"You look like a little purple bud in a bush of green leaves."

"Has my face paint smeared?" She ducked under the water before Mharina could respond. When she surfaced, she looked critically at her student. "You've been crying, my sweet. Fires! I've been so self-indulged. Here, take those clothes off and get into the bath. There is plenty of room, and the herbs will invigorate you."

Mharina felt shy as she removed her garments. But they were sweaty, and she raised them to her nose and wrinkled her face.

"Do they smell of fire?" Sa'gola asked, her tone abruptly serious. "Burn them. Throw them in the fire now."

"I could wash—"

"Now, Mharina. Burn them. All of them."

Mharina removed her underclothes and did as she was told. Then she walked quickly over and climbed into the tub. Sa'gola moved to accommodate her, and they lay, all but their heads submerged, arm and leg touching.

Mharina closed her eyes, and the tears erupted in erratic, uncontrolled sobs. Sa'gola moved and put her arm around the *calhei*, pulling her head until it cradled on the woman's chest. She whispered words that didn't make sense to Mharina, who just let the pain flow out of her.

It felt cleansing. The water became warmer, and, finally, the tears stopped. Mharina, eyes still closed, became conscious of the woman's breast against her, and her mind filled with thoughts of her mother. Somehow, this felt wrong, as though she was doing something that would hurt her mother's feelings.

She sat up and sniffed. Sa'gola watched her as she turned around in the bathtub, water sloshing over the top.

"Would you prefer to talk here or somewhere else?" Sa'gola asked, and Mharina wondered, not for the first time, if the woman could read her mind.

Mharina did not want to relinquish the warm, soft water. "Here is good."

"What do you want to know?"

"A lot," Mharina let out a nervous laugh. "But I don't know where to start."

"We don't need to cover everything in one go," Sa'gola replied, sitting up straighter, once again the teacher. "I am teaching you to use the elements, much as your father does. The Wycaans master the elements through words from their ancient language. Obviously, I don't understand it completely, but they have access to the power behind the words, when we see or hear only the word in our own languages.

"We channel the power through the moon. I think it is why only females can connect in this way. We can use these powers as you saw last night, but also to fold time and space. Do you remember how I appeared in the middle of the fight with the tutan?"

Mharina nodded, her mind reeling.

"You find this prospect exciting, I see. I fear that I'll teach you much, grow to love you, and, yet, you will escape me."

Mharina squirmed, and then, as she looked at Sa'gola, she could simply not bring herself to lie.

"If I could have it my way, my *ahdahr* would come, defeat this master, and free us. Then he would allow you to come back to Wycaan Island and be with me and teach me."

Sa'gola laughed. "Thank you for being honest, Mharina. It means a lot to me, and so do you. But happy endings can be very elusive."

Chapter Fifty Four

Sellia knew something was wrong as soon as she stepped outside and her eyes adjusted to the glare of the sun. Everything looked different, smelled different. The shack that they had slept in was still the same, but looked somehow out of place.

The trees were gone, and there was a forest in the distance. She turned sharply and saw the great mountain range behind her, but no sign of the fortress. In fact, the mountains looked somehow…cleaner, younger.

A wave of terror rose inside of her, and she felt challenged to breathe. Her hand moved to her chest, and she ran to a clump of nearby bushes and vomited. When she returned, she entered the hut and took her water skin.

The light began to stir the others while Sellia returned outside and washed her mouth and face. She began to breathe as she had seen Seanchai do countless times. No magical energy came to her, but she calmed down, and, by the time the others had come outside, she was ready to face them.

She sat on a rock a short distance away and watched as they squinted, went to relieve themselves, and gradually realized that something had gone terribly wrong. The three of them stood, conferring and gesticulating. Riona left the others and came to sit next to Sellia, while Pyre and Montclair drew their swords and went off in the opposite direction.

"Where are they going?" Sellia asked.

"To check things out and establish a perimeter. Are you okay?"

Sellia thought for a moment. "Whenever I was in dangerous situations before, death didn't worry me. Before Seanchai, I would dream of being reunited with my former mate, Dyrovas, and, even afterwards, it felt kind of noble: dying in service to the Wycaan. But now…" She paused and slowly shook her head.

"Now there is more at stake," Riona finished for her. "I think I know what you mean."

"Montclair?"

"The scoundrel, yes. I will blame him for this, too."

They both laughed, and Riona put her arm around Sellia. They sat together in silence until Montclair and Pyre returned. They both held dripping water skins, but neither was smiling.

"Well, the good news is that we seem to be alone here," Montclair said. "There is a waterhole and enough animal footprints to suggest we can hunt. Other than that…"

He scratched his head, realizing he had nothing more to add. Pyre gave Sellia her water skin, and the dark elfe gulped some water down. Then she wiped her mouth on her sleeve and looked up at Montclair.

"Other than that?"

Montclair exchanged glances with Pyre, and it was the young elfe who spoke this time.

"We don't have a clue where we are. It is so strange, yet so familiar."

They heard the sound of rumbling approaching, and then trumpeting. The four of them ran, half-crouching, into the nearby brush. There, they settled down, bows already noched, blades at the ready.

Slowly, a herd of beasts came into view. They were big, hairy and six-legged. Their necks were long, but they kept their heads low, weighed down by a single, twisted horn. The young, hornless creatures darted around awkwardly, their young enthusiasm too fast for their six legs.

"What in the goddess's name are those?" Montclair asked.

"I've seen these, or at least, pictures of them," Pyre said. "I think they are rhinosaurs or unisaurs, or something like that. They are extinct, but maintain a place in our stories."

"They don't look too extinct to me," Montclair declared. "Are they tasty?"

"You can't hunt them!" Riona exclaimed.

"Why not?"

"They're almost extinct."

Sellia looked at her. "Riona, they *are* extinct. We are trapped in a time prior to our own. Look. The fortress should be over there, and a forest in front of it. The mountain is jagged at its peaks, and hasn't experienced a serious eruption yet."

"How did we get here?" Riona asked.

"Good question," Sellia answered. "It doesn't seem the Emperor's style. He would have just imprisoned or killed us, I think. It might be the sorceress or some other creature with magic. I'm not sure the taragusii and the sorceress are all he has on his side."

"Why go to all this trouble though?" Montclair asked. "Looks pretty complicated to me – not that I understand magic."

"You're right, Sellia," Pyre answered, staring off at the herd. "The sorceress said she was training Mharina and that the twins were receiving instruction from Wycaans. Having us in the castle without the children knowing might prove difficult, and then maybe they wouldn't be such cooperative students."

"How would they discover us unless they are kept in the dungeons, too?" Montclair asked.

"The twins will be learning how to scry, I imagine," Pyre answered. "As for Mharina, we don't know what she might be learning, but, judging by what we see around us, I have a feeling it might be something very powerful, and I have little doubt Mharina will make an excellent student once she agrees to learn."

They all looked at Sellia, who had pulled her legs up to her chest and rested her chin on her knees. There were tears welling in her eyes.

"We have to get back," she whispered. "We can't just survive here and wait. He might never discover we are here or how to get us out."

Chapter Fifty Five

The red-winged eagle soared again above Odessiya. He had only planned to dreamwalk from his cave, but as soon as he entered the spirit world, he sensed a momentous change — a new energy — and needed to discover its source.

And so he took his eagle form, for it was swift and strong. He rode the wind streams, rested on hot air currents, and tore his way across the land. He glided from one thermal to another across the desert and soon spied the fishing port of Braithwaite, where they had met Montclair. It was a mere dot by the expanse of blue, the sea continuing beyond the eagle's keen eyesight.

The ice bear entered his mind and told of the great battle in the north and the disappearance of the firebreather. The Wycaan had led the offensive and won. Now he was hurrying south, often changing into bear form to speed his way.

Briefly, the eagle felt the presence of the firebreather, a cacophony of pain and rage. It was wounded, but not defeated. Its plan was unfolding, despite the setback. Beneath its struggle to maintain form and flight, and its anger at being outsmarted, lay a smug confidence that scared the eagle. For a brief moment the firebreather seemed aware of his presence and he drew back quickly.

Denalion woke up, panting. He stared up into the concerned face of Ricard's mother. She offered him a water skin.

"I fear I have kept you awake," he said at last. "My apologies."

She smiled, and took the hem of her tattered dress to mop his sweaty brow. He began to protest, but she moved a finger to her mouth and shushed him.

"It takes so much out of you, old one. Must you do this so often?"

"I must," he replied. "It remains all that I am good for."

"Are you really as old as you say?"

He laughed, but it became a sigh. "Probably older. Why are you here?"

"When I got near the village, the taragusii were tearing down houses and gathering people in the square. They planted their tendrils in a few of the women. They were looking for something, perhaps whoever killed the governor."

"What happens when they pierce you with their tendrils?"

"They see everything in your mind, and you often die from the intensity, the violation. They didn't seem to find what they wanted. I waited in the bushes."

"It was only the women they questioned?"

"Yes, and that made me wonder if they might be looking for me. I fear returning there."

"I am sorry. Hopefully this will be over soon." He grew uncomfortable under her stare. "I must step outside a moment and then try again."

"Twice in one night? That can't be safe." She had a worried look in her eyes.

"Probably not. Nonetheless, I walk the road I chose and do so in love."

He rose, and she reached out a hand to steady him. He almost jerked away in annoyance, seeing it as a reminder of his age, but it had been a caring gesture and he restrained himself.

When he returned, she gave him more water and some dried goat meat.

"Where did you get this?" he asked.

"Every family has a secret stash out in the woods. It's the times we live in."

He nodded as he chewed. Then he lay down again and closed his eyes.

The red-winged owl hooted down from its branch at the grizzly that was lapping at a stream, its thick tongue rolling water into its mouth.

"Seanchai. You do that very…well…very bear-ish." He hooted a chuckle, but stopped when the bear looked up. "You look terrible, my friend."

"I don't sleep much, Dreamwalker. Did you tell Maugwen to slip me a potion?"

"You must sleep," the red owl replied.

"My children—"

"—will not be rescued if their father arrives exhausted. I counseled Sellia in just the same way. Your children, as much as we can discern, are being well taken care of. The one who has them is kind, and there are Wycaans who train the twins. There is no need to hurry on their account."

"Are you with Sellia? Who else is there?"

"Sellia, Pyre, Riona and a fortune-sword have broken into the fortress to rescue the children and find a way to contact you."

"What?"

"Seanchai. I will try and reach them when we finish, but every attempt to reach someone risks my revelation to the sorceress."

"Sorceress? What are you talking about? Wait. There are Wycaans there?"

"I know very little, but Mharina is training with the sorceress, and yes, there are Wycaans. I am concerned for Sellia and the others."

"It will take me weeks to arrive," Seanchai said, "but it might take the Emperor longer if I inflicted any serious damage."

"He will heal quickly," the dreamwalker said, "I am not even sure how you can kill him at this point. Listen, Seanchai. I grow weary. Hear my council: I will seek out those inside the castle and let you know what I hear. Pace yourself and those with you unless I tell you otherwise."

"I will try," Seanchai replied. "I need to know how many are in the fortress."

"You will bring an army? Prince Shayth's?"

"No."

"The dwarves of Hothengold?"

"No," Seanchai repeated. "I want to know how many I will have to kill if any harm comes to my family."

"The Emperor will be there, the sorceress, the taragussi, and other Wycaans. You cannot come alone."

Seanchai frowned. "There are many reasons why Wycaans don't usually wed. History records the wrath that many have brought upon the people, but never has the land seen the wrath of a Wycaan ahdahr. If any harm has come to my children, well, it will be better if no friend is anywhere near."

Chapter Fifty Six

Ablack and white flycatcher chirped as it flew past, rolling in an arc to catch an insect in flight. Master Willowood and the twins sat in a small courtyard with a pond to their left, some ripening fruit trees to their right, and a sandy bed in front of them that someone had taken great care to rake in a wavy pattern.

"Look at this book," the elderly Wycaan elfe said, offering a thick tome that Ilan needed two hands to hold.

Though Master Willowood was old, her face was smooth, her ears beautifully pointed, and her hair a healthy white. She had told Senzia that she needed to work to keep her good looks and had laughed loudly. Senzia had thought of Denalion and how old he was. She was both impressed and intrigued.

"Are you as strong as Master Sythen?" she asked.

The old elfe frowned. "We are strong in different ways. But Master Sythen and I would not fight each other. We have been friends for many, many moons."

"My *ahdahr*, then?" Ilan said.

"Your father is apparently a proficient Wycaan by all accounts, but he is young and not without weaknesses."

"Weaknesses?" Ilan screwed up his face in a frown.

"Of course," the old elfe replied, stroking his arm. "You and your beautiful sisters, for starters." She laughed again. " But enough idle chitchat. Come, read from the book."

"Why? We all know how to read."

"But I want to hear you, and this is a special book."

Ilan sighed. "Okay. But this is a children's book, and we can read more grown up stories."

"Humor me, young *calhei*."

"Okay. 'He looked out over the valley and called to the wind spirit. *Moriarhtur, Moriarhtur,* I summon you.'"

"Excellent, and do you see the word *Moriarhtur* as well, Senzia?"

"Of course I do," Senzia said scornfully. "That is what is written there."

"My dear *calhei*, nothing is ever as it might seem." She looked up. A young woman was picking a few oranges from a tree nearby. "Come here, please," Master Willowood called, beckoning with a thin, spindly hand.

The girl hesitated, put her basket down, and ran over. "The purple lady sent me to pick the oranges, Master," she blurted, bowing deeply.

"And I'm sure you're doing a marvelous job. Can you read, child?"

"Yes, but not well, milady."

"Read this to us, please," Master Willowood said, thrusting out the book. "Just a few sentences."

The girl took the book, and Senzia could not be sure whether the weight of the tome or fear made it shake. "'H-he looked out over the v-valley and called to the wind spirit. Wind Spirit, Wind Spirit, I summon you.'"

Ilan went to correct her, but Master Willowood intervened. "Thank you, child, that is all. If the Lady Sa'gola questions you taking too long, by all means tell her I detained you."

"Thank you, Master." The girl curtsied and fled back to the trees.

"Will Sa'gola punish her?" Senzia asked.

The old elfe shrugged. "No one would dare be late for the purple lady without good reason. She is not to be trifled with. Studying with her, your sister has both a great opportunity and at the same time flirts with great danger."

"I think Sa'gola is beautiful," Ilan said.

"There's no question about that, *calhei*, but remember, nothing is ever what it seems. Now, you were quick to notice that the girl read the word Wind Spirit, for this is what she saw. She did not make a mistake, which is why I stopped you from correcting her.

"We saw the word *Moriarhtur*, which means Wind Spirit in the ancient language. Now, watch this."

Master Willowood stared at the sand bed in front of them and began repeating the word over and over again. "*Moriarhtur, Moriarhtur, Moriarhtur.*"

Slowly, the sand began to move – first only the grains on top, but then layers of sand – like the sandstorm they had encountered on the way here. Then Master Willowood lifted her hands and moved them in intricate circles. The sand spiraled up into a column before she let it settle again.

"What was that?" Ilan exclaimed, his eyes bulging.

"That was an old elfe showing off," Willowood said and laughed. "But it was also the foundation of Wycaan magic."

"We do magic?" Ilan asked, and Senzia noted his use of the word 'we'.

"It is not really magic. We direct the elements. Nature holds the power; we just leverage it."

She turned to the pond. "*Agamai, Agamai, Agamai,*" she chanted and again moved her hands upwards. A small fountain spouted for a little while.

When she turned back to the twins, Senzia saw her cheeks were flushed, and offered the old elfe a water skin.

"Thank you, my dear *calhei,*" Master Willowood said. "Now, you have work to do."

"Don't!" Mharina whispered when she and her sister were alone in their room. "It's too dangerous, and she is…"

"Is what?"

"Vulnerable right now. You saw how I was when I returned to you the other morning. Sa'gola is much worse. It wouldn't be fair—"

"Fair! Do you hear yourself?" Senzia frowned. "Listen. All you need to do is keep her busy. Stay at the waterfall as long as you can. That is all I ask. I'll take care of the rest."

"I don't think the Anwar is even there. She had it underground before."

"There is only one way to find out. I will be careful and quick. There is no chance she will find me."

"Senzia. She is very powerful. I have seen…"

Senzia thought of the Wycaan teacher's words: *No one would dare be late for the purple lady without good reason. She is not to be trifled with.*

"I'll be fine," she replied, but gulped.

Chapter Fifty Seven

"What are you doing, child? These are my rooms. You enter only with my permission."

Even though she was a small woman, Sa'gola cut an imposing image. She stood in the doorway, her hands on her tiny hips, shoulders hunched up.

Senzia turned slowly, taking time to force her breathing under control. She stared at the sorceress and suddenly felt very foolish. She had not prepared a cover story despite anticipating that she would be caught.

Their eyes locked, and it took all of Senzia's self-control not to look away. It was Sa'gola who relented, removing her hands from her hips and entering the room. She moved toward a table that overlooked the courtyard.

"Since you are having trouble coming up with a plausible excuse, I suggest you tell me the truth. The Master commands me to protect you, so how will I explain why I turned you into a cockroach or a guinea pig."

Despite herself, Senzia giggled.

"Bring the water pitcher and two glasses," Sa'gola said and sat down in one of two comfortable chairs next to a small table.

Though she was as graceful as ever, Senzia saw that the sorceress walked stiffly and carefully. She brought the water and poured a glass for Sa'gola, then for herself.

"Are you well?" she asked, trying to divert Sa'gola's attention.

"You and your sister are very courteous," she said by way of an answer. "Is this the way of all elves?"

Senzia shrugged. "It is the way we were brought up. I have not met many elves."

"So, why were you in my rooms?"

The elfe took a long sip of water, considering her answer. "Master Sythen says we should make everything a teachable moment. Let's see if you can work it out for yourself."

Sa'gola arched a purple-tinged eyebrow. "If I play your game, then you must promise to answer truthfully."

Senzia nodded, oddly intrigued by what she had set in motion.

"There is something in my rooms that you want. Something that you think will give you power."

Sa'gola paused, waiting for confirmation.

"Correct on the first. Incorrect on the second." Senzia leaned forward.

The woman frowned as she sipped her water.

"You are worried for your sister. You want to see if you can find out what she is learning and what happened to her the other night."

Senzia twisted a strand of her white hair. "I am worried about what you are doing to Mharina, but that is not my motivation right now."

Sa'gola smiled. "You seek something that I possess that will help you escape." Senzia didn't even have a chance to respond before Sa'gola slapped the table, upsetting her cup. "You saw me use the stone when we were traveling here. You want my Anwar."

Senzia pursed her lips and nodded. It had been so easy.

"What would you do once you found and understood the stone? Who would you contact?"

"You have discovered my goal. The game is finished. I don't have to answer."

Sa'gola pushed, unfazed. "Does your father have an Anwar? Or maybe the dreamwalker?"

Silence. Senzia picked up her glass and gulped water, sloshing a few drops onto her chin and shirt. She could feel Sa'gola reaching out to her mind with slow, soft movements. She felt an irrational urge to let her in to share whatever she wanted.

Guard your mind, Pyre had told her once while they had sparred on Wycaan Island. *If your opponent gets past your sword, there might be time to recover or limit the damage. But if they get past your mind, then all is lost.*

She missed Pyre. They had been special friends, sharing secrets. Was she dead on Wycaan Island? She would surely have fought the taragusii to defend the *calhei*.

Sa'gola tapped her long, purple-painted fingernails on the table.

"Is she an older sister?"

"Who?" Senzia asked, frantically setting up the walls in her mind that she had practiced with Pyre.

"The elfe. She trained and played with you. Is she your sister?"

"No. She was a friend of my *ahdahr*."

"Was?"

"She was on Wycaan Island when the taragusii attacked."

"You chew your lips when you are upset. I have noticed. You must learn to better mask your emotions when they make you vulnerable. Not all who were on that piece of rock died in the attack, my dear."

Senzia stared at her. "Pyre is alive? She is here, or on her way?"

"I never said that, child."

"You may not chew your lips, Sa'gola, but your eyes dart around while you search for a lie."

Sa'gola chuckled. "Very good. I shall work on that. I propose a trade of information. Why were you after the Anwar?"

"You first. I'm only a *calhei*. You're an adult. You need to set an example."

Sa'gola consented amicably. "Okay. Your friend Pyre has two Win Dao swords and a bow. She is a natural-born Wycaan, but her hair is not Wycaan white. She has not succeeded in completing her...what do you call it? Her transformation. Her eyes are not yet blue, either. I think something is holding her back."

"All that, I know," Senzia rolled her eyes. "What do you want me to tell you about the Anwar: that it is black and you can use it to communicate with another who has an Anwar?"

Sa'gola laughed again. "I like you, Senzia, I really do. But you are impulsive and did not allow me to finish. I was simply confirming that I have the right elfe. What I will impart to you is that she is alive and has hopes of rescuing you."

Senzia let out a deep sigh. "Thank you," she said. "I have had nightmares about her dying."

"Your turn now. On your honor."

Senzia took another deep drink of water. "I was trying to find the Anwar in order to connect with my *ahdahr*. He has a set of dwarf stones. Once, he accidentally entered a conversation between the Emperor and his general, and discovered that the Emperor planned to attack the dwarf capital."

"Good. That was an honest exchange. Now, for your information, I have wards around my room, similar to what you erected around your mind just before. Yes, I felt it. So you cannot enter without me knowing. Next time, you should just ask."

"Would you have let me see it?"

"Possibly, but you couldn't use it without the Master's permission. Would you like to ask him?"

Senzia almost answered yes. She was desperate to see her father, but if Sa'gola was offering her this, it could not be a good thing for him.

Then a large smile stretched across Senzia's face. "No I don't need to speak to my *ahdahr* anymore."

"Why not? You went to all this trouble."

"I went to all this trouble so that I could tell him we are here and ask him to come rescue us. But if you are willing for me to talk with him, it means he already knows. Thank you. You were right from the beginning. I should have just asked."

Sa'gola's face went from smiling to scowling to a hostile glare. She rose. "Thank you for your concern about my well-being."

Senzia walked smugly to the doorway, but then something occurred to her. She turned around. Sa'gola was now smiling, but it was strained.

"You said that Pyre is hoping to rescue me. Is she here?"

"She is an incomplete Wycaan. Master Sythen and the others would make short work of her. You should hope she isn't."

"Is she here?" Senzia asked again.

Sa'gola's smile pursed and her eyes glinted cruelly.

"Yes…and no. Goodnight, Senzia."

Chapter Fifty Eight

"Promise me you will not go alone, Wycaan," Prince Shindell said as they stood in the early morning gray. A young squire brought them both a steaming, dark beverage, its bitterness masked unsuccessfully by spices. Seanchai's was grateful for the warmth it provided, but he eyed the young man with suspicion. He was still jarred, not only by the discovery that his children and maybe Sellia were captive, but that there were still many in Shayth's court still loyal to the Emperor.

"Seanchai? If you do not promise me, I will drop everything and come with you."

"You must finish this battle. The Ice Clans run from something they fear as much as the Emperor. You must find out what it is and prepare."

"Then you promise?"

"I have Umnesilk and Narasilk with me. Even a Wycaan can't outrun a pictorian."

Both boars were already packed and waiting nearby. They stood, towering and impatient to leave, both agitated and full of energy.

"Maybe an elf cannot outrun them," Shayth replied, also staring at the huge boars, "but a bear could."

"Probably," Seanchai had absolutely considered transforming for the journey, especially since they would have to trek below the snowline before they could mount horses. He did not, however, respond to Shayth.

The prince continued. "Rhoddan will go with you, too. I have sent instructions to Shindellia to prepare troops to join you from there. Once this force returns to the capital, I will come with more men.

Shayth sipped his drink. "I have also sent word to the dwarves in Hothengold. I am sure Ballendir would appreciate an opportunity to spend time with you."

"Thank you," Seanchai said. "Denalion suggested last night that your uncle might not garrison a large number, but that some may be Wycaans. I don't understand who they are or why they side with him."

"Seanchai," Shayth ruffled his spiky hair, even more unruly at this hour. "It might be that you have not read all of the Wycaan histories."

"What do you mean?"

"Wycaans are highly trained and special, but carry the same flaws as the rest of us."

"There are good Wycaans and bad?" Seanchai was shocked by this idea.

"Well, let's face it: we know you, Mhari, Master Oxynei, and my uncle. That's only three-quarters good, and, frankly, I have my doubts about you."

Seanchai frowned at him, but Shayth was smiling and shaking his head. "All that training, all those great masters, and no one could teach you a sense of humor."

The prince sobered again. "You cannot arrive at Grogin alone and tired. You don't know what you will face, discounting my dear uncle."

Seanchai nodded, then frowned as he saw Maugwen approaching, a pile of bags on her shoulders. She stopped by Narasilk, who took the two biggest from her and strapped them to the horses.

"What is she doing?" Seanchai asked.

"She is joining you, at my request."

"You have more need of her. The battle here is not done and—"

"She is a skillful healer, but that is not the only reason I have asked her to go with you."

Seanchai waited expectantly for an answer.

"There is more to her than we know — than even she knows. She heals with energy, Seanchai. She might be of great service to you, and I don't mean with salves and bandages. I wouldn't send her from me lightly."

There was something in Shayth's tone that surprised Seanchai. But he never got the chance to pursue it.

"Whatcha boys gossiping about?" Maugwen asked as she approached. "Have you given him the bad news, Shayth?"

"I have commanded him to take you on pain of execution," Shayth taunted her back.

She laughed, took his steaming cup, and sipped. Seanchai shivered, remembering how Ilana would do this to him. He looked from the prince to the healer and back again. Two dear and wonderful friends.

"Finish your conversation, then," she replied. "I'll go hang with my two new friends."

They watched her walk over to the pictorians. She looked so small compared to the huge boars, but they were clearly the more intimidated.

"Shayth?" Seanchai began.

"Just go," the prince interrupted. "I will come as soon as I can." He patted Seanchai's arm and walked away.

They rested halfway down a steep gorge that would take them out of pictorian territory. The going had been slow and frustrating. The horses, burdened with supplies, were having the hardest time. Breaks were short because of the cold, and both Seanchai and Rhoddan were constantly massaging the horses before they restarted. The pictorians had offered to help, but they were too rough.

Here, Seanchai used his energy to warm some water. Maugwen added a few herbs, mint leaves, and something red and fiery that warmed their insides.

Seanchai sat alone, staring down into the valley before them. Even there, a white blanket covered everything. He was done with the snow, and his thoughts went to Wycaan Island, where, despite a distinct change of seasons, there was never harsh weather.

He thought of his children and Sellia incessantly, but now his mind went to those who had been on the island. He wondered how many had been butchered and whether their passing had been quick or torturous. He felt a deep sense of failure, and every time he glanced at Rhoddan, he sensed harsh judgment from his friend. Rhoddan would not openly accuse him, but it was there in his eyes.

"What are you playing with?" Maugwen approached with a cup in either hand.

He glanced down, unaware that he had taken the dwarf stones out of their pouch. "These were given to me by the priestess at the Borden Mountains." He held up the green one, clearly cut in half. Ilana had given the other half to Sellia. "I can find Sellia using this."

"How?"

Seanchai felt stupid. "Um. I don't know exactly. We've never had a cause to use it."

"Smart guy," Maugwen said, sipping her drink. "Those swords you wear - do you know how to sharpen them?"

She was joking but Seanchai just stared at his blades. "They never need sharpening. Wycaan perk."

She feigned a grimace. "Does your quiver refill itself with arrows?"

"It does."

"For real?"

Seanchai nodded.

"Must be pretty easy being a Wycaan," she said.

He turned and stared at her. She was trying to lift his spirits but he did not respond. Just then, Rhoddan called over for them to leave.

"Seanchai," Maugwen said, her tone serious now. She nodded over to Rhoddan as she stood up. "I know it's hard for you, but you aren't the only one hurting."

Chapter Fifty Nine

Seanchai couldn't believe he was actually missing the pure, white snow, but now the constant sleet dripping under his clothes made him irritable. If there was anything to look at on either side of the path, he could not tell. Thick fog rolled around them, and the ground beneath them was wet and stony. They might have been riding in a stream, for all Seanchai knew.

They should have taken a break, but, without shelter, no one seemed compelled to stop. It was a mistake, not for the riders, but the horses – particularly those that bore the pictorians. Everyone had two horses and alternated riding them each day. But Umnesilk and Narasilk switched horses when they broke for lunch so no horse would bear a pictorian for more than a few hours.

Umnesilk's black stallion had slipped on the rocks and gone lame. They ate fresh meat that night, but no one enjoyed the feast. After that, the pictorian took Maugwen's second horse; she was light enough to ride her mare every day it was surmised. Both pictorians also ran alongside their horses for long periods in the morning and again later in the day.

Seanchai could not get Umnesilk to speak to him. The former First Boar was brooding and refused to respond. Most times he rode in silence at the front of the party with Narasilk by his side.

"What will happen to his family while he's here?" Maugwen asked.

Seanchai sighed. "They are exiled. There are several young boars, and three females, including his mate. Whenever one of his brothers died, Umnesilk adopted their offspring. It consolidated his power base and kept his warriors loyal, knowing he would take care of their mates and pictorye should the worst happen.

"Shayth will take them with him when he heads back to Shindellia. For now, I think they will live within his camp."

"If Umnesilk had been executed, would they still have had to leave?" Maugwen asked.

"I was wondering that, too."

"You stirred things up," Maugwen grinned. "Just like old times."

"I wasn't going to let them kill him. He's a great leader. Even if he's not First Boar, the clans are weaker for his absence. It's stup–"

He reined up his horse sharply. The pictorians had stopped up ahead, and Umnesilk was glaring at him.

"Our way. You respect," he growled, and, considering the matter closed, pointed to a nearby tree.

A hanging body swayed in the breeze. Even from this distance, Seanchai could see it had been badly ravaged, and, as they neared, he saw wolf prints all around. He could not distinguish any discernable features.

Umnesilk nudged his horse over to the tree and tried to reach the rope with his axe. The body was purposely high to prevent it from being cut down, Seanchai thought.

"I got it," he said, freeing his lime green bow. He pulled an arrow, noched, and released.

The body thudded to the ground. Maugwen began to dismount, but Seanchai put a hand on her arm.

"We can't do anything. Let's keep going."

They had only gone a short while before finding a second corpse. This one hung by one leg, and its head had been bludgeoned. Seanchai could see this one was a male elf. Here, too, there were tracks of predators.

At the next tree, there were two *calhei*, probably not much older than Mharina. He cut these down and looked for a way to bury them.

"Serve better to find who do this," Umnesilk said. "Let wolves feast."

"They're *calhei*," Seanchai snapped.

"They dead," the pictorian replied, his tone even. "Go on. Maybe find who and stop them."

They passed six more corpses as they approached a small stone village. All had been elves, and two had been calhei. Seanchai felt his blood boiling.

The stone houses in the village showed signs of burning and vandalism. Broken, charred doors lay strewn on the ground or swung from rusty hinges.

Seanchai dismounted and signaled for the others to remain mounted. But both pictorians ignored his signal. He looked at them and frowned.

"We not comfortable riding, why you think we fight good on horses?" Umnesilk growled.

"Our job is to protect you," Narasilk seemed anxious to relieve the tension. "We can better do this on two legs."

Seanchai nodded.

"What look for?" Umnesilk asked.

"Survivors, and whoever did this."

"Seanchai," Rhoddan called. "Is this the work of a firebreather?"

The Wycaan stared around at the destruction and carnage.

"I don't think so," he finally said. "I'm not sure the village would have been left standing."

"Unless he wanted to leave you something."

Seanchai nodded as he entered a tall, old stone building. He found arches that suggested a corridor or cloisters; broken gargoyles; and large rocks, once skillfully hewn, strewn around.

"What this place?" Umnesilk asked, coming in after him.

"I don't know. Perhaps a place of worship, or maybe a meeting hall. I think…" He paused, convinced he had heard a whimper. "I think we should leave now," he said loudly, pulling Umnesilk into the shadows of the only standing wall.

Once concealed, Seanchai closed his eyes and scryed. They were there, a dozen or so people inside a stone tomb, huddled together and shaking. He opened his eyes and watched, horrified as Maugwen came in and approached the stone cube.

"Come out, little ones. We won't harm you. There are two elves in our party, both great warriors. It's okay."

She stepped back and waited. The far side of the tomb slowly opened, stones scraping. Gradually, they crawled out, led by a young elf wielding a long knife and trying not to let it shake from fear. He darted it around at Maugwen, and then Seanchai, who rather self-consciously pushed his hair away to show his ears.

The young elf smiled in relief, and then saw the hulking pictorians. He fainted.

Chapter Sixty

"We'll camp here tonight," Seanchai told the pictorians. "Please, check the boundaries of the village. See if there are any more survivors, and make sure the scum that did this aren't around." He looked to Narasilk. "Use your horn if you need help."

"I left the horn behind," Narasilk said and stole a glare at his uncle.

"Only take weapons when exiled," Umnesilk growled.

"Then roar. Rhoddan, go with them."

Umnesilk grunted. "One stay with you."

"And what am I, then?" Maugwen feigned irritation, raising her arms and flexing non-existent muscles. Umnesilk just huffed at her attempt to break the tension.

"Not warrior," he said and strode out of the ruins.

"I should kick his butt," Maugwen said, and everyone stared at her. "Watch it," she warned, pointing a finger in a wide arc at them all.

Rhoddan, ever loyal, laughed, and even Seanchai cracked a smile. The survivors looked on, mystified.

"Do you have food?" Rhoddan asked an elfe who had two small *calhei* clutching to her tattered skirts.

"A little," she replied, wariness in her voice.

"We will not take your food," Rhoddan continued, "but neither can we share what we have. It is measured and we travel fast."

"He be the Wycaan," the elfe said, bowing her head to Seanchai. "We will feed him."

"No," Seanchai said. "You honor me more by using your food to feed your people."

The elfe stared at him, confused.

"What is your name?"

"I be Miri."

"That is my wish, Miri," Seanchai tried a reassuring smile, but it seemed to confuse her all the more. He turned away.

"Maugwen?" Seanchai asked, remembering what had transpired in the rubble. "Can you scry?"

"No, that's Wycaan magic. Do I look like you? Wouldn't mind the hair," she brushed her black, unruly locks away, "but I would need all new clothes."

Seanchai, never one to get a joke, frowned. "Then how?"

Maugwen shook her head slightly and turned to face the woman, who had moved to join their conversation.

"Who did this?" Seanchai asked her.

"There be a large band of men who wander these parts," Miri replied. "They raid elf villages, take our produce, kill our elves, and sometimes..."

"Sometimes what?" Seanchai asked grimly. Miri paused and looked at Maugwen for help.

"There are no young elfes here, are there?" Maugwen whispered.

"No," Miri answered. "It be dangerous for me to stay, but the *calhei* need someone, need me."

Seanchai kicked a rock and immediately regretted it. He winced in pain and frustration.

"The men wear uniforms," Miri said. "Faded uniforms. We think they be deserters from the Emperor's army."

Seanchai almost corrected her but realized she did not know what had happened. This village was her world. Elves had been little more than slaves, without rights or protection for centuries. It was a harsh reminder of how they had grown up living in such fear.

He walked away and sat against the base of what had once been a statue. Rhoddan came and crouched next to him.

"We can't stay here," he murmured.

"We can't leave them. I am sworn to protect our people."

"You're on a mission with a greater purpose. For once, you are entitled to put your family first. Let's try and get a message to Shayth. Perhaps he can clean up here on his way back."

Seanchai shook his head, but said nothing.

The pictorians returned, dragging a dead goat and effectively ending further conversation between Rhoddan and Seanchai.

"What did you do?" Seanchai asked. "That is—"

"Already dead," Umnesilk interrupted. "Found others and will bring. No more elves dead. No men too." He turned to his nephew. "I guard first," he said, and strode outside.

Narasilk took the goat to Miri and helped her put it over a fire she had just lit. Then he returned to Seanchai and Rhoddan.

"Must be tough being with him right now," Rhoddan commented to Narasilk about Umnesilk.

"Uncle, great pictorian. Most best First Boar. Did what he did for clans to be together."

"But you don't agree with him," Seanchai said.

"He know best. I young, I have other solutions."

"What were they?"

"Rip off Arad'gug head."

Seanchai and Rhoddan both laughed, but Narasilk did not crack a smile. "See why he First Boar and me young?"

"Umnesilk did what he thought was right and honorable," Seanchai said. "He made a huge personal sacrifice to bring the clans together. But he is too great a boar to die like that. I could not stand aside and let him throw his life away for an ancient tradition – not after all we've been through, all we've achieved. Odessiya is fragile. It will be built upon the tenacity of wise leaders, and Umnesilk is one of the greatest leaders I have met. His people will realize that in time."

He noticed Narasilk and Rhoddan were looking behind him. He swiveled to find the former First Boar standing there.

"Pictorian affair," he said.

Seanchai sprung to his feet and stared up at his friend. "Sure, but just for the record, I meant every word, and I am as proud to be that former First Boar's friend now as I ever was. Nothing has changed between us…from my perspective, at least."

Umnesilk stared at him, then lowered his head and let out a huge sigh. Immediately, he jerked his massive head back up. "Horse come," he said and wheeled around.

Seanchai, Rhoddan, and Narasilk scurried after him. By the time they caught up, Umnesilk was holding the reins of a gray stallion with one hand and flexing his knuckles on the other. The horse looked dizzy, and a man lay on the ground on his back, groaning.

"Did you just punch him?" Rhoddan asked.

"If punch man, man dead. Punch horse. Not sure why man lie there. He fall very slow."

"You punched the horse!" Rhoddan exclaimed.

"Think best to have man alive to torture."

The man sat up, holding his head, still groaning. "What happened?" he mumbled.

"He punched your horse," Maugwen said from behind them. "Keep your hand away from that sword, or my little friend here might hit you next."

Rhoddan snickered, Seanchai had to cover his mouth, and the pictorians looked at her in bewilderment. The man did, too.

"Narasilk," Maugwen said. "Please help this gentleman inside?"

With one hand, Narasilk pulled the man to his feet, wobbling and heavy-headed.

"Sure he didn't take a blow to the head?" Rhoddan asked.

"Yes," Maugwen answered. "He's drunk."

The man reached for a small water skin, popped the top, and took a deep gulp. "Yep," he said, "'n plan to stay that way, 'specially round them bears."

Chapter Sixty One

Sellia stared into the crackling fire. Whatever wood they had gathered sent up sparks that danced into dense blackness. A small, pig-like creature roasted on a spit, and Sellia's job was to prevent it from burning. Riona had dug some plump roots to cook, as well.

Riona spent her time foraging for herbs and mushrooms she recognized, building up a stock of medicinal plants. She dried them and sealed them in skins of rabbits that they had caught.

Pyre busied herself hunting and reinforcing the hut. None of them know what kind of weather to expect, but for now it was warm and pleasant. She also spent a lot of time intensely training with sword and bow.

Montclair was the most insufferable. At first, he had put considerable effort into guarding the camp and formulating escape plans. When nothing attacked and any plan for them to escape that he formulated seemed destined for failure, he became bored and irritable.

Pyre, out of sympathy, suggested that they spar together. She made thin training guards from skins, but they were unwieldy, and Montclair told her repeatedly that he was worried he might harm her.

She suggested they start slowly, and he seemed to relax when his broadsword moved rhythmically through the air. Pyre defended herself with both her Win Dao swords and matched his moves with ease. When Montclair had to stop to wipe the dripping sweat and drink, Pyre was hardly flustered, apart from a small glow on her cheeks.

"Do you need a longer break?" Pyre asked as he squared up again quickly.

"No," he replied. "How about you?"

Pyre smiled. "I'm fine."

"Perhaps I can go a little harder?" he asked. "Call out if you want me to stop, okay?"

"Thank you," Pyre replied.

Montclair sped up his sword work, Pyre defended it easily, and the fortune-sword pushed harder.

His sword flashed in the setting sunlight, and his sweat-soaked shirt clung to his body. Pyre was also working hard, but she remained composed and focused. Faster and faster, Montclair swirled his sword, eventually grunting with exertion. Pyre responded, matching his speed, his moves, and his footwork.

Riona grew increasingly anxious. "Stop!" she called, and they both broke off.

Pyre made a show of drinking water and wiping her face, though all could see it was a show for Montclair's benefit. He had stripped off his shirt, his chest heaving from the exertion. Pyre turned away to avoid his gaze.

"Why…stop?" Montclair panted.

Sellia glanced at Riona, who was cautiously approaching, and stepped in for the assist.

"I don't need either of you getting wounded or exhausting yourselves in case we get attacked," she said. Montclair stared at her, confused. "I need one of you to come with me," she blurted out.

"Where?"

Sellia looked up, lost for an answer. Then she saw a thin sliver of smoke on the mountain peak. "Up there," she said.

Montclair followed her stare. "You want to climb that mountain? Why?"

"Can you see the smoke?" Sellia asked.

Neither Riona nor Montclair could, but Pyre, who shared superior elf vision with Sellia, nodded.

"I will come with you," she offered.

"I should," Montclair declared.

They all stared at Montclair. This was getting tricky.

"I need to do something," he said. "I could use the climb."

"Perhaps we should all go," Sellia ventured.

"I will stay here," Riona said. "I want to make sure we have enough herbs, and there is a lot of meat drying. We can't lose it, and if winter surprises us, we will be in serious trouble."

"You shouldn't be left alone," Montclair said. "I'll stay."

"I can stay if you want to go," Pyre added.

Riona rolled her eyes, and then turned to Sellia. "Do me a favor, and take them both."

"You sure you don't mind being alone?"

"I *want* to be alone. I'm not used to being in such close company, and if you don't all go, then I might be the one to leave for a while. Please. There's nothing around to worry about. I can sleep in the shed, and I am not defenseless."

They left in the graying dawn with minimal supplies. Sellia led, and they moved fast, surprising a large number of animals at the water hole. Sellia estimated that it would take the best part of a day to reach the foot of the mountains and another day to climb. She wanted to utilize the cool of the evening to make some progress in the ascent and then finish as much of it as they could before the morning heat kicked in.

Montclair seemed in good spirits as they walked. He asked Pyre about her training, and she explained how she had been taught in the Markwin Forest as she had grown up, and what she'd learned from Seanchai. Much of this was new to Sellia, as well.

"What is the difference between your teacher and you?" he asked Pyre innocuously. "He is not that much older."

Pyre bristled and did not answer directly, so Montclair asked her again. She stopped walking, pulled out her water skin, and drank deeply. Sellia watched her throat gulp.

"My hair is not as white. My eyes are not as blue," she said and wiped her mouth with her sleeve. "Every Wycaan transforms, even the natural-born. I am not natural born, though the Wycaan blood clearly flows through me. But I cannot transform, can barely move the elements, and…"

They waited as she stared at a rock nearby. Then she turned to walk.

"All I seem good at is fighting. Seanchai thinks I need some kind of catalyst, but it might be that I'm only what I am." She sounded so lost. "I might never become a Wycaan Master."

"Seanchai thinks very highly of you," Sellia felt compelled to say.

Pyre stopped and turned to her. "Your mate thinks highly of everyone. That is why we all love him. I offer him loyalty and friendship because we bonded when you both came into the west. But I fear that might be all I have to offer."

Sellia put a hand on Pyre's shoulder. "Seanchai loves everyone; that is true. But he reserves a special love for those whom he deems special. I know him better than you. Trust me.

"It wasn't that you brought him bowls of bloodwood nut soup. It was because, of all the Elves of the West, you best understood his drive to free his people. It was because, although you were only a *calhei*, you had the courage to stand up to the High Council and the brains to step back when you saw that your actions had galvanized others.

"I don't think being good with weapons, controlling elements, or changing into animals, is what makes a Wycaan." She moved her hand to Pyre's heart. "It is what is here, and Seanchai is wise enough to recognize that."

"Thank you," Pyre whispered and tears welled up in her eyes.

Riona watched them leave. She was not as relieved as she had made them think. She pulled back the sleeper log and laid a clump of dried grass and twigs on the glowing embers. Holding her hair behind her ears, she blew on it until it caught. Then she poured water into the curved rock and waited. When the fire had caught and the water was heating, she sat on a rock and stared at it.

"You can come out now," she finally called. "I am alone."

A figure stepped out from the trees. It was tall, but slumped, and shrouded in a gray sheet. It smelled of burnt flesh and wheezed.

Chapter Sixty Two

"I am a healer," she said, struggling to keep her voice calm. "Whatever or whoever you are, I am sworn to help you."

"If you knew who I was, my dear Riona, you would take that sling you have and slay me."

"How do you know my name?"

"Oh, I know much. May I sit, please?"

Riona signaled with her hand and began to stand.

"Don't get up."

"Let me see your wounds."

"Soon. For now, a cup of tea will be splendid."

Riona crouched by the small fire. The water steamed but did not boil. She looked around for something to cover it and quicken the process, but there was nothing.

"Are you in pain?" she asked.

"Yes. I have ways to control it, but such energy drains what little strength remains."

She glanced up at him. She could not discern anything about who he was from his voice or body language. His tone was tight, and she imagined he must be exerting considerable energy to hold himself together.

"Since you know my name, I assume you also are aware of my predicament. I think this bark comes from a tree in the willow family. If so, it can help manage pain, but I am uncertain of the plant life here and haven't tested it."

"I will drink it," he replied. "I trust your intuition. So should you."

She could not help feeling unnerved and took a deep breath as she tossed a handful of herbs into the water.

"Listen. I said I was sworn to help you, and I will as long as you don't threaten or attack any of us. Now, tell me who you are."

"I make no promises. I serve the Master who is fighting your Wycaan. But for now, neither knows we are here, and I am tired."

"If we fought, who would win?"

"I would."

"And if my friends were here?"

"It would make no difference. But this isn't how I want our conversation to go, Riona."

"How do you know me?"

"I know a lot. Sellia, your dark-skinned elfe, is consort to the Wycaan. Did you know that they bonded out of love of others and not each other?"

"What?"

"Sean…what is his name?"

"Seanchai."

"Ah, yes. We always referred to him as The Soft One," the man rasped a chuckle. "Anyway, Seanchai had another mate who grew up with Sellia. She made Sellia swear to mate with him once she died. Your Wycaan needs a mate because he is weak. It is a terrible flaw, and one that we are aware of and clearly ready to exploit."

"They still care about each other," Riona said, suddenly unsure if this was actually true. She had the feeling that whoever this was might know more than her.

"I think so too. She bore his children and–"

"*Calhei.*"

"What?"

"The children are called *calhei*. It's elven for children."

"Is that an important distinction to you?"

"It is." It was not, but Riona was grasping for a way to control the conversation. It was so disconcerting. She saw the water was boiling, filled a coarse piece of rock that they had chiseled into a crude bowl, and gave it to him.

"I have no way of removing the bark," she said. "Try not to ingest it."

He nodded. "Thank you. So, Sellia is bound to the Wycaan by their *calhei* but he is also close to the female Wycaan student, and she worships him."

"Pyre? She is very young. I think you are over-thinking this." But she did wonder as she sipped from her water skin. "How's the tea?"

"Bitter, but the warmth is helping."

"What happened to you?"

"I've been severely burnt by the fires that run deep in that mountain range." He nodded to the mountains that Sellia and the others were exploring.

"Is that smoke a sign that the mountain is about to erupt?"

"No. You'll know when that's about to happen, but still might not have the time to run far enough. I have seen it blow. It's magnificent."

"Sounds scary."

"Oh – that, too."

"Are you responsible for that smoke, then?"

"Yes."

"To draw my friends away?"

"Clever girl."

"I am a woman."

"Of course you are. My apologies. I'm as old as your dreamwalker, so there is a skewering of proportion."

"What would you have done if one of them had stayed with me?"

"Ensured they didn't get in my way."

"You would have killed them?" She was shocked by his honesty.

"Depends who stayed. Your lover would probably have tried to fight me. It would have been a slight inconvenience. You should be happy he went. He lives another day."

"He is a very good swordsman," Riona realized she was pouting.

"Of course he is. Still he is more fueled by his love for you. The *calhei* would present the biggest problem."

"*Calhei*?"

"Yes. She is young and unmated. Does that not—"

"Doesn't matter," Riona was flustered enough and not sure herself.

"She is Wycaan potential, so she would probably have proved a more difficult opponent. But they have all gone. You deserve the credit for that, and I thank you."

"How much of your body is burnt?"

"All of me."

She flinched. "I must make a gel to help your skin grow and keep it from becoming infected."

"I have it here," he produced a small clay jar.

"How did you know? Where did you find it?"

"I have supplies in Grogin. I was able to bring it here. The gel is very thick. You might have difficulty spreading it."

"Finish your tea, and we shall go to the waterhole. I have no dressing, but can wash what you wear, and the wounds will need cleaning."

"Thank you," he said, slowly rising.

Riona brought the rest of the tea. "It's going to be hard to undress you. The sheet has probably stuck to the burns and raw skin."

"It's going to be hard for you to look at," the man replied.

"I have treated many burns."

"Not like this."

He was right. At the water's edge, Riona removed her own clothes and led him into the waterhole. With his body submerged enough that she could still see what she was doing, she peeled off the sheet, hoping that the cold water would help numb him. The man cried out quietly in pain.

She had to drag him from the water, and when she laid him on a smooth rock, he passed in and out of consciousness. His entire body was burned, head to foot. He had no hair anywhere, and he barely looked human.

It occurred to her that maybe he was not human. She focused on her work, beginning with his head. At one point, he woke, and she had him sip more tea.

"Do not try and cover the whole body," he whispered. "Focus on the energy centers. Heal those, and I can spread their energy."

"You can direct this?"

"Yes. You know where the centers are?"

"I do," she said, stopping to drink some water and compose herself. He was right – she had never seen such destruction. There were only bones in some places. How could a man stay alive like this?

"I have remarkable powers, honed over centuries," he said.

Riona had not realized she had thought out loud. "How, though?" she whispered.

"Revenge is a powerful motive, healer."

"Who did this to you?" Riona felt apprehensive asking.

"Have you met the purple sorceress?"

"Briefly. She did this?"

"No. Her student did. The *calhei* you call Mharina. But they will both suffer for this before they die."

Riona dropped the water skin.

Chapter Sixty Three

Sellia wiped the sweat that dripped down her face, panting in her damp, clinging clothes. The air was thin this high up, and the rocks they were scrambling over were ominously warm. They were treading on a sleeping giant that had the capacity at any time to erupt with unimaginable fury.

She glanced behind her. Montclair's tanned, shirtless chest glistened. He had a nice body for a human, she thought – lean and defined from years of training. There were a few scars but they did not diminish his good looks. She hoped Riona was enjoying him. They could be dead tomorrow or stuck here for life. Either way, she felt concern for the young healer, something she had only acquired on this journey.

Her thoughts went to Seanchai guiltily. She had scarcely thought of him, beyond whether he was coming to rescue their children. She was so consumed by her fear for Mharina and the twins. Their relationship had become strained, as his absences lengthened. Of course she loved her children deeply and would not hesitate to die in their defense, but she was racked with guilt at not being a doting mother. She was fulfilling a role and, had to admit, was looking forward to them being older. Denalion had once summed it up: *you would rather be their best friend than their mother. They will appreciate that when they grow older.*

Denalion had been her rock in Seanchai's absence, but away from the Forest of Markwin and the powerful bloodwood trees, he had aged at an alarming rate. If they survived this, she would send him back to the forest that had nurtured him. Perhaps, she and the children would accompany him.

Was he still alive? Still trying to reach Seanchai or Rhoddan? She feared for the old elf, for what his failure to walk in their dreams might be doing to him. She feared he might do something rash, especially once he discovered they were gone, or if the children were in danger.

A warning click froze her, and she quickly knelt and crept ahead to where Pyre crouched near a rock. Pyre's face was bright red, her white hair wet and stringy. She was drinking from her water skin and it occurred to Sellia that they would be short of water. They waited for Montclair to join them.

"We are about forty paces from the source of the smoke," Pyre whispered. "It's a camp, but I can't hear anyone. There are only tracks of one two-legged individual. What do we do?"

Sellia pursed her lips. "I'm going to walk in and see if anyone is there. You hide nearby and be ready to jump in if I'm attacked."

"You want me to go?" Montclair offered. "That's what you pay me for."

She had actually forgotten that Montclair was being paid. Still, it was nice he offered. She thought of Riona and winced.

"No, but thank you. I might look less threatening than you."

Montclair arched an eyebrow wryly to show he was not sure, and both elfes smiled. It was nice to smile, Sellia thought, even in their circumstances.

"Give us a few moments to establish good positions," Pyre whispered.

She rose, and immediately fell backwards to avoid bumping into the person who suddenly stood before them.

"There is no need," the shrouded figure said. "I'm too weak to fight right now, and too powerful for you to win if we did. Please join me at the fire. I have more water."

He turned his back on them and appeared to float regally around the rock and toward his camp. The three glanced at each other and then followed. Moments later, they were seated on rocks around the fire.

The figure's movement was slow and deliberate. He sat and turned his head to Montclair.

"In the little cave, there are water skins. Please bring them out. I'm afraid the water is warm and tastes of minerals, but it will quench your thirst."

Montclair did so. When he offered a skin to their host, the man's cowl shook from side-to-side.

"I cannot. I'm not actually here."

They all stared and he appeared to laugh, judging by the shimmering of the sheet.

"I am, at this moment, in your camp." He saw Montclair tense. "Your healer tends me. She is in no danger. I appreciate her efforts and may spare her, if not the rest of you."

Sellia did not know how to process that. "Who are you? What are you ailing from?"

The man's cowl shuffled, suggesting he was now looking at her. "My entire body is burnt from the fires beneath us. Two females – a sorceress and a young she-elf – did this to me. The she-elf used sorceress's fire on me. I was distracted and she attacked from behind, otherwise she would not have succeeded and been long dead.

"You, too, are dark-skinned, so I assume she was your daughter."

"Mharina?" Sellia gasped. "No. She doesn't know how to…" She turned to Pyre. "You never taught her something like…"

"No," Pyre replied. "Mharina wouldn't know—"

"You are not her teacher now," the man replied. "She studies with the sorceress and—"

"Wait," Sellia interrupted. "You said she *was* my daughter."

"I did," he replied. "You have lost her to the sorceress. If Sa'gola doesn't kill her, then I will when I kill the sorceress."

"You will not," Sellia sprung to her feet, but the man held out his arms, two raw palms.

"First, may I remind you that I am not physically here, and—"

He looked down. Montclair had thrown a stone, which had gone through his body. "How rude."

"Just checking," Montclair grinned. "Impressive."

His smile was infectious, and the man seemed amused. "You need my help if you are to return to our time."

"You can get us back?" Sellia asked.

"I haven't tried yet. The sorceress and I laid this plan together. I need to heal first, and then I'll work it out. Be assured my help will come at a price."

"I have money," Sellia said, "Not with me, of course."

"I do not lack for riches or at least access to it if I cared for such things. My price will be one of your bodies. You are all young and fit, so I will let you choose."

"What will happen to the one chosen?"

"They will die, of course. But I assure you it'll be painless and for a very good cause."

Chapter Sixty Four

Mharina collapsed onto a rock, her chest heaving and fingers numb. Sa'gola slumped next to her and offered a water skin. The sorceress erupted in laughter at Mharina's loud gulping. The young elfe was desperate to drink as much water as possible.

The elfe laughed, too, and water splashed down her white shirt. She passed the water skin to her teacher. Sa'gola's skin was beautiful, accentuated by a sheen of sweat. Though pale next to Mharina's dark skin, she glistened in the light of the torches, and her own black sleeveless top complemented the color of her skin.

Sa'gola had recovered from her wounds over the past few moon cycles and was once more moving with ease and grace. She had intensified Mharina's training, and now, for the first time, they traveled out from Grogin to another mountain.

They walked through deep tunnels, and Mharina was unsure how far they had come. All the time, she trained, nurturing the fire and learning how to disappear. She could move air, pushing small rocks off of bigger ones, and, once, Sa'gola had allowed her student to enter her mind.

It had been an amazing experience. Mharina felt as though she was actually touching the woman. Though she was a short distance away, she could feel the woman's skin, her heat, and her heart beating.

At that moment, Sa'gola had repelled her, and Mharina gasped, as she understood the implications.

"I could have…"

"Yes," Sa'gola answered. "That was very impressive," Sa'gola said. "I thought you would be able to feel my skin, hair, and body temperature, but that was advanced stuff, reaching so deep inside of me. Do you understand why I pushed you out?"

"I could have…stopped your heart?"

"Yes," Sa'gola stared hard at her, standing very close. "It's not something to ever use lightly. To be able to kill is a privilege and a responsibility. As much as I love you, Mharina, and I love you very much, I will kill you if I ever discover you abuse this. Do you understand?"

Mharina gulped and, unable to speak, nodded. It was, she had to admit, as scary as it was exhilarating. She realized she was shaking and suddenly found herself in Sa'gola's tight embrace. Although she was a small woman, Sa'gola engulfed the elfe, blanketing her with protection. Her arms were strong, and the *calhei* did not want to leave her embrace.

When they did separate, Mharina had a question. "Can I use that same power to heal? Can I start a heart that has stopped?"

"It depends how long ago the heart stopped. If the rest of the body does not receive blood, it can collapse. But, yes, you have the potential to do so."

Mharina reflected on the training she had been receiving.

"What are you thinking, young one?"

"Can the minerals you taught me that poison and influence behavior be used to heal, too?"

"Yes and we will go through those uses thoroughly when we return to Grogin."

Mharina nodded. "Why did we leave the fortress? Are you not supposed to be guarding us or something?"

Sa'gola smiled. "There are the Wycaans, too. The Master has many in his service. But he returned to Grogin two days ago, and we left with his permission. We will return soon. He is looking forward to meeting you, Senzia, and Ilan."

"We will meet him? What's he like?"

Sa'gola thought for a moment. "He is terrible and amazing. He is very, very smart. Always remember that, Mharina. He never does *anything* without forethought. He can make you feel so special and then destroy you if you disappoint him. He can be a kind uncle one moment and a ruthless animal the next."

Mharina frowned, thinking. "You fear him and admire him."

"Yes. It's why I am alive and one of his close advisors."

"Are you his slave? Do you stay because you have no choice?"

"Yes and no. I have my own home far from here, where I am but a myth to the people who live there. They pay homage to me with gifts of food and fuel. It is an honor to them to give to the Purple Woman in the Mist and, in return, I care for them. I have defended them from marauders, helped them give birth, and saved their children when they were ravaged by disease.

"I keep this world far away from anyone's eyes. Ithea and the Master know the place exists, but not where it is. I am careful to hide my trail, but I always come when the Master has need."

"Could you defeat him?"

"I doubt it, and neither can I imagine ever wanting to consider it."

"What if he fights my *ahdahr*?"

"The best Wycaan will win. So far, your father has twice vanquished the Master. That is twice more than any other adversary. He will also have the other Wycaans to contend with. While they are perhaps past their prime, they remain formidable."

"The Emperor fought my *ahdahr's* teacher, Mhari, a few times and neither prevailed."

"Perhaps. But maybe he let her get away because he doesn't want to lose a worthy adversary. It is lonely enough being so powerful. To know there is no one in existence like you sounds horrible."

"Are there others like you?" Mharina asked. "Or are you all alone?"

Sa'gola smiled and stroked the elfe's black hair. "Yes," she replied. "We would be a powerful order if ever we joined together, but we don't. I will tell you more about them another time."

"Sa'gola? When my *ahdahr* and the Emperor fight, will you go to the Emperor's aid if he is losing?"

"I imagine I would, my sweet."

"And if the Emperor decided to kill me, or Senzia and Ilan, would you stand by and let him?"

The woman frowned. "I don't know. I never thought I would ever question him." Her voice trailed off and then abruptly she sat up straight and her voice became harsh. "This conversation never happened, Mharina. Do you understand?"

Mharina looked carefully into Sa'gola's eyes and then put her arms around the diminutive woman, nuzzling her head in the woman's smooth neck.

"Thank you," she whispered.

Chapter Sixty Five

Ilan's favorite lessons were with Master Goldspiere, and it had nothing to do with the fact that Ilan was the same height as the Wycaan dwarf. Master Goldspiere had been grumpy at first, but when he saw that Ilan was genuinely interested in the endless potential of minerals, explosives, and in the path of the stars, he soon warmed to Ilan and, within a month, was allowing Ilan to assist with experiments.

Master Goldspiere worked in a huge cavern deep in the bowels of the mountain, mixing different minerals to create explosives, smoke, and even an energy that produced heat far more efficiently than wood. He made careful notes, clearly thrilled when Ilan was not only happy to record the results, but soon offered correlations with incredible memory and clarity.

The experiments often went awry, and, more than once, Ilan returned with singed hair or a sooty face, but he was inevitably smiling and excited to tell his sisters what had transpired.

Master Goldspiere also took Ilan up through a steep vertical corridor from the cavern that opened out to one of the mountain peaks. Here, the dwarf had designed an instrument with two transparent crystals at either end of a long tube. It enabled them to see stars that weren't visible to the naked eye. It was Ilan who suggested they use crystals of different thickness to see further. His teacher was skeptical, but let him try, and soon the two of them were complimenting each other with ideas and refinements until they could see different distances with almost equal sharpness.

Ilan begged the dwarf to let him bring his sisters to look through the crystals, so one night, while Mharina was away with Sa'gola, Senzia joined them, munching crackers and cheese and looking at different stars. It was Ilan who explained to his sister, directed her, and answered her questions.

Goldspiere, hovered in the background, and Ilan sensed his teacher was disapproving. He tried even harder to explain and include the dwarf, but as the evening wore on, his teacher became increasingly moody.

"He is worried about you being here," Ilan hypothesized to Senzia as the dwarf enveloped himself in a thick cloud of pipe smoke instead of answering a question.

"No – it is his return," Senzia said, and the dwarf jerked his head around to look at her. "They are all like this – all our teachers."

"What are you talking about?" Ilan was irritated his sister knew something he didn't. This was *his* show tonight.

"Am I right?" Senzia asked Goldspiere.

The dwarf nodded.

"You all fear him." She did not pose this as a question.

"He has lifted us each out of obscurity and given us back our pride. Soon, we will return to Odessiya and take our rightful places at the heads of civilized society. Do you have any idea how long it has been since I stood in the great halls of Hothengold, the capital of the dwarf nation?"

"None of that explains why you're all so afraid of him," Senzia remarked.

Goldspiere puffed more smoke into the air and stood abruptly. "We must return. It is late, and you have a big day tomorrow."

"We do?" Ilan asked, feeling a tinge of apprehension.

"Tomorrow, you will meet the Master."

"But Mharina is away," the young elf replied. She always knew what to say when he didn't.

"He knows," Goldspiere replied and began his descent.

Fresh, clean garments had been laid out for the twins when they woke in the morning. At breakfast, they sat with Masters Goldspiere, Sythen, and Willowood. The elderly elfe instructed them on how to approach the Emperor while she nibbled on a bit of cheese and a chunk of bread.

"You are to answer truthfully at all times. He will know if you hide the truth."

"But what if we don't know an answer?" Ilan felt a sharp pit in his stomach.

"You can tell him that. You're young, and he will understand."

"What if he asks something about our *ahdahr*? Something that might give him an advantage?" Senzia asked.

The three Wycaans glanced at each other.

"You are prisoners here," Master Sythen said, stroking his white beard. "You are treated well because the Master sees value in teaching you, but he will get whatever information he needs in the end."

Ilan dropped his cup and whimpered. He looked at his sister, wondering what they might know that the Emperor would torture them for.

"M–maybe we should wait for Mharina," he mumbled. "Perhaps the Emperor doesn't know she's away."

The three Wycaans chuckled, and Master Goldspiere ruffled his hair.

"You'll be fine," Master Willowood said. "Be honest. Be polite. You are children, and–"

"*Calhei*," Senzia corrected her. "And *ahdahr* means father, in case you have forgotten that, too. You must have also forgotten that my *ahdahr* freed *our* people from the Emperor you serve."

"Be honest. Be polite," Master Willowood repeated, undaunted. "The game that is being played out here is beyond you. No one – especially the Emperor and your parents – would expect you to try and change the course of the game."

But Senzia was angry and glared at the Wycaan elfe.

"Do you not feel any guilt?" she accused. "Our ears are pointed like yours, and the one who comes to rescue us is elven, too."

"You are young and cannot understand the complexity of–"

"Answer me," Senzia shouted and sprung to her feet. The entire hall was captivated. "You are a Wycaan elfe. You–"

"And you are not Wycaan yet!" Master Willowood rose, and, though old, she looked fearsome.

Ilan whimpered, but his sister stood her ground, her small hands on her hips. When she spoke, her voice was quiet but powerful.

"No, I am not," she hissed, "but if I become one, it will be because I am proud of my *ahdahr's* actions and hope I can follow in his footsteps as a free Wycaan elfe, proud of every action she takes and serving the people, not using them to my own advantage."

Master Willowood's eyes bulged, and Ilan was sure she was going to explode. But Senzia did not move, did not lower her eyes, did not budge.

"Young *calhei*," Master Sythen said quietly, but firmly. "Return to your room and await the Master's summons."

Chapter Sixty Six

The man burped, winced, and glanced at the pictorians. "Am I still drunk?"

"What's your name?" Rhoddan asked.

"Had many. Why?"

"Did you have anything to do with what happened here?" Seanchai interrupted waspishly.

The man shied away. "Take it easy. I don't usually harm people, unless they cheat me."

"Cheat you?"

"Yeah – cards, yeh know? Drinking is just part of the…" He hiccupped again. "'scuse me, fellas. Anyway, I don't gamble with elves. They don't come into the bars 'round these parts."

Seanchai loomed over him. "Do you know the men who have been slaughtering elves around here?"

When the man shrugged, Seanchai grabbed his collar and lifted him off his feet.

"I could kill you a dozen ways before your next burp," Seanchai said. "They" – he nodded to Umnesilk and Narasilk – "would be even less gracious. Do you understand?"

The man glanced from one to another. "Kinda. What do yeh want?"

"I want to meet the ones who did this, and you are going to take me to them."

"They'll skin me alive if I do."

"Then pray they aren't alive to find you when I'm finished."

"There're about forty of them. Trained soldiers, too."

Seanchai nodded to Umnesilk, and both pictorians took a step nearer.

"Okay. Okay. I help you, but then you take me with you."

"We're not going anywhere nice," Rhoddan said. "Ever heard of the Fortress of Grogin?"

"Yeah." The man creased his brow. "I grew up in Braithwaite. But it was an old, deserted ruin. People said it was haunted and that the folks in the villages around it were zombies."

"Can you take us there by the shortest route?" Rhoddan said.

"Betcha I can, for the right sort of compensation. I'm a man of business, you know."

"Then I have a business proposal for you," Rhoddan said. "You will take us to the people doing this. Then you will take us to Braithwaite, and possibly the fortress."

"What's in it for me?"

Umnesilk offered a rather theatrical growl.

"My friends here will not rip you apart."

The woman, Miri, watched them leave in the morning. When Seanchai promised he would deal with the gang who attacked them, she offered a defeated shrug. She looked exhausted and he wanted to offer her more, but there was nothing to do besides what he planned.

Their new guide, Shifron, led them on a two-day journey to a town called Alsbright. Alsbright was the capital of the region and boasted a thriving market where farmers and craftsmen hawked their produce and wares. The market backed into a quarter whose inhabitants were experts at separating the merchants and farmers from the money they had just earned.

Along with the bars and gambling joints, all of which Shifron seemed to be banned from, they found an amphitheater. It was late afternoon, and people drifted in, betting and buying food on sticks.

"What are they gambling on?" Rhoddan asked from beneath his hood.

"You won't want to know," Shifron replied, glancing at Seanchai, also hidden deep inside his cowl.

"What?" he growled.

"People. On who will win in a fight."

"Do they fight to the death?"

"Of course. I mean – yes, I'm afraid they do."

"Are the fighters all elves?" Seanchai asked.

"The losers are. There are a few men who fight. They are usually well-armed and well-trained mercenaries, and they always win."

"Who runs it?"

"It's a group of them. You won't find them easily."

"I won't need to," Seanchai said and began to push his way through the throng.

People turned to complain, but the sight of four big, hooded, heavily armed warriors was enough to change their minds.

Kneeling inside the arena were two rows of bare-chested elves. Some were dozing under the hot sun; many were bruised and swollen. When he got closer, Seanchai saw that their legs were chained.

He turned to Rhoddan. "Other than storming in and killing everyone, do you have an idea?"

"Not really," Rhoddan said. "Send a message to Shayth. Let him deal with it. He comes with an army, and you have your family to consider."

"I can't just walk away from this."

"I know you can't. But they may be too broken to join us even if we get weapons into their hands."

A cheer went up as a huge, bare-chested man stamped into the ring. He carried a long, thick sword. Behind him were five more men, all wearing red scarves around their heads and carrying a sword or axe.

"I see pointy-ears in our beautiful arena," he boomed. "I smell elf stench. I don't like that."

A cheer went up around the stands.

"How much will you pay us to kill them for you?"

People threw coins into the ring. A wave of glinting metal rained down.

"Bring me my coins, scum," the man bellowed, cutting the elves' chains. "The one who brings the most will live."

The audience laughed and pointed at the elves, who scampered around in a panic, kicking and biting each other. The men looked on, arms folded and muscles bulging.

"The bets are on how long it will take them to kill all the elves," Shifron whispered. "You get money back according to how close your guess was."

It did not take long for the elves to collect all the coins and dump them into a burlap sack. The man held the sack high above his head.

"I didn't notice who won," he said, to the great amusement of the crowd. "What a shame. These little buggers worked so very hard." More laughter. "What shall we do, I wonder?"

His men unsheathed their blades in regimented unison.

"What shall we do?" the man repeated as the elves backed into a cowering huddle.

An arrow tore through the burlap, and the coins spilled out. The crowd went silent at the sight of two hooded figures standing there, one passing a lime green bow to Shifron, who shrank into the crowd.

"I believe," said the other figure, "that the game is to bet on how long until the last elf in the ring is dead." Rhoddan walked into the middle, between the elves and the men, and removed his hood, showing everyone his pointed ears.

"Now, my friend and I are new around here and find these rules somewhat … restricting. How about all this money goes to whoever is still standing after the fight instead? It might be the poor elves who do not seem to have any weapons, or it might be the big, strong men who," he leaned forward theatrically, "don't actually look so brave now they are facing armed elves."

He drew his blade. "Seems to me that these might not be big brave men, but cowards, deserters from the army judging by their rags and their stench. Or is that the smell of fear?"

He whirled his broadsword. "Of course, there are six of them and only two of us armed. But before we begin, let me share something with you from the world outside your fair region.

"The Emperor was defeated. The elves are no longer underclass slaves. There is freedom in the land, and justice, too. So after we finish here and these elves return to their families, I strongly recommend that you change your ways, and quickly.

"You see," Rhoddan's voice reached the entire crowd, "an army led by Prince Shindell himself is coming from the north, and he now knows that part of his kingdom is disrespecting his rule. I know the prince very well, and he takes great exception to being disrespected."

The leader advanced, his sword glistening in the sun. "But who is going to show us this justice today, elf, while your army is far away?"

Seanchai stepped forward, unclasping his cloak and letting it fall behind him. He pulled out his Win Dao swords, the rasp of metal leaving scabbard ringing around the arena.

"I am," he hissed.

CHAPTER SIXTY SEVEN

Seanchai's swords whistled through the air, quickly felling the muscular men with his rage and his blades. Rhoddan found the leader a worthy opponent, and they sparred for a short while before the man began to slow.

"Who taught an elf to fight so well?" the man panted.

"Other elves," Rhoddan replied, "elves who are strong, free, and brave warriors every one."

The man raised his sword to attack, but, as he came forward, he crashed to the ground. His legs were wound in a chain. Seanchai held the other end.

"I want him alive," Seanchai snarled, and Rhoddan knew better than to argue when his friend was in this mood.

Seanchai turned to face a now-quiet crowd. "The world has moved on. Odessiya is a civilized society, and there is no room for racism or slavery. Prince Shindell will be here in days." He turned to the elves, who had returned to sit in their two rows and were watching him submissively.

"You are free. Go back to your villages and your families."

Not one moved, and Seanchai glanced at Rhoddan, who gathered up most of the coins in what was left of the burlap sack and took it to the elves. "This should help you," he said. "Your business is done here."

One of them rose. "Not quite," he said quietly.

He walked over, picked up a sword, and approached the leader.

"Kneel," he said, his voice still quiet. Others rose and took other weapons scattered on the ground.

"Never," the man said.

The elf walked around him, and the man shuffled unevenly, chains still wrapped around his legs. A hammer smashed into his knees from behind, and he crumpled.

Seanchai moved to intervene, but Rhoddan stopped him. "We should go," he whispered.

"There's going to be a bloodbath," Seanchai said, and stepped in front of the elf with the broadsword.

"You have done us a great service," the elf said. "Stories will be told of what happened here and we will never forget you. But we need to regain our own self-respect. They killed my *calhei* and my mate…"

"Only those who directly wronged you," Seanchai insisted. "Promise me that you will not attack their women or children."

"They attacked ours," the elf shouted, spittle forming at the side of his mouth. "They tortured and raped them."

"But you know better," Seanchai's voice was soft, but firm. "Swear to me, or I will stop you. You know I can."

The elf looked at him. "Where do you find the power to forgive? When, all your life, they have insulted you, denigrated you, and killed your dear ones, where do you find the power?"

Seanchai opened his mouth, but had no answer. From nowhere, Maugwen stepped up and put a hand on the man's arm.

"You find it in the future you always dreamed of." She raised her voice, and it carried on the power of her words. "Now is the time when you must decide. The easy path to take is revenge. Justice must be handed out to those who committed these atrocities, but it is not justice when meted out upon the innocent. If they die, so will a part of you."

Other elves and humans gathered around them – the poor and the slaves. Maugwen turned and addressed them all.

"If you kill the innocent, you are no better than these butchers. You have endured so much, but you cannot bring back your dear ones. Choose the right path, and you will honor their memory with a just and fair society."

She turned back to the elf with the broadsword and looked into his eyes. "You cannot bring her back," she repeated. "But you can honor her memory and her life, and you can regain your self-respect."

The arena was quiet. The elf slowly nodded. Then he stepped away and swung the heavy sword in an arc. It severed the man's head from his shoulders. The elf watched as the body slowly fell forward and blood pooled into the dust.

"Very well," he said. "We will try. I hope the prince comes soon."

"*Your dreams are full of anger,*" the red owl hooted. "*What happened?*"

"*It is a long story,*" the young grizzly replied from where it sat on the warm rock. "*What news do you have of my family, Dreamwalker?*"

"*The children are well. They are being trained, and it is challenging for them. Apparently, the Wycaans there feel a need to teach them as quickly as possible. But something has happened to Mharina. The sorceress, Sa'gola, is teaching her. They are very close, but I sense that*"

Mharina has experienced something monumental. I don't believe Sa'gola perpetrated it, but whatever happened seems to have bonded them. Mharina is growing up fast."

"Is the Emperor teaching them?"

The Emperor has returned; I can sense it. There is much energy around him, and Mharina tells me that the other Wycaans and the sorceress are all channeling considerable energy into him to help him heal. I do not think he is teaching them, for now at least.

"He awaits you, Seanchai, and it seems he has a trap ready. I do not know what it is, but I fear he was never really committed to killing you until now. But he has your children. If he cannot bend you to his service, then he has others now that he can train."

"What else, Denalion? What news of Sellia and the others?"

The owl sighed. "I don't know. I cannot find them in the dreamworld. If they are captured, I should be able to reach them."

"Maybe there is a shield around them like the one that prevented you from reaching us."

"But I knew you were there. I could sense you. If they were alive, I would know. I could feel you and Rhoddan and the healer, even if I could not talk with you. Do you understand? I fear they—"

"They're alive, my friend – at least, Sellia is."

"How do you know?"

"I cannot tell you, just in case. But I know."

"I don't understand why they refrain from hunting me. The Emperor and sorceress know who I am. She entered a dream of Mharina's. It is very strange. I have walked in the fortress, my friend. I have been able to explore most places. I am convinced Sellia and the others are not physically there."

Seanchai nodded. "Perhaps he wants you to believe Sellia is dead, and for you to inform me. They would want me angry and careless.

Continue to search for them, but be cautious. You are all the children have to cling to for hope. You must stay free as long as you can."

"Seanchai. I fear something has happened."

"It hasn't, my dear friend — not yet."

Seanchai woke with a start, clenching the green half stone in his fist. It was pulsating.

"I'm coming, Sellia," he whispered to the stone. "For you, too, my love."

Chapter Sixty Eight

"I have met the twins, Sa'gola. I am pleased with their progress and their mentality. You have done well as have the Wycaans."

"Thank you, Master." Sa'gola was still on one knee, head bowed. She had not been told to rise, which was strange.

"The little girl seems somewhat strong-headed," the Emperor said before popping a grape into his mouth.

"Senzia is very independent and mature for her age. I suspect she will be the hardest to train, but the better Wycaan in the end."

"The boy is weak like his father."

"I have not met his father."

"You will soon. I have another mission for you. But first, tell me about the older girl. I have not met her yet. What does she do all day?"

"She is with me. I teach her things and—"

"Things?" He laughed, a thin, cynical cackle. "Do you teach her to cook and sew?"

Sa'gola raised her head. "Have I done something to displease you, my master?"

The sound of masticated grapes was all that broke the silence, but finally he spoke, preempted by a heavy sigh.

"Rise, my beauty. I am weary and in pain. Come sit with me."

Sa'gola rose and moved to a stool next to the throne. A bony hand descended and rested on her shoulder. Its touch was light and cold.

"What happened, my lord?"

"He outsmarted me. I, with all this experience, was defeated by a pup."

"Hardly defeated, Master. Just a setback."

The hand tightened on her shoulder. "It should never have happened," he hissed. "I underestimated him. Once is understandable – twice, inexcusable."

Sa'gola moved around to face him better, but the hand, though twisted, did not leave her skin.

"We must plan ahead, Master. Perhaps we should not be so eager to bring him here. If your long-term plans concern the children, why bring him at all?"

"I have had similar thoughts. Where is Ithea?"

"I have been wondering that, myself."

"Have you two been fighting?"

Sa'gola did not answer.

"Sa'gola?"

"He has been increasingly aggressive. I stay away from him." She turned her head and shoulder from him.

"Could he move you to kill him?" The Emperor's voice was soft.

"Yes. If he ever crossed the line, I would not hesitate."

He squeezed her shoulder, his sharp nail pressing into her skin. She was not sure how to take the gesture and remained quiet. The Emperor leaned back and drank from a large goblet.

"I will also meet your young apprentice and decide if it is prudent that she continue to study with you."

"As you wish, Master. I am fond of her. She has a lot of spirit."

"Good. I like them that way, as you know." He drank some more. "I grow tired and must rest. You must prepare to leave. I want you to lure the Wycaan away from his friends, but do not kill them. I want the pictorian. I hold him responsible for General Tarlach's death, and he will pay for his betrayal at Hothengold."

"Am I going to be able to face the Wycaan, Master?"

"I do not want you to fight him, though you should be prepared to defend yourself. If you must, kill him, but you are a different kind of adversary than what he is used to. I would prefer that you seduce and incarcerate him. Make sure he knows that only you and Ithea know how to free his mate. And point out that we do not know where Ithea is, which makes you very important for everyone concerned."

"When shall I leave?"

"In two days. He will be close to Braithwaite, and I will feel stronger."

"You are a furry cub?"

The grizzly stood up on its hind legs, but the rocks in the river were smooth and slippery. It wobbled a bit, went back to all fours, and left the water.

"I'm a grizzly," he said. "But not a very good one."

Sa'gola laughed. "I'm a woman," she said and twirled, allowing the purple stripe that went across her black hair to ripple. "I was so focused on entering your dream, I didn't think to go the animal route."

"How did you enter my dreams? Are you a dreamwalker?"

"I walk in many worlds and in many forms. Here..." she transformed into a peacock and raised beautiful purple and blue feathers. "Better?"

Seanchai shook his fur, and water splayed in all directions. "Sorry," he said when the peacock ruffled its feathers.

"You defeated the Emperor in his firebreather form as an ungainly cub?" she asked. "Impressive."

"I'm a grizzly," he growled.

"Oh, yes – so you said. I still think you're cute. When I finish with you, I might stuff you and keep you in my bed." When the bear did not laugh, she frowned. "That was a joke. Do you have a better sense of humor as an elf?"

Seanchai just grunted. "You're the sorceress. You stole my children. If you harm them—"

"I am extremely fond of them, Wycaan. Mharina and I are very close. Senzia is coming into her own; with your powers and your mate's temperament, she's an intriguing combination. And Ilan might never be a warrior, but he is very smart. I would not want to harm them, myself, but it is hardly in my hands."

"You serve him?"

The peacock seemed to bristle at this and didn't respond for a few moments. "We all serve him eventually, Wycaan, and you will, too, if you wish to stay alive."

"What happened to Mharina? She was involved in something frightening."

"How do you know?"

"What happened?" Seanchai insisted.

"She saved me when I was being beaten. She is…a very loyal student."

The bear studied her for an uncomfortable amount of time. The peacock felt a chilly wind ruffle her feathers.

"Come to Braithwaite, Seanchai. Come alone and in elf form. No one must know you're coming. If I see anyone else — and I will be looking — we won't meet."

"Who will be there?"

"It may well be just me."

"Are you powerful enough to defeat me?"

"I come with considerable experience."

"Will you be alone, as well?" he asked.

"I believe that is the plan," she replied, arching her long neck. "No one knows where we're meeting except him, you, and me."

The bear stared at her. "This is a test," he observed. "You love my daughter very much. Teaching her has become your life's work."

"I don't know what you are talk–"

"She is the daughter you never had," Seanchai continued. "She is the daughter denied to you."

The peacock ruffled its feathers furiously. "You have no id–"

"The test is not mine, Sa'gola, it's yours. The Emperor tests your subservience to him against the elfe you love. If you kill me, then you prove your loyalty, knowing that Mharina will never forgive you. Maybe she will even seek revenge. If you don't, then I will deprive the Emperor of one of his most dangerous servants."

"I will see you in Braithwaite."

"And what will you choose, Sa'gola? Death waits down either path. Your master is always several moves ahead of the game. Seems to me that the ensnarer is also the ensnared."

"Braithwaite," the sorceress snarled and vanished.

Chapter Sixty Nine

The tiny, red mouse scurried through endless corridors, his tiny paws sore from the uncompromising stone. He had spent many nights now exploring the fortress. The kitchens were a good place to spend time, drawn by the smell of fresh and aged cheese. But there were other mice there and, well, it was complicated.

The mouse had explored what it believed was every part of the dungeons. However, he couldn't be sure for there were tunnels and catacombs that went deep into the mountain. But he remained convinced that Sellia and the others were not there because he had failed to enter their dreams. They were not here, and he was running out of time. Seanchai would soon arrive, and if Denalion couldn't find Sellia, then he was sure she would be used as bait to defeat Seanchai.

He saw Mharina walking down the corridor. He often went to the children's room, though he dare not reveal himself. He would watch them talk and sleep, and his heart grew heavy. They were growing up fast, and would never again be the *calhei* that he had taught these past few years.

Senzia, in particular, was becoming an enigma. She had immense power like her father, but she lacked his softer side. She was formidable like her mother and already challenging her teachers' limits.

Denalion feared for Mharina the most. She was an elfe now, and she carried a heavy weight on her young shoulders. He knew something had happened and saw lines that should not be on such a youthful face. Now the dreamwalker could see it, too, in the way she spoke and treated her brother and sister. She was more distant and impatient.

He followed Mharina now as she returned to the sorceress's chambers. She was there all the time, leaving only to eat and sleep with her siblings. Mharina was training harder than the twins, and this too scared Denalion, because he had no idea what she was learning.

He entered the sorceress's room through the vent to the unlit fireplace and saw the two on the balcony. Mharina was taller than Sa'gola now, but it was still the sorceress who had her arms around the elfe.

"I cannot tell you where or for how long," she was saying. "The Master sends me on missions all the time."

"Why can't I accompany you? I could continue learning while we travel."

"I would like that, too," Sa'gola replied, stroking the elfe's dark hair. "I do not seek to be apart from you. But you are important for Ilan and Senzia. Their training is intensifying, and they will have need for you soon."

"He is coming, then?" Mharina asked.

"I don't know where your father is, and probably would not tell you even if I did. Now, I leave in the morning, and I want a good meal beforehand. Come, let's pick up the twins and go eat. I have something special prepared."

When they left, the mouse sniffed carefully. He suspected all kind of wards in place to prevent unwanted guests. But now that he was already inside, perhaps he would be undetected.

He scurried from one part of the room to another. The bedroom, and the bag that Sa'gola had packed, yielded no clues. He was about to leave when he noticed a slit at the bottom of part of a wall.

He scampered over, tail swishing and nose twitching in anticipation. A small stone or gem was preventing a hidden door from closing all the way to the ground. He could see a pale light on the other side. The slit was barely big enough for a small mouse to squeeze through, which explained why Sa'gola must have missed it. Still, he really must cut down on the cheese, he thought.

The room was hexagon-shaped and lined with shelves groaning from piles of books and jars. The fire pit featured a cauldron hanging over it. Near the solitary window sat a lectern with a chair and a pile of books.

He scurried up the chair and jumped onto the lectern. The open book was old and smelled worse than some of the cheese he had scavenged around the kitchens. He wiggled his nose as he climbed onto the book and struggled to focus on the letters. The language was an ancient elven dialect, but he was able to discern much from the root of the words.

It seemed to be about time and traveling. Was this how the sorceress moved from place to place? There was a whole paragraph about maintaining tunnels between times, about keeping them open. No – it was not about traveling, he realized. It was about keeping a way open to travel between different time periods.

He tried to turn the page, but his little claws could not grasp the brittle pages. He sighed and, looking around for something to leverage a page, suddenly found himself staring into the dark eyes of a black and purple cat licking its claws. He gasped, and his fur stood up on end.

"I'm impressed," the cat purred. "But why do you think I would not have wards to protect my most sacred workroom?"

The mouse twitched his whiskers and looked around furtively for an escape. The door was now open enough for a cat to stalk through.

"There is no escape now," the cat continued. "And you were so close."

"This is where you have them? Sellia and the others are in another world? Why? It seems like so much trouble."

"It is intricate magic, I must admit, and needed two of us to stabilize."

"So you can bring them back?"

"Yes. I can also send you there." The cat licked its lips. "But right now, I have an overwhelming desire to eat you. A rat, ugh."

"A mouse," Denalion pouted, despite himself.

The door in the wall opened all the way, and Mharina stepped in. "Sa'gola? Where are you?"

The cat turned to the door, and the mouse skipped onto its tail and jumped down while it was distracted. The cat chased him across the room. The mouse squeaked at Mharina, who instinctively raised her foot and let him pass.

The cat raced past her and chased after the mouse. Mharina stared, frowning, at the wake of the chase, and then went to the lectern to see if there was any damage. She stared at the open page of the book and whispered a word. Then she read the whole passage before her, and the next page, and the next.

Chapter Seventy

R iona screamed when she saw the little red mouse. She was not generally scared of rodents, but neither was she used to them appearing out of thin air. This mouse fell from the tree stump, then put the tip of his tail into its mouth and squealed.

The healer recovered enough to realize that the creature was hurt. She cautiously approached, not wanting to scare it off. "I can help you, little one. Did a cat bite your tail?"

"How did you guess?" the mouse wondered aloud, and Riona, not much of a screamer, screamed again. "I'm sorry, dear," he continued. "Turn around. This can sometimes be awkward."

Riona turned around and blinked furiously to confirm she was awake and that her eyes were not about to fall out.

"You can turn around now," Denalion said, and when she did, he was struggling to tie a piece of cloth around his waist. Unperturbed, she leapt at him with open arms, and he allowed her to fall into his embrace.

"It's so good to see you, Dreamwalker."

"It is good to see you, too, but maybe you could see less of me. Do you have some clothes?" Denalion's voice was muffled in her hair.

Riona let him go, and then could not help but giggle. Denalion had always seemed so regal to her. Before her now stood a pale, scrawny, old body topped with a bright red mop of hair. She took her cloak, wrapped it around him, and guided him to sit down.

"You look tired," she said. "Sleep. It will be dark soon, and the others will probably return in the morning."

"Some tea would be nice," Denalion yawned.

Riona added some small twigs and dried moss to the embers she had kept all day and blew on them. By the time she had heated water, the old elf was curled up and fast asleep. Riona stared at the deep creases on his face. He was so ancient, she thought – so weak, yet so strong.

She drank his tea and realized she had given him her cloak. She went over, gently lifted it, and curled up underneath it with him. He unconsciously made room for her and draped a bony arm over her.

"Dyfellion," she heard him mutter from far away in a dream. The leaves in the trees above them rustled. "Dyfellion, my one love."

When Sellia, Pyre, and Montclair returned to the camp the next night, Denalion and Riona were already sitting by the fire, sipping tea. After they all updated each other, they spent considerable time trying to decide whether Ithea had really been in two places simultaneously.

"It begs the question whether he is truly in this world at all," Montclair said.

"He is," Riona answered. "I treated his wounds."

"Maybe that was a mistake," he mused.

Riona wiggled out of his embrace; they had been sitting on a log together. "I'm a healer," she said, her voice cold.

Montclair raised his hands, palms facing her. "Okay. So you would heal the Emperor if he was lying in front of you?"

"She swore the healer's oath," Denalion answered. Montclair harrumphed, but Denalion was looking at Sellia. "Do you want me to go to him?"

"Do you think he is who he says he is? Can he get us back?"

"Yes. The sorceress mentioned there were two of them who had initially stabilized this... this time tunnel. I believe he is the other."

"What are you suggesting?" Pyre demanded.

"Ithea demands a body as a price to get us back to the fortress and the children."

"Why you?" Pyre sprung up. "You are Denalion the Dreamwalker. You are a wise elder of the Elves of the West, a unique individual, an Ancient."

"I aspire to be wise, thank you, and am indeed an elder. But I'm also very old and have no desire to live forever. There are those who wait for me in the Eternal Forests, and I will go to them in peace."

"Dyfellion?" Riona said. "Who was she?"

Denalion stared, his mouth dropped open.

"When you held me last night, while you slept, you said her name, over and over again."

The old elf frowned, but did not have a chance to speak.

"Dyfellion?" Pyre's mouth hung open. "One of the greatest Wycaans of our time. She helped Seanchai with his transformation into a bear. She was a black panther. So beautiful." She smiled, losing herself in memory. Then, just as abruptly, she recovered. "But if anyone should sacrifice their life it should be me. I am not a fully evolved Wycaan and probably never will be. There were teachers in the Forest of Markwin who said I would never—"

"They were fools!" Denalion snapped, and his ruddy complexion became even hotter. "You have an independent streak in you. It is what drew you to Seanchai, and him to you. We just need to find how to unlock the Wycaan Master inside of you. It requires a different key than the ones those teachers use."

"And until then, you are our best warrior," Sellia added.

Montclair cleared his throat.

"When she spars with you," Riona said, "she not only protects herself, but also your delicate ego."

Montclair looked from one female to the next. All three were smiling in a way that already had his ego deflating.

"There are many pieces to our puzzle," Denalion said to the fortune-sword. "And you are an important piece." He looked at Pyre. "We will find another way."

"But my children," Sellia said. "I feel like I lose them a little more every day. The twins become Wycaans, and Mharina a sorceress."

"The twins were always destined to become Wycaans," Denalion replied.

"But there are different kinds of Wycaans, as we are clearly learning. The Emperor does not appear to be the only bad Wycaan egg as we always thought."

"I know it is hard, Sellia," Denalion said quietly, "but you must trust your children. Their father is coming, and when he has rescued them, he will help them walk the right path. You must trust Seanchai, too."

There was a heavy silence before Sellia spoke. "I do," she whispered.

"If we're not going to give this Ithea a body, he will be angry. He might try to take one of us against our will. We do not know how to kill him." Denalion looked at Riona. "Did he say who wounded him?"

Riona had not imparted this part earlier. Now she glanced at Sellia, who was already looking vulnerable. "He said it was Mharina."

"What?!" Sellia exclaimed.

"Which is why I have an interesting proposition for you," Ithea said, and they all jumped.

He was still wrapped in his shawl and walked slowly to the fire, where he took a seat on a log by Denalion.

"No insult meant, old one, but I wouldn't want your body. It's not much of an improvement on what I already have."

Denalion shrugged. "I try to keep in shape," he said.

Ithea stared at Sellia across the fire. "When I return – and I stress *when* and not *if* – I plan to kill your daughter and her foolish teacher. Only the Master can treat me as she did. But if you give me your body, then maybe I will spare your daughter. I don't really want to be a she-elf–"

"An elfe," Sellia hissed.

"Ah yes. It would take some getting used to, but your body looks adequate."

They all bristled at the comment, and Montclair's hand wrapped around the hilt of his sword.

"Walk away, sir," he said.

Ithea forced all the muscles in his face to lift in a semblance of a smile. "Pathetic," he said, and rose.

They watched him move into the trees and disappear. Then all eyes turned on Sellia.

"You can't be seriously thinking about it," Pyre said.

"Depriving the children of their mother is not a solution," Riona added.

"And we don't even know if he would keep his word," Denalion sighed.

Sellia rose. "I need to be alone. I need to think," she said, and retreated to the far side of the clearing to lay against a rock, her eyes closed as she let the rays of the sun bask upon her face. But closed eyes could not stop the tears rolling silently down her cheeks.

Chapter Seventy One

Sa'gola opened her eyes and blinked. Then she sighed and closed them again, allowing her comfortable bed to envelop her. It was not usually so difficult to step into someone's dreams. She had done it many times to glean information or to put fear into a person. She had entered humans, elves, dwarves, and giants, as well as many different animals.

But the Wycaan had the most complex mind she had ever encountered. He was strong and had built defenses around himself, which she had expected. Usually, she broke someone down as soon as she discovered his or her fatal flaw: ego, lack of confidence, guilt, weakness etcetera.

This one, however, seemed to have a balance of everything. He had strengths and weaknesses, power and vulnerability. She sensed that he had the capacity to be both fearsome and compassionate. And then it occurred to her: the elf had within him *ha'yzun*, the balance. It made him powerful and unpredictable, full of potential and full of flaws.

She wondered whether he was aware of what this meant. He had studied with a chain of teachers, but each time their training had been cut short. They had honed him to defeat the Master and done little else.

Furthermore, she had found something disturbingly familiar inside the elf. The Wycaan was a mixture of Mharina,

Senzia, and Ilan. Not surprising in and of itself, but this was the first time that Sa'gola had gotten close to children, especially Mharina, and the connections took her a bit off guard.

Mharina.

Sa'gola reached out with her mind into the room. Mharina sat in a chair, awake. Slowly, Sa'gola stretched and feigned a yawn. Then she opened her eyes, blinking, and slowly rose.

"Mharina? What are you doing here?"

The girl looked at her, but did not smile or move. Sa'gola felt hurt. Is this how a mother felt? She rose, sat back against the cool stone wall, and shook out her hair. There was a foul taste in her mouth.

"I slept deeply. Please, bring me some water and a leaf to chew on."

Mharina rose and brought what her teacher required. Sa'gola sipped the water and waited. But the elfe was not going to talk first.

"I'm too tired to play games," Sa'gola said, realizing that she was also very hungry. "Why am I receiving the silent treatment? I didn't kill the mouse. Your precious dreamwalker lives. I spared him."

"Then I want to see him."

"Do you?" Sa'gola felt an edge in her voice and took another drink. "He is a powerful elf. He is somewhere safe, but imprisoned. He is not, as far as I know, in any danger." She thought for a moment. "At least, no more than he was in this world."

"I know where he is," Mharina said, steel in her voice.

Sa'gola put the water skin to her mouth and drank slowly, composing herself. "And where is that, my dear?"

"Is that where you imprisoned my mother, and Riona, and Pyre?"

"You ignored my question."

"Is it?"

Sa'gola took another swig, trying to work out what to say. Finally, she just nodded.

"Did you do this alone?"

"No. The Master made the decision and his other options were far less pleasant."

"Who else was involved?"

"Why?"

"It would be easier for me to vent my anger on them."

Sa'gola spilled the water as she laughed.

"What's so funny?" Mharina demanded.

"My dear. You already have. There was Ithea and myself. I'm afraid I'm your only reachable target."

Mharina rose, walked over to a window, and peered out. Sa'gola got out of her bed, wrapped a shawl around herself, and joined Mharina at the window. The chilly stone under her bare feet sharpened her senses. Mharina turned to face her, and her expression was of a lost child.

"If I killed him, can you still get my mother and friends back?"

Sa'gola reached out and brought the elfe into her embrace, guiding her head onto her shoulder. Mharina shook.

"I believe I can," she whispered, rubbing the tips of her student's ears. "I have been further studying the magic involved. This is why the book was open. But only the Master can decide if and when I will."

Mharina disengaged from the embrace and perched on the ledge of the window. She brought her knees up and buried her head in her thighs. And she cried. Sa'gola bit her lip and felt a wave of emotion – a desire to soothe the elfe, comfort her, and make it all right.

"I have an idea. I cannot bring them out without the Master's permission. But he did not expressly order me to prevent you from observing them. Would you like that?"

Mharina looked up, her eyes red and puffy. Her lips quivered, and she nodded. Mharina took her hand and led her out of her chambers.

They took a route that Mharina was beginning to recognize. This time, however, they walked in tense silence. They brought several unlit fire sticks and, as the ones mounted on the walls became less frequent, they lit the ones they carried, one by one.

When they arrived at the sorceress's cavern, Sa'gola instructed the elfe to light the torches within it. Mharina complied without comment.

"Now close your eyes."

"Why?" Mharina asked, rather too sharply.

Sa'gola stared at her. "You are my student. You will show me respect."

"I didn't know you had imprisoned my mother and my friends."

"I have you imprisoned, and your siblings, too. You know who I serve and what responsibilities I have. You study with me because you yearn for the knowledge I possess."

Mharina could not hide the look she knew was spreading across her face. Sa'gola, however, frowned.

"What is it, my *calhei*?"

When Mharina spoke, her voice was soft and vulnerable. "It's not just for the knowledge," she said.

When it occurred to the sorceress what she meant, Sa'gola was at a loss for what to say. She took a deep breath.

"Let's try and navigate our way through this. We stand against each other, but we can also stand together."

"How could that possibly work?" Mharina asked.

The sorceress smiled beautifully. "I have no idea. Now please. I do not want you to see where I hide certain things. Close your eyes."

Mharina did as she was told and gasped when she was directed to look. On a metal ring, held up by three carved legs, sat a black stone.

"Your Anwar," Mharina said. "You'll let me…"

"Come. Look into the stone and clearly visualize your mother, just her. Good. Is that her?"

"Yes," Mharina whispered.

"She's beautiful," Sa'gola answered, purposefully neglecting to mention that this was not the first time she had seen her. "You look so like her."

Mharina grinned. "I wish," she said, curling a loose strand of hair behind a pointed ear.

"Who are the others?"

"That is Pyre behind her."

"She is Wycaan, too?"

"Yes," it occurred to Mharina that she might not want to be so free with her information. "Yes, she is. And the dark-haired woman is Riona. She's a healer."

"Her face is so pale."

"Isn't it?" Mharina giggled. "When she first came to Wycaan Island, we thought she was a ghost."

"Where is she from?"

"I don't know," Mharina replied, safe in the knowledge that she really did not know. "She is very closed and, though my *ahdahr* values her, she has no friends."

"I think you're wrong," Sa'gola replied. "Come around this side. Do you see that handsome man? There is something between them."

"How do you know?"

"When you get to a certain age, you notice these things. Who is he?"

"I've never seen him before," Mharina answered. "I don't think he was ever at Wycaan Island. Look. There is Denalion. He has aged, and – is he injured?"

"I'm afraid that might be my fault. He was the mouse I chased when you came into my chambers before. I caught him by digging a claw into his tail. Sorry."

Mharina could not help but laugh. "You should respect your elders, too," she said. "It is cat etiquette." They both laughed.

"We need to go," Sa'gola said at last.

She turned away to gather the cloth she kept the Anwar in as Mharina walked around the stone. She whirled when Mharina gasped, and saw the elfe stood with both hands over her mouth.

"What is it? What do you see?"

"Him. He was there, in the trees, shrouded in the cloak we used."

Sa'gola did not ask whom. She knew, and came quickly. The scene in the Anwar moved rapidly as she sought out Ithea, tracking him with her mind. She caught glimpses of him as he weaved himself out of her vision, magic against magic, but she harbored no doubts. When she looked up at her student, Mharina's face was hard.

"You said they were not in any danger."

"I didn't know," Sa'gola whispered, and Mharina knew she was telling the truth, because she could hear the fear in the purple woman's voice.

Chapter Seventy Two

Seanchai sat staring into the dying fire, hugging a mug of his resuscitating danseng tea. Umnesilk was guarding the last shift, but they rarely spoke these days. The Wycaan mulled over his dream. It had been real, he knew, and he had to go to meet this sorceress in the fishing port.

He stood up and walked over to the towering boar.

"I am going on myself," he said, and Umnesilk turned his massive head but did not speak. Seanchai continued. "I had a dream and must meet someone near Grogin."

"*Unsek?*" The pictorians had a name for the dreamwalker, and Seanchai had discovered that Denalion was known and held in high esteem by Umnesilk's people.

"No, but one similar."

"Similar?"

"Similar, but more dangerous. I need you to help me. I will turn into the bear and, you will strap my weapons and clothes to my back. Then you will all continue to the fortress without me."

"Where you meet?"

"I cannot tell you, and I must go alone. It's the only way to save my *calhei.*"

The huge boar nodded. "I angry with you. But you friend."

"Thank you. I know it hasn't been easy between us, but I feel the same. Listen. If I do not meet you at the fortress, you must wait for Shayth. None of you can defeat the Emperor, and if there are Wycaans and a sorceress, too, it will be a massacre. Also, the Emperor will not have forgotten how you took your boars and left his army at Hothengold. You will not be well received. Do not get near him. Wait for Shayth."

Umnesilk nodded. "Shayth good fighter, but only human."

"I know. I'm just hoping that… There are two others in all this who may be able to… Maybe the army can be a distraction while…someone sneaks in or something."

The huge pictorian frowned. "Sounds not like good plan, Wycaan. You must come if to rescue family. Or many die."

"You're always fun to talk to, my friend. I'm going to transform now. Keep an eye on Maugwen, okay?"

"She special?"

"She's special," Seanchai said. "But I doubt if she is special enough or even aware of her potential. I will be there. Now, I want to be gone before everyone wakes."

It felt good to run, the earth vibrant beneath his paws, as he pounded steadily along. The grizzly knew the way instinctively. Animals cleared from his path, predators and prey. All recognized that here ran a determined grizzly, one that would suffer no one to bar his way. As dusk fell, he heard the call of other bears. He turned and followed the cries.

Two brown bears waited on a mountainside near a cave. When Seanchai looked toward the cave, the female bristled, and he smiled to himself at the cries of newborn cubs. Outside the cave, a small, pig-like animal lay bloodied and still between the male's paws. When the grizzly sniffed it, the other bears stepped back. He yipped his gratitude and tore into the meat. He was starving. It tasted right – strange, but right.

When he had finished, the male stepped forward and nodded for Seanchai to follow him. Without help through the range, the grizzly would have gone around these mountains, not knowing the way. The brown bear ran into the night with absolute certainty. Finally, it signaled for the grizzly to rest and sat on its haunches to guard.

When the grizzly woke in the chilly dawn, two bluebirds chirped nearby. The brown bear was still sitting guard. They continued deep into the mountains and, with the sun at its zenith, surprised a sleepy herd of mountain goats. They fell upon the goats and each ate one.

Later, the brown bear let out a series of deep grunts, waited, and received no reply. A while later, as they descended toward the plains, the brown stopped and grunted again. This time, they heard a faint response drift over the plain. At the edge of the flat grassland, they drank from a stream. The brown stood staring, one paw held above the water with claws extended. The grizzly pretended not to watch, but was fascinated. When the claws flashed into the water, the grizzly knew its guide had caught a scaled one, and a struggling rainbow-colored fish glistened in the sun before disappearing into the brown's mouth.

The brown yipped to the grizzly, asking why it was not feeding. The grizzly nodded toward the plain, suggesting it was impatient rather than admitting to being a terrible hunter. The brown caught a second, and then set off onto the grasslands. When it reached a rock protruding through the rich green, the brown bounded up onto it. The grizzly followed, and this time, his guide's cries were returned by four dots on the horizon coming toward them. The brown nodded in their direction, and then turned to leave.

The grizzly grunted, and the brown stopped. The bigger bear approached and yipped, putting its head to the others. The brown bear yipped back, then turned and began running back to the mountains. It was eager to return to its mate and cubs, the grizzly surmised, and sighed deeply.

The four black bears met the grizzly and surrounded him as they took him further south. They slept in a forest with the rest of the black bear pack. Others had hunted, and several goats and a big, brown-haired buffalo lay ready. The pack stood near the goats and watched as the grizzly sniffed the prey. Then it clenched the buffalo with its teeth and dragged it to an old black bear, clearly the leader.

The grizzly grunted, turned to a goat instead, and ate. The sound of bears' surprise was soon lost in the munching and cracking of bones. Four cubs made a game of trying to steal food from their elders. They were warned to leave the grizzly alone and did so, but the old leader allowed them to eat from the rich red meat of the buffalo.

It was three more days before the grizzly, led by interchanging black bears, reached a ridge and stared down on the bright blue of the ocean. It was a beautiful sight, the water sparkling like sun-kissed jewels.

The black bears took their leave. This was two-leggeds' territory, and the grizzly could smell men, elves, and others. He turned to thank his guides, but they were already heading home. He watched them go and threw back his head, crying out to the entire bear nation. He doubted they heard him, but hoped, just maybe, they did.

Chapter Seventy Three

Seanchai had never remained in bear form for so long. He had been a grizzly…totally…and he had enjoyed it immensely. So much so that it actually felt strange and cumbersome to transform back into an elf.

He took the bundle that Umnesilk had tied to his bear body and dressed. His boots, comfortable and of high quality, felt restrictive in a way they hadn't before. He strapped his Win Dao swords to his back along with his quiver and bow.

He walked across the rocky terrain, twice encountering – and shying away from – a road. It had been many years since Seanchai had felt a need for stealth, but this was not Odessiya. Whoever was meeting him in Braithwaite may well have an ambush planned; if it were truly the Emperor, he would have several plans in place.

That night, Seanchai camped under a large rock with his swords kept close. He did not light a fire. But it proved a restless night, and not because no one guarded him. Seanchai had reached out to Denalion and failed to find him. They had weaved several ways to connect that only the two of them knew. The silence scared him.

He searched the different levels of the dream world and the conscious. He reached out to animals. He even dared enter the minds of villagers near the fortress without their permission.

He found a mother mourning the death of her son, and she allowed him in, thinking he was Denalion.

"He is my teacher and friend," Seanchai said. "I must speak with him. Can you help me?"

"What if you work for the Master?"

"Then you are as good as dead. But I do not. How can I prove it to you?"

The woman thought, and then told of her son's loss. When she had finished, tears streamed down her face. Seanchai, the dreamwalker, closed his eyes and murmured *Ahuvah, Ahuvah.* Waves of warm energy flooded into her until she sighed deeply.

"You cannot take away the pain, but I thank you. I fear for the dreamwalker. He is old, yet he walked many nights to be with the children, and in the daytime he went to figure out what has happened to your wife and her group."

"Did he find them?"

"No. When we last spoke, he planned to enter the sorceress's chambers and look for clues. I asked how and he said he'd walk in. No one would stop him. But I think someone did. I know people inside, and no one has seen him or even heard anything about him. Neither have they seen or heard of your wife and her company. They did not even make it to the dungeons, or I would have heard. I don't think the dreamwalker understood the power of the Master, the Priest, or the sorceress."

"Priest?"

"Yes. He is powerful beyond my imagination, surpassed only by the Master."

"Is the sorceress that good?"

The old woman shrugged. "I'm a simple woman. We fear the white-haired ones and the taragusii. The Priest and the Sorceress are beyond them, and towering above all is the Master."

"Hope may not be lost," Seanchai said. "Twice I have beaten the Master, though I fear him to be the stronger. But there is always hope."

"Hope?" she smiled. "It has long left this land."

The following night, Seanchai tried again to find the dreamwalker. Still, there was no sign of him. When the Wycaan woke, he reached into his pouch and took the green stone. It glowed faintly.

Seanchai now followed the road as it wound its way down toward the ocean. He drew his hood over his head as wagons and travelers passed by. A tall, well-armed figure like him was ignored or given a wide berth.

Ahead, a man, woman, child, and a babe in the mother's arms stood near a wagon. The man was struggling to lift the side of his cart and replace the wheel. His donkey stared ahead, apathetic.

Seanchai stopped. "I'll lift it. You fit the wheel."

The woman backed away, clutching the small child as she retreated. The man said nothing, but quickly fitted the wheel.

"I 'ave no money," he mumbled.

"I do not want reward, my friend." Seanchai started to walk away.

"Wait," the man called. "We 'ave a little bread an—"

His wife hissed something unintelligible.

"I have enough supplies and will soon be in Braithwaite," Seanchai answered. Do you live there?"

The man nodded. Seanchai returned to him. "Then if you wish to pay me for my help, let your family ride, and tell me of the town while we walk."

"Whatcha wanna know? Whatcha want there?"

As they walked, Seanchai wove a story of looking for business. His father grew grapes, and they were looking for a market for their wine. The man nodded, offered advice, immediately contradicted himself, and rambled a bit. Seanchai interrupted and asked about crime.

"A big fella like y'rself wiv weapons ain't gotta worry. Them elves have a hard time, and any who fink 'emselves tough. If yah threaten, be ready to do it, know what I mean? If yah ain't, best shaddup.

"If yah 'ave money, keep it 'idden and spend it wisely. Them dock's are the wors'. Don't wanna do business there, tho' most o' the moneys there, but not worth it until yah know yah ways around."

Seanchai listened carefully, nodding. He realized he didn't know who he would meet, or where. He thought it would be the purple sorceress, but he had a hard time imagining such a diminutive woman walking through the docks.

"I'm looking for a woman," he said.

The woman tutted from the cart, and the man laughed. "Course yah ar, strapping lad. Why not? Ain't married, eh? Then's okay."

He laughed again, and Seanchai glanced back to see the man's wife all red-faced in the wagon. The man enjoyed his joke and even slapped Seanchai on the back.

"The woman I'm looking for is small. She has a pale face, black and purple hair, and purple around her eyes. Do you…"

The man had stopped laughing and was now almost shaking. "Leave us," he said. "Walk ahead. Go on. We thank yah for yah help, but we ain't mixing with the likes o' yah. Scat. Go on now. I got the babe to look out for."

Seanchai took a few steps backwards, still facing them, and held out his palms. "I don't know–"

"Go," the woman shrieked. "You'll get us killed."

Seanchai turned around and walked on, a tight pit forming in his stomach.

Chapter Seventy Four

Seanchai made his way into the fishing port of Braithwaite. His head was buried deep inside his cowl, but all his senses were on alert. The town was dense, with one building leaning on another. Many were in disrepair, and often the windows were boarded up. The smell of rotting fish was everywhere, and the piercing squawks of seagulls carried through the air.

He scryed every alleyway and building, seeking out anyone who might be lying in wait. A small boy of about Ilan's age was following him, and not doing a great job being discreet.

The elf made his way toward the docks, drawn by the fresh, salty sea air. It was late afternoon, and the town seemed empty. The fishing boats were still at sea, and everyone land-bound sought refuge from the hot sun.

He was hungry and thirsty. He stopped at a small establishment with a statue of a blue fish welcoming him at the entrance. Inside, it was dark and dense, and Seanchai chose a table near the front. Any other customers had to be further inside.

A big woman shuffled up, rolls of fat collecting under her chin and hanging from her arms. She carried two skins. "Whatcha drink? Beer or water?"

"Water, if you please."

It did not seem to please her as she tossed the lighter brown skin onto the table and produced a cup from her apron.

"Gotta eat, if only drinking water."

"I *am* hungry. I'll have your freshest fish. There is a boy outside following me. Prepare a plate for him as well."

The woman grunted something, and then retreated. Seanchai tried to see further inside the eating establishment, but the glare from the street made it impossible. He did not like the idea of not knowing who was nearby.

A younger woman, her hair carelessly bundled in a scarf, brought him a large plate with chopped whitefish; thin, square fried dough; and an assortment of chopped vegetables. She put an empty plate in front of Seanchai and a second one opposite. Then she looked around for a second person.

"There is a boy outside. Please invite him in. He wears dirty brown clothes and a whiter turban."

She frowned. "Them scum ain't good to know. Just try 'n take your money. 'e 'as friends nearby, I betcha."

"I appreciate the warning. But if that's the case, he might as well be where I can see him."

She cocked her head, but nodded and went outside when Seanchai stared at her. When she returned, she pushed the boy toward the table.

"Sit," Seanchai said.

"Whatcha want?"

"Well, for a start, I am hungry, and have no idea how to eat this food."

The boy had dark, sunburnt skin, and his smile was genuine. "Want me to show yah?"

"Please."

The boy laughed. "And yah paying, right?"

"For the food, not the lesson."

The boy nodded. "Awright," he said. "Since yah new in town, I guess I can let yah. Watch."

He took a square of dough onto his plate and added layers of fish and vegetables, leaving out the dark green strings. Then he added a gray sauce and deftly wrapped it into a roll. Seanchai attempted to do the same. The boy laughed, and then quickly covered his mouth.

"What about the green strings?"

"It's seaweed, very 'ealthy. Me mum makes us eat it. She ain't 'ere, though, so…"

Seanchai took some and chewed on it. "Very salty," he said, and took a long drink of water.

"Make yah a big man, me mum says. Sure you ain't been scoffing it since yah a tyke?"

The Wycaan grinned. "First time near the sea," he admitted.

"Really? There are other places? Like what?"

"Well. I grew up in a big forest, surrounded by trees. I have crossed mountains, deserts, and ice plains."

The boy's eyes grew big. "Ice plains?"

"Everything is covered in snow, a world of white. It gets so cold that the water freezes." Seanchai folded a second wrap. The boy was on his third. "Eat your seaweed. I don't want to make your mother angry."

"You good with that bow?"

"Yes."

"How good?"

"Very."

"And you fight with two swords?"

"Yes."

"Why?"

"Got two hands." Seanchai couldn't help trying to make the boy laugh. He missed his *calhei*.

"What's the best way to fight?"

"The best fight is one you don't have to have."

The boy rolled his brown eyes. "Sound like me mum, but wiv fancy words. You good, I bet."

Seanchai laughed. "I'm alive. Now, tell me: why are you following me?"

"Who said I's following yah?"

"I did, and I bought you food."

The big woman came to the table and glared at the boy. Then she turned to Seanchai. "You plan to pay for this?"

Seanchai looked at the boy and then at the empty plate. "You still hungry?" He did not wait for an answer. "Another plate, please," he said to the woman. "And a double serving of the sea weed."

"Pay first," the woman said. "Four hangans or six draktans."

Seanchai handed her the coins, and she left.

"You work for her?" he asked, and the boy stared at the retreating woman. "I mean the Purple Lady."

The boy's eyes grew large.

"That's okay. You're in no danger. My business is with her, not you. What are you supposed to do?"

"Follow yah. Make sure yah okay. Know where yah sleep. In the morning, I need to take yah to see 'er."

"Where?"

"I show yah. By the docks."

They ate some more, and Seanchai asked the woman to wrap the rest. She brought a large leaf and deftly tied it up with twine. Seanchai handed the package to the boy.

"Take it home. Give it to your mother. Tell her there is extra seaweed inside."

"Thanks. Yah gonna sleep around here?"

"Is it safe?"

"Not really. I take yah back into town."

"Are you safe walking around the town? It's getting dark?"

The boy produced a purple stone on a length of twine. "Shows I work for the Purple Witch. No one'll mess with 'er, so no one'll mess with me. Why yah wanna see 'er so bad?"

"I plan to mess with her," Seanchai said. "Her master has my *cal*–children."

"She has a master?" This seems amazing to the boy. "Listen. You've been nice wiv the food and me following yah. She's a very powerful witch, I tell yah."

"You see my swords and bow," Seanchai said. "They're the least effective of my weapons."

The boy leaned forward. "But a wise man tells me that the best fight is one you don't have to have."

Seanchai laughed. "You learn quickly."

"So should yah. No one crosses the Purple Witch. She's small and beautiful. Every gang man and criminal and politician would gladly force 'er to their bed, but she walks the docks at night and 'ard men cross the street to avoid 'er. Yah understanding?"

"I do. Thank you. But they have my children."

The boy nodded. "Me mum says she fight anyone who 'urts me."

"She's very brave."

"No, she ain't. But she's smart," the boy replied.

"Why?"

"I stay outta trouble 'cause I know if she fight, she be dead. Parents don't understand."

"They do," Seanchai said, leaning forward. "They understand the love for the ones they bring into this world. Love is a powerful weapon, my friend, and the love a parent has for their children is the most powerful there is."

The boy looked at him, his eyes big and sad. "Sorry, mister. But if yah gonna mess wiv the Purple Lady, love ain't gonna be enough."

Chapter Seventy Five

"He could not have gotten past me! I'm awake and alert. No one ever gets past me!" Montclair yelled at everyone and glared at Ithea, who was now sitting against a tree trunk and smiling.

"But he did get past you," Pyre said, her arms folded across her chest.

"He is old and wounded," Sellia added. "It couldn't have been easy for him to pass you silently."

"And I thought we could trust you," Riona sighed. She may be falling in love with Montclair, but that would not stop her from making fun of him.

"Impossible." Montclair glared at the old man, shrouded in his white sheet.

Then he glared at each of the females in his party and stomped off into the trees, but returned immediately. They all burst out laughing, and this woke Denalion.

"What strange sound is this?" he asked, yawning as he struggled to sit up.

"Go back to sleep, old one," Riona said, bringing him water. "You toiled all night."

"Not to any success," Denalion said. "There must be a way to reach back into our time."

"There is not," Ithea said, his voice raspy. "May I have some water, too?"

Riona brought him a skin.

A thin, brittle hand reached out, shaking, and took the water skin. The top disappeared into the cowl, and he gulped audibly. When he finished, it fell to the ground.

"I did not mean to drop it," he said.

"It's okay," Riona replied and retrieved the skin.

Denalion came and sat next to Ithea. "Is it really possible to return? You designed this together with Sa'gola?"

"I orchestrated this corridor between time with a little help from the purple sorceress."

"The obstruction: is it both ways?" Denalion asked.

Ithea thought. "I presume so, but have never tried. Who will save you, though? The Wycaan elf?" He scoffed, and everyone bristled.

The silence was broken only by the sound of water boiling. Riona made tea, carefully mixing from her growing supply of herbs. She sat next to Montclair and shared her cup with him. He put an arm around her, and neither seemed embarrassed that the others saw.

"We are moving on," Sellia told Ithea.

"Which way?" When no one answered, he asked: "Do you think I can't track you?"

"Do you think we should make it easy for you?" Sellia snapped.

Ithea shrugged. "Fair point. Off you go then. I will come to you soon and hope by then you have made your choice."

They followed the river downstream in silence.

"We need to lose him," Sellia said.

"We already have," Montclair replied.

"No, we haven't," Denalion said. "He doesn't need to physically follow us but maybe that is to our advantage." They all stopped and looked at him. "When he meets me in the dream world, he might not be the most experienced."

"But he is more powerful than you, no?" Pyre said, the fear clear in her voice.

Denalion put a hand on her shoulder. "I doubt I can kill him, but I may be able to weaken him. If he survived the sorceress and Mharina, though —"

"Don't mention them in the same breath," Sellia hissed. "She is my daughter. I gave birth and sustenance to her. She is mine."

Denalion walked past Pyre and Riona to face Sellia. "Mharina is very much her own elfe now, Sellia," Denalion said. "While I'm sure she will make the right decision when the time comes, things will never be the same, ever."

"Why are you telling me this?"

"Because I might not have the opportunity when the time comes." He faced the others. "I will meet him in the dream world. I don't expect to survive the night."

A snarl from behind silenced them all. A second growl answered it.

"We should find higher ground," Montclair declared, drawing his sword.

Sellia noched an arrow, Pyre drew her Win Dao swords, while Riona tensed her sling, a stone already in the leather pouch.

"Up there," Montclair pointed to a couple of rocks hidden in shadow.

They made their way over slowly, listening to the growls now coming from all around them.

"There," Pyre nodded to a cave partially hidden by a huge, withered oak tree. They reached the cave without seeing their hunters. It was small and dank. As they entered, Montclair sheathed his sword and snapped small branches from the tree outside. The snapping sound was ominous in the dark space.

Pyre sheathed her swords, but glanced at Sellia. "Keep your bowstring taut and cover us."

As Sellia kept watch, they quickly dropped their packs in the back of the cave.

A sharp crunch echoed off the stone walls.

"Bones," Montclair muttered. "This place has already served as a tomb."

Sellia apart, they all gathered wood, darting to the tree and back to safety. Riona yanked dry grasses, and they soon had a pile in the cave.

"I will sleep," Denalion said, his voice quiet. "I may not awaken." He turned to Sellia. "Tell the children…tell them…"

Tears glistened in his eyes. Sellia took him in her arms. "I will," she whispered.

He turned to Pyre and Riona. "You share much in common. One uses all her strength to deny who she is, and the other to become who she so desperately wants to be. All will happen in time. Your destinies lie before you. Walk in confidence."

They both hugged him, and tears mixed. Then the dreamwalker turned to Montclair and patted his arm. "Love requires more skill than the sword. Fight to keep her if you will, but be good to her."

Montclair nodded. Denalion shuffled to the back of the cave, lay down, and wrapped himself in his cloak. The darkness swallowed Denalion, last Dreamwalker of the Elves of the West.

Chapter Seventy Six

As dusk gathered, the party took turns to try and sleep, but no one could find rest. They heard the growls, the scuffling, and as the day drew on, the howls. The pack was getting bigger, excited at the prospect of fresh meat.

Sellia stared out, caught fleeting glimpses of them, and sighed at the prospect of a long and dangerous night. She could hear Montclair sharpening his already finely honed blade and the occasional swish of Pyre's Win Dao swords, all typical preparations the world over in the hours before battle. She had been here before, in many guerilla-type fights and the battles at Galbrieth, Hothengold, and the Cliftean Pass. Each time, however, she had fought beside Seanchai. This was different and, though surrounded by friends, she suddenly felt very alone.

Deep in her thoughts, she was surprised to see Riona sitting next to her. "How are you holding up?"

"I hate the waiting," Sellia replied, her eyes never leaving the slope in front of them. "I always do. How about you?"

Riona sighed and stared out into the gathering darkness. She hooked a strand of hair behind her round ear. "I don't know. Dying never seemed to burden me. We all die at our appointed time, but now it feels different." She nodded toward Montclair.

"I do," Sellia said. "Tell me a story to pass the time – a true story."

Riona bristled. "I have kept it inside me for so long. Why should I let it out now?"

"Because this might be your last chance," Sellia said as Pyre and Montclair came over to join them. The elfe stared at Montclair. "You know everything, don't you? You knew before the two of you were together."

Montclair did not answer. He just looked at Riona and waited for her.

"No," she said at last. "I made a decision a long time ago that I would live in anonymity. I'm ready to die that way, as well."

"Shame," Sellia said. "We could do with a story to pass the–."

"There is no time," Pyre sprung to her feet, an arrow leaving her bow even as she rose.

A single howl of pain was followed by a frenzy of yelps. About twenty giant wolfheids came bounding toward them on all fours. Sellia had seen these distorted creatures when they had attacked and wounded her, before Seanchai had rescued her. It was the first time they had met since he had completed his transformation into a Wycaan.

Sellia and Pyre released arrow after arrow, each hitting their mark. The huge wolfheids were easy targets. When one broke through and sprung at them, Montclair took two steps forward and swung his broadsword in a wide arc, cutting straight through the animal's neck. The head fell in its place, but the body continued, gushing a torrid stream of purple blood over both elfes. The fortune-sword twisted round and stabbed at another piercing the dark mark on its forehead. Blood gushed out. It never got closer.

The wolfheids retreated to regroup and, over the next two hours, they charged relentlessly, their numbers never seeming to diminish. When the arrows and sling stones were exhausted,

Sellia, Riona, Pyre, and Montclair drew their blades with one hand and held burning torches in the other.

They repelled two more wolfheid assaults, but not without price. They were all exhausted. Montclair had a nasty gash on his sword arm, and Riona was concussed and holding her rib cage. Pyre stepped in front of them, her swords a blur, and a mound of dead beasts soon piled at her feet.

Sellia knew they couldn't continue much longer. She could barely lift her long knife. But she looked at Pyre and gasped. Everyone was exhausted, but the young elfe stood erect, chest heaving. Her Win Dao swords glimmered blue, purple blood dripping from the blades onto the dust. Pyre turned, her gray-white hair swirling, and when her eyes met Sellia's, she smiled. Her voice was deep and powerful.

"I am no Wycaan Master, but for a precious moment I can feel what it might be like. The energy pulsates through me."

Sellia nodded, too exhausted to comment. The giant wolfheids were gathering in front of them, about forty strides away. They were no longer frightened of arrows and knew they had their prey.

Pyre brought the final moss and branches to the mouth of the cave. They would set it alight when the wolfheids next attacked. It might help take down a few more, but it would not be enough.

"Where are you, old one? Did you not come to confront me?"
"Why must they die?" Denalion asked from within the mist.
"Everyone dies."

"They are important to me. Who are you to decide their fate?"

"Really, Dreamwalker? I was told you are old and wise, so you know how it works. When one of us dies, it is monumental. When it is one of them, it is nature."

"Have you never loved someone, never desired to make them happy, to see them succeed?"

"There are those I have used and enjoyed during their servitude. But what you talk about is weak, stupid, and mortal."

"I am mortal, as are you."

"Not really. And not like them. Look at your friends, Dreamwalker. They are weak and puny. I planned to take the man's body, but I am impressed with the young elfe. She fights with great spirit and skill."

A snort of derision came out of the mist.

"Are we to fight now or wait until my packwolves have killed your friends?"

There was silence. Ithea raised a singed eyebrow.

From deep within the mist, almost faint, yet clearly distant, came a deep growl.

Sellia watched the wolfheids move closer. But then, they stopped, ears perked and snouts sniffing. Suddenly, a younger one turned on the wolfheid next to it, sinking its jaws into the animal's neck. Immediately, several more beasts began to fight, breaking the line of attack.

But the leader, a shoulder taller than the others, approached with teeth barred. He was followed by a half dozen more wolfheids. Sellia raised her long, bloodied knife. Montclair did the same, but his arm wound made the thick broadsword shake.

Pyre stepped forward to have enough room to swing her two swords.

As the leader crouched to attack, a roar came from above the cave, vibrating the walls. A giant red wolf leapt upon the leader. A loud crack, and the leader crumbled to the ground. The red wasted no time and leapt at another.

With the pack in disarray, Sellia raised her torch. "Attack," she yelled, and, flanked by Montclair and Pyre, ran forward to stand with the red.

It was over in minutes. Any wounded beast was killed, while those who could, fled, howling and yipping as they ran. The giant red wolf turned to Pyre, its sides heaving, bloody saliva drooling from its mouth.

Run.

The voice was clear in Pyre's head.

"Denalion," she panted.

Go now. Take the healer. He comes. I will wait for him, but I won't hold him up for long.

"Denalion–"

We have said our goodbyes, my young Wycaan warrior. Guide them to safety if you can.

"I love you, Denalion." Tears rolled down her face.

I have always loved you, too, Pyre, ever since I helped my granddaughter give birth to you. Now please, go and become the Wycaan that you aspire to be.

And the great red wolf turned his back and walked into the brush to meet his death.

Chapter Seventy Seven

The boy led Seanchai through the docks to the foot of a pier. Though it was early, the waterfront was already bustling. Most fishing boats had left, but a few were still casting off, and the cries of captains' orders pierced the fog, even as it seemed to muffle their voices and the squawks of the ever-hungry seagulls.

Old men, women, and children were opening stalls at the marketplace, scrubbing trays and preparing to receive the catch they would later sell. Here and there, smoking cauldrons of a dark, pungent drink was being sold, and Seanchai bought a long, thin loaf of crispy bread. He tore a third off for himself and gave the rest wordlessly to the boy.

He chewed the soft inside of the loaf and stared out at a rickety pier that disappeared into the fog.

"This is where the Purple Lady told me to leave yah," the boy said, his mouth stuffed with bread. "She'll be waiting."

"How do you know?" Seanchai asked.

"Said so. Purple Lady don't lie."

"Thank you," Seanchai said and extended his hand. The boy stared at it, and then shook it. When Seanchai released the boy's hand, it held a small cloth bag half full of coins. "Spend it wisely," Seanchai said in a low voice. "I think you are too smart to waste it."

The boy's eyes grew wide. "Thank yah, sir, and please, don't anger 'er." Then he pocketed the bag, turned, and disappeared into the crowd.

Seanchai watched him go, adjusted his bow and swords, then wrapped his cloak around himself and stepped, somewhat gingerly, onto the pier.

The rickety structure rocked with each wave and rhythmically groaned under Seanchai's weight. His boots thudded damply, and he found himself pleased that the pier was long. He had time to balance himself.

Unlike the adjacent piers that still had boats moored, this pier had no boats attached and no evidence that anyone had been here. No one, apparently, desired to share a pier with the Purple Lady.

Seanchai walked slowly, taking his time, weighing every step, and every possible scenario. He doubted she would try to fight him. The children were still hostage, and the Emperor would surely not want someone else to kill Seanchai.

He could not conceive any other option than to go with her if she asked. But if that's what she wanted, why had they not just instructed him to head to Grogin? He stepped on a plank of wood, which snapped, but he hopped ahead. When he turned back to look down at the offending plank, he saw that the fog now obscured his view of the docks. He turned and continued walking, feeling that he was being cut off from the world.

Eventually, his sharp, elven eyes saw a boat's silhouette. As it became more defined, he saw it was flat, with a small cabin near the rear. Its single mast had a dirty white sail tied tightly around it. In the front of the boat there was a large flat area with benches around the side.

She stood next to the boat with her back to him, shrouded in a purple cloak with two diagonal black stripes down the rear. She straightened as he approached.

He stopped several strides from her, waiting for her to turn and face him, wanting her to make the first move. Sa'gola did not turn. She just removed her hood and shook out her long dark hair.

"Thank you for coming," she said.

"I found your request hard to refuse," Seanchai replied. "How are my *calhei*?"

"They are well and truly wonderful. The Wycaans tell me Ilan has an aptitude for science and mineralogy, and Senzia will be very powerful. Mharina says her sister combines her mother's spirit with your wisdom. Would you agree?"

"A parent is not objective about such things," Seanchai answered, realizing he was biting his lower lip.

"I know Mharina the best. I am teaching her myself, and she's an excellent pupil."

Seanchai snorted. "You think you can know my *calhei* in just a few months?"

Sa'gola turned, an engaging smile on her face. "Why, yes, I do. I have seen her in situations that you have not. She has grown up a lot, seen many things – too many, you would no doubt think."

"And you have my wife and friends?"

"We do. They are alive, as far as I know, but they are in a dangerous situation we did not anticipate. Come. We will talk more on the boat."

She stepped gracefully onto the stern of the boat. It rocked, but she did not falter. She waited expectantly, knowing he had little choice but to follow.

The boat rocked when Seanchai climbed aboard, as well, and he needed to steady himself. Sa'gola, he noticed, was stable and at ease.

"It's a small boat, but sturdy," she said. 'Still, you might want to watch your step. Please unfasten the rope there."

Seanchai leaned over and unraveled the mooring rope. It was tied around a black block of wood, carved crudely into a fish's head. The boat immediately began to glide through the water away from the quay. The Wycaan looked around, confused. The sail was furled, and he felt no wind. Neither were there any oarsmen. The boat simply moved. He looked up. Sa'gola had her arms folded across her chest, smiling.

"Impressive," he conceded.

"Thank you."

She was beautiful, Seanchai thought. Though small, he could feel her confidence and power. Sa'gola closed her eyes and raised her head as if smelling the scent of the ocean.

"I love water, though I serve the fire. Is that strange? What is your element?"

"A Wycaan trains with all the elements. I'm equally comfortable with water and fire, tree and wind, but my training has been erratic. Your master has a habit of killing my teachers."

"Really? He killed them?"

"Not exactly," Seanchai said, feeling foolish. "But had we not been fighting him, they would be alive."

"Then maybe you all err in fighting him and should surrender."

"Do you not fight him in some way? Are there not some secrets you keep from him to delude yourself into thinking you are still free?"

Sa'gola laughed, a throaty, attractive sound, and flicked her curly hair back. It was an intriguing movement.

"I do not fight the Master, because he is more powerful than me."

"Not true," Seanchai retorted.

The sorceress' face went serious. "Do not presume to understand me. We have only just met. The Master has known me for years, trusts me, and I him."

"True, I don't know you, but I know him. If you think he trusts you then you delude yourself. He will use you as long as you further his plans, but will not hesitate to destroy you when he has no further use for you, especially if he believes that you are a potential threat. No. You serve him because…"

Sa'gola was eyeing him now, her black eyes intense. Seanchai was tempted to scry, but knew he would be repelled. Then a smile crept across his face.

"I know. It's because he has not threatened something dear to you. If he did, you would fight and try to destroy him."

Sa'gola just stared at Seanchai, then turned away and looked out on the water and the mist.

Chapter Seventy Eight

S eanchai moved to a bench, adjusted his swords, and sat down. "You know, it's not just about him and me anymore."

"What do you mean?"

"The day he kidnapped my children, everything changed. The twins study with Wycaans, you say, but I wonder if they are truly Wycaan."

"What do you mean? They have white hair and are unbearably arrogant. Is there more to your sort?"

Seanchai laughed and was surprised to see this pleased Sa'gola.

"Where do they come from? Apart from the Elves of the West, the Wycaans were thought to be destroyed, with one or two notable exceptions."

Sa'gola turned to him. The sun momentarily pierced through the fog and, though it offered no warmth, it lit up the sorceress's face. She was truly beautiful, Seanchai thought – and young. Or was she? Everything about her suggested she possessed considerable experience. He blushed when he realized she had caught him staring.

"I'm sorry," he said.

She smiled. "I know how I look. I have seen hunger on the faces of many men, but never an elf."

"I-I have a mate," Seanchai stammered, looking down at his boots.

"Of course you do. Sellia is beautiful and strong. Tell me how you got together."

Seanchai turned away.

"Do elves have their marriages arranged for them by parents or elders? You don't love each other that way – I can tell. Who brought you together?"

"The elfe we both loved. She is dead, but foresaw her own end and begged us to be together."

"So you do it to honor her memory? That's sweet, if somewhat tragic."

"I have grown to love Sellia, and I hope she feels the same way."

Sa'gola laughed – an eerie sound in the mist that enveloped them. "That sounds…dutiful, on both your parts. Your true love did this because she knew you were weak, I presume, She was probably very strong and smart. She was able to manipulate you to fulfill your destiny and needed to ensure that someone would be there for you when she died. What was her name?"

"Ilana."

"Ah, and who is Senzia is named after? Sellia's true love? Did she have to leave him for you?"

"Senzia is named after Sellia's mother, and no, her mate died a few years before we met."

"And Mharina is, I understand, named after your first teacher. She is most proud of her name."

Sa'gola's voice softened when she mentioned Mharina, and Seanchai was drawn out of his reverie.

"Tell me about your relationship with Mharina," he said.

"I am her teacher."

"No," Seanchai said. "It's more than that."

"You might not want the truth," Sa'gola said and arched a thin eyebrow from where it perched above her purple eyeliner.

"Then we waste our time. I thought you were…"

"What?"

"I don't know," he looked away. "I felt we were sharing something, like we were…" he paused as he realized what he was thinking. "We are very similar, Sa'gola, you and I. Both have immense power, but are destined to play roles that we have come to terms with rather than enjoy."

"You assume much, Wycaan."

"What are you hiding, then? Tell me about Mharina."

"If you really want to know, your daughter and I are *very* close. We spend all of our time together, except when she checks in on the twins or the Master has a task for me."

"What do you teach her? Dark magic?"

"Feminine magic, fueled by sun, blood, and fire. Men think they draw their power from the sun and fire as women do from the moon and water, but they are mistaken. Nothing is ever quite so simple. As I told you, I am comfortable using any element. You ask which I prefer? Whichever it takes to defeat my enemies."

"So what makes teaching Mharina so special?" he persisted.

"*She* does," Sa'gola responded. "She has, I understand, some of you in her, but a great deal of her mother. It's a shame that I did not meet Sellia earlier. Perhaps she might have found happiness in my arms and love, rather than searching for it in duty."

She paused and waited for his response.

"We're talking about Mharina. What do you teach her? Who are you, Sa'gola?"

"I come from an ancient order far from here, beyond the boundaries and knowledge of Odessiya. Those in my order are all females–"

"All human?"

"No, all races. Like your Wycaan order it is about the individual, not the shape of their ears. But no male has ever survived our training, and I suspect one never will."

"How do you perpetuate your order?" Seanchai inquired, blushing as he asked.

"We find suitable males, take what we need from them, and leave their shells to die."

Seanchai laughed.

"Why is that funny?" Sa'gola asked.

He turned to her and smiled wryly. "It's just that you have the audacity to judge my relationship with Sellia when it seems quite civilized compared to your order."

To her credit, Sa'gola laughed, as well. "True," she conceded, "but my order is honest in what we do. There are no illusions. You and Sellia live a lie, and the sad part is that you have even begun to believe it yourselves. Men are weak when faced with a beautiful woman who wants him to take her. They think they are invincible, but, in fact, they are at their most vulnerable. What could they give up that is more sacred than their chance to create life?"

"It's the ultimate magic," Seanchai said.

Sa'gola nodded. "It is also expected that each sorceress apprentice a worthy young female in the craft. A powerful bond forms between teacher and student, something you might have felt yourself with your teachers. Among our order, it is intense. You are ready to die for each other, to kill for each other, to–"

Seanchai sprung to his feet. "Has Mharina killed for you? Denalion sensed–"

"Sit down," Sa'gola's voice growled with power, and Seanchai felt himself pulled back down to the bench. He felt his heart constrict and his breath catch.

"Did you make her kill someone?"

"It was not like that. She came across me being beaten, and the magic rose inside of her, a wave of fury. She had never before succeeded in bringing the fire forth, but it was a catalyst. She should not have even been there. But she just might have saved my life."

"She's so young. She–"

"She is not so young, Wycaan. You are her father and have no perspective. How old were you when you first killed someone?"

Seanchai's mind went back to when he charged a patrol of soldiers who had captured Rhoddan, even before he had met Uncle and begun his training. He winced. It sounded all too similar. He had unleashed a power inside of him that he never knew existed in order to save a friend. Sa'gola studied him.

"Seanchai, I already told you." Her voice was soft. "She saw me being brutalized, and the rage rose."

"Why, I should–" Seanchai had not even noticed he was on his feet again.

"No," Sa'gola's voice resonated with power. "You cannot harm me. Your mate and friends are incarcerated and in danger. Only two people know how to free them. I am one of them."

"Then I will find the other." He could feel his power rising, the energy of sea and fog coursing through him."

"The other is the one your daughter killed."

Seanchai panted. "I will find a way to reach them. You'll not destroy my family."

"If you kill me, you risk losing something far more than a mate who bonded with you out of duty. You risk losing your daughter."

Seanchai's nostrils flared. He flicked back his cloak, wrapped his hands around the hilts of his Win Dao swords, and drew them with a chilling rasp of blade on scabbard.

"You will not take my daughter from me."

"You *are* correct about one thing, Seanchai. We are very similar, you and I: pawns in the Master's plan for Odessiya. But there is one fundamental difference that sets us apart. You are bound to your family and weak. I am ruthless and know my place."

His chest heaving, Seanchai raised his swords. Sa'gola didn't know if it was to attack or sheathe them, but she didn't hesitate. Two purple flames left the sorceress' fingertips and ripped into Seanchai's chest. They were followed by two more bursts, this time pure white fire. He staggered back to the edge of the boat, staring at her, eyes bulging, and swords now sheathed. Then, as the fog began to shroud his shoulders, the Wycaan fell slowly backwards into the water.

There was a crisp splash as the sea embraced him, and then silence.

Sa'gola just stood there, fingers still stretched out before her, chest heaving. She had thought he was about to attack her. Men do that. But she knew now he was not. But he was going to take her apprentice away from her. That was not possible. She stared out over the water, but it was not his face that she saw.

"Mharina," she whispered. "Forgive me."

Chapter Seventy Nine

Pyre led them away from the cave and the carnage, howls echoing in their wake. She sheathed her Win Dao swords and drew her bow, noching an arrow, noticing that she only had two left. She wished there had been time to retrieve some from the wolfheids.

A groan from Riona made her stop and turn. The healer was always pale, but now her face looked wraith-like. Montclair had an arm around her and was supporting her as they walked. Sellia, her bow also ready, brought up the rear.

"She needs to rest," Montclair said. "I think she cracked a rib."

Pyre turned around and looked at the healer. "I'm sorry, but we can't stop. Ithea is coming, and Denalion won't be able to hold him back for long."

Riona nodded and guzzled the water Montclair gave her, letting half drip down her chin. Pyre disappeared into the brush and returned with a rough walking stick.

"I can support her," Montclair snapped.

"We might yet have need of your sword," Pyre answered, giving the stick to Riona.

"Not sure we will, the way you wielded yours," Montclair answered. "You were possessed."

"Can I take that as a compliment?"

"I can still whip you, *calhei*," Montclair grinned. "Experience counts for something."

They all laughed, but Pyre could tell he was genuinely impressed, and she was a little surprised at how important that was to her.

"Thank you," she said.

"Where are we going?" Sellia asked from the rear.

"Up there," Pyre said.

They all stared at the mountain where, one day in the future, Grogin would be built.

"His camp is there," Sellia was alarmed.

"I know," Pyre replied. "It is more defensible against wolfheids."

"But he will surely find us."

"He will find us, anyway," Pyre replied. "But there is a reason he chose that place for his camp. I want to know what it is."

Montclair shook his head. "Face it. We are alone with only a psychopath and deformed, possessed wolves for company."

Pyre wheeled on him and grabbed his collar, venting her frustration and exhaustion on him. "Not forever. I believe in Seanchai. I have seen him do great things, and I know he will never give up on his mate, his children, or his friends."

There was only the sound of her heavy breathing. She looked down to the ground in shame.

Montclair gently removed her hands from his shirt. "I'm sorry," he said. "Lead the way."

As they climbed the mountain, Sellia reflected on what was happening. Pyre, exhilarated by the fight, had taken over leadership of the party. Sellia had no doubt the young Wycaan was doing this subconsciously, but regardless, she exuded an undeniable sense of confidence and power. Sellia was pleased with Pyre's newfound confidence, but her power felt familiar... reminiscent. Like Seanchai.

But something deeper disturbed her. Pyre had absolute belief in Seanchai – that he would risk it all for them. Sellia did not share this belief, and the revelation hit her hard. She knew he would try and rescue the children, but she wasn't so sure he'd come for her if he didn't know where she was. He might decide she had backed off and returned to Wycaan Island. He might simply decide to do what was safest for their children.

As the day moved on and they climbed higher, Sellia fell into a depression; a sense of hopelessness swallowed her up. She might never see her children again, or Seanchai. All the complaints and resentment at the time and energy she had portioned out to the four of them fell away. In that moment she realized how much they were an integral part of her.

"I never got to tell them," she murmured.

"What?" Riona and Montclair, in front of her, stopped and turned around.

Sellia had not even realized she had spoken out loud. She watched concern replace pain in the healer's expression.

"It's nothing," Sellia said.

"You rarely get to say goodbye," Riona said, her voice soft. "It makes everything so much more difficult, so incomplete."

Sellia stared at her and nodded. "Things have not been good between Seanchai and me of late. He's always gone, leaving me with the school and the children. And Mharina started to push back against me before she was taken, as if she sensed my inner resentment."

"She knows you love her," Riona put a hand on Sellia's shoulder.

Pyre had walked back to join them. "As does Seanchai," she said.

Anger flared out of Sellia's depression. "Have you ever heard him say so?"

"N-no," Pyre replied, abruptly transformed back into the young elfe she was. "He rarely talked about you, unless it was about your mastery of the bow or stories from your past."

"And that is all we had left: stories from the past." Sellia pushed past them all. "After all these years, I'm still just standing in for Ilana."

"Sellia," Riona's voice was strong, and when the elfe turned, she saw the effort Riona had to put in to stand up straight, a hand on her rib cage. "It is a long, dark path you are going down. We do not have the time or strength for it. You will get your chance to tell him, Mharina, and the twins how you feel about them. Hold yourself together."

Sellia glared at her. She knew Riona was right, but that wasn't the point. She turned and resumed her own steep climb.

"Take another step, and I'll shoot." Pyre woke when she heard Montclair's clear command and jumped to her feet, her blanket flying, her hands unsheathing her swords in one well-practiced movement.

She turned, the blades of her Win Dao swords glistening in the early morning light, her body crouched and ready to spring.

"Denalion!" she exclaimed. "Montclair? What are you doing?"

The fortune-sword was holding Pyre's bow noched, the bowstring taut. About twenty paces in front of him stood Denalion, his red hair flaming in the sunlight that bathed him.

"Keep your swords out," Montclair growled as she began to sheathe them. "This is the old elf's body, but it is not him inside."

Pyre edged forward, her swords poised to parry and thrust. Montclair was right. The old elf's body was too erect and awkward.

Sellia moved into the clearing, the steep, volcanic rock behind them and a sheer drop to either side. Her bow was also noched and ready.

"Speak," she commanded.

The elf smiled, a familiar expression, but the voice, cold and dry, left no doubt. "The puny human is right. My body failed me, but this one is an inadequate replacement, old and worn. I require another."

"Is Denalion dead?" Pyre asked.

Ithea frowned. "Hard to say. He put up a credible fight and then, well I'm not sure. It felt as if he fled. But please don't get your hopes up. No spirit can successfully travel without a body for its base. If he is alive and out there somewhere, he is but an old wisp. Listen for his whispers in the winds, on the mountainside, and other poetic garbage like that, if it makes you feel better.

"But, as I said, I require a new body." He looked at Riona, resting against a rock, a thin sheen of sweat on her face. "Oh, my. Did my puppies hurt her? Shame."

He continued to stare at Riona and frown. As he did, she drew the curved dagger from her boot. The hilt was a black stone, smooth and shiny. The blade was sharp and engraved with runes.

"You will try to kill me with that?" He laughed.

"No," Riona replied, her voice cold. "I will take my own life before you possess me. You can't enter one who is dead."

Montclair began to move toward her to object, but then realized he could not relinquish his place.

Ithea barely glanced at him. "What a shame the male is the weakest of you. His body would be easiest to possess." He turned to Pyre. "And you are almost a true Wycaan. Our union might be interesting, but I have never tried to enter a Wycaan. It could become complicated and a risk if I have no back up plan."

He turned to Sellia. "Now, you are a beautiful creature: strong-spirited and smart. I think we can do great things together."

And Ithea took a step forward.

CHAPTER EIGHTY

Though it took Sa'gola only a short while to return to the fortress at Grogin, it felt like forever. She had remained on the boat for a considerable amount of time, staring out into the murky water. Even as the fog lifted, the water remained dark and ominous…and still.

The Master had been clear that she was to capture Seanchai and keep him away from the fortress. Killing him had been a last option. She had laid plans to transfer him to the same time as his mate and friends. She had not come here to kill him.

But he had goaded her in a way much different than other adversaries had. She sat heavily on the bow of the boat. Small bubbles rose where he sank, but gradually slowed to an occasional pop and then ceased completely. Seanchai had not tried to kill her or possess her. But he had threatened to take her acolyte from her. He was going to drive a wedge between her and Mharina, to turn the young elfe against her.

Her rage had come from deep within – from an emotional, long-buried part of her psyche. It had been hidden so well that when it erupted, she had not been prepared. But that was the point. Survival and protection was everything. When the fire left her fingertips, it was not the usual purple, but white-hot and pure. What had instinctually left her body was the most powerful force she possessed. Nothing could stand in the face of it, and even if he was still alive after the impact, the Wycaan had still sunk, unconscious, to the ocean bed.

Moving only two fingers, Sa'gola slowly turned the boat around and let it glide her back to the fishing port. Once firmly on solid ground, she walked out of Braithwaite and, having checked that no one was watching her, disappeared.

Back in her chambers, Sa'gola collapsed onto her bed and closed her eyes. She was exhausted and fell asleep immediately. When Mharina woke her, she thought she had only just lain down, but it was a fresh morning.

She could feel the steamy heat of a drawn bath. As she stood up, she wobbled and blinked in surprise. Mharina immediately steadied her and began to unlace her clothes and remove her boots.

"I slept in my boots," Sa'gola exclaimed.

"You did. I thought to remove them when I came here earlier, but didn't want to wake you. You seemed exhausted, and I knew you would not have long to rest.

"Why?"

"Master Sythen told me to bring you at noon before the Emperor."

"Call him Master, little one. The title Emperor is loaded for him, given that he has lost Odessiya."

Mharina shrugged. "I am his prisoner. His ego is not my concern. Come; you should bathe."

"Even so," Sa'gola said, "you do not want to incur his wrath. Remember: he is, at all times, the most powerful one in the room."

Mharina nodded, guided her Sa'gola to the bath, and helped her in.

"Do you want to join me?" Sa'gola asked. They had shared a bath a few times, and the sorceress treasured the intimacy.

"No," Mharina perched on the edge of the stone tub. "Where did you go?"

"I am to report back to the Master. If you're invited to the meeting, you will hear then." She closed her eyes. "Leave me now. I need to think."

Mharina had not actually met the Emperor yet, a point that Ilan and Senzia made clear at regular intervals. They had apparently sat with him plenty of times, where he had told them stories of the Wycaan Order and taken a great interest in their studies. When they showed him their exercises or a new achievement, he was extremely complimentary, and they both admitted to looking forward to his summonses.

Sa'gola came to Mharina's room and immediately told her to change clothes. Sa'gola, herself, was resplendent in a purple dress cut low over her chest, but still hiding the scars on her back. A large purple stone surrounded by smaller black ones hung at her cleavage. Over an arm, she carried a dress that she offered to Mharina.

"What is this?" The elfe was taken aback.

"You are no longer a *calhei*, and you should dress appropriately to meet the Master."

"Did Senzia and Ilan receive clothes specially to meet him?"

"I am not concerned with them at this time. You are my student, and how you carry yourself reflects upon me."

A little while later, Mharina presented herself to her teacher. She wore a tight, black dress that hugged her small body. There was high slit from the bottom, which made her feel she would be able to run if needed.

"Beautiful," Sa'gola said when she saw her. "Turn around."

She did, and Sa'gola clasped a small chain around her neck. A small black stone hung there, simple and shiny.

"Thank you," Mharina said as she looked at herself in the mirror. Then she turned and hugged her teacher.

"It is plain, but you are only at the beginning of your journey. Come. The Master should not be kept waiting."

They walked together through the main hall. Servants, taragusii, and fortune-swords all made way for them with reverence. Mharina felt herself walking straighter and realized she enjoyed the feeling of power the two of them emanated.

A pair of large taragusii guarded the tall wooden door. When Sa'gola and Mharina approached, the guards opened the two doors with graceful synchronicity. Inside the Master's hall, the conversation ceased, and all gathered looked at them.

A large stone table dominated the room. It was shiny white marble, dense, and clearly heavy. High-backed wooden chairs surrounded the table. To the left of the highest chair at the head of the table sat Master Sythen, his cloak matching the red band that bound his white hair tightly behind his round ears. His huge broadsword hung in its sheath from the back of his chair. Next to him sat Master Willowood, the old elfe, her white hair contained in a tight bun. She had not been seen much since her very public argument with Senzia, which Senzia and Ilan had described to Mharina a dozen times each.

Master Goldspiere, the dwarf Wycaan, had been standing to one side, and when he came to the table, Mharina saw that he had left a huge, black, triangular stone that sat on a beautiful golden stand, sculptured to resemble a tree with hanging leaves.

"An Anwar," Mharina heard herself say unwittingly.

"Indeed, child," a voice said from the window. A figure, silhouetted by the sunlight, began to move toward them.

Sa'gola went down on one knee and bowed her head. She gently pulled Mharina down with her.

"I believe you are quite familiar with the Anwar," the Emperor continued, his voice rich and deep. "There are only six believed to have survived the Age of Misted Times. Sa'gola has one. There is one in a monastery near Galbrieth, another with the dwarf high priestess, and a small one with your father. Mine makes five, and the sixth remains elusive. We know it exists, but so far, Master Goldspiere has failed to locate it."

The dwarf shuffled in his big chair. "'Tis very frustrating, milord," he said, his hands clasping each other tightly.

"Your teacher has not allowed you free access to her Anwar on my orders because it possesses great, ancient power. One this size could be used as a great weapon, and should always be guarded. But today, perhaps you will get to look into the Anwar, or perhaps you will die.

Chapter Eighty One

M harina made every effort not to show how his threat had impacted her.

"I would, of course, like use of the Anwar, Master." The words stuck in her throat, but she forced them out. She needed his cooperation and, certainly, his Anwar.

"Rise, both of you. Take your seats."

Mharina sat at the table next to Sa'gola, facing Master Willowood, who forced a smile.

"You are not a member of my council, Mharina," the Emperor said. He was a mass of white: his clothes, hair, and turban. It made his blue eyes extra prominent. "You are here today because I deem it pertinent. Naturally, you must master your craft and show great loyalty and deeds to join the council. Now, tell me, how do you like your studies and teacher?"

Mharina swallowed hard. "I enjoy learning so much and in such depth. I look forward to mastering my craft, as you say, and using it to do good in the world."

There were a few condescending smiles at this last comment. Mharina felt her anger rising.

"And your teacher?" the Emperor said. "How do you feel about her?"

Mharina blushed and stared at Sa'gola, resplendent in her purple makeup; dark, shiny hair; and beautiful smile.

"The truth," Sa'gola murmured.

The elfe turned back to the Emperor at the other end of the table. "I have great respect for her knowledge and skills. I love studying with her. She is caring and conscientious. She is strict, yet encourages me to make mistakes so that I may learn from them."

"Do you feel close to her?" the Emperor asked.

Mharina felt Sa'gola tense, though she didn't think anyone else noticed. "Yes," she said clearly. "I love her very much, but…"

"But what?"

Mharina looked down at the table, feeling the Emperor's eyes piercing into her. "Tell me the truth, girl. But what?"

She glanced at Sa'gola but found no help. She turned back to the Emperor. "But I am your prisoner. My brother and sister are your prisoners. My mother and teachers are in danger there." She nodded to the Anwar. "My *ahdahr* leads a large host to fight you and will probably kill Sa'gola. I am not, as you surely appreciate, in a good position."

The Emperor nodded approval. "A fair answer. Your mother and her friends were foolish to come alone. They are imprisoned, but I am not aware they are in danger."

"Then you might not know everything you think you do," Mharina snapped.

There was coughing and shuffling around the table. Mharina felt her body go cold in a sweeping wave from her feet up to her chest.

"You will address me respectfully at all times," the Emperor said. "You are smart enough to know that you are my prisoner; be smart enough to know that, as well."

The cold drained from her, and she felt her blood racing through to warm her extremities. She tried to speak, but could only nod.

"I am glad you so enjoy being with Sa'gola. She is very special and does not offer her love to anyone as intensely as she has to you. Remember that well, child." The Emperor turned to Sa'gola. "Is he dead?"

"Regrettably, he is."

"Regrettably?"

"I think he could have served you better alive. I did not plan to kill him."

There was quiet around the table, and Mharina realized that they were all waiting for her reaction. She felt her chest tighten and mustered all her strength to turn to Sa'gola. Her eyes were already filling with tears.

"Who…did…you…kill?" she whispered.

"I'm sorry, Mharina. He drew his swords and left me no choice."

Mharina sprung up, her hand covering her mouth. She turned and ran to the doors, but they would not open. She struggled fruitlessly, shaking the ancient timbers with her fury. Then she took a step back and raised her arms. But the fire never came. She could feel it churning inside, but it was being contained.

She whirled around. The Emperor stood with his palms facing her.

"You will not summon the fire in my presence without my express permission," he said quietly. "Return to your seat."

Mharina walked slowly, numbly, her stomach and chest tight. But she did not return to her seat. Instead, she walked around the table. Master Sythen rose, unsheathing his sword, but the Emperor put a hand on his shoulder and guided him back to his seat.

Mharina did not approach the Emperor, but continued toward the Anwar. It was getting increasingly harder to put one foot before the other. He was slowing her down, but not stopping her.

"I told you to sit down, *she-elf*," the Emperor ordered.

Mharina saw Master Willowood stiffen at his words. The young elfe caught her eye, but continued to drag herself forward.

"I must see it," she cried between clenched teeth.

The Emperor relented, and she fell forward from his release. "Very well. Look. Confirm it. You sit." This last command had been directed at Sa'gola, and Mharina approached the stone alone.

Fixing an image of her father in her mind, she scryed through the stone. All she saw was ocean – a dark, murky expanse of water – with fog closing in around her.

"Was it at sea?" Her voice was small, and she had to force the words out. "Surrounded by fog?"

"It was," Sa'gola answered.

Mharina stifled the pain about to erupt and focused on her mother. What she saw made her gasp. Riona was laid against a rock, her eyes closed – unconscious, perhaps. Montclair lay across her, a burn along his back and his legs bent at grotesque angles.

Denalion was shooting bolts of white fire at them. But it could not be him; the body language was wrong – never mind that he was attacking Pyre. She deflected his bolts, moving her Win Dao swords in a blur, but she was clearly on the back foot, nearing a precipice with each step. Mharina saw her mother lay on the edge of the precipice, half her body over the edge. There was desperation in Pyre's eyes.

"Give me her body," a strange voice said from inside Denalion. "You are dead, she-elf."

Mharina whirled around. "Save them," she cried.

The Emperor closed his eyes and smiled. "Is that Ithea inside the red elf's body? Ha! He is resilient, is he not? Did you destroy his body but leave his spirit intact, Sa'gola? Rather careless."

"I killed him," Mharina snarled, walking toward him.

"Apparently not very well," the Emperor guffawed.

Before she knew it, orange bolts of fire were erupting from her at the Emperor. The first blast skimmed his shoulder, and he wheeled around. The next volleys missed, giving the Emperor time to flick his hand and send Mharina flying into the wall. She cried on impact, but did not fall to the floor. He was pinning her to the wall from across the room.

"Your father was naive, pathetic, and not fit to rule. He was an elf, and an elf should know his place. Maybe you want to join your spineless father in the land of failure."

As he raised his hands, Master Willowood sprung to her feet. Stamping one foot into the stone ground, she pushed, and the Emperor spiraled against his chair. He turned and stared at her.

The Emperor glared. "After all I've done for you. Why now?"

"All this time that I've been your faithful servant, I'd forgotten that I am also an elfe, and a Wycaan."

Her eyes bulged open as Master Sythen's large blade pierced through her back and out her chest. Scarlet blood pooled on the white stone table and dripped to the floor. She staggered forward, the sword still inside her, and made her way toward Mharina, hand outstretched.

"Tell...your...sister...I-I...remembered...in the...end."

She fell to the floor with a resounding thud and the scratching rasp of the blade on stone.

Chapter Eighty Two

The old elfe lay on the stone floor, blood spreading out from her chest. Still pinned to the wall, Mharina rolled her eyes to look at the Emperor as he approached.

"That was unexpected, don't you think?" the Emperor sneered. "To think pointed ears still mean something after a lifetime of servitude."

He laughed and his mockery brought tears to the young elfe's eyes.

"They do," Mharina said, struggling against the invisible bond, "and that is why you have always and will always fail – because you cannot comprehend."

"Yes, offer me words of wisdom before you die, little she-elf, please."

"All races – elf, human, dwarf, pictorian – are all equal, and, if some rise higher, it is not because of the shape of their ears, but the quality of their heart."

The Emperor erupted in laughter again – a mean sound that echoed back from the high roof. "And who told you that? Let me guess: your poor, dead father? An elf who lacked spine and vision. Only a total fool would say–"

A flash of purple light enveloped the Emperor, freezing him mid-sentence, his arms poised above his head. The air around him sizzled and crackled, as small golden sparks left his fingertips but could not pierce the purple. Sa'gola came and stood in front of him. When she spoke, her voice was quiet and void of emotion.

"I was the total fool who said that."

She flicked her hands, and the great Anwar flew at the purple bubble that held the Emperor. It smashed against him, and the very foundation of Grogin shook as the purple light flashed and a deep, black void encased it and then seemed to absorb the purple until the light and the Emperor disappeared into the great stone. Sa'gola calmly kept her distance and motioned with her hands directing the Anwar out of the window. The sorceress then moved to the window and watched the bubble and stone bounce down the side of the mountain. When there was a loud crash from below, Mharina fell to the ground, released from the Emperor's bonds, and gasped with pain as she struggled to stand up.

Sa'gola whirled on Master Sythen, but the tall man had sheathed his sword. "Enough deaths," he said, his voice weary.

"Sa'gola," Mharina gasped, pulling herself up by leveraging the stand that had held the Anwar. "My mother, please."

Sa'gola, chest heaving from exertion, turned and stared at Mharina for a long moment, not moving.

"Please, Sa'gola. I'll do anything. I'll-I'll be your slave."

"Not my slave," Sa'gola panted. "Swear that you will be my student: live with me, learn from me, and stay with me until you complete your training. You will be my pupil, companion, and friend. Swear it in your own ancient tongue."

"You killed my *ahdahr*," Mharina cried, tears finally falling down her cheeks.

"I did, and I regret it. I will spare the rest of your family and friends, but you must swear."

Mharina blinked and took a deep breath. "I do. *Ashbar*. Save them." She stared at the shattered window, where the Emperor had gone hurtling through. "But the Anwar…"

Sa'gola leapt forward and grabbed the black stone around Mharina's neck, the sixth Anwar. She poured bright purple light into the small Anwar, more and more. Mharina felt the stone grow heavy and hot. Still Sa'gola kept it up, mingling strange words with guttural sounds. Then, roaring with power, she threw the purple fire across the room. Sellia screamed as she hit the floor; Riona, too. Montclair fell on top of the healer. Pyre landed on the table and somersaulted onto the ground, her Win Dao swords flashing as she sought Ithea.

When she could not see him, she charged Master Sythen, but Mharina cried out for her to stop. Then she ran to her mother. Sellia was streaked with blood and scratches, but smiled through tears as she took her daughter into her arms.

Sa'gola moved to Riona, who was writhing in pain and laid her hands on the healer. Montclair sat up and rubbed his head.

"I'll get the twins," Mharina shouted with delight and ran to the door.

She stopped suddenly. "Sa'gola, the guards are gone."

Master Sythen ran past her, and she followed. The castle was empty save for a few confused servants and the muted sound of battle. Mharina started calling out for Ilan and Senzia. She eventually found them hiding in a chimney, black soot covering them. Taking their hands, she led them back to their mother.

Deep in Sellia's embrace, Mharina broke the news about Seanchai. She did not share details; only that he was killed at sea. They cried, all four of them, arms entwined, as Sa'gola looked on, her face inscrutable.

Rhoddan led the charge through the gates. A few fortune-swords offered half-hearted resistance, but soon surrendered when their masters and the taragusii did not come to fight with them. Ballendir, who had marched his troops from Hothengold for two relentless days and nights, led his dwarves as they swarmed to secure the outer ramparts and marshaled the prisoners.

Rhoddan swept onwards, his broadsword destroying any who stood in his path. Umnesilk and Narasilk flanked him, great axes at the ready. They entered the keep and bounded up the stairs. A tall Wycaan with a pure white beard met them outside the Emperor's hall. His sword was sheathed, his hands extended to his side, palms facing Rhoddan in surrender.

A short while later, Sellia broke the news to him. Rhoddan stumbled backwards, shaking his head.

"Seanchai is not dead," he screamed. "The Emperor lied to you. He didn't–"

"It was not the Emperor," Sa'gola said, her voice calm but firm. "Come, sit down. I will tell you how it happened." She explained meeting Seanchai at Braithwaite and taking him out to sea.

Rhoddan sprung up and drew his sword. Sa'gola did not move from her seat, but Mharina, her eyes red and face swollen, came around the table and stood in front of Sa'gola, facing him.

"You were my *ahdahr's* best friend," she said, her voice breaking. "You were with him from the beginning. What would he tell you to do now?"

Rhoddan stared at her, the tip of his sword shaking for the first time since childhood. "But I am not, and could never be, Seanchai. Get out of my way, Mharina."

She shook her head. "My *ahdahr* always kept his word. You know this to be true more than anyone. I will follow in his footsteps and keep mine. Sa'gola saved my mother, Riona, and Pyre, and I swore in return to continue as her student and to defend her."

"What?" Sellia jumped to her feet.

"I am going with Sa'gola to continue my training."

"No. You are coming home with me," Sellia said.

"I am no longer a *calhei*, mother. I made my choice. I made it to save you, and I do not regret it. I swore in the ancient language and accept my destiny."

Sa'gola rose. "I will be in my quarters. I must prepare to leave."

"Where are you taking her?" Sellia demanded, panic in her voice.

"Somewhere safe," Sa'gola said. "Somewhere she will learn to fulfill her incredible potential."

"Why? Why are you doing this? It's over." Sellia was shaking her head. "What cruelty is this?"

Sa'gola leaned on the table. "This is not over, Sellia. The Emperor is dead, maybe. I believe the ancient power of the Anwar consumed him. Ithea is trapped, maybe, and even without them, there are many evil powers in this world. There are few of us alive who can take on this fight. Mharina might become one of them.

"I have seen the your daughter's potential and maybe she will fulfill your mate's vision. I cannot bring him back, but I can help sow the seeds of his legacy."

She turned and walked out the room. Sellia stared after her.

"It's not over?" she mumbled.

Epilogue

Rhoddan led his stallion out through the castle gates. It was still dark and a thin gray tinged the horizon. His horse's hooves clicked on the cobbled ground and echoed up against the arches he passed under. His thick cloak was wrapped around him, and crisp breaths of steam puffed from his mouth.

He had charged the pictorians and Ballendir's troops with escorting the family back to Wycaan Island. Montclair was going, too, as well as the Wycaan swordsman and dwarf. There was enough protection without him. He guided his horse across the bridge.

On the other side, he saw a hooded figure mounted, and a second horse laden with supplies. The figure was armed with a bow and two swords. He thought it was the one they called Master Sythen and was annoyed that the man was reneging on his agreement.

Rhoddan mounted his horse, which snorted as it trotted to the end of the bridge. The second figure moved its horse into step.

"I ride alone," Rhoddan growled.

"As do I," Pyre replied. "But we travel the same road."

"You don't know where I'm going."

"To find Seanchai, dead or alive. You are as inextricably linked to him as I am."

"Why would I bother? The sorceress said that if he did not die from her flames, he drowned."

"He may well have died from her fire," Pyre conceded, "but he is Wycaan. He did not drown. He told us both of his transformation ceremony, of the ley lake under the mountain."

And the two of them rode out of Grogin in comfortable silence.

Author's Note:

Dear Friend,

If you have got this far – I thank you – it has been quite a journey. If you are angry, fearful, or wanting to throw this book into the fire, I take full responsibility...unless you are reading an ebook and then you really shouldn't throw your eReader around.

This was the hardest Wycaan Master book that I have written this far. I wrote it as a parent and it was as much a rollercoaster for me as I'm sure it was for you. If you cried, got angry, or apprehensive, well, I walked with you ever step of the way.

But life moves on and all we can hope for in the end is that we leave our legacy and sow the seeds for a better place, whether we are kings or knights, peasants or Wycaan Masters.

At the time of writing, I am already one-third into the first draft of Book 5 – tentatively titled *Calhei No More* – and I hope you will join me as the legacy plays out. I cannot say where this story is taking us. There always seems to be twists and turns that even I don't anticipate until they are on paper. But wherever it goes, I trust in its path. I hope you will too.

The world of epic fantasy is thriving, and there are many great authors producing fine novels to choose from. I thank you for taking the time to read *Sacrificial Flame* and the Wycaan Master series.

If we meet upon the road or at a tavern, let us meet as companions and tell tales of old times: of battles won, love lost, and alliances formed.

    If we do not meet, feel free to contact me at anelfwriter@ gmail.com or sign up for my weekly blog post at http://www. elfwriter.com. I also tweet at @elfwriter. Please consider leaving a brief review of this book online – I really appreciate it!

Thank you again,

Alon
http://www.alonshalev.com

NON-FANTASY NOVELS BY ALON SHALEV:

Unwanted Heroes (Three Clover Press, 2012)
A Gardener's Tale (Three Clover Press, 2011)
The Accidental Activist (Three Clover Press, 2010)

BOOK 5

CALHEI NO MORE

Anticipated Publication Date: January 2015

PROLOGUE

T here is more than one kind of elf, but history favors those who are fair of skin and would claim the moral high ground. Why would it not? For those who won and seized power, those who destroyed and conquered, were the ones who wrote the histories. Is it not this way the world over?

The stories tell of tall, thin, lithe elves, many with snow-white hair and a love for the earth. They fight with delicate swords and bows of polished wood. They honor the land, the trees, and the different races. They exhort fanciful notions of equality and noble living.

But history has a conveniently bad memory. It shies from their transgressions, ignores their elitism and forgives their transgressions. When their moral compass is spun, they unsheathe their swords and wield their contempt upon all who do not bow down and comply.

Such was it when these fair elves came to Odessiya before the rise of men and dwarves. The white-haired ones tell how they discovered and claimed the land, finding a beautiful unspoiled mix of blue rivers, mighty mountains, lush plains, and majestic forests. They mention the massive herds of bullists, buffalo-like creatures still shaggy and fat, that crossed the deserts providing food and skins. They spoke of the great cats that trailed and hunted the multiplicity of animals, of the precious metals and the wealth that was abundant.

But they never spoke of the Ashen Elves who already lived there, who had in fact lived there for centuries and saw the land as their own.

These aboriginal elves shared pointed ears but little else. They were dark of hair and their complexion gray. Their songs tell how they were formed in the bowels of the great fire mountains. They roamed the land, following the herds and the seasons. They were great warriors and those who crossed their paths regretted it, but they never sought out other races to subjugate.

And they were different from the newcomers in one crucial aspect: they had no magic.

Those who came over the seas from the west never accepted the true elves of Odessiya, the gray ones. Perhaps it was their complexion, their nomadic desires, or their lack of magic. But the Ashen Elves never begged to be taken in, for they shared the pride of all elves, and when called to bend the knee, they rebelled.

Great battles were fought, great treachery unleashed and, though the Western elves came with great numbers, they faced a warrior-like people familiar and able to leverage the land.

The difference was the magic, and once unleashed, it took control of the fair elves and fueled their craving for superiority.

However, the magic belongs to no people, serves no race, and it was the magic that eventually saved the Ashen Elves. Manipulating its wielders, the gray elves were banished to another dimension, buried under the great mountains far to the north of Odessiya. They became isolated from time and history, and finally from legend, itself.

But, though time was as frozen as the terrain around them, the gray elves trained hard and became even stronger warriors. And the magic saw them, pitied them, and nurtured them.

The Ashen Elves became one again with the mountains, growing muscles as hard as rock, a temperament to match any eruption, and the dogged tenacity of the lava flow. They became hard of body and hard of heart. But deep within themselves they buried their fear, their shame, their elven essence, and allowed the desire for revenge to grow.

Then one day, a white-haired stranger with round ears came and sat with them. He heard their stories and understood. He guided and helped them refine their magic, and he promised to one day return and help the Ashen Elves to fulfill their destiny.

And so the time nears when the gray elves will develop their magical art to such an extent that will they will break the chains that retrains them. Then they will descend upon the land of Odessiya and usurp the usurper, because the land belongs to no one and the Stewards of Odessiya will regain their life, their honor, and will have their revenge.

From The Chronicles of Tarth, Priest of The Ashen Elves of Ardien.

Publisher's Disclaimer:

Tourmaline Books have not, at this time of writing, edited or approved the material for Book 5 and reserve the right to change any and all of what is shared here with the reader.